T0129214

A Particular Darkness

The Katrina Williams Novels by Robert Dunn

A Living Grave

A Particular Darkness

A Particular Darkness

A Katrina Williams Mystery

Robert E. Dunn

LYRICAL UNDERGROUND
Kensington Publishing Corp.
www.kensingtonbooks.com

LYRICAL UNDERGROUND BOOKS are published by

Kensington Publishing Corp.
119 West 40th Street
New York, NY 10018

First Electronic Edition: September 2017
eISBN-13: 978-1-60183-809-4
eISBN-10: 1-60183-809-3

First Print Edition: September 2017
ISBN-13: 978-1-60183-810-0
ISBN-10: 1-60183-810-7

Printed in the United States of America

For my mother, Mary. Military spouses and families serve right alongside their enlisted, noncoms, and officers.

ACKNOWLEDGMENTS

No story turns into a book without a team of people. Unfortunately I don't know many of those people. Nonetheless, I appreciate and acknowledge the efforts of everyone at Lyrical Press who worked to bring this second Katrina Williams story out into the world. Between book one and book two were some changes in the people involved. Thank you to my first editor, the man who brought me into the Lyrical Press shop, Peter Senftleben. And deep thanks to my new editor, Martin Biro, for being patient as I tried to finish this book.

I also want to express my appreciation for the efforts and support of Erin Al-Mehairi. She helped me get the word out, and that is no small thing.

Chapter 1

Life is quicksilver, seemingly all shimmer and joy, but in truth a slippery dream-fluid, impossible to hold. I lost my husband, Nelson Solomon, fifteen months after we married. It wasn't unexpected, but that doesn't mean it wasn't terrible. He was a Marine and an artist and funny and kind . . . I married him even though I knew he was sick from the effects of chemical exposure during the first Gulf War. It was the best, and worst, risk I'd ever taken.

Loss of a love. Grief. Sorrow. Burdens—but not the reason I was sitting across from a therapist. I had a host of other burdens. Issues my therapist calls them. We have a difficult relationship. I can't say she realizes that. The difficulties are mine. For one thing, she's the kind of perfect woman who just sets me on edge. I'm in jeans and pointy-toed boots with a two-inch riding heel, and I'm spilling my life out to a woman in a skirt with stockings that peek through the toes of red pumps with four-inch heels. We're very different. She tells me that we're not, but how can you believe anything a therapist says?

My presence in therapy is mandated as a condition for keeping my job as a sheriff's detective in Taney County, Missouri. They say I drink too much and have a tendency to violate departmental policies on the use of force. I haven't had a drink since the night fourteen-year-old Carrie Owens bled out in my arms. It was the same night my friend Billy Blevins was almost beaten to death by meth-cooking bikers. It was also the night I shot and killed a gangster for kidnapping and shooting Nelson. There may be an issue with violence, but it's not mine alone. We live in a dangerous world. That's a lesson I learned as an MP and soldier in Iraq, not in therapy.

The therapist and I talked a while about my job and the fact that

I've had no black marks against me since that night. Just when I think there are no more surprises, she uncrossed her pretty legs and re-crossed them, right over left. I tried not to be jealous. Dr. Regina Kurtz is the kind of woman I'll never be, perfect hair, perfect make-up. I imagined she wore pearls and slinky black dresses to the kind of parties that have always intimidated me. She looked like an actress playing the part of a therapist on TV. Even her name annoyed me the way it echoed my own, Regina to my Katrina. People sometimes called me Hurricane for obvious reasons. I bet no one called Regina anything other than Dr. Kurtz.

"How are you dealing with the money issues?" she asked me.

"Why?"

"It must be a big change."

"Bigger than the other changes?"

"Different from the other big changes. But big or small, changes all have an effect," she said. "What effect is that one having?"

It wasn't as easy a question as one might think. Money changes everything. Most of the people in my life know about that like they know about breathing underwater. My problem *was* different and she knows it. The question isn't about bills or living on a salary. She was asking about the fortune that Nelson's death left me responsible for. It's the one thing I hold against the man.

I told her about the problems of licensing and keeping control of the images Nelson created. I shared my feelings of corked-up confusion, anger, and the chainsaw visions I got when talking with lawyers who took millions of dollars for granted. She almost smiled. When I told her, I thought they hid behind their job as a shield from care and responsibility, she didn't smile. Her face froze into that waiting-for-the-other-slingback-pump-to-drop look she gets.

I didn't bite.

After the session I went out to my truck. It was new-to-me new. My old truck had been fine but after I married Nelson, there was so much money and he needed something roomier for our trips to the hospital. Dr. Kurtz said I have an intimate acquaintance with ratio-nalization. At least I didn't buy straight-from-the-dealer new. It was an off-lease GMC 2500 all-terrain, with every option—a work truck covered in leather and luxury. Nelson said it was me, tough and pretty. Then he added, "Just the right kind of pretty."

He knew how to make sure a girl knew she was being flirted with.

I climbed into the truck and stared out the window for a long time.

One of the changes I had made in my life since Nelson passed was my therapy schedule. Before his death, I went on Thursday mornings, but just after he died, I stopped. And I had remained stopped, as well as off work for a long time. Going back to work required that I return to the sessions, and I really needed to get back to work. My new schedule brought me in on Monday afternoons and the one I just finished was my eighth since going back.

Eight weeks in and I still hated the change. Always before, before Nelson and before perhaps a small amount of perspective, I would attend my session, and depending on how it went, gorge on the kind of breakfast I'm sure the good doctor never indulged in. Often I would meet my father and we'd talk over plates of biscuits and gravy. I'd met him for dinner after the last couple of appointments, but he was out of town this week. That wasn't the real problem though. It was the fact that after sessions and breakfasts, I would go back to work.

That afternoon, sitting and staring out at a slow-draining parking lot, I had no place to go. At least no place that needed me there. My Uncle Orson ran a boat dock and floating bait shop. He was always glad to see me, but . . . in mid-March, the shop was cold and clammy when the water still had its winter chill on.

My other option was to go to Moonshines—a distillery restaurant overlooking Lake Taneycomo in Branson. My restaurant. At least the majority interest in it was mine. The rest was a complicated mess involving more lawyers and clients whom I don't actually know. Another of the ways Nelson had changed my life.

I was saved from a decision when my phone rang. That was not exactly uncommon, but the fact that it wasn't the ringtone of the department put it squarely into the surprise category. The fact that work is the only programmed ringtone says a lot more about me than I liked to admit.

The phone's display showed *Billy*—my friend and a deputy with the department.

"How quickly can you get to Black Fork Cove?" Billy asked without bothering to say hello.

"Is there even a road to get there?" Black Fork was an isolated notch in Table Rock Lake where two small creeks drained. It was barely in the state of Missouri let alone in Taney County. "And why?"

"Come down through that housing development," he said. "They put in the road before it went under."

"That doesn't get to the lake," I answered.

"There's a field. Then a trail."

"Great. You never said why."

"It's important, Hurricane."

That was something he didn't need to say. I knew Billy. If he was asking me to come to the ass-end of the county after duty hours, it was important. If he wasn't bothering to say anything else, it was because of a reason he didn't want to share at the moment, but I didn't need to worry about.

"I'm in Springfield." I didn't say where in Springfield. I was pretty sure I didn't need to.

"Can you leave now?"

His was the best offer I had. "Yeah," I said. "I can."

The late afternoon was spring-warm so the windows could come down a bit. Too cold for all the way, but way too nice to be closed in. Even the way I drive, it took well over an hour and a half to get through Springfield traffic and down to Table Rock. Full dark had fallen by the time I got to the stretch of abandoned asphalt called Lake Forest Road. When the road ran out I didn't bother to stop. The developer had walked away when the economy tanked in 2008 and left the end of the pavement a jagged edge dribbling into a graded lot. Since then the lot had become overgrown with weeds, but remained distinct from the green belt that surrounded the lakeshore. I could see a flashlight bobbing around and a truck with a rack of lights pointing into the thick wall of junipers and grape vine.

When my truck passed over the road end and into the field I flashed my lights and the flashlight waved in response. I'd found Billy.

"Thanks for coming," he said through the open window as soon as I stopped. "I really didn't want to call anyone else."

"Sure you didn't." I handed over a XXX-large soda I'd picked up at a convenience store. Billy was a fiend for soda pop and I was his enabler. Usually it was payment for helping me out on a case. Sometimes though you simply wanted people to know you think about them.

His eyes brightened and his grin broadened until it was brighter than the off-road lights on his truck's roll bar. "You're a gem," he said after his first long pull on the straw. He took another drink. "See? That's why I call you. No one else knows me like you do."

"No one else would come," I replied drily. "Now tell me what this is all about."

"What else would I call a woman out into the moonlight at the lake side for? A body."

"Billy, I'm not even on call tonight."

"I know. But a friend called me and I called a friend."

"Me?"

"Close enough." He laughed a bit. More than I thought it deserved.

"Okay." I climbed down out of the truck and left the lights on, pointed at the same spot as Billy's lights. There was a small black gap sliced into the tree line there, the head of a trail.

The passenger door on Billy's truck opened and a shadow without a source moved.

"Who's there?" I reached to the small of my back to set my hand on the weapon there.

"That's my friend." Billy waved the shadow over. "Damon, come over here."

The shadow moved quickly to the front of the truck and I must have twitched because Billy called out, "Take it slow and easy. Hurricane is jumpy tonight."

When the shadow moved into the direct line of the off-road lights, it became a man—a shirtless black man, with very dark skin. He moved closer and I was struck by the play of light on his body. Despite the cool weather he was beaded with wetness that made a sheen on his chest and abdomen like crude oil on cast iron.

"Why doesn't he have a shirt?" I asked. "It's kind of cold for that."

He passed through the bank of light and back into the gloom between vehicles. When he crossed the bumper of my truck, he held out a hand.

"Damon Tarique," Billy said, "meet Katrina Williams."

"The Hurricane," Damon said, then he added, "Ma'am."

Assumptions. I guess we all have them and I guess I failed Enlightenment 101. Seeing the extreme darkness of the man's skin, and

his tall, lean physique I expected to hear an accent, perhaps the lilt-
ing, soft cadences I'd heard from Eritreans or Somalis. I wouldn't
have been surprised by something that sent my ears to the Caribbean.
What I got was middle of anywhere, America. I tried not to be disappointed and wondered briefly if that made me a racist.

"Billy has told me a lot about you." Tarique said.

I shook his hand. "A lot?"

"Billy's a talker."

A note of accent crept in, but it was only an accent because it
came from him. He sounded like me. Or Billy. Or any of the people
I'd spent most of my life around.

Expectations.

"Let's get down to the water," Billy said. "We don't want to spend
all night."

I nodded in the direction of my rear passenger door and said to
Damon, "There's a jacket in the truck if you want it."

"Thanks." He went right for it.

"So where do you two know each other from?"

"Iraq." Billy said the word and looked away. He knew something
of what happened to me over there. Probably more than he wanted
me to realize and he was uncomfortable talking about that place in
front of me. It used to make me feel a lot more than uncomfortable.
"Damon was a Ranger. I patched him up a few times."

That was part of what made me uncomfortable. When I was Lieutenant Williams, an Army MP, something had happened. Something
that left me naked and bleeding beside a road. The one tiny piece of
that day I can recall without terror was the care I got in the back of a
Humvee from a medic. Not so long ago, when my life began falling
apart all over again, I began to think that Billy might have been that
medic. He's never said anything to make me believe one way or the
other. I don't have the guts to ask. Just another one of those compli-
cations.

"You can always tell military," I said.

The truck door slammed. Damon came back around into the light
wearing a flannel-lined denim jacket. It was Nelson's.

"Thanks," he said rubbing his arms. "It was getting cold."

For some reason the action gave me goose flesh and made the
short hair on the back of my neck stand up. More than that, I began to
feel angry.

"Let's go," Billy said again. This time he didn't wait.

Damon gave me a little *after-you* gesture and I fell in with him bringing up the rear. "You grow up around here?" I asked him over my shoulder.

"Just on the other side of the border."

"Little Rock?" That made sense.

"No, ma'am. Eureka Springs," he answered, once again taking down my expectations.

"I'm surprised." Ahead of me Billy paused at the transition from wispy weeds to thigh high scrub. He cast the beam of his flashlight around until he found the bare dirt of the trail.

"Because you think only good ol' boys come from hereabouts?"

I looked back and caught him grinning before I started down the track after Billy again.

"Well . . ."

"Ha!" The laugh was a good-natured sound. "Billy was right about you."

"What did Billy say?"

Billy jumped in. "He said you knew when to keep your mouth shut and keep walking. But he was wrong."

"Keep sucking your soda," I told him. "You invited me."

"It's my fault," Damon said.

"What is?" My question came fast and sharp. If you bring a cop out into the woods and say there's a body, don't be surprised to find everything you say scrutinized.

"Billy's mood. The whole night."

"It's not your fault." Billy told him. "You did the right thing calling."

"The right thing would have been calling the regular cops. I called you. That's my fault."

"I am a regular cop." Billy said it like he'd had the conversation a million times. "We both are."

"Why didn't you call 911?" I asked him. Then to Billy I asked, "And why did you call me?"

"He didn't want to get in trouble," Billy answered.

"You found the body?" I asked Damon.

"Yeah."

"Do you have anything to do with it being there?"

"I know you got to ask." He lifted his chin at Billy. "He asked the same thing. But I didn't. And it wasn't why I didn't call the regular cops."

"I *am* a regular cop." Billy said.

"You know what I mean."

"Yeah, I'm a pretty regular cop too." I told him. "If you thought Billy could keep you clear of things you should have—"

"I'm not trying to keep clear of nothing to do with the dead dude. That has nothing to do with me. It's the fish."

"Fish?" I asked.

"Don't ask," Billy chimed in. "Just wait to see."

It wasn't a long wait, but it was a wait spent tramping through thick overgrowth at night. By the time we reached the edge of the water I swore I could feel ticks crawling over every bit of my skin. Even though it was too early in the spring for the parasites, I'd still check carefully when I got home. Then it hit me that there was no one there to help with those odd little tasks married people share. Thoughts like that came unbidden but never unexpected. I had a history of going to the dark places without much warning.

Usually I went to a patch of dirt in Iraq—a spot so dry and bare it was as if the earth had been rubbed raw and left to scab over. I could feel the dark pulling me in, and I reached up to touch the small crescent of scar tissue that curled out of my eyebrow and curved along the outer corner of my eye socket on the left side. It was a habit and a warning to myself. I only did it when things bothered me.

At the end of a therapy day I'd been called out into the woods by the lake to investigate a body and, possibly, be manipulated by a friend. What was there to be bothered about?

"Over here." Billy gestured with his flashlight and turned off trail to follow the lapping lake bank.

A reflection came back from the beam. It was dull at first, the aluminum of a boat. It brightened when the light struck the registration letters.

"Whose boat?" I asked.

"It's mine." Damon answered. "That spot, with the flat rock is a good place to clean my fish and make a camp."

As we got closer the smell rose slowly, but hit suddenly. I almost retched. Billy took a drink of soda like it had no effect on him.

"Don't you smell that?" I asked it like an accusation. How could anyone walk into that miasma sucking on a sugary drink?

"I was already here once. I got used to it."

Damon didn't seem too bothered either. We kept following the bank closer to the boat and deeper into the foulness. It became a physical thing when we hit the flies. Their sound came first, then the blind bumping of their bodies against my skin. I waved a hand trying to keep my face clear as they landed and crawled on me.

Any cop will tell you what's worst about the job. They will tell you different things because it's a job full of worsts. Way up on that list are dead bodies. I never knew until that night that the dead bodies of fish were in the top ten.

Billy's flashlight was paused on a pile of gutted and rotting fish. The pile almost appeared to be one large organism, with dozens of eyes and one thick, pale white skin that wriggled continuously. Maggots. The living cloud of flies swept down to walk the pile, then like a startled flock of hellish birds they took flight, their tiny bodies flashing green iridescence in the light beam. Carrion eaters hard at their task.

"You did this?" I turned to look at Damon.

He shook his head.

"Look closer," Billy said, passing the light over the pile again, then settling it on a large carcass at the edge.

I could see the fish: a body, a tail, one eye gone milky and staring like it had caught a ghost in its last vision. But there was something else. Something wrong. The proportions weren't right or the light was bad. It was a bit of MC Escher art, fish that were kind of fish, but kind of not fish, and my mind couldn't see what my eyes were looking at.

Billy reached in with his foot and used the toe of his boot to lift a long bone. As soon as he did things fell into place.

"It's a paddlefish," I said.

The bit he'd moved with his boot wasn't a bone, it was a long, spoon-shaped snout.

Paddlefish are an ancient species with a skeleton of cartilage like sharks and noses almost half the length of their body sticking out front. I knew that because my uncle liked to tell fish stories and he'd caught one in this same lake that had weighed over eighty pounds. But that was about all I knew.

"Why?" I asked.

"Who knows?" Billy let the blue-white snout fall off his toe.

I turned to look at Damon.

He raised his hands in front of his chest and waved them like he could wave away suspicion. "No, ma'am. Not me. I didn't have nothing to do with this."

"Then who?"

"Probably this guy." Billy swept the flashlight's beam from the writhing pile of maggots and fish into the lake. There was a man, bundled into a cocoon of monofilament netting, face down in the water. He had long black hair that made the skin, every bit as pale as the bellies of the fish, look even more colorless.

One thing stood out though. On the upper part of his exposed arm was a tattoo I recognized instantly. It was a shield framing an eagle head and underneath it was a ribbon that read AIRBORNE.

For a few moments it was like my head had turned inside out. The darkness that surrounded us was within me. The buzzing of flies and lapping of water occupied the nighttime vacuum. The sounds were the invisible stars reflecting on waves with no substance. I was the dead soldier, but my grave was dry, my bonds were the long tracks of wounds inflicted by combat knives. It was a memory beyond memory that remained always on the doorstep of my perception. My life was slowly bleeding away into the dirt of Iraq even as my body was being buried by blowing dust. The drowning sensation I felt was the pooling of blood in my lungs.

"Hurricane." It was a call from a million miles away and just as many years. "Hurricane!"

Suddenly Billy was there. Or I was back and he'd always been there. His face was confusing because it seemed out of order. I was supposed to see him later, in the back of the Humvee. He would say, *everything will be all right.*

"Hurricane," he said again waving the flashlight in my face.

"What?" I shielded my eyes as I snapped at him.

"Are you okay?"

"I'm just thinking about things. Get that light out of my face and back on the body."

He did and the beam centered on the tattoo.

"Damon," I waved at him to come stand beside me. "You recognize that tattoo?"

He came reluctantly trying hard to avoid looking at the bloated, misshapen person in the netting. "Airborne," he said then quickly turned back away.

"And you were . . ."

"I was Airborne."

"Tell me everything."

He looked at Billy quickly. There was no telling if it was for reassurance or help. He got neither.

"This is the start of the hard road, Damon." Billy told him. "Just man up and walk it."

Damon seemed to take the advice to heart. He straightened his spine and turned back to face me then said, "Ma'am . . ."

I straightened my own back and looked him in the eyes as he told his story.

"I was fishing, like I said. I was grabbin' for paddlefish out there." He pointed into the darkness and the breaking reflections of the moon on the water. "There's a good spot. One of my favorites. Anyway, I got one, a big one and brought it in. When I got here the smell hit me. I've smelled worse. That was other times, other places. I know you understand *that*. I was okay until I put a foot down on a gutted fish and fell."

Helping the story along, Billy turned the flashlight beam again and set it on two pieces of soggy fabric. One was a light jacket heaped onto a rock and the other was a T-shirt hanging from a prickly shrub. Both looked to have been covered in blood and slime.

"Your shirt and jacket?" It was a needless question, but I asked anyway.

"I got rotting fish guts and blood all over me."

I nodded, understanding. But Damon either missed it or misunderstood it.

"That pile isn't all of it." He sounded a little desperate his tone and pace rising. At the same time I noticed him rubbing his arms through the jacket again like he was unable to get warm. "There are fish scattered. It was a horrible sight to see and it reminded me . . ."

"Of what?" I prodded.

"*Things*."

I understood him completely.

"Take a deep breath then go on."

He didn't take the breath. "I went over there." He pointed and

Billy directed the light. "'Cause I saw the rope." A rock was holding down a braided line that trailed from the mud into the water. The far end of it was coiled around the neck of the man in the net. "I pulled it thinking there might be some fish on it. Live fish. I was going to let them go if I could."

"Let them go?"

"I'd kind of lost my appetite for fish by then. I woulda put out the one that I'd caught, but it was too bad caught. I got it in the belly."

"Does that matter?"

Damon heard the question, but he heard it in a different way than spoken. Either that or he was hearing memory. "Matter?" he asked. When he turned his eyes to gaze right into mine, even in the darkness, I could see the firefight he was seeing. "Of course it matters. How could it not matter when a friend takes one in the guts?"

"Damon." I spoke calmly and quietly. "Damon. We're talking about fish."

Like pulling a switch something of the light of battle went out and the man came back. I wondered if that was what people see when I went away. Then for some reason, vanity, denial, or simply wishful, stupid thinking, I had the thought that I could hide it better.

"You get that don't you?" I asked, still in the careful voice. "Fish."

"I get it," he said.

I could see the last moment of the transition, where Damon changed places with his earlier self in his posture. At the same time he stood straight again and relaxed.

Billy put the light on the back of his friend's head. It made a black silhouette with a halo of mist around it. "Are you okay to go on, man?"

"I'm fine."

"I was just asking about the fish," I said, hoping to steer him a little closer to now. "Why did it matter that you got one in the belly?"

"You know about fish grabbing?"

"I know about sucker grabbing. I've seen it done in rivers."

"Same thing," he said. "Use big, bare hooks to snag the fish and pull it in. In a clear river you can put a rag on the line so you see it. When the fish swims over"—he jerked his arms upward like he was pulling on an invisible pole—"in the lake you can't see. You just find good spots and hope. You do it because suckers and paddlefish are basically filter feeders, sucking tiny plants and bugs in and catching it all in their throats. They don't take bait. The suckers are hardy with thick scales. The paddlefish have slick, thin skin. But with either one, the belly is the soft spot. It's easy to kill 'em or hurt 'em bad bringing one in."

"You don't hurt them if you can help it."

"I don't hurt anything anymore if I can help it."

I gave him a few seconds to breathe and relax. Then I said, "That doesn't tell me why you didn't call 911."

Damon shrugged looking down at his feet or the fish on the ground.

"You know I have to ask you again, Damon. You find a body and you call your friend to what? Help you cover it up? Give you an alibi?"

Billy laughed and I wondered what was so funny.

"No." Damon shot a look over at Billy who kept chuckling at him. "I called Billy because I thought he could help me with my fish."

"What do you mean, help you with your fish?"

"Tell her," Billy told his friend.

"I didn't want to get in trouble for it."

"Get in trouble for what?" I was getting tired. I can understand the troubles of vets. I have more than my own share, but dealing with those issues in others was exhausting.

"With the game warden. The season doesn't start until tomorrow."

"You found a dead man and a pile of fish and you were worried about getting a ticket for starting the season early?"

Billy started laughing again.

"Well when you put it like that it sounds bad," Damon said.

"Yeah," I told him, "It does and I can't see any other way to put it." I turned and put my gaze on Billy. "And why'd you drag me into this?"

"Mike Resnick," he answered.

"Oh."

"Billy said your friend is a conservation agent," Damon explained. We thought maybe."

"Unbelievable."

Chapter 2

I was the one with *Detective* in front of my name so I made the calls that put the machineries of death into motion. Bureaucracy and guns are a terrible and almost irresistible force when combined, but the monster they make is slower than most people realize.

While we waited, I pulled out a pen and my pad to sketch out the scene. There would be photographs, a million details taken and categorized with digital precision. A sketch, my own sketches anyway, fixed things in my mind. I drew out the scene and added notes around each element. I noted the rope, its length and type, and the fact that it was cut and left to fray on the end rather than being tied off.

I even drew out the pile of fish and marked the individual animals that were left out of the pile. In the end I couldn't resist the urge to draw little dots of flies and adding the word, *Buzz*. What I ended up with was a series of pictures that were what I saw, not necessarily what was objectively there. Along with it I noted times and names and anything I could think of that related. When I asked Billy to shine his light on the bow of the boat so I could copy the registration number, Damon seemed to get a little nervous.

When I stepped inside to look around he asked, "You really need to do that?"

"You have something to hide?" I asked in way of an answer.

"Everybody's got something to hide from government eyes."

"Government?" I asked. "Not cops?"

The light was focused in the boat but Damon was standing on a point of shore that left him between the scattered light of the Milky Way reflecting on the lake and me. He was like a relief sculpture carved from obsidian, black over black.

"You need a warrant," he said.

I looked over the top of the flashlight at Billy. His face was worried and grim. He locked his gaze with mine and refused to turn toward his friend.

"No, Damon. I don't."

"Billy?" Damon's voice was quiet, but insistent.

What was grim in Billy's face fell into a soft embarrassment. He kept the light in the boat but finally turned to Damon. "This is a crime scene. You were the first one here. That's all the probable cause in the world. I'm sorry."

"Unreasonable search and seizure—"

"That's what I'm telling you man, it doesn't get any more reasonable than this."

"And Reno said kids were in danger at Waco too." Damon's anger was fully bloomed. His body was taut and his voice had gotten as cold as the accusation behind it.

I stood up straight with my legs wide to keep balance. With the boat half in and half out of the water the keel was rocking on mud and the transom was bobbing on waves. It was an unsteady platform that matched perfectly my feelings about our conversation. I stared silently at Damon for a moment, trying to sweep thoughts and words into a sensible pile. I didn't want to search his boat but I had to. On the other hand, his nervousness demanded that I take a good hard look. If I had a third hand I'd have put into it a whole host of government errors and myths of black helicopters. I'd tie them all up with a bow made out of the lack of after-service counseling for vets because I was beginning to think I understood what was going on.

Billy had the sense to take the flashlight beam from the boat and put it on Damon. But because the man was his friend he didn't have it centered in his face. He wasn't blinding Damon but he was making sure I could see his hands. At the same time, Billy moved his right hand down to the weapon at his hip.

Either Damon saw Billy ready his gun grip or he knew from experience the tension we were feeling. "Oh. So that's how it is?" It wasn't really a question. "You violate a man's home when he tries to do the right thing?"

"Not your home, Damon." Billy spoke calmly, slowly, but he kept both the light and his gun hand steady. "Just your boat."

"The boat is his home," I said.

"What?"

"Put the light back here in the boat."

"Man, screw you both." Damon's voice was weak with resignation. "And the horses you rode in on," he added quietly as Billy moved the light back to the boat.

Along with a pole and tackle box there was a small suitcase and a sleeping bag under a tarp in the bow of the boat. Sitting in a cup holder duct taped to the edge of the boat was a bottle of water with a toothbrush secured to it by a rubber band. Tucked back by the transom was a small camp stove. In the built-in storage compartments were plastic tubs filled with various soups, stews, and a full case of store-brand pork and beans.

As I looked I also tried to keep an eye on Billy. I didn't feel any more threat coming from Damon, but Billy still had a hand on his service weapon and a shamed look on his face. Mental conflict can lead to all kinds of bad situations when cops and guns are involved.

"Relax." I spoke quietly hoping my voice wouldn't carry to Damon.

I saw Billy's hand move away from the gun but he didn't look at me. He didn't look at his friend either. He looked into the boat and it was clear the shame he felt was for more than being party to searching his friend's stuff. He had not known that Damon was living on the boat. He was questioning how good a friend he had been and why Damon had never trusted him enough to ask for help. Guilt can be like a spider web you walk through and never see coming.

I went through his belongings as carefully as I could. Pretty much everything on the boat was a case of tetanus waiting to happen. Doing it in the dark with one flashlight wasn't making the search any easier. No matter how thorough I was, the job would have to be done again, either in daylight or in a lighted garage. Damon wasn't getting his home back tonight.

"Is there anything you want to point me to or anything you need to tell me?" I asked Damon.

He didn't answer. I didn't expect him to. I knew a million guys like him, coming out of the military not quite broken but not quite right either. Squeezed just a little out of shape by the use they endured. You go in thinking it's about your country, the flag and apple pie, and all that stuff. But they actually train all that out of you and replace it with routines and muscle memory, with ideas about the unit or the squad, the corps or the wing or any other—*greater good*. In the end, you learn for yourself that it's just the guy next to you, your friends who live and die for you and you for them. In the end they put you out, out of the unit, out of the friendships, out of the system and expect you to find your own way back to mom and apple pie and sanity.

It was something I understood even though the entire system had been turned against me. Maybe that was why I could still see the government as something more banal than evil. It's a blind giant and a child at the same time, playing with blocks then kicking them over but not evil. That's a label reserved for the people who direct the giant. But like the saying goes, guns don't kill people . . . neither do governments. People kill people.

"Damon."

"I got nothing to say," he answered.

"I'm going to open your tackle box." I told him to give him a last chance. If I were keeping a gun here on the boat that would be where I'd put it.

He said nothing.

The two-part lid of the plastic box opened up and spread out with trays of hooks, and jigs, lures and artificial worms. Below that was a panel holding lead weights, line, and tools. I lifted the panel and there it was.

The revolver was old but in good condition. It was a J. C. Higgins nine-shot .22. My father had one almost exactly like it but his had the long barrel. Damon's was short barreled. Stuffed in alongside the gun, was a cheap cell phone in a zipper bag with a couple of prepaid cards. Under everything was a bundle that looked to be old letters and photos. They were wrapped in rubber bands.

I lifted the revolver out by the trigger guard and held it up so light showed through the cylinder. It wasn't loaded. It smelled of oil too. Either he had shot the guy in the water and sat down to clean his gun or the pistol had not been fired recently.

"You should have said something," I told Damon. "It would have helped."

"I should have kept my mouth shut and left this place. That was the only thing would have helped me."

I had Damon in my truck, cuffed and quiet, while I waited for the rest of officialdom to arrive. Billy remained with the body and boat.

The first to show up in the darkness were the on-duty deputies.

They drove fast with lights and sirens more to liven up a boring shift than for any need to clear a path. The cars looked like UFOs in the distance, hugging the earth and bringing the thrill of action. It always seems a bit of a letdown when the cars park and the men with guns amble over pulling their belts from under their guts.

Deputies secured the scene, staking out a perimeter and taping it off as our evidence technician arrived. He'd been dragged out of bed and from the looks of it by the hair. At least he'd had the sense to be carrying a thermos of coffee along with his camera and gear box.

There was one surprise. Before anyone else arrived the sheriff showed up. Charles Benson—Chuck to his friends and everyone in the county seemed to be his friend—had been the sheriff for a long time. He'd lost his wife, Emily, not long before Nelson died and the years were looking pretty heavy on him since then. He didn't sleep much lately so any late night call more interesting than a traffic accident got his attention.

His SUV arrived without the lights or sounds of emergency. After he parked though, strobes from the deputy's cars hit the reflective decals of the star and SHERIFF TANEY COUNTY logo. They shimmered and pulsed in the darkness making the crime scene appear more like an election rally. It made me wonder if he would run again and what that could mean for my job.

When the sheriff passed through the tape, he ambled as well. It's a thing with men in this part of the country, I decided.

"Whaddya got?" he asked as he approached. Canting his head the brim of his hat gestured toward the lake. "Floater?"

"Not exactly," I answered. "How are you doing?"

"I'll tell you, Hurricane. I'm just too tired and too old for this shit."

Sheriff Benson was the kindest man around and a good politician but he was at the same time a poster boy for the rural, white sheriff cliché. When he was worked up he spoke like the good ol' boy he was at heart. That wasn't a problem with most of his constituency. Lately though, since Emily had been buried, I noticed that he controlled it a little less. Or maybe more things simply twisted his nerves.

"Thinking about retiring?" I asked gingerly.

"Thinkin' I'm tired of people asking about it."

"Things have changed since Emily passed."

"Don't I know it—"

"You've changed, Chuck."

"Oh hell, girl." He tilted his hat and looked around the way some men will scan the area for a good place to spit their tobacco juice. The sheriff was looking to see who might be close enough to hear. "I haven't changed. I'm just a little . . . raw. You been there. You're the one should be retirin'. You have something waiting. Why you haven't told me to kiss your ass and gone is beyond me."

We'd had this conversation before. Several times as a matter of fact. But it was like interrogation, as much about what *wasn't* said as was.

"I'm afraid you would pucker up."

He laughed, a good hard sound that brayed over the field and died in the border of trees. "Well we are who we are, are we not?" That pretty much said everything not said.

"Yes sir," I answered. "But no one says you have to be it in the middle of the night. You have a soft bed at home."

"You saw the casket I picked out for Emily."

"Yes, sir."

"It was padded thick with satin and draped with her favorite comforter. I figure a bed won't be more comfortable than that. And I'll goddamned tell you, my bed is no less cold or lonely than a grave. I don't want to be in it anymore."

"I know."

"You do?" He looked at me. He looked hard, without challenge or rancor but deep in thought. "I know you do," he finally admitted. "Do you know I think about being buried with her? I had the plot dug deep so we'll share the same space, not lie side by side."

"I do."

"Which?"

"Both. But mostly I know you think about being close to her. You think about how life isn't life and you imagine a rest."

"Imagine?"

"That's not how I meant—"

He waved a dismissive hand and pulled the brim of his gray, felt Stetson down. "Tell me about the floater."

I smiled. Gently, but I still pointed the expression out into the darkness. He'd lost his mood for sympathy.

"Well . . ." I took a cleansing breath. "Like I said, it's not exactly a floater. The body was wrapped in a net and put in the water."

"COD?"

"We won't have cause of death until the coroner's report. There's nothing obvious but it is dark and he is waterlogged and tied up in a net. We just can't see that much. I'm afraid it might be drowning."

"Afraid?"

"Have you ever experienced trying to breathe liquid?" I asked, thinking of my lungs filling with my own blood, drowning in the desert. "I wouldn't wish that on most anyone."

"'*Most* anyone,'" he echoed and emphasized. The sheriff knew a lot about me.

"He was a soldier. Airborne by the tattoo on his upper-right arm."

"Who called it in?"

"That's a story in itself." I didn't really want to go into it. The sheriff did. So after giving him a short version I told him, "Damon Tarique, the guy who found the body was Airborne too. And a Ranger. *And* he had a gun. But I don't think it had been fired. He's cuffed and in my truck."

"Connected?"

"Damon and the dead guy?" I shrugged. The sheriff nodded. It would bear looking into.

"Back up and tell me about the fish."

Headlights appeared on the horizon. After a moment a set of emergency lights joined them. It was the coroner's van coming to collect the body.

"You want to see things before we get the body in a bag?"

He shook his head and I excused myself long enough to guide the van to where we needed it and to ask two deputies to assist in recovery.

When I returned to the sheriff he asked, "Shouldn't you be down there supervising?"

"You think they need me?"

"No. But you never know."

"That's a mouthful."

He quirked a brow. "Okay. Tell me about the fish."

I did. I showed him the notes and sketches I'd made. He held my pad so headlights illuminated it and flipped through the pages.

When he handed the pad back he asked, "The boys wanted you to call the game warden?"

"I'm friendly with Mike Resnick. We went to high school together. They thought I could talk to him and keep Damon from getting a ticket."

"You think that was the real reason?"

"No. I think Damon was simply afraid of getting pulled into the system. He called his friend the Deputy Sheriff without thinking things through. There were a couple of times he mentioned the real cops."

"Is he stupid?"

"I think maybe confused about some things. He's been living on the boat and in campsites. But I genuinely think he was more afraid of the conservation agent than of the Taney County Sheriff's Department."

"Which means you don't think he's our killer."

I shook my head.

"Then what do you think?"

"At this point"—I put up my hands and gestured around at the vehicles pointing their lights into the woods—"I think we investigate."

More headlights appeared on the road. I recognized the vehicle that pulled up, well behind the official units.

Sheriff Benson knew the car as well. "Riley Yates," he said. "I bet his wife was pissed he got up for this."

"Are you going to talk to him?"

"What else for an old sheriff but to talk to the press? You're here to work. I'm just . . . here." He waved as Riley got out of his car.

Riley waved back and waited politely beside his fender for the sheriff to come over. There's a lot to be said about how things are done in smaller communities.

"One thing though," the sheriff said to me. "I think you should call that friend of yours."

"Resnick?"

"A game warden will be a lot of help on this."

"I was going to call in the morning. See what they wanted to do about the fish if anything."

"Call him or someone on duty tonight. They'll want to see this and we'll need them."

"Why?"

"I think"—he let the thought dissolve into a smile without any joy in it—"I think I'm an old man who may not know as much as he thinks he does. Bring in the Conservation Department. If I'm right, it'll help. If I'm completely wrong, at least they'll take care of the fish."

He turned and began his amble, waving as he went, "Riley Yates," he hollered across the space. "What brings you out of your bed on this chilly evening? You know someone might be back home trying to slip in and keep Junie warm."

"That's why I'm here making sure you're at work," the reporter called back.

They laughed and fell into talking more quietly. I pulled out my phone.

Before dialing I took a moment for myself. I don't care who you are, nights like this one have an effect on you. There was no place to look except up that wasn't streaked with blue and red comets from the emergency vehicles. The sky directly overhead though, was clear. So clear it showed itself to be the absence that it was. Not black. Just nothing. Into nothing had been cast a spray of shattered light. I reached up with my empty hand, stretching to touch the shine or the void. The beauty of it made me think of Bob Dylan and I wanted to dance beneath the diamond sky. It was a sad longing, just like the song. And a feeling you can't imagine ever experiencing again but you can't imagine living without either.

I lowered my arm and my hand was so empty I knew I had touched the nothing, but fallen far short of the diamonds. If I thought any more about it I was going to cry or laugh. So I dialed the phone.

It took Mike a few rings to pick up and when he did he wasn't too happy to hear about a pile of fish that was just barely in his state. When I asked him what was so special about paddlefish though he perked up.

"Paddlefish?" he asked. "You're sure?"

"Look like catfish with long bills instead of whiskers."

"Close enough." He actually sounded a bit excited and he must have been because he was there in twenty minutes.

Mike arrived in a truck pulling a boat and trailer just as the body was coming out of the woods. I noticed his boat had just been pulled from the water—the bilge drain was still dripping and it was dragging a tie-down strap. Sticking over the bow of the boat was a gaff and a long gigging pole. When he got out of the truck he went back to the boat and trailer to tuck away the loose bits and shift some boxes and poles around.

He stopped the busy work when the body reached the asphalt. It was in a black bag and strapped to a lift board carried by the coroner's assistant and two deputies. He watched the procession for a moment leaning on the gunnel of his boat to make some notes in a pad before he came over to me. Mike didn't amble. He was the kind of guy who looked exactly like what he was—half cop and half biologist who spent most of his life outside. When he came toward me his stride was long and determined like he had someplace to be and something to do once he got there. If my Uncle Orson had been there he would have said the man was there to kick ass and take names. It was the kind of description Mike would have liked.

"Did we drag you out of the water?" I asked.

"It's where I live," he answered then pointed back to the boat. "Home's a bit crowded right now, illegal trot lines, jug fishing, gigging. Seems like all the evidence I collect has hooks and barbs."

"Better you than me," I told him sincerely.

"Is that the poacher?" Mike asked canting his head in the direction of the body bag being transferred to a gurney.

"Poacher?" That was a surprise and I guess I let it show in my voice. "They poach paddlefish?"

"Well, technically, any harvesting of wildlife out of season or without the proper license is poaching. But *this* is something else entirely. You didn't know?"

"Know what?"

"About paddlefish and caviar."

"Is it anything like 'The Walrus and the Carpenter'?" I asked.

"What?"

"It's a—"

His brows came together in bewilderment. "I don't even see how those things can go together."

"It's nothing." I tried to dismiss the confusion and my attempt at whimsy. "It's a poem. It's nothing."

"A poem?" Mike stared at me. There was no mistaking the appraisal in his eyes.

"From *Through the Looking-Glass*," I explained. "*Alice in Wonderland*?"

"People are talking, Hurricane."

"What? What's that mean?"

"Some are saying you're off your game. That you're not the Hurricane you used to be."

"Yeah? Well maybe that's a good thing."

Mike looked away then kind of shrug-nodded before letting his gaze fall to the dark asphalt. "It's just what some people are saying."

"Because I mention a poem?" I waited for an answer but when nothing came I said, "What's next? Jokes about how women cops can only do their jobs three weeks a month?"

"That's not what I'm saying."

"Then what are you saying?" I was mad and he could hear it. The sheriff and Riley could hear it too. They stopped their friendly banter to look at us. At me that is. I didn't care.

"I'm just—"

"What?"

"Some people are—"

"I notice that none of those people are coming and saying it to my face."

Even in the darkness I could see his face darken with a flush of shame. "There's no reason to try to pick a fight." It was a weak and defensive refutation.

"Tell it to your mirror. I was in a pretty good mood for a woman standing in the middle of a murder scene. I was thinking about Bob Dylan and 'Mr. Tambourine Man' and just trying not to be weighed down by death and all the other shit in my life. You get me?" I stepped closer, deliberately invading his personal space. "One little comment about a poem and you warn me about—what? That I'm a different person after my husband died? Or maybe it's because of the money? The guys think I should be back at the art gallery and hosting tea parties and acting like a good woman?"

"Forget it," he said sounding almost desperate. "Can you just take me to the fish and show me what's going on?"

I didn't say anything then. I spun around and started walking toward the opening in the trees so fast that Mike had to catch up. I was practically stomping through the woods. At one point I pushed past a low branch, holding it back then releasing it to whip back into Mike's chest and face.

Once we arrived at the scene we ducked under the tape posted by the deputies.

Billy was still there talking to the evidence tech. "I thought there was a bear coming down the trail," he called out once he saw us.

I ignored him and pointed over to the pile of fish. "There it is," I told Mike. "Check it out."

He walked past me and raised a hand to Billy. "There *is* a bear," he said. Then, in a whisper that still carried in the quiet and the empty space between the trees and the water, he asked, "What's *her* problem?"

"What happened?" I saw Billy glancing over to me and he saw me notice.

"I was talking about the fish and she asked me something about a walrus and a carpenter. I tried to tell her, as a friend, maybe she shouldn't be at work. I mean what are you supposed to say to something like that?"

"Next time she says anything about 'The Walrus and The Carpenter'," Billy said with another glance my way. "Ask her, *why is a raven like a writing desk?*" After that he grinned and I could tell it was for me.

That was all it took to open the fist of anger that was clenched in my chest. Someone who gets me. And that set a whole other flock of feelings to stir around my heart. Those feelings were a lot more confusing than anger and honestly a lot less welcome.

"So what do you think?" I asked as I walked over without stomping. To ignore, I'd decided was the best policy. "Are these the fish you expected? And what do they have to do with caviar?"

Mike stood straight and tense, waiting, I'm sure, for me to turn back into some female PMS demon. When he didn't answer right away I asked again, "Mike, what do you think?"

"Are we good?" he asked. "You know I wasn't trying to . . ."

I arched my eyebrows and tilted my head slightly in question.

". . . anything," he finished.

"No problem at all, Mike. I might have overreacted. And I'm sorry."

Billy was grinning, clearly having a good time.

I nodded in the direction of the tech placing little rulers for scale next to muddy tracks. "Maybe you could make yourself useful," I told him. "Then we can get out of here sometime tonight."

He went but he kept grinning. I thought I was safe but he simply couldn't help himself. "By the way," Billy said. "You owe me a soda."

Chapter 3

One thing that truly astounded me about Mike Resnick that night was his reaction to the smell. It's something that everyone who has to spend any time around death knows—you get used to the smell. When I'd first encountered this scent though, I had my doubts. Dead and rotting fish has its own special place in the pantheon of horrific odors. The river Styx, I imagined, was nothing more or less than the flowing soup of rotten fish. I had been surprised to realize that I had in fact gotten so used to the stink of the pile, I noticed it only when I thought about it. And I tried pretty hard not to think about it.

Mike never mentioned the smell. He never waved a hand at the cloud of buzzing flies. And in a gesture that seemed to be a terrible temptation of fate, he reached, barehanded, into the pile and sorted through fish carcasses. Once he'd seen all he wanted to see, he casually wiped his slimy hands on the thighs of his jeans. It wasn't enough even for him I guess because he rubbed his fingers together then took a couple of steps to the edge of the water. There he squatted and dipped his hands in to wash them off.

"I see you looking," he said. "I spend half my life with fish guts on my hands."

"I'm not saying anything."

"You don't have to." Mike stood and whipped his wet arms over the lake water slinging the clinging drops away. "I guess we all have our own quirks."

"I guess so."

"I never picked up much about poetry."

I nodded, understanding the process of easing into being sorry. "And I never picked up too much about paddlefish and caviar."

"Then let me tell you." He extended a still moist and I was certain, stinking and probably sticky hand. "Friends" His grin was bright and challenging—still the awkward country boy I knew in school.

I took his hand and shook. "Friends."

He laughed. "I can't believe you shook. I was sure you wouldn't."

"Tell me about the fish, Mike."

Still chuckling he pointed at the pile. "They're not all paddlefish. Most are, and since they are a smaller part of the population it was the paddlefish they were after."

"Then why have different kinds?"

"I didn't see any hook marks and you can't catch these animals with bait so what I think we have is someone electrofishing."

I shook my head. "I've never heard of anything like that."

"You need a boat with a small generator or a bank of batteries." He spread his hands and pointed down with the index finger of each hand. "You have two electrodes and dip them into the water then— zap." Mike jerked his hands and waggled his fingers demonstrating a shock. "It's like a stun gun in the water. Fish float up. You net them."

"Then why a mix of fish? Why don't you get only the ones you want?"

"Because all these fish float up and if you're doing it at night, which the poachers do, you sometimes get the wrong ones. That's why there was a mix of male and female paddlefish in there too."

"How can you tell male from female and what does it matter?"

"It matters a lot to the fish and to the poachers. To the fish, well, it just makes life interesting. The poachers though are only there for the eggs. They only want the females. If you look at the pile, you'll see some split open. Female. The smaller ones, male, were just left to rot."

"Okay. But what about the whole caviar thing? Caviar comes from sturgeon and Russia, right."

"That's what everyone thinks. Actually there are sturgeon here in the U.S. The thing is though, the roe of paddlefish is basically identical. Maybe there are fish egg connoisseurs out there that can tell the difference but enough people can't."

"Caviar's expensive isn't it?"

"And that's what it's all about. Money. Missouri paddlefish roe can go for thirty-three hundred to thirty-five hundred."

"For each fish?" I was stunned as I looked over at the pile and tried to do a calculation. If only a quarter of those were female . . .

"No." Mike interrupted my math. "Per ounce."

It was my case. I didn't want it but that's the way it goes sometimes. Beware of doing favors for friends. I asked the sheriff if he would put Billy on the clock retroactively from the time he arrived at the scene. It was more than generosity. Having him on duty allowed me to stick him with the chore of impounding Damon's boat. That was something else I didn't want to do. There wasn't much choice. We already had his pistol and the boat needed a much more thorough search than we could do by flashlight. Billy had to take the boat to a landing and have another deputy bring a trailer to get it secured in impound. When I told him, I wondered if he'd noticed the engine. Damon's boat was sixteen feet long and you would have expected it to have at least a twenty-five-horsepower engine. The things you learn working summers on the dock. It had an ancient Johnson nine-horse engine. It would be slow going to get it to the nearest boat landing.

I don't know why but I took a little pleasure in giving Billy the all-night chore. When I did it, I would have smiled and said it was what he got for dragging me into this mess. A few minutes later though I was thinking about his comment to Mike about the raven and the writing desk. It was nice that he understood, but it kind of annoyed me at the same time. More than annoyed, it was like an itch under my bra that I couldn't do anything about in polite company. I didn't know why it bothered me and not knowing only made it worse.

Sticking Billy with the chores left me with Damon. The simple thing would have been to have him taken in and held. Simple and easy but not right. I didn't believe he killed the man in the lake. Mike didn't even give him the ticket for fishing out of season. The problem was I'd just sent his home off to impound.

I could tell by the tilt of his head against the truck window he'd dozed off waiting. I opened the driver's side door carefully but his head popped up instantly. You have to be careful how you wake a combat veteran. Someone is likely to get hurt.

"You doing okay?" I asked him.

His response was to show me his cuffed hands.

"Sorry about that." I pulled my keys and released the bonds on his wrists. "You're a suspect. There's no way around it."

"Then why're you cutting me loose?"

"I'm not. I just took the cuffs off." He nodded and I got the impression that he had a deep understanding of the variables of freedom. "There are a couple of ways we can go."

"Any of them keep me out of jail?" It much less a question than a resignation.

"As a matter of fact . . ." I started the truck and let him think about it for a second.

"Yeah? Well?"

"The problem is one of situation," I told him. "Yours."

"I don't get it."

"You don't have a home because we took away your boat." I dropped the truck into gear. "Even if we hadn't, that boat is not the kind of living arrangement I would want to send you back into."

"It's what I got," he said. "Sometimes we take what we got."

"Don't I know it," I agreed. "But why?"

"Why what? Why's a stunningly handsome, dark-skinned, urban American going homeless in the country music, Caucasian capital of the country?"

I stared at him for a moment. In the dash light, his skin had a gunmetal shine but the angles of his face were hard edged and matched the sullen tone of his voice. "You're not that handsome," I said.

Damon smiled and eased back into the seat. Once he'd made the decision I wasn't an enemy, the chip disappeared from his shoulder. "It's a nice truck." He cast his eyes around the cab then added, "It's a lot of truck for a woman."

"I'm a lot of woman."

He laughed. It was short and quiet. The chip was gone but not the caution. "Billy said you were a good one."

"A good what?"

"Person. Nothing weird or gossipy. He's not like that."

"I know. He's a good one too. One of the best."

"I think he'd like to hear you say that."

I had the feeling of having been caught in a trap. To get away from it I moved my foot from the brake to the gas and twisted the wheel around sharply bringing the truck back to the road. "So where to?" I asked him.

"Not jail."

"Before I promise that, tell me why. Why are you living on a boat?"

"The water."

"What about it?"

"I feel better on the water. The motion. The sound. Even the cold and the smells, damp wood rotting, fish spawning, bait . . . It all soothes me."

"You served . . . ?"

"Two tours. Iraq. Protecting troops against insurgent snipers and gathering intel."

"This is about as far from that world as you can get."

"Exactly." He watched the road crawling through headlights for long moments but I was certain it wasn't asphalt or the Ozarks he was seeing. "Water is like a moat. Something between me and that world."

I let him have the privacy of his memory until he looked up at me with a question in his eyes.

"Okay," I said. "Not jail."

Once he was relaxed, that is to say once he wasn't looking at a murder scene, having his home searched, and once he wasn't heading to jail, Damon was an easy guy to talk with and like. He didn't want to talk about his service experience but neither did I. Mostly we talked about the lake and Billy. I was beginning to think one of us had an ulterior motive for that when I pulled into the parking lot in front of my Uncle Orson's boat dock. It was late but the lights within the shop and the bare bulbs strung through the boat slips were on.

"Come on," I told Damon pointing ahead to the suspended walkway that tethered the dock to the shore.

"What are we doing here?" he asked, suspicion rising back up into his voice.

"You're going to meet the family." I didn't stop at the screen door but I shouted. "Uncle Orson!" The shop was cluttered with shelves and fishing gear. It hummed too, with the sounds of refrigerators and the pumps in the live bait wells. Behind me the screen door slapped closed and the old spring *twanged* like an out-of-tune guitar string. Damon was still standing on the other side of it looking in. "Orson!"

My shout was louder that time and carried out the far side of the shop.

"You don't have to shout," my uncle hollered back at me. "I'm right here cooking dinner." Through the rusted mesh of a window screen his head appeared from behind the grill top. Grill was a generous description. It was a fifty-five gallon drum halved on its side and welded to a frame. When it burned through Uncle Orson simply cut a new barrel and welded it in. I know he never cleaned out the coals and I kind of doubted that he ever cleaned the steel grating he cooked on. "Chicken," he proclaimed as though it explained everything that needed to be said.

"I want you to meet someone." I turned and Damon was still standing on the far side of the screen door. I had to backtrack and push it open and all but drag him through. "Come on," I told him, "come meet the black sheep in my family."

"Black sheep?"

"He was a Marine."

That was when Uncle Orson pushed through the door on his side. "Do I hear you taking the name of the corps in vain? Who's this?" He wiped his hands on one of the wash faded shop towels he used when cooking.

"Damon Tarique, Army Airborne, Ranger, meet my uncle, Master Gunnery Sergeant Orson Williams."

Orson put out his big hand, "Retired."

Damon shook but his eyes were wary. He appeared to be thinking jail would have been better or at least more in line with what he'd expected.

"Ranger huh?" Orson shook quickly and dropped the grip. He had a lot of experience with edgy soldiers. "That's a tough row to hoe. I'm glad to meet you. Chicken?"

"What?" Damon almost choked on the word, but at the same time his face sharpened into something you didn't want pointed at you.

My uncle ignored the look. "You like barbecued chicken? I hit it with my own spicy cayenne rub on the skin and slip garlic butter with rosemary and parsley under it. I'm roasting some ears of corn too and summer squash."

"It sounds pretty good."

"Oh, it's better than pretty good, Ranger. It's damn good. But if I'd of known you were coming it would have been a T-bone."

That seemed to break a spell. Damon smiled and laughed a little.

Uncle Orson pointed him to the table and chairs in the corner and almost shoved him in. "Beer," he said then pointed at me and added, "and a soda pop." Next he pointed to Damon. "You a beer man?"

"Oh hell yeah," Damon answered and for the first time that night sounded almost happy. Once the beers were open he loosened up even more and followed Uncle Orson out to the grill to help. They talked and got along easily the way a lot of veterans do. It was more than that and exactly what I'd hoped too.

Orson had a way with other vets. He recognized wounds that were sometimes so deep the sufferer didn't even know they were there. Then he did the best thing. He found a way to talk, and get them to talk, without preaching. Shared experience. Orson was haunted by the glow of flaming hooches, entire villages he'd set alight with a cigarette lighter. Occasionally he talked about the waves that rippled through elephant grass in the downward wash of Huey helicopters like they were the ripples of the lake he continued to live on. When he got drunk enough, not a rare occurrence, he would talk about the call-and-response nature of an ambush. Two different voices, the AK-47s barking and M16s popping, in firefly flashes across an invisible trail in a jungle of black.

Both he and my father had gone to that war and come back changed. Uncle Orson—Gunnery Sergeant Orson Williams, USMC, drank and remembered. My father, Lt. Colonel Clement Williams, US Army, Retired, a Phoenix Project intelligence officer, went to re-unions and stood at the wall. Sometimes I think Orson's way is healthier.

"We have a problem," I said as Damon and Uncle Orson returned with heaping plates of food.

"What's that?" Uncle Orson asked, setting down his platter of chicken and lifting his beer.

Damon set down the corn and squash and some foil wrapped potatoes. He didn't ask anything or even look at me.

"Damon needs some things I thought you could help him out with."

"Yeah, I saw that comin'," Uncle Orson said once he swallowed his gulp of beer.

"I'm not askin' for anything." Damon looked at the food as he spoke, not at either of us.

"I'm asking. And not just for you." I speared a chicken quarter and plopped it on Damon's plate. "Uncle Orson, you need some help since I took Clare off to work at Moonshines." I reached across the table and dropped a quarter chicken on his plate. "Damon needs not to be in jail."

"Jail?" Orson was more curious than worried. He dropped a corn-cob in front of Damon.

"He found a body tonight on the lake. Technically he has to be a suspect but"—I looked at Damon and gave him an exaggerated shrug—"that seems unlikely. However we did have to impound his boat."

"You can't just let him go home? Or get bail or whatever you do in cases like this?"

"The boat is home." Damon was staring at the food in front of him like a teenaged boy presented with his first girly magazine, as though he knew it was an illusion but hungered for it all the more because of it. "It's all I have." The statement was as naked as the hunger in his eyes.

That was when I realized that he'd probably not eaten this well in a long time. Still he was listening to us talk with his hands in his lap. A perfect guest.

Uncle Orson noticed the same thing at the same time but he acted quicker. "Dig in," he said tearing the leg from the thigh and lifting it to his mouth. He wasn't that hungry. He was making it okay for Damon to eat, and he did. He bit into the thigh meat without bothering to separate the sections. Before he'd even chewed it he had the corn to his mouth grinding away at the cob with his front teeth.

Orson shoved some squash off onto Damon's plate and I added a potato. Together, we shoved the butter dish, salt and pepper shakers, and a bottle of barbecue sauce at him. It was like family and funny, a good moment that would have been made perfect, some small voice in my head whispered, if I had a drink of the beer myself.

It was a cold water thought as shocking as the kind of laugh that says nothing is funny at all coming from out of the darkness. Why, at times like this, do I think of my desire to drink easier than I think of my husband?

Stupid question. I knew it and I knew the insidious nature of sim-ply asking why. Addiction is the whisper itself as well as the whisperer. I took a drink of my orange soda and concentrated on the face of Nelson Solomon.

His face let me smile.

"So what so you need?" Uncle Orson asked.

I couldn't tell if the question was for Damon or me but he was chewing ravenously so I said. "How about if you let him work on the dock for a bit? He likes being on the water."

Even shoveling the food in Damon managed to nod at that.

"In exchange for your spare room," I said.

Uncle Orson lived on the second level of the dock above the bait shop. It was a cozy two-bedroom apartment. There was also a docked houseboat on the slip side but I claimed that whenever I stayed over. Which had not been since I was last drunk I realized.

"And a little food, I imagine," Uncle Orson added.

"I'm not sure you can afford to feed him," I said and we laughed.

Damon put down the chicken and wiped a napkin at his face revealing a sheepish grin. "I would be grateful, sir," he said. "And I would work hard."

"I don't doubt it." Orson stood and went to the cooler behind the bar and pulled out a couple of more beers and another soda. "I do not doubt it for a minute," he said again, then added, "we'll give it a try."

The two men, combat veterans from different wars had an instant connection. I didn't have any worries that things would work out and both would benefit. As a matter of fact, by the time dinner was over and we were clearing the dishes I was beginning to feel like I was the one holding things back.

I put my empty soda bottles in the recycle bin. Uncle Orson had gone green while his old friend Clarence Bolin had been helping him out. Clare was a closet Democrat and an old bootlegger. Who else would I put in charge of the distillery at Moonshines when I needed someone to run the business?

It was a work night, late for a sober girl, and I had every intention of heading home. I needed sleep. Needing isn't the same as wanting. I was wide awake. Besides, my sleep was never the rest I hoped for. Thinking of Clare and Moonshines reminded me that I owed the place a visit.

That time I drove slowly, in no hurry of any kind and cherishing the quiet darkness. The stars still paid no attention to me.

It was as lively within Moonshines as it had been quiet outside under the indifferent stars. Walking in the door had become a joy since I turned over the reins to Clare. Aside from his talents with distilling, he looked like what the tourists expected, a hillbilly in overalls with a big gut and chicken legs. I'd gotten him to dress a little better on the floor, but the whiskers and belly remained.

"Hurricane," he called out to me as I stepped into the bar.

"Clare," I called back. "Don't call me that."

He grinned and without saying so, ignored the request as he always did. "I want you to meet someone." He took me by the arm and literally pulled me along. His other arm he put out in front as he walked like he was both clearing a path and presenting whatever was at the end of it. "My brother, Roscoe."

At the bar was a man that was like a fun-house reflection of Clare only in a mirror that made things better than real life. Roscoe stood and offered his hand. All the parts were there, it was just that the brothers had done something different with them. Rather than a big belly he had a barrel chest. Clare's slightly bowed, poultry-legged look was turned almost unnaturally straight, lean more than skinny. Up top was the real difference, they had the same basic face, but the eyes were... frightening and beautiful. Clare had brown eyes. His brother had eyes of browns. Roscoe's right iris was chestnut, streaked with a center band the color of a worn but still shining penny. It was a stunning cat's eye pattern made all the more dramatic by its absence in the left. It didn't mean the other side was less intriguing. There, was a mosaic of broken shards ranging from shattered brown quartz to beer-bottle green. Looking into those eyes was like touching a hot stove. You only did it quickly and rarely. And, I suspect, you remained wary the rest of your life.

"Hello," I managed to say and I was proud of myself for getting that out. I shook his hand.

When I released it, Roscoe lifted his hand up and pushed back a tumbling cascade of pewter hair. His brother grinned at him then at me from under a tarnished crew cut. The two of them were different sides of an old silver dollar—men from another age who wore the time differently. Clare I imagined as the heads side, burnished and worn, maybe from the thumb of someone hoping for luck. Comfort. Roscoe was tails, a more intricate engraving, still shining with the pressure of being struck and all sharp edges. If I'd flipped that coin I would have wished for heads every time. Clare was a man who put me at ease. In just a few seconds I saw Roscoe as the spinning fall of the coin itself, unpredictable chance.

"This is Katrina Williams, detective with the Sheriff's Department, Orson Williams's niece, and the owner of Moonshines."

"Howdy," Roscoe said, cowboy without the drawl. "Very pleased to meet you."

"I didn't even know Clare had a brother."

His smile was a trickle, slight and crooked compared with the raging grin of Clare.

"He's my big brother," Clare said bubbling with pride. "And famous too."

"Now that's not really true." Roscoe's smile, at first a cautious upward angle, turned down into a humble line. There was still a tiny flick at the corners that said he enjoyed the attention.

"You've probably heard of him, Reverend Roscoe Bolin and the Starry Night Traveling Salvation Show."

I had. Before Clare had even gotten the title out, my gaze had returned to those eyes and looked away again. Roscoe had the look of a firebrand and the reputation of a modern day John Brown.

"Revolution wears a black frock coat," I said.

The smile ticked upward. "You read the news magazines."

"Mostly in waiting rooms," I answered "But that one was hard to miss. Mixing politics and religion. I bet you don't get invited to a lot of dinner parties."

He laughed with good humor then said, "I didn't mix it. In fact, I don't think it has even been unmixed. They are like the front and back of one shirt that we all wear."

"Yeah, but you keep talking about an independent Palestine. Redrawing all kinds of borders. You even said religion could not be the only consideration for any government. I thought it was against the rules for you guys to rattle cages in Israel."

"The Middle East is a place of turmoil and historic rage. The first step to fixing it is denying the fairy tale that any one group is absolutely right."

"Wait, isn't that—"

"I'm talking about borders and land use, not faith." He guessed my path and cut me off.

"Fair enough. What about all the talk about a Kurdish state with freedom of religion? That had to make you some enemies. They say you're rewriting the rules of evangelical Protestantism."

"That's a mouthful isn't it?" He grinned with dull teeth and bright eyes. "But if I am, it's for the better, I hope." He downshifted from grin to smile and opened his jacket wide. "And it's not a frock coat. It's a wool blend summer-weight from Sears."

"But you can see the comparison?" I pointed to his shirt and then down to his boots and back up. "And all those to Johnny Cash. The whole man-in-black thing?"

"I do." He smiled and released his jacket to let it fall into place. "People like to make comparisons. Don't they, Hurricane?"

Yeah, I deserved that. "Please, sit." I gestured to the stool he had occupied until my arrival and I sat beside him. "You're doing a show here?"

"Despite the name, we don't do shows. We hold testimony. We call the lost to home. And we shout the praise that heals us all from within."

"Sounds like a heck of a show."

He nodded and the smile went to a, you-caught-me smirk. "It is. The band is something else. Gospel, bluegrass, and down-home country with a little more gospel. I hope you come join us."

"I'm not much of a joiner," I said expecting the Reverend to either give up politely or to give me the evangelical sales pitch.

He did neither. "I couldn't get a permit for within Branson city limits," he told me.

The shift of focus caught me a little off guard and I wondered if that was intentional. "I can see how that might be tough."

Clare had slipped away and was now behind the bar. He put a bottle of orange soda in front of me then opened it, brushing off the clinging flakes of ice. He didn't bother to set out a glass. For his brother he opened up a mason jar of Moonshines' best and topped off his highball glass then dropped in two fresh cubes. Even the ice for the drinks was Clare's special recipe. He used filtered and distilled water in ice trays. He claimed it tasted better than the machine ice. I don't know about that, but they look good. The cubes were clear as crystals in the colorless liquid.

Roscoe didn't seem to notice. As soon as Clare's hands went back to his side of the bar the elder Bolin was bringing the glass to his lips.

After the taste he made kind of a gasp-sigh sound of pleasure. "This is good." He nodded with approval and sucked at his upper lip as though there was some left over. "A lot better than what you cooked out in the woods," he said to his brother.

"Don't I know it?" Clare started screwing the lid back down on the jar, but Roscoe rattled his glass gently. The lid came off and the glass was given a liberal splash.

"Is that a preacher's drink or a revolutionary's?" I asked.

"Just a man's" he answered. "Our Lord, who provided wine for the feast, would, I believe, have enjoyed whiskey." He took a sip savoring it then added, "In moderation."

I held up my orange soda and tilted it in his direction. "Here's to moderation." After we each took a drink I said, "So no city permit? But that's not stopping you is it?"

"Things are much more agreeable in the county," Roscoe said. "A friend and follower has provided a bit of pasture land, twenty acres of alfalfa he's willing to see trampled for us to put on a week's worth of the Lord's work."

"Well I wish you good luck with that."

"And speaking of the Lord's work . . ."

You didn't need to be a prophet to see what was coming there. I held up my soda like a personal talisman and said, "Nope."

Roscoe smiled and turned his entire aspect on me. It was all contrasts, silver hair and black clothing, eyes, both bright and dark, and something deeper that I immediately thought of as will and acceptance.

"No," I said again. "No, no, no, no." Just in case I wasn't clear.

His face and the contrasts hidden within merged into one single dissonance between felicity and something else. Anger? Pity? I couldn't guess. I didn't try.

My phone rang, startling me. The second time in one day and neither one the sheriff's office. Even though the call wasn't the SO, it was once again work. This time the caller was Mike Resnick.

"Hurricane, can we get together and talk?" I glanced at Roscoe. He was nursing his drink, watching me like he knew more about me than I did. "Yeah," I said. "I'm at Moonshines if you want to meet."

After disconnecting I held up my empty bottle to Clare and shook it. Before I had set it back on the bar he was there holding out a new orange soda.

"Sticking around?" he asked.

"Yes," I said. "I'm meeting a conservation agent."

"Are you sure you want to do that in public?" Roscoe asked.

The brothers laughed and the similarity between them, the feeling, and the sound was uncanny.

Clare leaned on the bar with his big gut under the rail and his elbows on the top. "Game wardens are never very popular around here."

"Anywhere," the elder Bolin added.

The pair of them chuckled again. Clare reminded his brother about a fishing story from their youth. I didn't listen. I watched them. So much was the same. So much was different. Just like his brother Clare was an ordained minister—Assemblies of God. I wondered if Roscoe had ever distilled whiskey in the woods. But I had the feeling that the similarities were surface features only. Clare was a man I trusted completely. His brother was a lit fuse that kept me feeling on edge. One of the problems with my life was that I was always wanting to see the fireworks.

They laughed again and pulled me out of my thoughts.

"The last time I was caught over my limit the fine cost me almost a hundred dollars." Clare said.

"Tax collectors and game wardens, the cost of modern life." Roscoe finished up.

"What about cops?" I asked.

"Usually, cops too." He chortled his amusement with me. "But you're not a cop. You're the hurricane."

I'd almost come to terms with that nickname like you come to terms with Jehovah's Witnesses. You don't fight and they go away a lot quicker.

"You're the sheriff's stealth bomber."

"That's right, Hurricane." Clare said grinning. "Everyone *tut-tuts* about the things you do, but the county is glad to have their big-ass, lady cop."

"I thought I'd asked you to stop staring at my ass."

"Not staring; just using a figure of speech."

"Either way, keep my figure out of it." I pushed the soda bottle aside and told Clare. "I think I'm all soda-popped out. Would you pour me up an iced tea?"

"Iced tea, coming up. Lemon. No sugar." He stepped away from the bar and started around to the gate side. "What kind of southern girl are you?"

"I'm no girl, you keep reminding me. I'm a hurricane."

"So why does a sheriff's deputy need to meet a conservation agent this late at the local watering hole?" the Reverend asked me. "I hope it's something about which I should disapprove. Clare tells me you could use a little life in your life." Behind the wink and good humor was a kind of current. Roscoe Bolin was the sort of man who couldn't ever turn off the intensity, I decided. I chalked it up to the eyes and the hair, to the fact he was a firebrand preacher. Like his brother, there was something there that was hard to dislike.

I smiled at the joke. "He does, does he?"

Behind the bar Clare shoved a glass into the ice bin. I was getting the machine ice, not the good, clear stuff he uses for company and big spenders. He squeezed in a lemon wedge and poured the tea. It was fresh and still warm. The ice cracked like tiny glaciers in the glass when the liquid hit it. As he passed it over he told me, "Good for what ails you."

"That's a tough promise for a glass of tea." It was wonderful, cooling and watering down from dark brown to amber in the time it took me to raise the glass for a first taste.

"So?" Clare pressed his brother's question.

When I sat the glass down I toyed with it between my palms. It was already sweating and I liked the feel of cold water on my dry skin. Drunks learn tricks to distract themselves if they are going to hang out in bars.

"So you're as much a fisherman as your little brother?" I asked the Reverend Bolin.

"We grew up fishing. And I can say without being accused of undue pride, I'm a much better fisherman."

"Don't let him tell stories," Clare spoke to me but grinned at his brother. "He's only better at the fisher-of-men thing. I never had the calling he did, but I have definitely caught more fish."

Before they could get too deep into familial reminiscing I asked, "You know anything about poaching paddlefish?"

Roscoe looked a little caught by the change in direction. He took a sip from his glass, seeming to think the new topic over. Clare mulled it over with genuine interest. "I know it's a big, *illegal* business that's a danger to the population."

"Danger?" I stopped with my glass poised at my lips. "What do you mean, like the meth trade?"

"Sure. I guess," he answered thinking it through. "I've heard of people fighting over it. The eggs go for a fortune. But I was thinking of the *fish* population. I was always more of a catfish man. I never saw why anyone would waste their time on a paddlefish."

I had the feeling that I'd spoiled a family moment with my question.

Clare must have felt the same way because he turned to Roscoe and tried to bring back his enthusiasm by asking, "Do you remember that big catfish we caught up above Powersite that time? It took both of us to bring it in."

It didn't work. Roscoe nodded quietly, but didn't get pulled back in.

I took my drink and kept my gaze on him over the top of my glass. I savored the flavor and when I sat the tumbler back on the bar it was almost half-empty. "Fish population?"

"Yeah." Clare gave his brother some space and gave his attention back to me. "Paddlefish are an ancient species. No bones. Cartilage. Like sharks."

"Okay. I've heard that."

"There're not that many places left for them, and if you don't manage the population in the lakes they'll be gone."

I took another long drink of tea and braced myself. Clare was surprisingly green and forward thinking for an old-time country guy. Sometimes my ignorance of his causes brought him up on a soapbox. This time I was pretty sure what my next question would put me in for, but I wanted to know.

"What's it matter?" I asked. "Aren't there plenty more fish in the lakes, trout, bass, crappie, catfish . . ."

Clare looked at me as if I had walked naked into Sunday services.

But before he could say anything a voice from behind me answered. "You would lose your business." It was Mike.

Clare nodded and asked, "Beer?" It wasn't so much a question as a statement of expectation. I hadn't realized they knew each other so well.

"Please," Mike said as he sat next to me. "Did I interrupt the lesson in conservation?"

"Not so much as turned it into an economics lesson," I responded.

"You want to fill in the blanks? You know I'm just a cop and, from what I hear, the token loose cannon."

"Yep." He said as Clare handed over a bottle without a glass. "I've heard that too." He looked at Clare and took a drink.

"Whatever." I gave Clare a look myself. It said, *One of these days, Alice.* And I'm pretty sure he understood the subtext to the subtext was, *Bang, zoom, to the moon.* Out loud I said, "Just tell me about the fish."

"It's all about the fish." Mike looked at me serious as a girl who missed her first period after prom. "This whole area is about the fish and fishing. You take it away and you lose a quarter of the economy like a stack of dominos from the lake to every business in the region."

"Okay," I said. "I can understand that, but how do you lose the fish? We're talking about one kind out of several. And—it's the one most people don't even know about."

"You're talking about fish. *I'm* talking about a system. It's like asking what happens when you take the police out of a city. The city and other people are still there but how long will it work? Or nurses? Or teachers? Mechanics—"

"Or distillers of fine spirits," Clare chimed in.

"Okay it takes a village," I said. "Thanks Oprah. But we're still talking about fish."

"We're talking about a healthy eco-system. How many cogs do you need in a clock?"

I shrugged.

"If you take a couple out maybe it still works well enough that you'd never know until that one moment you really need to be on time."

"Forget I asked," I told him. "I'm already tired of fish stories."

"Too bad," Mike said. Then he took a drink like it was some kind of dramatic pause. "Because I have one I think you'll like."

"Only if it's going to get this body off my plate."

"It just might." Mike pulled a paper from his shirt pocket and set it on the bar between us. "The body's name is Daniel Boone."

"You're kidding me." I picked up the printout. It was an intake form from the Benton County, Missouri Sheriff's Department. The booking photo showed a youngish man, probably early twenties. His black hair was cut high and tight. Military. Aside from his hair, the image also showed a split lip and bruised eye. The important thing was nothing in his face. He was shirtless and there on the top of his right shoulder was the Airborne eagle tattoo. Just visible on the left was a smaller tattoo. It mimicked the Army tab that read RANGER. "Daniel William Boone," I read from the form. "They named him Daniel Boone? Who would do that to a kid?"

"You'd be surprised." Mike reached over to tap at the paper. His finger pointed out the box with Daniel Boone's address. His town of residence was listed as Boonville. "That part of the state is full of Boones and all of them claim relation to the great bear killer. A lot of his family moved to Missouri before the Civil War."

"The town was originally called Booneslick because there was a salt lick some of the Boone family used for their cattle," Clare added. "It's right next door to Boone County. The family brought slaves and tobacco farming. That whole area was the heart of what they called Little Dixie."

"Enough history lessons." I used the form to point at Mike. "How did you find this? And how did you do it so quickly?"

"There are only so many arrests for wildlife poaching and even fewer for paddlefish. And I already knew that the town of Warsaw has the highest rate of those arrests in the state. It wasn't that big a pile to dig through."

"Okay," I conceded. "It helps but it opens up a whole other can of pain in my butt."

"I thought you'd be pleased."

"I haven't been pleased in a long time."

"Sounds like a personal problem to me." Mike grinned over his beer at Clare who glared back at him like he'd told a dirty joke to someone's grandmother. It took Mike a second to remember the whole widow thing. When he did, he pulled the bottle from his lips, spilling an amber trail, and sputtered. "I didn't mean . . . Oh God, Hurricane . . . I—"

"At least you didn't offer to do the job for me."

He laughed. It came out half nervous and maybe a quarter amused. I didn't know what the last little part of it was, but it was a bit too loud and hard-edged. I didn't say anything. I did keep staring at him while I took another long drink from my tea. It kept him feeling foolish, which was fine with me. I wasn't quite ready to let him off that hook.

"Let me see that." Clare, who had been glaring at Mike since his attempt at being funny, picked up the printout I'd left on the bar.

"So, uh," Mike seemed to be having difficulty finding something to say. "How's uh . . . I mean did you get Damon settled?"

"You know Damon?"

"Billy told me you had him in custody. I've cited him a few times. Small stuff. Never had the heart to hit him with a big fine."

"He's with my Uncle Orson," I said and lifted my glass.

"I know that guy." Clare flicked the page in his hand.

I almost choked on the last drops of my tea. "You're kidding me," I managed to say, mostly without spraying liquid.

"He was here a couple of days ago." Clare pointed to the picture, tracing out imaginary lines around the head. "He had long hair but I'm pretty sure it was him. He came into town with Roscoe."

I turned and looked down the row of empty barstools. Reverend Bolin was gone.

Chapter 4

Morning crawled through my window amber-eyed and cat-like in its quiet. It needn't have bothered I wasn't there. I was in bed but a thousand miles away and almost a decade in the past. My past. Most of the night I had been there, the sweat that stained the sheets a cold echo of the blood I had left in the dirt of Iraq. People who don't know talk about PTSD in terms of nightmares and soldiers living on the street. In my experience, there are few nightmares, instead there are moments of transport, actual reliving, not dreaming, of terror. My experience tells me also that the ones on the street are simply the peaks of mountains sticking up from under mist. The rest of us are hidden and living in the mist with you. With, but separate.

There was a time, a time before . . . everything, when I was a normal young woman, a little taller than average but pretty enough even if it's me saying it. I had long legs and white skin that bloomed with pale freckles in the summer sun. My hair, a dark auburn from fall until spring, burned under clear skies to the color of bright pennies.

Then I'd gone to war. It was a time when women were not supposed to be in combat but no one told the Taliban or the hundreds of other tribesmen gleefully living in the thirteenth century. There were no lines, and we were fighting people who wore no uniforms. Shia were fighting Sunni. Warlords were battling over villages and trade routes for oil and Afghan opium. Former Red Guards were pitted against Iranian militia insurgents. And all of them were fighting us.

It turned out that in that stew of loyalties, money alliances, flags, and faiths, all the men could find one thing to agree on—their disdain, if not outright hatred, for women. Even the men in my own unit.

I'd been dragged out of camp and raped by two superior officers who seemed to feel that any woman who dared demand a place at the table, deserved to be treated like a dog under it. They left me for dead in the blowing brown Iraqi dust. The dirt I stained with my blood and despair even as it blew like airy rivers over a mud wall, trying to bury me from the sight of men. I'd crept out of the soil of my living grave and stumbled, scared and mute like the monster's bride, right into the path of an insurgent vehicle.

I'd been saved—that is my life, the breathing, heart beating, basic functions of my body had been saved—by the appearance of an American patrol. The wide-eyed boy, a-nineteen-year-old, Army medic who patched me up and told me "Everything would be okay," went on to become Deputy William Blevins—Billy. At least in my mind. A year ago, I'd helped him save a girl and her arm after a car accident. That was when I learned Billy had been a medic in the Army. I still don't know if he was *the* medic. He's never said. And I won't ask. What I did, rather than asking, was to run a check. What does that say about me? The same thing it says about all former military police and sheriff's detectives, probably, that we don't trust well.

Billy was deployed there at the time.

It's his face I remember but remembering is a hard thing that my mind sometimes dresses up in prettier clothing. I believe it was Billy and that was enough for understanding if not for sharing.

If I had spent my night bleeding into dry ground and watching the birth of the scars that track my body I might have greeted the sun with a sense of liberation. That particular battle, no matter how I sound, and despite the concerns of my therapist, I'd left behind me. It came in blowing dusts of memory that intruded into my day-to-day but, mostly, I lived without it coloring my every thought.

Still—

Before the sun had come sneaking on cat feet through my window the world I was living in was that war, years past. So when the light found me, it illuminated the face of Billy over my bloody body. It shone through his head and the fuzz of his cropped hair like a crown of light and peered through his eyes, his kind eyes.

Billy said, "You'll be okay. Everything will be all right . . ."

Then he was gone and I was lying back in my bed. I wasn't alone. The past year was with me.

It had been a rough, but wonderful time when I'd met Nelson Solomon. Like a river flow, he tumbled and smoothed the ragged rocks that my brain insisted on chewing daily. When I wanted to drink, he helped me both with his need and his strength. His need because a man as sick as he got at the end requires a lot of care and attention. His strength because he kept his promise to me and fought to the end.

"Everything will be all right . . ."

After Billy spoke and after his voice and the grind of Humvee tires echoed in the chambers of my past, Nelson was lying next to me in the wet sheets, incredibly close but not touching. He was temptation and terror. I knew that if I reached for him, if I admitted the loss and the devastation by contact, he would become, a corpse decaying beside me. All my love and all my loss would be experienced again in a momentary rotting of flesh. My bed—my life—was a grave.

I didn't move. I didn't reach to relive my loss and the sun slowly dispelled it.

Once the ghosts were all gone, and I had the courage and strength to put my legs under me again, I showered and dressed feeling like I was the haunt. The house was Nelson's. It was a prefab log cabin but about as rustic as an art museum. It was filled with Nelson's own art that he'd collected from friends I'd never met. In the big living room I paused. It was a large, open space with a glass wall that stuck out like the prow of a ship over the cliff face that dropped a hundred feet to the lake below. I could never walk straight through it, not since Nelson passed. To the side, between the fireplace and kitchen was a spattered drop that defined his workspace. Still standing within it was his easel and his last painting. It was of him and me in two rowboats on greenish-blue water. My boat and I were in the light. Nelson was in shadow. I was close to shore and he was adrift, far from me, out of reach. I hated it. I loved it. But I looked at it every morning when I came out of an empty bedroom and went to my job.

I called in to dispatch and let them know I was on the clock, but not going directly into the SO. Instead, I logged myself as making a visit to the Starry Night Traveling Salvation Show.

An early spring morning in the Ozarks can be almost anything. That one was almost everything. To the east was orange rubbing into turquoise and sunlight. To the west was a line of clouds as dark as the night I'd just spent. The border between them clashed and roiled. It curled like a fishhook to the south where it took on the green cast of hail. I didn't see, but could feel thunder. It was perfect weather.

The tents were set up on the south side of Lake Taneycomo in an empty pasture that had a clear view of the water. An old bit of property, it had to have been in someone's family for many years, the ground was too valuable now for anyone to leave agricultural. It was a developer's dream.

I drove through the cut-away barbed wire and parked in the trampled grass. It had taken almost half an hour to get through the twisting roads from the cliffs over Branson to the far side of Forsyth. In that time, the fishhook in the clouds had circled around and filled almost all of the sky. Wind was whipping the canvas and harried looking men whose shirtsleeves were already rolled for labor were running about tying the loose ends. I noticed almost all of them had the look of ex-military. There's no crib sheet for picking them out. But there is something, a discipline in the movement and a distance in the gaze. Part of it's the hair. A lot of guys get out and let their hair grow as a big *screw you* to the rules they had to live by while enlisted. These guys were all lean, and hard, and ratty in a way that screamed pissed-off vet to me. Some of my favorite people and some of my least favorite.

There were a few women around but they were all small and brown. They were Hispanic in a way that said something south of Mexico. They were girls really and they looked scared. I wondered if it was the building storm or the men that had them looking like black-eyed rabbits ready to bolt.

"Hey!" someone shouted. I looked around and a lanky-looking man was tromping through the grass in my direction. "Hey," he shouted through the wind again. This time the call followed his pointed finger to a knot of men working to tame a bit of flapping tent.

That time one of the men looked up.

"Reverend says to get over there to the north side of the big tent," the approaching man pointed and shouted again. "Put down another stake for each pole and double-line them." Then he turned, shifting his pointing finger to me. "You can't be here." He was still shouting.

Once he got close enough I could see he wasn't a man at all. He was a teenager. The kid was tall and rough edged in a way that gave the impression of a little dog trying to bully the world back. He wore torn jeans and a denim jacket with the sleeves cut off over a flannel shirt. The shirt cuffs were rolled exposing thin arms decorated with homemade tattoos. I guessed seventeen and that was being generous considering his smooth face.

"Hey!" he called again, waving as though it was possible I didn't see him.

I opened my jacket to show the shield on my belt. It was all the shout I needed.

The tall boy stopped and stared for a moment. I could see the thoughts behind his eyes. People who share an adversarial history with law enforcement always do the same heavy math in their heads when confronted with cops. You can literally see them calculating the odds of being arrested and for what versus those of just being asked uncomfortable questions. Mixed in is always the complex word problem, to run or not. That unaccustomed concentration betrays them and they always end up feeling targeted by cops who have seen those equations worked out a million times before.

He looked like he wanted to say something then he cocked a leg and moved it back ready to turn and run.

"I'm looking for Roscoe Bolin," I told him. "No need to be skittish."

"Who's skittish?" He didn't come any closer. "The Reverend?"

"Yes. The Reverend Bolin. Looks like God in a black suit. The one who just said to double-line the tent ties."

"Whatcha want with 'em?"

I walked toward him. My hand still held back the tail of my jacket showing my badge. That was distraction from the fact of its resting on the end of a metal telescoping baton. He didn't know where to look, at the badge or my face. He seemed uncomfortable with either choice and decided to look away at where the other men had run behind the big tent.

"What I want is between him and me. What's your name?"

"Why?"

"Courtesy."

"You didn't tell me your name."

"You mama didn't teach you to introduce yourself to a lady?"

"You're a cop." He said it like he had found some magic loophole in manners.

"I'm both."

He heard the warning in my voice and dropped the smile he was working at. I waited and he got fidgety and confused.

"What?" The question blurted out seemingly on its own.

"Your name?" The first bit of distant thunder rumbled in the sky. I wondered if the coincidence of it helped.

"Dewey." He said it hard, like the name had been pried from his mouth. After that it was as if he was deflating with words and anger. "You got it? I'm Dewey Boone. Like a man ain't got a right to walk around without being talked down to and water-boarded. Jack—boot—thugs. And I got rights. Don't think I don't know my rights. I got a Fifth Amendment right not to tell you anything. Fifth Amendment and don't tread on me. There's the Second Amendment too. I got a right to defend myself."

If I didn't jump in I could see that little tirade building up a head of steam. So I cut him off asking, "Are you related to Daniel Boone?"

Dewey stopped his rant like he'd had his plug pulled. He didn't relax though. If anything his body took on an added tension, a rictus of restrained energy like a man holding a charged wire. His eyes kept moving. They looked from my shield to my face to my boots and back up. They couldn't seem to settle, dancing like the lid on a boiling pot and, when they lifted all the way up, steam escaped. Suspicion.

I pulled the print of the intake form with the booking photo of Daniel Boone on it from my pocked and unfolded it.

"What you got?" His eyes narrowed.

"A picture."

"I don't need a picture."

Thunder charged again and for the first time I caught sight of a pale flashing in the darkened clouds.

I held the photo up anyway. "This man. Do you know him?"

"I told you I don't need a damn picture. Where is he? Arrested? He gets a phone call, don't he? He ain't called. We can get a lawyer. Don't think we can't. There ain't no getting away with this. We have rights—"

"We?"

"Me and my brother. We have rights. You can't keep him. You can't spirit him away in the night. We are citizens and free men—"

"Daniel Boone?" I shook the picture in front of him to try for a little focus. "This man?" When Dewey looked away I stepped around and put the paper in front of him again. "Is this your brother?"

"You know that already. Why else would you be here? You come for me now, ain't you? This is how it starts. Rounding up the citizens." The energy that locked his limbs released and Dewey stood straight, a mimicry of standing at attention and stared right into my eyes. "I ain't gonna go. You got no charges and no cause."

Before he could begin again about his rights and the Constitution, I lowered the paper and tried to soften my own eyes. I stepped back and said as gently as I could, "Mr. Boone, I'm sorry." That stopped him. No matter how much you hate or fear the government, when someone with a badge shows up to say they're sorry, you know it's bad news.

The clouds that had been creeping were running. Lightning pulsed within them and the wind hit, cold and moist. I could smell the rain and the waft of clean air.

"How bad is it?" The question was quiet and knowing. It said *bad news was not entirely unexpected, but please, bring me hope.* I've heard it spoken a thousand ways in a thousand voices.

"I'm sorry . . ." I began again.

Dewey nodded and a trembling began in his lips. It spread quickly through his body and he looked for a moment like he might collapse. He didn't. At least not on the outside. "He's dead?" It came out as a question. He wasn't really asking.

"Yes, Mr. Boone. I'm sorry."

"Was he drunk?"

"What?"

"I've told him. Scolded him. Mama did too, over and over. *Don't drink on the road,* she'd tell him. *It'll be the death of you.*"

"Mr. Boone."

Lightning bolted from the lowered black front clouds to the ground. It looked far away. Not that far, because thunder followed nearly instantly. The scent of the ozone blew through.

"But he loved drivin' fast. And sometimes I think he loved being drunk more than anything else." His misty recollections congealed back into suspicion as he looked back from the grass up to my eyes. "I don't believe it." It was a pronouncement, a statement of truth and denial at the same time. "I don't believe it. I won't. He can't be gone."

"It wasn't a car accident, Mr. Boone." I let that stand out there between us for a moment, a damaged fence between two bad neighbors who can't see to a mending. Then I said again, "I'm sorry."

"I don't—" Then he did. Understanding blossomed in his face and the roots of the flower reached into his gut. "Who?" he asked. "How?"

"Who?" I echoed the question and regretted the edge that was in my voice. Dewey was a kid attuned to suspicion and I feared setting him off again.

"Who did it?"

I was surprised by the reaction or lack of it. For the first time he seemed like a rational person. He was smaller than he'd been at first. Before he seemed puffed, one of those fish that turns itself into a ball with all the spines. Once the knowledge that his brother had been murdered settled on his shoulders, the armor of his anger and suspicion drooped, all wet paper. The boy was revealed.

"Did someone mean him harm?" I asked.

A hard roll of wind hit us. The canvas of the tents flapped more loudly. Lines that had been pulled extra taut hummed in the air. More people came out of trailers and tents to work the ropes. When the gust slowed to a crawl, it carried a new smell from the nearby lake. The new scent was of old wet wood and rich mud, spawning fish and deep water just turning over for the season. It was decay and fecundity.

"It's a hard world, detective." The thought was strong. The words themselves were so soft they were nearly carried away by the wind.

Before I could ask anything more a shout came from behind him. I looked up to see a man marching with a bit of a limp across the undulating grass. He appeared to have come from the largest and nicest trailer and not happy to be sent out into the weather.

"Dewey!" the man shouted again this time it reached us clearly and Dewey turned. "What the hell? I told you to get to work and check all the tents before the storm. Not make time with the local—"

I could imagine what kind of local I was, but the man stopped shouting. Maybe he noticed my badge or he saw how Dewey was looking. Either way he shut his mouth and turned to run back to the big RV. His limp was much more pronounced as he ran.

"Dewey," I said it as gently as I could. "Would you come down to the station to talk with me?"

He shook his head. "I can't, can I." The statement was said as something obvious, something he imagined I had to understand.

I wasn't sure if I did or not. Then the door to the RV opened and Reverend Roscoe Bolin, dressed all in black, came out. He was followed by a gaunt-looking man with a dark complexion and a walrus mustache blacker than anything the Reverend had on. He struck me as Middle Eastern and probably moneyed by his features and bearing.

Roscoe walked over followed by the man who had been shouting at Dewey a moment before. The mustached man, remained by the RV and smoked.

"You can," I told Dewey. "You really need to. You want to help figure this out don't you?"

"I can't figure nothin' out no more."

Lighting ripped the bottom of the black clouds, ragged, bright fingers that were there, then gone leaving a rumble of falling barrels on an oak floor. Hard drops of rain hit me, one on my cheek and one down the open collar of my shirt. Both rolled down my skin, fat, cold tears.

"Hurricane," Roscoe called.

I looked up and nodded to him then I turned back to Dewey. "It's important, Dewey. I want to find out who hurt your brother."

He wanted to say something, but never got the words out. The Reverend came trotting up behind him again cheerfully calling, "Hurricane."

"Detective," I said.

He stopped and dropped the smile.

"It's Detective Williams." I explained. "This is an official visit."

Without a beat, without hesitation at all, Roscoe asked, "What's happened, Dewey?"

"Daniel is dead." I noticed he took care to pronounce his brother's name fully, not Dan'el as I would have expected. "Killed," he added.

"We'll take care of it," Roscoe told him, again, without hesitation or surprise. To punctuate the statement, thunder once more scattered above our heads.

"What do you mean, *you'll* take care of it, Reverend?" I wasn't surprised when Roscoe ignored my questions.

Instead, he put his hand on Dewey's shoulder turning him to meet his eyes. Without looking at me he answered. "We'll take care of the arrangements. We'll have a funeral for your brother right here and have him taken home for interment among friends and family. Does that sound all right, Dewey?"

Dewey Boone shrugged. I thought for a moment, he was turning to look at me. The Reverend's hands visibly tightened and turned Dewey by the shoulders.

"Come back to the trailer," Roscoe told him. "We'll talk. We'll get things going for poor Daniel." He turned the boy around then pushed to get him moving.

I couldn't see Dewey's eyes, but I saw his body stiffen and his feet stop as though he had walked into a wall. I didn't need to see his eyes to see that he was looking at the dark man beside the RV door.

The dark man, with two fingers pinched at the butt, flicked his cigarette away and opened the door.

"Who's that?" I asked.

Roscoe heard me; that was clear. Again he ignored me just as clearly. I caught the look at the corner of his eye and the resolute turning away. "Go to Massoud," he said, pushing Dewey ahead of him.

As they walked, I put out a hand to touch the Reverend's arm. I was going to say that I still wanted to talk to Dewey or to ask that he come down to the station and make a statement. I didn't get the chance. The big man who had brought Roscoe out of the RV stepped in between us and pushed my hand away.

I guess my bad reputation hadn't gotten around to him yet.

A lot of civilians don't understand how broad the rules about assaulting a police officer are and how they're always slanted in favor of the cop. A lot of people, like, I believed, the man in front of me, do know. But they think I'm a woman before they think I'm a cop. It's their mistake.

As soon as the big man interposed himself between the Reverend and me, I let him come, leading with his right hand on my left wrist. With the edge of my boot heel I stepped down on the outer toes of his foot and pushed my body in. It looked like an accident when he fell on his butt. No one believed how it looked.

"Careful," I told him. Then I stepped around without bothering to look down at him. I had the Reverend's eye.

He glanced down and kind of smiled as he looked back. Above and behind me lightning flashed and I saw it echo in the brighter shards of his eyes. No thunder followed but hard, cold bullets of rain began to fall. I could hear them hitting the tent canvas each drop spaced so far apart it could have been a slow motion telegraph warning of what was to come.

"I still need to speak with Dewey about his brother, if you don't mind Reverend."

"Of course," he answered keeping his guiding hand on the young man's shoulders. "May I ask, is this in the official capacity of interviewing a suspect or a talk to gather information from the bereaved family member?"

The big guy had gotten up and was standing close, an offended dog waiting to be let off the leash. I let him wait while I considered.

"I ask," Roscoe continued, "So I know what to tell the lawyer we'll be providing him with."

"Mr. Boone is a family member." I conceded.

"Then will tomorrow be soon enough for him to speak with you?"

I tucked the paper I'd been holding in one jacket pocket and pulled a business card from another. "Tomorrow would be great," I said holding out the card to the kid.

It wasn't until he got a nudge from the Reverend that Dewey reached to accept the card.

"We'll call," the Reverend assured me. I was already moving.

The big guy had been standing too close to my back on the left waiting to front me as I turned. I didn't turn I backed up leading with my elbow. He took it right below the sternum and woofed out his air as I kept pushing back. His feet were planted wide. The thinking, I assume, was that I would be intimidated if he appeared even larger and more solid when I turned. It was a mistake on a lot of levels, mostly because he wasn't ready to move. His balance was wrong. His feet weren't ready for me to press him again and, again, he went down. Ass and elbows.

"What's your name?" I asked looking down on him.

He tried looking around me to the Reverend.

"This doesn't concern your boss," I told him. "This is about you."

Rain that had pattered began to drop steady. The front had arrived. Thick, hard droplets hit the ground kicking up dust, raising an earthy, spring smell.

The big guy tried scooting back. I stepped forward putting my pointy-toe boot right between his thighs.

"Let me guess." I pretended to think it through. "Your last name is Boone?"

"Silas is my cousin." Dewey said from behind me. I couldn't tell if he was trying to help me or Silas.

"Shut up, Dewey," Silas scolded. "You don't need to be tellin' the cops anything."

I scooched my boot forward so my toe was a real threat to his tender bits, then I said, "No. You shut up, Silas. I've had about enough of you."

A wet lick of wind ran though the grounds and popped the tents. It died in ripples, but carried a steady, thickening rain. I didn't much care. I was ready to make a point or two. I would have if it weren't for the hail that began falling. It came in a fast firing rage that tattooed the ground, the tents, and vehicles with white pellets.

"Silas Boone," I mulled as I stepped away. "I'll be looking into that."

I trotted off to my truck hoping the hail wasn't doing any damage to the hood.

Chapter 5

The sheriff had his feet up on his desk and his eyes pointed to the window when I came in. At first I assumed he was watching the spring storm blowing through the tops of trees. Then I realized he wasn't looking outside but inside—at the picture of his late wife Emily on the windowsill.

"It's a mother fucker, Hurricane," he said without looking at me.

The language was like hearing a new, strange noise from your engine on a familiar stretch of road, wrong and disconcerting. Not the word itself. The sheriff was a man who cursed loudly and often, but almost always for impact. In anger or deep pain I've heard him use every word in the book. Those times, he's considered me—one of the highest honors a man like him can bestow—just one of the guys. Other times, quiet, talking-across-the-desk times, he still thought of me as a lady and curbed his language. It was a strange contrast and had to be a difficult balancing act, but one I actually admired. One I appreciated.

This was different.

"God damn it." He spoke quietly. Still I heard the slight quaver in his voice. "Damn it all to son-of-a-bitching hell."

I closed the door.

"Are you all right, sir?"

He snorted a derisive little laugh through his nose then lifted a balled tissue to dab under his glasses. "There isn't a lot of all right left in life these days, young lady."

"You should speak to someone." I stunned myself with words I never thought I would say after my own hatred of therapy. "Maybe not the same woman I'm seeing," I added.

"I'm talking to you."

"I was thinking of a professional."

"I know what you were thinking. But I'm just sad. I've earned a little of that and saved up a lot more besides. After Vietnam I thought I'd never be sad again. And I wasn't until . . . Now I feel like I can't remember the last time I was happy."

He let his dirty boots fall from the desk to clop loudly on the floor then sat up in his chair and looked at me. It was a deep look that reminded me he knew almost all my secrets. It reassured me also that he had never shared them with anyone.

"You can't have my job," he stated simply. "You can't handle it."

"What?" I didn't know whether to be offended or relieved then I wondered why he thought I wanted it.

"You're a fine and tough woman, but you're tempered too hard for the politics. And you have too much going on in your life. You're too rich for one thing and people would wonder what you're up to."

"Sir, I—"

"Don't worry about it. I know it's not something you were planning." He pointed at the chairs in front of his desk. "Sit down; you're bothering me."

I sat.

"But I want you to think about it. So you won't be thinking I let you down."

"I could never think that."

"Never say never." He used the wadded tissue to touch at his nose. "It's important what you leave behind and who you leave to carry on."

I didn't know what to say but he seemed to expect something so I nodded.

"You can't be sheriff, Hurricane. Hell being Hurricane is about half the reason you can't. The other half is a million other reasons we don't need to talk about. But the thing is, the department needs you."

"Needs?"

He laughed, and he grinned but his eyes were still shining a little from the tears. "Hell, it's kind of hard for me to say too. But it's true. I know I said you should retire and play with the money your husband left you. You'd be good at it, but you wouldn't be happy. It wouldn't be good for the department either."

"You've been thinking about this."

"A lot. Like I said, it's important."

"Why now?" I asked. "Why are you making plans now? You said you were sick of people asking you about it."

"I am. But I got to thinking, maybe they were seeing things I didn't. Then I thought, fuck them." He laughed like he had the past night in the field, full and loud. "And I thought, who wants to spend what time they have left worrying about this shit? Dead guys and piles of fish? But I don't want to abandon it either. I plan to leave it better than I found it. I need you to do that."

"I'll help anyway I can." I decided I was relieved. The sheriff was right about everything, except maybe the department needing me. I tried counting how many mandated therapy sessions I had left. If I *was* sheriff I could probably get out of those.

"What do you think of Blevins?"

"In what way," I asked, imagining I sounded as if I was hedging some bets.

"He could do it."

"Do what?"

"Win an election."

"I'm not sure that's much a part of his thinking."

"Yeah. I imagine you're right about that. I think you could make it a part."

I scowled. "Why me? You just said the reason I'm not suited for the job was that I'm not political."

The sheriff sat and looked at me like I had missed something important. He stared so long that his expression evolved as the question hung on the wall, pornography in a museum waiting for comment. In the end his expression lightened and seemed to be half calling me an idiot and half enjoying the joke at my expense.

Finally he said, "It would be a favor to me if you would talk to him when the time comes."

"Of course," I said still a bit confused. "But while I'm here . . ."

We talked for another several minutes about the death of Daniel Boone and the status of the investigation. There was a time I gave him notes on yellow legal paper instead of e-mail because I was sure he would read the actual pages sitting on his desk. More recently I've taken to talking things through with him face to face, then following up with e-mail so I could copy it to the case file. I'd actually thought I was doing it because it worked better for both of us. Talking to him that day, I wondered if I might have lied to myself. He was hearing. I didn't know how deeply he was listening. When he turned back to the picture on the sill, I saw all the yesterdays come into his eyes.

Once I returned to my desk, I wrote careful notes and added them to the case file with a copy to the sheriff. I printed them out as well and dropped the copy into the box on his closed door.

People watch TV and read books that make a cop's life look like either nonstop shootouts or miracles of modern science that require only a few keystrokes. The truth is much more boring and way slower. I had no autopsy results because we're not a large department with those kind of resources in town. Daniel Boone's body had been taken to a private forensics and pathology lab in another county. They wouldn't even get to it until tomorrow.

Since I couldn't work the evidence I needed to work the people. I started with Silas Boone.

He left big footprints. Silas had been involved with county and state systems almost since he could walk. Family services. Juvenile courts. Just like his cousin Daniel, he had a lot of history with the Conservation Department too. No criminal prosecutions. A lot of fines. Then he disappeared into the military system. Ordinarily that would be easy too, but there was something wrong. Nothing was coming up except his basic record. Induction date, ratings, and rankings—no service locations or Criminal Investigation Division records. There was one bit of interesting information. Silas had been wounded. The location had been redacted, but there were some gruesome details. Aside from that, his documentation was sterile. I found it impossible to believe that he'd been a model soldier, and the absence of documentation was all the confirmation I needed. A cleaned record was worse than anything that could have been logged.

My next call was to my father. He picked up on the first ring like he'd been waiting for my call, but when he spoke it was clear he'd been waiting for someone else.

"The hearing is out until nine tomorrow morning. How about dinner and something—"

"Dad?" I had to cut him off afraid of where that question was going.

"Katrina?"

"You know most people look at the display on their phone before answering. It's not like the old days."

"What do you know about the old days? And I was expecting a call."

"Yes. I picked up on that. Who is she?" My father and Uncle Orson both delighted in trying to get me married off before I met Nelson. I never missed a chance for a little payback. And they took it good-naturedly. When I asked who she was, I expected the usual response, some made-up name, sexy in a cartoonish sort of way, Babette or Trixie LaRue. Once when I made a joke about him finding a date on one of his trips to DC, he said he was meeting someone named Hillary. Then he told me it had to be a secret and that if I said anything a Secret Service man would be knocking on my door.

He simply asked, "Is everything okay?"

"You're not going to tell me?"

"There's nothing to tell. I'm on the Hill and working."

His evasion was about as subtle as a bullhorn at a funeral. I couldn't wait to tell Uncle Orson all about it, but it wasn't the time to rake Dad over the coals. "I need help with a case."

It took just a couple of minutes to explain everything and what I needed to know. He said he'd get right back to me with the information.

He would too. There was no doubt about that. When Dad said he was *on the Hill* that meant hearings and testifying. Not for him. He'd served in Army Intelligence during Vietnam, in something called the Phoenix program. After the war, he continued working intel with a different kind of thrust. He was one of the guys that senators or CEOs of military contractors could call to talk to generals and vice versa. It's a peculiar aspect of our military industrial combine that the different parts kept secrets from each other. Dad was basically a spy and liaison for all sides with business cards that say consultant. So if he's on the Hill he's helping someone say the right thing. And if he says he can get me information tucked into military databases, he can.

Again, life is not like a TV show. Dad didn't call back with all the right answers in the next two minutes. I did paperwork and caught up on some of the many other cases I had. I found a stolen boat with a series of eight phone calls and asking a deputy to check the last lead. While that was going on, I took a call from a pawnshop owner in Branson who was worried some of what he'd purchased might be stolen. I sent a deputy to check it out. There was a report of a stolen car that turned out to be a lover's revenge. She trashed the car, spray painted some choice words on it, then parked it in front of the other woman's home.

After all of that action I was ready for lunch.

Most of the actual storm front had past. We were on the trailing edge and the clouds were thinner with the glow of sun showing through them. The dread and darkness I'd woken with had lifted also. I decided I was probably safe around normal people. Not that there are many of those I care to be around. I went to Uncle Orson's dock to see what he had on the grill.

When I arrived, Damon was moving chicken halves, brats, and Kielbasa sausages around the grate. Standing beside him with a squirt bottle to douse flare-ups in his game warden's uniform was Mike Resnick. I watched the pair working through the screened windows as Uncle Orson finished up with a customer buying salmon eggs and Velveeta, trout bait.

"What's going on out there?" I nodded in the direction of the grill as the customer went out the other door.

"He showed up here about twenty minutes ago. Scared off three customers. When I asked what he wanted he just mumbled something about hoping to catch you and talk. I tried to send him to the station but he wanted to wait."

"That sounds a little odd."

"It sounds a little *personal*." Uncle Orson made sure he got all the meaning he could into the last word.

Some things I'm just a little slow to pick up on. *Personal* things for instance. So I stared at him longer than most people would trying to understand.

He helped me out by nodding at me then in the direction of Mike and saying again, "*Personal*."

"Oh." I got it. "Oh no," I said again. "It's not like that."

"Why not, something wrong with him?"

"No. I mean—that's not the issue. That's not anything. It's not like that. He's helping with the investigation."

"Is that what the kids are calling it now?"

I laughed. "What?" Then I really laughed. "You are such an old man, you know that?"

"Maybe so," he responded. "But at least I know when someone's interested in this fine, droopy, white behind." Uncle Orson shimmied his hips and stuck his butt out to try and pretend he had moves.

"Yeah? When was the last time that happened?"

"That's not really fair since all the women around here know you're the only girl for me."

"Sweet, sweet lies, but I appreciate every one, Uncle Orson. And later, remind me to tell you about Daddy and some woman in DC."

At first I thought he was rolling his eyes at me but instead, Uncle Orson looked away. He turned so I couldn't see his face and pointed toward Mike. "You better get to him quick. I think the sausages are done and the chicken will be there soon."

"I see how it is," I told him. "I'm always the last to know."

Forget helping me with the investigation; I needed to have a long talk with my father.

I pushed my way through the screen door to the dock side of the shop. The long, rusted spring twanged then slapped the door closed behind me rattling the frame.

"Hey, Hurricane," Damon called cheerfully.

Mike stepped back looking a bit embarrassed. He waved with the squirt bottle in his hand and said, "Katrina."

Suddenly I was afraid that my uncle was right. Mike had something personal on his mind. The tough thing was I didn't know exactly how I felt about that. I'd never thought of Mike in any kind of romantic context. I'd actually stopped thinking of my entire life in any kind of romantic context. *What does that say?*

"Were you looking for me?" The question sounded careful as I asked it but as soon as it was out there, seemed a dangerous invitation.

"Yeah. Kind of, I guess." He set the bottle down and looked at Damon.

Damon looked down and studied the chicken carefully.

I reached up and touched the scar at the end of my left eyebrow.

"I just wanted to follow up on the Daniel Boone thing. See if the information helped at all."

"And cook sausages?" I asked him.

"And cook sausages," Mike tried to joke. It came out a little flat and unnatural sounding.

There was obviously something else on his mind and I was not making it easier on him. He had a little boyish charm fumbling with his words and looking hopeful but I really wasn't in the mood.

Would I ever be in the mood again, I had to ask myself. Then, I had to wonder, exactly what mood I was thinking of? Romance or—

"Have you had any action on the poaching angle?" Mike interrupted my self-interrogation.

"No." My answer came slow.

Mike watched me. Damon looked up from the chicken. He smiled slightly. It was the kind of expression that said he knew something I wanted to know, but was having fun keeping it to himself.

I massaged the hard ribbon of flesh at my eye. I could feel the water under the dock, liquid earth, like the dust that had flowed over a mud wall in Iraq trying to bury me. It was too much and suddenly I wanted to hit someone. Anger lives in me, a parasite waiting for the weaker moments to spit acid and fire into my guts. It's a drunk's feeling, and a survivor's burden. When it happens, the blood of the creature that burns my insides pumps into my veins, a mainline of whiskey. A beautiful excuse.

If it came when I needed it, or rose up on command—

But it doesn't. It comes unbidden and unexpected, Tourette's of the soul.

I wanted to drink. I wanted to rage and fight. But I had enough sense left in me to really want to hide in shame and cry.

When I opened my clenched eyes I realized that I had left off touching the minor scar at my eye and had reached my hand under the collar of my shirt. There I had been tracing the top of a long track that wound from my clavicle, around and through my left breast.

Both of the men were staring now. In the grill, flames were surging unchecked over the chicken, blackening the skin.

I don't recall if I said anything. I know I left, because the next thing I knew I was pulling into the parking lot of the Taney County Sheriff. When I did, it was with relief that I wasn't waking drunk someplace. It was also with the sure knowledge that I was not ready for romance.

But it's an adage in my life, a secret tattooed in my heart by experience that nothing is ever easy, and things never work the way I need them to.

Silas Boone was standing beside a big black SUV smoking a hand-rolled cigarette and letting the new sun bloom on him. When I'd seen him before I took him in as big. I saw then that there was more to it than that. He was big in an awkward, gangling sort of way. He was tall. What I had first assumed to be muscle looked through the tight, threadbare, and black T-shirt to be all sinew. If anything, he looked like a scarecrow on steroids and he was staring at me.

The parasite in my gut surged with joy.

I fought the rush of adrenaline and wicked happiness. I didn't want to want the conflict, but still I hoped—

"Look who it is," Silas said as soon as I stepped out of the truck. He pulled the wet and wrinkled cigarette from his lips and tossed it aside.

"You *don't* want to do this," I told him carefully. Clearly.

"Do what? Talk? I'm just standing here, in the parking lot, minding my own business." He pulled at the tattered neck of his shirt like he was popping the collar. "Just doin' my own thing."

Silas was putting on a show. I was trying to figure out who it was for when he glanced back at the SUV. It was backed into the parking space and his jacket was bundled on the hood. In the center, nestled in the folds and covered by a leather sleeve, was the shine of glass. There was a lens. Behind it, of course, would be a camera.

He was looking for an incident. Probably an excuse to get me to lay off or justification for keeping me at arm's length.

I couldn't help it. I was hoping for a little justification of my own.

After he made sure he was lined up for the camera Silas came forward.

I opened my jacket letting my badge show again. Not because I thought it would make him think about things, but because I hoped it would piss him off just a little more. And it covered the fact that I was resting my hand on the telescoping baton at my hip.

"Mr. Boone, you need to return to your vehicle." I spoke up both for effect and to be heard on the recording.

He stepped closer and held up his hands showing them empty. At that point we were both playing to the camera.

"What are you going to do if I don't?"

He was so close I could smell him, sweat and old tobacco. He was dirty and seemed to take pride in it. That was something I'd encountered before. A lot of bikers will wear a cut that's been urinated and spat upon by every member of the club for twenty years and never once wash it. Some guys just seem to think there is something special in their personal ape funk.

"The way I see it, I don't have to comply if there is no matter of threat or safety." He still projected his words. "Or are you threatening me?" At that point Silas, with his back to the camera grinned at me. Subtlety wasn't his strength he was telegraphing his coming slur. Still it surprised me. He looked down the front of my shirt then whispered, "Gonna show me them big ol' titties if I don't?"

Even if my skin wasn't so pale, it would have flushed. The heat crawled up from where he stared to burn across my neck and face. Within my belly, the parasite danced in anticipation.

I held back.

Not because I was a cop. Not because I had come to the realization that the impending violence was mine to avoid. Honest to God, I was savoring it. I held back to let the feeling build, to let Silas dig his hole a little deeper.

And he did.

He held up his hands. At the same time he eased forward. From behind, on camera I could imagine that it looked like surrender or supplication. From in front it was an aggressive pressing in on my space accompanied by a renewed leer down my body.

Men like Silas Boone always seem to be born knowing how to shame and degrade women. They know the effect of their words and the grinning appraisal of bodies. Making themselves seem greater by diminishing what they desire. Control and loathing.

When his eyes returned to mine he licked his lips and glanced back down my collar.

"Your skin's not as perfect as you act, is it?" He waggled his fingers—suggestively to me—to the camera, in demonstration of empty hands. Then he leaned to the side a little and peeked deeper under my collar. "In fact, there's a little pink line that goes someplace . . ." He looked at my eyes again. "Someplace special?"

His grin bloomed, tobacco stained and stinking.

"In fact," he went on, "I like a woman with scars. Like that little one by your eye."

His right hand eased forward almost pointing. Almost touching my hair. Instead he gestured with a finger. A flip that suggested flicking the hair aside to fully reveal the ragged line at my eye.

The thing in my body surged. It pumped itself into my chest and arm it charged the muscles in my legs and hands. I kept it from my face though.

Silas Boone, all testosterone and hate, could cut through the good graces of better women than I with a wink. Since I had not responded yet. That is, since I had not been sucked into initiating an act of violence against him, he tried a little harder.

"You're quiet now ain't you? Not so loud mouth? Or maybe you know that's how I like it with a bitch like you?" He made a sound in the back of his throat that was a growl and an obscenity at the same time. "You just lay there and let me see all the scars. And you open up that big one between your legs for me." Without moving any closer he lifted his face and twitched his nose. He wasn't any closer at all but my experience was of his nose, tracking over my body, an inch from my skin, smelling me.

"Yeaaah," he moaned the word out in a long exhalation. "And that little one on your eye—" His tongue flicked out as he mocked licking my scar. "And you just lay there as I fu—"

"Can you?" I asked the question hard and cut him off just as he was getting to the high point of his act.

"What?"

"Can you?" That time I asked the question simply and let it hang. There could be no doubt of my meaning or the challenge in it. Men who know how to leer at women and make them feel small, have their own weaknesses. Even the best men seem to have the same weaknesses dangling between their legs.

The thing about intimidation, it's really a war of information. You need to know what makes someone fight or falter. Silas had been guessing and nearly hitting the mark with me. He seemed to have a lot of experience cowing women. But I don't push as easy as I might have once. Women who fight through, then against their own military, to serve despite all the men who say you are something less— something worse than nothing—those women don't push easy at all.

There was something else I had going for me. I had more information than he did. His file didn't say a lot but it did contain records of his injury.

Just as he looked ready to say something I beat him to it. "You don't have much of a limp."

His open mouth snapped shut. Then, as if he couldn't help himself, he asked, "The fuck you talkin' about?"

"The limp you ended up with after that IED explosion." I let it sink in that I knew about the explosion. I watched him wonder what else I knew. "A lot of guys don't come back from those." I looked down and made it obvious where I was looking. "It must be hard with so much muscle loss." And I looked back into his eyes to say, "So much scar tissue."

"You don't know shit. You don't know what the fuck you're talking about."

I had the hook in his mouth and I set it. "So can you?"

"What?" He spit the word out. It was a useless exclamation. Silas knew what I was asking and he knew what I knew.

Still I pressed. "You know. Can you?" Then I smiled. It was small but sweet. Just sweet enough to burn. "You lost a lot more than muscle, didn't you, Silas?" I wasn't proud of myself but I said more. "Some might feel like less than a man without their—"

He broke and the thing in my belly pounced, red of tooth and claw and I loved it.

Silas didn't swing. He curled his hand, fingers under and knuckles out and went for a throat punch. If he'd connected he would have put me down. He didn't because he was sucked into his own trap of rage and humiliation. That and the fact that I was ready.

As his hand arched in I turned my left shoulder away and raised my right arm. The blow went behind my neck. I levered over my right, trapping his arm with my shoulder and elbow then gripped the hand with my left locking him against me. That was when I had the chance to be cruel.

I took it.

With us shoulder to shoulder, Silas off balance, and me set on my planted left leg, I raised my right foot and kicked the stacked heel, aiming for the side of his bent knee. I missed the knee striking higher up the thigh. Even though it came through my boot heel and traveled up my leg in a moment of anger, I knew the feeling was wrong. There was almost no flesh to cushion the impact. I hit his thigh and struck bone. With so much muscle loss it was amazing the man could walk at all. When he screamed and dropped, I had to wonder if I'd finished the job started by the IED.

It should have been over. There was a little guilt in me about his leg. That was mind thought. Gut thought, the churning lust to spread my own pain onto others, was actually disappointed at how easy it had been.

That was when Silas gave me a gift.

He'd reached down once he'd collapsed. I had thought he was nursing his wound but instead he raised his pant leg and pulled a knife from his boot. It was a cheap tactical knife, the kind you can buy at a convenience store for three dollars. He flicked it open. The blade had a sharp point and an edge that transitioned into brutal serrations at the back half.

I don't know what he thought he was going to do with it, especially from the ground. I never gave him the chance to show me. When he raised the weapon, I grabbed his wrist with my left hand and twisted holding the blade up and away from my body. I had a moment to hope it showed on the camera before I pulled the baton with my right hand and brought it down on his elbow.

He was strong and stubborn, I'll give him that. He didn't drop the weapon. Instead of using the baton again, I jerked my knee up and planted it into his grimacing face. His nose broke with a solid crunch and blood stained my jeans.

Silas opened his hand and the knife dropped. That time I hoped that the camera didn't catch the satisfied smile on my face.

Chapter 6

Reverend Roscoe Bolin was standing in the common area outside the sheriff's office speaking in grand gestures to Sheriff Benson when I came in pushing a cuffed and bloody Silas Boone ahead of me. Silas was walking on his own but slowly. His limp had become an awkward one-sided hop.

Roscoe stopped what I assumed was either a sermon or a tirade and looked at the pair of us. There was a kind of appraisal in his eyes, but I didn't see any surprise. "Silas," he called. Then to me, "What happened here?"

I grabbed several tissues from the box on the reception counter and dabbed at my knee. Then I wiped some of the blood from Silas's face. I wasn't very gentle with his nose.

"Silas Boone, is under arrest for assaulting an officer."

"That can't be," the Reverend said, speaking to the sheriff. "Mr. Boone works for me. He's the soul of restraint. Besides he would never hit a woman. Sheriff, this is exactly what I was talking about. Detective Williams and Silas had a little brush-up this morning."

"How about it, Hurricane?" Sheriff Benson asked me in a tired-sounding tone that still managed to be official. "I'm sure there was a reason behind this."

"Isn't there always?" I asked.

"You know what I mean," he answered. "A good one."

I pulled from my pocket a small digital video recorder and tossed it over. "Judge for yourself. I think Boone planned on getting me to take a swing at him. Maybe put it up on the Internet? Maybe look for a big cash settlement. But I think that will show that either his soul, or his restraint, needs a little reinforcement." Then I turned back to

Roscoe. "You should see if that lawyer you got for Dewey might give you a two-for-one deal."

The Reverend didn't bother to look at Silas. He looked at the sheriff.

"Reverend Bolin here tells me, Dewey Boone has disappeared," the sheriff explained.

Roscoe nodded. "It's why we came in. To tell you that he ran off from the show and wouldn't be here to talk to you."

I pushed Silas into a chair then used a fresh tissue to wipe at my hands. "Why'd he run?" I asked.

"I don' know." The Reverend shrugged and ran spread fingers through his thick hair as if in deep thought. "Unless he had a guilty conscience."

"Guilty about what?" I asked him still dabbing at my hands. "I thought he was your friend, Reverend. This morning you were taking care of everything like family. Now you're tossing him under the church bus?"

"I'm not tossing anyone under any bus. I'm only saying I don't know why he ran away."

"Convenience?" I tossed the tissue in the trash. "Yours or his though . . . I don't know." I asked the sheriff to watch Silas and went to the restroom to splash a little water on my face and breathe. When I came out the Reverend was gone and Sheriff Benson had called EMTs. He detailed a deputy to escort Silas to the hospital and to bring him back to jail once released. Then he said, "Let's have a look at this video."

He played it over twice with both of us watching the tiny screen built onto the camera. "You got away with it," the sheriff said shutting the camera off.

"What do you mean, *got away*? He tried to take my head off."

"Yeah," he nodded thoughtfully. "He did."

"So?"

"So, you're a good cop."

"That's a problem?"

"I'm just an elected man. You know that."

I nodded back at him. It was more to show him I was listening than anything else because I could tell he was saying something he thought was important. I was probably the only one of his subordinates that got the benefit of so much of his wisdom.

"But I hire good cops." Neither of us was nodding then. His gaze had a real, come-to-Jesus lock on my eyes. "And I keep them on, even when there is a lot of pressure to"—without looking away, he sliced his flat hand through the air between us—"cut 'em loose."

"You saw the video."

"I saw the video. I saw a little more too."

We both waited for a moment. It was a long moment full of a lot of screaming silence.

He spoke first. "What do you think I expect of a *good* cop when I see that video?"

I remained still.

"I expect to see a de-escalation. I expect to see my detective make every effort to avoid that kind of conflict. I don't expect to see her eager for it."

"Not eager—"

"Oh that dog don't hunt, Hurricane. I don't know what you said to him, but it wasn't any kind of sweetness and light."

"Is that what you want?"

"I want you to talk. I want you to occasionally soothe some ruffled feathers not pluck the fucking rooster every time it crosses your path." The stare he hit me with was a dare to say anything.

I didn't.

When his breathing calmed, the sheriff said, "Take the rest of the day."

"But—"

"And tomorrow."

"I'm—"

"You're what?"

"I'm sorry." I was too. Not when I did it but I was honestly sorry I had disappointed someone who believed in me and the better nature I sometimes thought I had given to the dirt of Iraq.

"You're goddamned right you are."

"But there's something going on here."

"That's what I'm telling you."

"Not with me. Why did Silas Boone try to set me up? And why did a kid we had no reason to suspect, run? I think someone is telling us not to look at one hand and waving a big red flag with the other."

"I think it's not your problem for a couple of days. Houseman can take over for now."

He went into his office and closed the door.

I went out to my truck but didn't start it. The parasite inside me was born out of the violence inflicted upon me by two men who were supposed to be comrades. They pulled me out of my bunk in the middle of the night, took me to a secluded spot beside an empty road and raped me. Not content with the simple act, they cut and brutalized my body for the crime of being a woman in the men's club of war.

That thing—the parasite—a child of hate and fear, loves only violence. Sometimes I think I need it. Sometimes it terrifies me. Always, when it is sated and curls back to sleep in the pit of my body, it leaves me mired in the past and fearful of the present.

I didn't want to drive because my hands were trembling. My eyes were seeing the brown dirt of a wasted country and the dark stain of my own blood seeping into it.

Brown.

Browns.

Misty snakes of wind, sidewinding along patched and broken asphalt, slithering over a mud wall to cover my life as though my presence in the dun-colored world were somehow shameful.

When I see the world turning to shades of old shit, I have to wait. It's something I've learned. If I got into the truck and drove there was a huge chance I would wake someplace, drunk, with no memory of how I got from here to there.

That was the price I paid for the pleasure of bringing a little perspective into the life of Silas Boone.

It was worth it.

After an hour or so of standing against the washed out winds of my past, I got behind the wheel. There were many safe places for me to go. My home held no liquor. Uncle Orson's bait shop was filled with cheap pints and beer. It also had Uncle Orson. Moonshines, a bar was equally safe because of Clare. The old men in my life looked out for me. Maybe that's a pattern but I didn't want to examine it very carefully.

I don't recall what lies I told myself, but I didn't go to any of the places I knew were safe. Or maybe I simply needed a different kind of safety. When I got out of the truck again the sun was setting, and I was parked in the grass outside the big tent of the Starry Night Traveling Salvation Show.

In the far western distance, old storm clouds were throwing themselves into a dying sun. Their deaths were rendered pink, purple, and red. All the rest of the sky was a dark gloaming of ancient blue. There was the moon and a single star. Venus? The tent, under impending night, was blazing with light and color. I went in to find a technical rehearsal going on. On the stage Reverend Bolin was striding from corner to corner pointing to theatrical lights high up on support poles. As he went, a man followed him around. Every time they spotted a shadow they both yelled at another man on a ladder among the lighting instruments.

In the far back of the tent, there was yet another pair of technicians working over a big audio console.

Everywhere there were young women running in and out doing smaller tasks. Some were hanging bunting. Some lining up chairs. Half a dozen were raking the cropped grass for every last clipping or bit of trash. I counted fourteen of them. In all the activity it was hard to miss the few men who stood around the perimeter. Their grim faces were shaded by sunglasses but they all echoed Silas Boone in aspect. They were ex-military men and they were on the job. The question was, what job?

If they were hard to miss they certainly didn't miss me. It wasn't obvious. They were watching me without looking directly at me. When I wandered to the audio table their bodies shifted slightly. It was a subtle give away. Behind their sunglasses their eyes followed while their faces remained turned to an imaginary middle distance.

At the front apron of the stage, one of the girls draping red, white, and blue bunting fell from a chair. Her surprised scream caught the attention of everyone inside the tent. I noticed that the men outside didn't seem to react at all.

The girl looked to be twelve or thirteen, it was hard to judge—they all seemed small. Two other girls had come to her aid and were already helping her up when Reverend Bolin jumped down from the stage. When he appeared among them, the two girls scattered like bait fish in front of a shark. The girl who had fallen was left alone to face him.

It was a strange moment. Even from where I was I could feel the girl's fear. From the Reverend I felt something else but couldn't pin it down. Roscoe put his hand on the girl's chin and directed her face upward to his. He spoke softly and she nodded making his arm echo and amplify the motion.

There was a pressure coming from the front of the stage. A wall of energy that kept me pushed back and immobile. I feared what I might see, a secret signal of sin or a bursting of rage onto a child. But I couldn't move. I couldn't look away. My body remained like a coiled and locked spring, waiting for the trigger that would set me free. I had no reason to believe that Reverend Bolin was mistreating the girls. However, my experiences have left me more ready to believe the worst, than to blindly accept the good intentions of any authority.

Reverend Bolin released the girl then bent to pick up the chair she'd fallen from. It was an old folding chair made of peeling wood. Nothing like the shining rows of new metal chairs set out for the audience. He hefted the seat as if weighing it against something in memory, then raised it up and shattered it on the stage lip. He raised it two more times, breaking the offending object into shards that scattered from his anger just like the two girls had.

Roscoe threw aside the bits remaining in his hands then turned his head to the lights and bellowed out a word that made me think he was actually insane, "Banjo!"

"Banjo!" he shouted again. It was a Charlton Heston sound. The effort made his hair flow around his head and shoulders like mercury.

The man who had been looking for shadows with Roscoe when I first came in appeared from behind a giant, rough-hewn cross center stage. "What?" he shouted back.

When Roscoe turned to fix the other man in his focus, his hair shook and caught the light again making it appear that he was radiating light. "Banjo," he said, still almost howling. "I told you we needed ladders, or stepping stools for the girls."

Banjo spread his hands in surrender saying, "I asked for the money to buy some last week. I asked for that, and to buy some sizing and muslin to fix the flats you were yelling about. Massoud sicced Silas on me. So don't be yelling at me until you figure out who's running this show."

Without waiting for a response, Banjo turned and went back behind the cross. I noticed for the first time that the huge prop was moving. It was being hoisted up from behind.

Roscoe brushed aside the few remaining splinters that rested on the stage floor before lifting the silent and scared girl up. Then he sat beside her with an arm over her shoulders.

He spoke to her. His quiet words were eaten up by the distance and general noise of the tent but I could tell she was listening. As she listened she seemed less afraid.

I hadn't realized until then that I'd been holding my breath for a long time.

There was a pop and a sizzle on the sound system, then a piano run I knew instantly as Floyd Cramer, then a slow hum from the backup singers before Elvis launched into the gospel, jubilee number, "Run On." It started loud before the tech pulled it down to almost a whisper. It was like wind celebrating in the background.

The girl snuggled under Roscoe's arm and smiled. He kept talking to her. Behind them the cross continued to grow and rise into the tent's peaks. Someone I couldn't see shouted and the stage lights shifted then changed again going through the show cues one by one.

Wind, cool and clean, rushed in and billowed the canvas out.

The girl on the stage with the Reverend was laughing.

That same unknown someone shouted again and a spot lit up the downstage lip where the pair were sitting. The girl grinned and giggled. Her teeth gleamed in her dark face pressed into the Reverend's black shirt. Her eyes shined.

Another shift of the lights and everything but the front key and a backlight, focused directly on the pair, went out.

Elvis finished his song.

The girl, still grinning, gave Roscoe a hug and hopped off the stage to run out of the tent.

Then the Reverend, looked up, directly at me. His eyes, even from the length of the tent, crackled with broken-glass sparks. The hair that had seemed to flow, was solidified into a white mane that haloed his head. While his face reflected light, his clothing absorbed it. He stood from the stage, more Reverend than Roscoe and I understood why he had a following.

"Hurricane," he said. I heard him clearly even though he seemed to speak quietly again. "Katrina," He corrected. Then he beckoned. "Please, come talk to me."

Another gust of wind came in under the peaked roof and swirled. I went up the aisle.

When I got close, he asked, "Official?"

For some reason the word confused me and the only thing I could think to say was, "What?"

"Official business?" he asked helpfully.

"Some," I answered carefully. I looked around and we suddenly seemed to be alone. The techs working lights and audio were gone. The big cross was upright and motionless. No sound came from behind it. Most telling of all, the men with sunglasses and hard faces were gone too. "Some," I added, "maybe not."

"Let's get the official out of the way, what do you say?"

I nodded, more to clear my head than to agree. "Dewey?"

"Your guess is as good as mine."

"I doubt that, Reverend."

He nodded this time adding a slight, I wondered if smug, smile. "I told all I know back at the sheriff's office."

"Tell me about the fish." It wasn't planned. It was simply the first thing to come out of my mouth. My mind was so muddled by the day, I was lucky what I said was an actual sentence.

It had an effect though. The Reverend's confident smile drooped. His eyes' hard shine went soft. "Fish?" Confusion came out in the question.

"The fish Dewey's brother Daniel was poaching. Is that what he was killed for?"

"I don't"—he looked around for help but we were alone—"I don't know what you're talking about."

"Why are you upset?"

"I'm not upset. I just don't know."

"What don't you know?"

"Daniel was poaching fish."

"Are you asking me or telling me, Reverend?"

He shrugged and that made it clear. His confusion was real. I doubted that he knew much about the killing. But that shrug was false—a lie.

"How could I?"

"It was something he had a long history with," I pressed. "He was catching paddlefish and harvesting their eggs for a kind of domestic caviar."

"I don't know anything about his fish egg business."

That—I didn't believe. First, he didn't react at all to the idea of paddlefish producing caviar. That made me think he was completely familiar with, what I considered, an unfamiliar concept. And second, "Why did you say, business?"

"What are you talking about?" His head jerked sideways.

"You said, 'his fish egg business.' I said he was poaching, you said he had a business."

"Is that what you wanted? In your official capacity? To talk to me about fish."

"I think the fish are why he was killed. But not the *Why*. Do you know what I mean?"

There was no wind then. It had gone still and the tent filled with lights was getting hot.

"I don't." Roscoe said stepping back. When his legs touched the stage, he sat down once again in the light. "This is what I know." With his hands spread he presented the stage and tent in his defense. "Everything else—*out there*"—he pointed hard, thick fingers outward, beyond the confines of canvas—"remains out there."

"Even murder?"

"Justice is your job. Vengeance is the Lord's. I'm, just a shepherd."

I stared at him as hard as I could. It wasn't easy. Looking into those eyes was like staring at the moon reflected in moving water; you knew there was something beautiful there, but didn't know if it was too broken to ever really see.

For his part, the Reverend Roscoe Bolin didn't seem bothered at all by my gaze. He'd changed a bit in my view though. The fire had dampened but not the heat. It was still banked behind the eyes. He smiled and I thought perhaps I was seeing what the little girl saw a few minutes before.

"So . . ." he opened. "*Un*-officially?"

I considered that. I didn't know why I'd even suggested anything other than an investigatory reason for my being there.

He stared.

I *did* know. I didn't want him to know. I'd been drawn to the idea of comfort and forgiveness. The idea was not the man. And that realization was footsteps over my grave—a cold, lonely passage that had no connection to the spirit hiding within.

"Nothing," I said.

"Nothing? I don't believe that."

"Belief . . ." I sighed the word out, then tried to look stronger than I felt. That's not the truth. I tried to look stronger than my need for belief. "Well, that's your job isn't it?"

Roscoe nodded and smiled and that time I was sure I was seeing the same smile the girl had seen. I realized that the Reverend and Roscoe might be two different men.

"I'm duty bound to take the position that belief is the job of us all."

"Now that's the evangelical zeal I expected."

He laughed and his hair shook, the silver lion at play. "I didn't say what belief."

"I thought you were duty bound?"

"Only to speak the truth. And when there is no truth to be had, I speak what I believe. And I'm not so sure telling others that their faith is wrong is what I believe anymore."

"Are you confessing to me?"

"We're just talking. That's what you were looking for wasn't it? Talk. It's a long walk from official to what troubles you. I may not be the one to share it with you. But you need to take it."

"Free advice?"

"Always worth what you pay."

"What's Dewey running away from?"

My change of direction didn't surprise him at all. Or it didn't seem to. "What are we all running from?" Roscoe asked right back.

"Not murder."

"Are you so sure?"

"What do you mean?"

"He's running from his brother's death." He spread his hands out in front of him and held them like he was trying to hold on to truth itself. It was the kind of gesture that said *this is it, the real thing, and it doesn't get more real.* "Everyone is running. To or from something— it doesn't matter. Only we know what's chasing us." Roscoe put his hands down, and I was sure it was Roscoe not the Reverend. Then he said, "There's a girl."

It was full-on dark and the day's accumulated heat was radiated into a sky that had become filled with stars by the time I returned to the office. Technically I was off duty. More accurately and less technically, I was on administrative leave for a cooling down. The technical part was that Sheriff Benson hadn't taken my shield or weapon so it was more of a time-out. Still I shouldn't have been pushing it or his patience, but things change when kids are involved.

Dewey was seventeen, just as I had guessed. The girl he was with, Sartaña, an indigenous Aymara girl from Peru, was fifteen. It turned out that the Starry Night Traveling Salvation Show was smuggling refugees out of the Peruvian conflict zones under the cover of mission trips. It was a situation that raised more questions than it answered but my concern was finding the pair of runaways before anything happened. After that, I'd sort out Dewey's involvement with his brother.

I didn't believe Dewey participated in what happened but I was absolutely certain he knew more than he was letting on. Then there was the split personality of the Reverend's entire enterprise. Refugees and ex-military? It was not a very comfortable mix and definitely not one designed to ensure salvation. There was one other concerning aspect to that. When I asked Reverend Bolin about that charity that relocated the girls, he said only, "Massoud handles that."

The feeling of spiders creeping down my spine was the only evidence I had for thinking it was a problem. One thing I've learned, usually too late, is to listen when my nerves tell me something is wrong.

We're a large department for a rural sheriff's office but a small force by any other standards. Branson, the largest, and best-known city in the county has its own police department. Over twenty percent of the county is within the Mark Twain National Forest—federal land and federal jurisdiction. So after dark we're pretty quiet. The deputies patrol. They respond to calls mostly from the road. That means the office is quiet except for dispatch and the cleaning crew.

I dug into routine paperwork. Having it done would make the official return to duty less daunting. After filling out my logs, and putting my case notes in the file, I found the inventory from Damon's boat. Fishing tackle and canned food, blankets, and toothpaste—nothing but his pistol was of interest. I wrote a note releasing everything but the .22 revolver and cell phone from evidence. I needed to pull the logs from the cell number. Something else to add to the to-do list. On the inventory, along with CONTENTS OF TACKLE BOX—VARIOUS, was a notation, PHOTOS AND LETTERS—PERSONAL. I remembered the bundle. His pictures were all from deployment and the letters were probably the same. Still they needed to be checked. I revised the release to keep the gun, the cell phone and his letters in evidence. I didn't see any reason to keep a veteran's pictures of his buddies. All of it was a just-in-case hold back. Damon wasn't high on my list for suspects.

While I worked, I called the sheriff to tell him what I was doing. I didn't want to create any more of a problem than I already had. He was in a better mood. Or at least a calmer one. He took the information and got off the phone without any advice or gripes. Maybe he was running out of steam.

I thought of his talk about retiring and the suggestion that Billy run for the office. I didn't know how I felt about that. Billy was a complicated subject for me. That made me think of Mike. Mike was not complicated. He was easy and undemanding, and I was pretty sure, interested.

Was I? I was afraid to even consider it, but the idea had become background noise in my mind—relationship elevator music. It was like when you have something to remember or figure out but your mind just won't find the right path. If you get busy, your brain will puzzle it out for you and the answer will pop into your head when you least expect it.

What popped into my head was terrifying.

I'd been a widow for a year. I was just settling into that and managing to not melt down on a daily basis. The last thing I needed was to have romance rear its ugly head into my life.

Wasn't it?

I was sure giving a lot of thought to something I didn't want.

My computer finished its boot-up and I bent to work, instantly feeling more relaxed.

I issued a BOLO, be-on-the-look-out, for the two kids with what information I had. I did a records search and found Dewey had a juvenile record. No surprise. It was actually not as bad as I thought. Most of his defensiveness and mistrust of authority probably came from his brother and cousin. There was no father listed. The surprise came when I tried to contact his mother.

I called the listed phone number to find someone genuinely surprised by the call. They claimed not to be or to have ever heard of Cheryl Boone. When I asked, the woman said she'd had that number for over a year.

More digging told a story between the records. Cheryl Boone was gone. She wasn't in jail. She wasn't listed as missing or dead. Her appearance in her own legal life simply stopped. If she had gone missing, someone would have filed a report. I checked family services and found Dewey again. His jacket listed his parents as *Whereabouts unknown.* He was presumed abandoned.

From there I returned to military records and was not very surprised to find the same kinds of redactions in Daniel Boone's file as I'd discovered in Silas Boone's. There was one detail that fit neatly into place. A year and a half earlier, Daniel had been granted a family hardship discharge. I learned two things. He'd come home to take responsibility for his brother. And he was connected to Silas by more than blood.

I did another search. Sometimes coincidences are just that. The 101st Airborne Division is a formation of over twenty thousand men in a number of combined brigades and regiments. The possibility of encountering Screaming Eagle veterans anywhere in the country was pretty high. My own military police unit was attached to the 502nd Infantry Regiment, part of the 101st when I was in Iraq. But the chances of finding connected soldiers and connected crimes in one place stretches coincidence pretty thin, and it got a lot thinner when I pulled up the records of Staff Sergeant Damon Tarique.

Redacted.

Sometimes, when you hit an obstacle, the best thing is to trust that other roads lead to where you need to be. I put away my growing pile of notes on the men involved and concentrated instead on the girls. It was my thinking that anytime people come into the country as refugees, there have to be hurdles. In most cases, hurdles are paperwork, and paper trails are the friend of any investigation. I started by writing a long e-mail to a friend. Marion Combs was a social worker for the Division of Family Services. We'd met when I worked on an earlier case involving one of the kids she worked to protect. It was a failure that changed us both.

In my note, I gave her everything I had on Massoud and the girls from Peru. It wasn't a long note. Long enough for her to start looking, I hoped. Since Marion had a history with Sheriff Benson, she always called him Chuck, I told her about his despair and plans to retire. I felt a bit like sharing was gossiping. Marion wouldn't take it that way. It was my issue. I can't say my intentions were entirely pure though. The history the two of them shared was a youthful romance. If anyone could inject a little life into the sheriff it was Marion.

When my note finished, I paused before sending. The part about charities and kids was fine. Marion would jump on that and find roads I didn't even know existed. The other part—the meddling in the sheriff's life—that worried me a little. What is it they say about good intentions and the road to hell? I shook off the thought. If I was going to hell it wouldn't be for trying to spark up a couple of sexagenarians. I hit Send. I felt pretty good about it too.

I was about to kill the computer and go out the door to find Damon for a little talk when the e-mail program refreshed. I had a new message. It was a preliminary report from the forensics contractor who was doing the autopsy on Daniel Boone. After all the usual caveats and disclaimers noting the tests yet to be performed and lab results to return, it said death was probably the result of drowning. It also indicated wounds that suggested violence. There was a laceration and impact wound on the skull. In addition, there were a series of puncture wounds in the abdomen. They were small in diameter but ragged. The included photo showed three holes in a perfect line spread about two inches apart. The last notation was the most chilling. Cuts and abrasions in the skin from the nylon net were *perimortem*—at the time of death. He was wrapped in the net and put under to drown.

Chapter 7

The sheriff's office was in Forsyth and my uncle's dock was in Rockaway Beach. It wasn't a great distance but even with recent improvements the roads were twisting and dark. It was a twenty-minute drive in daylight. It took me less than fifteen. I was wishing the entire way that it was summer so I could have had the windows down to feel the air.

I pulled up to park at the head of the dock's ramp. In summer the lot would be full of vehicles. That time of year, and that time of night, I expected to be the only visitor. Expectations are kind of like worries, almost always there and pretty much always useless. There was a big Dodge Ram with a boat and trailer parked sideways. The logo of the State of Missouri Conservation Department glowed with reflected light on the driver's side door.

Mike was at the dock again.

I was glad.

It hit me hard. The sensation of desire rolled over me like the blush I'd felt the first time I saw a man naked. It was an almost mirror-image sensation too. I experienced a wave of want, and shame, fear and arousal, and guilt, all of it accompanied by images in my head that really would have made me blush.

I sat in the truck without shutting it off. I looked at the world through the windows, the strings of clear bulbs around the dock, their reflections in the water and the millions of tiny bursts of starlight in the undulating blackness at the center of the lake. Above, there was the spray of the Milky Way and a single line of dark clouds way south. All around were shades of black with crystals of white. The only colors were the mismatched green and red trim on the dock and the bold stripes on the boats bobbing in their slips.

I wanted more color.

My mind unlatched with an almost audible *click*.

I wanted more color.

Not in the night around me, but in my life. For a very long time the spectrum of my life had been defined by shades of brown. The dust of a violent country and the mud made from my blood and horror. Nelson had come into my life and shown me the other colors were still there. But he'd passed without my blooming back into the world. I'd traded my grave for his and wrapped myself up again.

I wanted more color. It was the same as saying I wanted to live. And for the first time in a long while, that didn't seem like a betrayal to anyone.

"What's happened to you?" Uncle Orson hit me with the question as soon as I walked into the shop. Then he handed over a root beer still crusted with ice. He'd seen me coming.

"What do you mean?" I smelled the mist coming from the open mouth of the bottle. The carbon dioxide burned my nose and the rich scent soothed it. "I'm smiling." I said. "I'm in a good mood. Why do you think something's happened?"

"That's why. I haven't see in you in a good mood since . . ."

"I know." I smiled to let him off the hook before putting the bottle to my lips and taking a long pull of the fizzing liquid. When I lowered it, the bottle spit at me a little and I wiped my mouth with the back of my hand. "I haven't been in a good mood *since* . . ." I let the thought and the words fade but I looked over to the wall behind Orson. There was a calendar there. Each month was one of Nelson's paintings. It always displayed April from two years before. The image was of a deep river valley from the unseen mountain peak. Flowers in a riot of yellows over green defined one side of the river. On the other were furrowed fields in muted golds bordered by aspen and pine. Through the middle, meandered the river washed in too many colors to count.

Nelson had tried to give him an original painting but Uncle Orson said a bait shop was no place for that. I think he just loved that one too much. Nelson had signed it for him though and the page hasn't been turned since.

"What's changed?"

I considered the question before drinking more of the root beer. As I drank, I considered some more. There wasn't an answer. I didn't even try. "This is amazing," I said once I lowered the bottle. That was when I noticed there was no label. It was in a plain, amber bottle.

"Clare sent it over," Uncle Orson explained. "Homemade."

"No more moonshine?"

"No point. He's got the biggest still in the state at the restaurant and a license to cook. I think some of the thrill has gone out of it for him."

"I'm afraid I'm going to have other less than thrilling news for him."

"What's that?"

I almost shared my concerns about the Reverend's church. Then I held back. There is no one who helps me think things through better than Uncle Orson, but he'd known Roscoe all his life too. I wasn't sure I was ready to open up that bag of snakes yet.

"How's Damon working out for you?"

Two changes of subject. I could see Uncle Orson keeping count.

"He's a worker."

"But?"

"Not a complaint in the world."

"Buuut?" I dragged the sound out as I raised the bottle again.

"His sidekick has been here a couple of hours. What are you going to do about that?"

"Who says I have to do anything?"

"Fish or cut bait. There's no tourists in life."

"Yeah, well . . ." I took a drink from the bottle and finished it. "I don't know what to do about Mike either. He's a nice guy . . ."

"The most damning of faint praises." Orson took the bottle from me and set it under the counter.

"Are there more?" I asked.

"There are, but not for now."

"Think I can't handle my root beer?"

"I think I don't want to hear you belching like a sailor on a bender when you go out and talk to that guy."

Right on cue I burped and let it come out loud. "Like that?" I laughed.

"Nice." He pointed out the door to the slip side. "They're out on the houseboat."

I was still laughing to myself and feeling good when I went through the door. The largest slip on the dock was devoted to a houseboat belonging to Uncle Orson—my home away from home and when I'd been drinking, the hole I was most likely to hide in. It was set away from the shop by a broad walkway and the tanks for the gas pump.

I wasn't sneaking. I didn't even think I was walking quietly. But I don't guess anyone heard me coming.

When I stepped around the stern of the houseboat, Mike and Damon were on the deck locked in an embrace. Their kiss was furious and hungry.

They didn't hear me leave either.

My phone began ringing almost as soon as I got back into my truck. It was my father calling back. I didn't answer.

When he called the second time, I was over by the Powersite Dam. The third time he called, I had no idea where I was.

I suppose I should have been grateful for having missed the embarrassment of whatever I would have said to Mike. I wasn't in a grateful mood anymore. I wasn't in any kind of mood. Everything was numb. There were simply too many emotions and thoughts for me to keep anything straight. So I kept driving.

How could I have been so foolish?

How could I have been so needy?

After an hour on the road and three more calls ignored, I began laughing. Life is kind of a bitch, but sometimes she has a sense of humor. It's just me who's a little slow on getting the joke. What I'm not, is slow to learn. She doesn't have to hit me with a hammer.

Finding my way home at close to midnight I made a decision. No more thoughts of romance. No more men, period.

Once I made it to the house, exhaustion set in. I'd barely slept the night before and it had been a very long day. I didn't even make it to bed. Not that I tried. The big leather couch and the afghan that always laid over it were calling my name.

The phone kept ringing every hour and I kept ignoring it until my sleep was deep enough that the sound couldn't make it through. I was still sleeping at ten a.m. because I was still, technically, on administrative leave. That was a call I couldn't ignore.

The dispatch number is the only contact in my phone programed with a special ring tone. It sounds like an old-fashioned phone, a shrill trilling that has never failed to wake me. As soon as I heard it that morning, I thought of the BOLO for Dewey and the girl, Sartaña.

"Doreen?" I answered using the name of our daytime dispatcher.

"You need to get your ass in here," the sheriff responded. "And I mean light it on fire."

I walked into the Taney County Sheriff's office wearing the same clothes I had the day before. I'd managed to wrangle my hair into a ponytail and brush my teeth, but it wasn't until I was walking in that I noticed the dried blood on the knee of my jeans. There was no chance the call-in wasn't related to Silas Boone.

Billy was in the office sucking soda from one of his favorite thermal cups. It was the size of a coffee pot. He smiled when he saw me. It struck me that he always did and I always looked forward to it. That brought to mind the promise I'd made to myself the night before, which brought on a whole other slew of memories and I was suddenly, absolutely sure that he knew how close I'd come to suggesting a date with a gay man.

Those thoughts tangled my already cluttered mind. I wished I had Billy's huge mug filled with steaming, black coffee. Then I was at the sheriff's door.

With a quick look back at Billy and a deep breath I went in.

Even though the call had been abrupt and gruff, even though I had come running I hadn't been worried about the meeting. The sheriff, no matter how angry he might get at me, had shown many times and ways, he had my back. I expected a lawyer, maybe a few accusations and harsh words. The reality of my expectations were of a typical pain in the butt.

Reality and expectations rarely share the same bed.

When I opened the door two men stood from the chairs in front of the sheriff's desk. One was wearing his class-A Army uniform, the other, a good, but worn suit. Both men were large and black, cut from the same military mold. The suit had to be FBI and it took no leap for me to recognize Army CID.

Reality just killed my expectations and buried the body in a shallow grave.

The next thing I noticed, there was not a third seat. It was going to be a stand-up conversation. That's the wrong word. They would speak and I was expected to listen. Short, not-so-sweet.

"Come in Hurricane," Sheriff Benson said. He remained seated. "This is Timothy Givens." With an open hand he indicated the man in the suit. "And *this* gentleman"—he added the emphasis because he was well aware of my difficult relationship with the Army Criminal Investigations Division—"is Captain Alastair Keene, Criminal Investigations Division."

I nodded. They didn't.

"This is Detective Katrina Williams."

"We know Detective Williams," Keene, the CID man said.

For the first time I noticed he was holding a manila folder. Once he spoke he dropped it on the sheriff's desk. It was thick and ragged-looking as though it had gotten a lot of attention over the years. There was no doubt I was the subject of that file.

"Silas Boone?" I asked ignoring the file and the attitude that went with it.

"The subject of a cooperative, and ongoing investigation," Givens chimed in. He had an attitude too.

That was when I finally realized there was an elephant in the room. And it there's one thing I have problems with, one of many things I have to admit, it is being able to keep my mouth shut about pachyderms in the corner.

"You said 'cooperative.'" I said it to Givens, not quite an accusation.

"Yes." His response was, in the same sense, not quite encouragement to dig deeper. Not that I needed encouragement.

"Who's cooperating?" I asked.

This time Keene jumped in. "We expect full cooperation from your department—"

I jumped too. "That's not what he said." I stared hard at Timothy Givens. "You said it was a cooperative investigation, and you weren't talking about cooperation with us."

I let it sit there a moment hoping he would say something. He didn't.

"This is an Army investigation," Keene said.

"But you're not Army are you?" I asked of Givens. "So who are you? FBI? ATF?"

He didn't react at all.

"Homeland?"

There was the smallest twitch on his face.

"Let's call it Homeland then," I said and I probably sounded smug.

"Look." Captain Keene had a glare to go along with the hostility in his voice. He'd definitely read my file. "Let's make this easy."

Between dealing with secrets and the Army again, I was already getting my back up. "Is that the official motto of the CID?" I asked him before he could say exactly what easy was. "Make it easy. Screw the hard work of investigating. To hell with the victim. Just bury the problem."

"We're not here about your past issues—" he tried to cut in but I wasn't finished with my dance yet.

"Bullshit." These guys always set me off. I was angry, enraged as a matter of fact. But the words came out cold, as flat and challenging as Kansas by wagon.

Their reaction was almost as absurdly level, just a few steps higher. These guys, all the feds I'd ever met, were used to the locals treating them with a kind of reverence. It was something I didn't have in me to give.

Givens deigned to speak first and tried to remaster the exchange. "This isn't about you."

"Fuck you." I said it right to his face and looking straight into his eyes. One thing you learn as a woman in the military is that you have to talk to the boys like a boy. Girls may enlist in the Army, but it's the bitch that survives the experience.

I looked from him to Keene, then said, "And your little buckaroo. If it wasn't about me, you wouldn't have brought that file. If it wasn't about me, this would have been a phone call. You're here because you've decided I don't play well with others and you want me out of the game."

"Fair enough." It was the captain. He said it calmly and as a matter of fact. The glare he kept pointed at me didn't come out in his voice. I hadn't really rattled his cage at all. Givens looked a little set back on his heels like I'd spit in his face. In a sense I did.

I guess we knew who the lead horse was. "You're out," Keene continued. "Boone needs to be cut loose and you're not going to go near him. We're here to make it clear because you have a bad history with the CID."

"The way I put it is the CID has a bad history with me. Did you even read the file or are all you guys so into the party line that you always toe up to protect the Army ahead of the soldier?"

He leaned in to speak, making his voice a mimicry of his eyes. It was intimidation 101. "What happened to you then, has nothing to do with now."

"That's why you'll never be a real cop," I said without backing away. Then I eased in, not showy and forceful like him. I made it slow, without urgency. I didn't want him to back away. I wanted him to feel me when I spoke again. "It's why you'll be a rubber stamp your whole life."

"The hell are you talking about?" he asked, his voice backed down even if he didn't.

"You just can't understand that what happened to me then will always have everything to do with now. For the rest of my life."

"Maybe you should—"

"Get over it?" I cut him off, both his words and the smug curl that was just creeping into his lips. "Deal with it?" I eased closer until my breasts were brushing the lapels of his uniform. I like to think of it as an intimate encroachment. It makes men uneasy in a nonsexual context. "Live with it?" I asked letting my voice drop in volume, not tone. "I bet you say that to all the girls."

Captain Keene stepped back. There was no curl on his lips, smug or otherwise.

As he did, Givens moved forward with a hand out like he was going to put it on my shoulder. He didn't. He had the sense to keep it up just above my shirt, gesturing rather than pushing. I decided that he was the smart one of the pair.

"Can we take it down a notch? Maybe two?" Givens imposed himself in front of the captain and forced him back rather than trying to get me moving.

Definitely smarter.

He looked at the sheriff for help but my boss was sitting back in his chair watching the show. If I knew Chuck Benson, and I was pretty sure I did, he called me at their insistence and took a little joy in knowing what would happen. The only thing that really bothered me about that was knowing I was completely predictable.

Givens got his Army counterpart moved and slightly settled, then he gave his attention to me. "You mind letting me in on what the issue is?"

"You didn't read my file?"

"I didn't read anything about you. I just came to let everyone know that there was an ongoing federal investigation dealing with your boy, Silas Boone. You tossing him in jail has complicated things and we need it fixed."

The way he said *federal investigation* made me wonder if I'd been wrong about thinking he was with Homeland. Maybe Justice was his niche. Just for a moment I wondered about the tic in his face when I'd mentioned Homeland Security. What was that? My imagination? Or was he sharp enough to throw me off with a twitch?

Maybe I could do a little throwing of my own.

I looked over at the sheriff and asked him, "Anyone happen to mention that ongoing investigation also includes our homicide, Daniel Boone, and Damon Tarique?"

"Tarique's the fellow . . ." No one ever said Sheriff Chuck Benson wasn't good at his job or a man slow to put things together. He was about to say, *over at your uncle's place,* I was sure of that. He caught the look in my eyes and his words at the same time.

"Yeah, he was there at the lake." I picked up for him. "He was the one who found the body."

"Wait." It was Givens' turn to get bent. It made me feel good. "You're saying Daniel Boone is dead and Tarique is involved?"

"He picks up quick, don't he?" the sheriff asked. "College I'd guess."

"This isn't a joke." Givens's words came out like the bark of an angry dog. He fired them full force at the sheriff even leaning over the desk to get his wrath a little closer. "Why is this the first time we're hearing this?" He'd finished barking and settled into a growl.

Sheriff Benson let the smile freeze on his face then he stood. He was an old dog who wouldn't bark. He'd just bite without telling anyone it was coming. "Boy—"

"Boy?" The echo came instantly from Givens and it came with heat.

"Kid, then," the sheriff shot back. Then he kept firing. "Child. Little, snotty-nosed, pissant—son of a bitch, if you like that better."

Givens opened his mouth to say something but my boss kept going and it was my turn to stand back and watch the show. "The first thing is—don't you dare imagine I'm some Jim Crow country sheriff. Getting' all pissy about assumptions is how you get your ass kicked. No matter what color a man is. And second, you're running your big federal investigation in my county without telling me. Just how the holy, dancing hell are we supposed to know to let you in on our investigation? And third"—he included both men in his gaze—"if you can't answer the questions or state your case with a civil tongue, I will hold the lady's purse while she makes you question why your mama brought you into this world."

Sheriff Benson was a colorful and genuine man who I fell in love with a little more just then.

Still, you could almost smell the testosterone in the room.

"What's it going to be?" I asked. "A cooperative investigation, *including* the Sheriff's Department—or do we all do our own thing?"

"This is the way it's going to be," Captain Keene said as he stepped up to stand side by side with Givens. Both of them kept their gaze on the sheriff, ignoring me. It didn't hurt my feelings. "There's only going to be one investigation. Ours. Anything you know, anything you learn, anything that happens—you will bring to us. Everything you have going on that affects our investigation, you stop. As of now." Keene turned to look at me finally and asked, "What do you think of that?"

I didn't have to say anything. The sheriff said it all. "I think you boys know how to work a door, don't you?"

The stunned look on their faces had nothing to do with racial sensitivity this time.

"You can't do that," Givens said.

"Seems like he just did," I told him.

"This is federal jurisdiction," Givens said it like it was as heavy as gold and twice as precious.

"No one is disputing that," the sheriff said as he came around his desk pointing at the door. "And your respective agencies"—he looked at Givens very specifically—"whatever they are, will get all the cooperation they deserve."

Both Givens and Captain Keene stood their ground. Sheriff Benson stopped once he'd rounded his desk, then looked at the tattered file still sitting where it had been laid in evidence of my . . . what exactly? Failures? Disloyalty? As far as the Army seemed to be concerned, the worst thing I ever did was to ask to be treated as a human being.

The sheriff picked the file up and, for a moment, seemed to be taking the weight of it, then he handed it to me. I knew the weight of it. I passed it on to Captain Keene who looked at it, then at me like we were symptom and disease together.

"*Cooperation,*" the sheriff said it again. "It's a two-way street. And like I said, you will get everything this side has to give."

I was still watching Keene. His mouth began twisting and the small wrinkles at the corners of his eyes bunched.

"As soon as I get a call from your supervisors," the sheriff added.

Keene's smile hung from his face not even half-birthed and dead. Mine spread lively and free.

"We'll discuss the nature of cooperation and your particular skills at bringing it about with local law enforcement," the sheriff finished up.

Keene was ready to fight. The smile that died on his lips had rotted into a snarling quiver. I'd seen it before and the sheriff had played it perfectly. Career military officers function like precision timepieces in the confines of their hierarchy. Out in the real world where the roads are bumpy and the lines aren't so clear, their rusted skills of give-and-take put them at a disadvantage. It couldn't have happened to a nicer guy.

Givens put a hand on Keene's shoulder and said softly, "Come on. Let's not make things worse."

Like I'd said earlier, he was the smarter one.

Givens backed up through the door keeping a hand on Captain Keene's shoulder. Keene went but he had the appearance of someone who wanted to spit out an old wad of tobacco.

"Don't let that door hit you in the ass as you go," Sheriff Benson said as they headed for the building's exit. "Or do. I don't really care," he added just to me. Then, without much breath between thoughts he said, "I'm sorry about that. I knew that fellow would make it a pissing match. I just didn't know it would get so . . ." he searched for the perfect word to sum it all up. He didn't find it so he simply said, "Pissy."

"It was bound to happen," I told him and hoped my tone was more forgiving than it sounded to me. "He was right. The CID and I have a history of issues."

"We're going to cut Silas Boone loose."

"What? No. You can't."

"We'll have to. You know it. The feds will make it happen with or without me. We can let him sweat it out tonight and open the door in the morning. Besides, if he's already out when the honcho over those peckerwoods calls me, I'll have a lot more room on my plate for chewing their asses off."

"Maybe. But I don't have to be here to do it. I'm still off duty."

"That's a good thing too. I imagine we'll let his lawyer think we're afraid of how that arrest went when we let his boy walk. It'll look good if you even take a couple of more days."

I looked and could tell by the gaze that I got back, it wasn't a suggestion. I didn't fight. "Thanks," I said.

"For what? Making you a scapegoat?"

"For backing me up with those two. For always having my back." I had a thought that had been tingling just behind my ears. It wasn't a good one and it wasn't one I completely understood. I just knew that it had to come out before I could really get a handle on it and sooner was better than later. "I'm not sure"—I turned and looked away from the sheriff—"I'm not sure Billy could have done that."

"Done what? Send those guys packing?"

"Stood up for me. Not like that."

He laughed. It was a quick and tentative cluck, like he'd never found anything to laugh about before and was just trying the sound on for size. Then he did it again and the cluck bloomed into a full-on hen's cackle. It was the kind of laugh you associate with old movies and ancient men dancing after they discovered gold in them thar hills.

"Sometimes—" he started then let the laugh take him over again. When it settled he picked it up. "Sometimes—I swear, girl—sometimes you're dumber than a box of rocks."

"What?"

"Why do you really think I talked Billy Blevins over with you?"

"I don't know," I said feeling pretty flustered and actually ambushed. "You said—"

"That boy . . ." Sheriff Benson thought about that then laughed again. "He does look like a boy and that soda pop don't help things, but he's a man. And he's a man who would do anything for you. He'd do the right thing for this department. He'd give his life for anyone of us. But he'd do anything for you."

It was a stunning revelation. Not just the statement of Billy's feeling, but that it was so obvious to the sheriff and I'd never known. Or had I? There had been moments. There had been a time before I married Nelson.

"No," I said and I hit it like a nail to fix the truth of it. "Billy and I are friends."

"Hurricane—Katrina," I hated the sound of both names because they were said with such sadness and sympathy. Understanding even, and that only made it worse. "You don't really have friends, do you?"

I flushed with heat and I knew a red blush was spreading up my neck and into my face. I kept turned away from the sheriff. I wouldn't have blushed if it wasn't true.

"You know people and they know you, *but* it's all on the surface. I'm about the closest thing you have to a real friend and I'm an old man. All the friends you have are old men, me, that old moonshiner, Clare Bolin, even your uncle. How many people in this world do you really trust? And how many of them are men over sixty?"

"Billy is . . ." I didn't have anything to put in the end of that sentence. Billy was a mirage to me, a ghost of war as much as a solid person in my life.

"Billy Blevins is not who you think he is," the sheriff said out loud what I was thinking. "He's not what you think or imagine."

"How can you know what I think?" It was a weak refutation, a child's argument against the truth.

"Do you?"

"Do I what?"

"Do you even know what you think?"

I didn't say anything. I wasn't feeling guilty for sending that note to Marion or sticking my fingers into the sheriff's life anymore. That was sure.

"It's a serious question, Katrina."

I remembered a conversation I'd had with Billy in that time before I'd married Nelson Solomon. The world was falling apart and Billy was there to scrape together my pieces and keep me from making all my mistakes even bigger. I'd found out some surprising things about him, he was moonlighting at Moonshines, singing on the outdoor stage. Everything seemed to be changing as I got closer to Nelson. I'd said something to Billy about us being friends but there were so many things I didn't know about him. He said that I'd never asked. It wasn't an accusation. Just a fact.

"I can't—" I started. Then I had nowhere to go with the sentence. "Billy and I aren't—" I didn't know where that was going either. "I think you're mistaken."

Sheriff Benson didn't say anything right out. The look on his face called me an idiot though.

"He should have said something," I said.

"Oh I think he did. I'd say he said about a million somethings, but you're always inside your own head talking too loud to yourself."

"What's that supposed to mean?"

He sighed. "It means you don't listen."

Chapter 8

Sheriff Benson had given me a lot to think about. The gift that keeps on giving and annoying. I forgot it all once I got out to my truck and found six more calls from my father waiting on the phone I'd left behind. I'd lost count of how many times he'd actually called but the number of messages was easy to remember. There were none.

That time I called him back.

"It's about guns and you should stay clear," he said instead of hello. "CID is sending someone and they are not your biggest fan."

"I already met Captain Keene, the feeling is pretty mutual," I told him. "What do you mean it's about guns?"

"*Guns,*" he emphasized. "Military weapons. I don't want to talk about it over the phone but there is something big and dirty going on."

"Well, what else is new?" I asked because I was always good with sarcasm.

Or at least I thought I was. Dad didn't pick up on it. Instead he said, "Something else I need to talk with you about. But also not on the phone."

"That sounds ominous."

"I hope you won't think so when you hear it."

He was talking about a woman. The woman from DC.

My finger was stroking along the ridge of scar by my eye before I was even aware of my unease. "I'm looking forward to it," I lied.

"Listen sweetheart . . ."

"Tell me about the guns," I said.

"Nothing is clear yet and that's a message itself. Documentation of military weapons is precise. The fact that some arms are missing is not nearly as disturbing as the intentional destruction of the paper trail." He paused and I could feel the turmoil of his other thoughts through the phone. "We'll talk more when I get there."

Off the phone I wondered why it bothered me so much that Dad would be seeing someone. And I thought about some of what the sheriff had said to me. When I started the truck and got on the road I was angry. Not simple anger, I was pissed off in the way I had been when confronted by Keene and that file but without the clear target. I wanted to be able to hold my feelings in my hand and examine them one by one in the light.

Why was I angry at Dad?

Why was I angry at Billy?

The truth, and I had at least enough self-awareness to see part of it, was that I wasn't angry at them. So much of the anger in my life was a gun pointed right at my heart. There was a long string tied to the trigger that led back to the moments of violence that I couldn't get past. But the hard thing—the dangerous thing—was that the string was tangled through my life, wrapped around thoughts and actions, the furniture of living. Any wrong move would trip over that string and put a fresh round of rage right into my heart.

As it does so often in my life the world closed in. It was hot, brown, and dirty with hate. The world hated me. Crawled over my skin and into my wounds, a slow burial. It wanted to devour me and spit me into the grave at the same instant. The filthy, crawling mist of sand that drank my dripping blood had the power to make me less. I was less than myself, less than human. I was a woman in the male world that despised me, taking joy in the long cuts the two men had put on my skin. Dirt matted in the gaping wound where a superior officer had run the edge of a KA-BAR knife around my breast, almost severing it. The dust of Iraq, wasted, brown hate, muddied the stab wound in my buttocks. The two men, officers, comrades, had attacked what was woman about me. Their assault was an open door for the dirt of the grave.

My concentration was on myself, focused inward with nothing left to spare for defending the outer walls or for driving. It wasn't until the truck was slowing to a stop that I realized how split from my body I'd become.

Automatic driving, something we all experience when our minds wander to deeper thoughts and the road is easy. All of a sudden we notice that miles have passed since we were last aware of the road and wonder, astounded, how we made it that far. There are some of us though that take it further. The automatic action becomes more of a functional blackout and it shows not the easy road, but the roads we are most desperate for.

I had pulled into the parking lot of a liquor store.

I was actually imagining the burn of whiskey down my throat and the wondrous bloom of its heat into my belly. Whiskey was like a religion to me. It offered a transformation, a miraculous change in my gut from heat, to peace. But the peace was a lie. As far as I was concerned, exactly like religion.

If I hadn't seen the car parked in the next lot over I might have gone in. God help me, I wanted to go in. But, surprisingly, I wanted to rake Keene and Givens over the coals even more.

They were in a rental car. A generic SUV that was nothing more than a high-riding station wagon. I never would have noticed them if they weren't two black men. The Ozarks is kind of a homogenous place. Even Branson, a tourist destination, attracted mostly white faces to country music shows and corn pone gospel reviews. Not that that was a surprise to anyone. It did work against two black investigators being able to surveil me without being noticed.

My first thought was to drive on. I could spend the whole day if I wanted to, leading them nowhere. I didn't trust myself though. Not the way I was feeling. Not with the gritty feel of old dirt still on my skin. Besides, I thought, why were they following me? Then I realized it had to be for Damon. They had been surprised that I knew about him, and he was certainly involved in their investigation. Being a live-off-the-grid kind of guy, he had to be hard to keep track of. I was their way of finding him.

Twisting the rearview mirror around to see what was around, I found my answer. The lot they were parked in belonged to one of the older shows. Imagine *Hee-Haw* and the *Lawrence Welk Show* having a baby raised by George Wallace. I called dispatch to look up the number for me.

They weren't friends as the sheriff pointed out. Not that I would have claimed the two men who came out of the theater a few minutes later and approached the rental car from front and behind. But I had known them for a while. Kyle and Keith were two brothers who barely made it out of high school and firmly believed that white men could no longer get a fair shake in America. They were security guards at the Ozark's Hillbilly Road Show and I'd had to deal with them more than once because of their enthusiasm for the job.

There was a moment when I felt bad using race against the men. More than that, I'd stacked the deck when I called the box office and said there were two black men in the parking lot who had made suggestive comments to my teenaged daughter. I had done almost the same thing to another CID officer a while back when I ditched him at a redneck bar and told the locals he had been following me. Is race-baiting in self-defense racist? I didn't really know the answer to that, but I was willing to use the tools at hand. Still I felt bad enough that I didn't stick around to watch.

It did lift my spirits to see a ball bat-sized club shatter the headlight of the rental car as I drove away. Off-handedly I hoped everyone would be all right, but the truth was, both groups could stand lessons in tolerance. I turned on the radio and actually danced a little in my seat to an oldie from KC and the Sunshine Band. I was feeling pretty good by the time I parked in front of Uncle Orson's dock ramp.

This time Mike was not visiting and I found Damon netting dead minnows from the live well. He was in an even better mood than I had been getting into.

"Never seen a man smile so big about scooping dead fish from a tank before."

"A happy man can be happy no matter the task," he answered broadening his smile. "And it's something I thought I had lost forever."

"The happy?"

"Yes. I was sure I had left it in Iraq."

I nodded and looked over his shoulder where the edges of my vision were hazing up with creeping dirt. I shook my head trying to physically throw off something I knew was not physical at all. It worked—to a degree.

"That country has stolen a lot of happiness." I shook my head again and reached up to stroke my scar. My mood, the exuberant, car-radio good feeling, was blowing off my skin in a wind only I could feel. But I was fighting it. "I'm glad you got yours back. And I have an idea about the source of this new spirit."

Damon stopped and stood up straight. In his hand, the net with several shining silver fish, dead and dying, dripped. He didn't look so happy anymore.

"It's all right," I spoke to him gently and remembered the sound of the young medic telling me I would be all right in the back of a Humvee. That was when I noticed that my head was roaring with the sound of hard tires on broken asphalt. "Everything will be all right," I said again and slipped away into my own memories.

There, in the remembering, the medic is Billy Blevins. More and more I hope that memory is true. And hoping is the answer to the question of why I never asked him if he was the one who cleaned my wounds and reassured me with a kind voice that everything would be all right. His presence makes the memory better. I can't bear to give that up to the truth.

"Everything will be all right."

My words echoed Billy's and for a moment I saw my filthy sliced-up body through his eyes.

He'd cut my clothes off. I was naked except for my boots but there was no sneer or contempt from him. Medics are the best people in the world.

"What?" Damon's question came from years and miles away, pulling me out of the vision.

"Everything will be all right," I said again but there must have been something in my voice or my face that conflicted with that thought.

Damon dropped the net. I watched it fall and the spilling of the small fish. They fell away like tiny, crystal meteors splashing into the tank and scattering the living minnows. Most floated back up, silent and motionless, but a couple, as if given hope by the return to water. Tried swimming.

Damon had his hands on my shoulders and was urging me around the tank to an old kitchen chair that stayed in the corner. I didn't want to go. I wanted to see if the wounded minnows came back to life. It seemed important at the moment.

"I've been where you are," Someone was saying. It must have been Damon. "An' I still go there too. You'll be fine, Hurricane. You're going to be just fine."

"Everything will be all right," I said, correcting him. Then I asked, "Billy? Is it really you?"

After that I don't remember much except crying. I'm pretty sure I asked for some whiskey. Uncle Orson still had some jars of moon-shine that Clare had made before he went straight and worked for me. I wanted it. I wanted to drink until Iraq and everything that happened was sweated out of my skin.

They told me later that Damon had called Orson in from where he was working on the dock. Together they moved me into the bed on the houseboat. The next thing I knew was that the sun was setting. I knew that because of the bloody-knuckle sky I saw out the window that always faced west. I didn't know which sunset it was. Was it the end of the same day or had more passed?

The sky went from fresh blood, to old, to black as I watched; I didn't move until I heard footsteps on the dock outside. Through the floor of the boat I felt as much as heard Uncle Orson's heavy step aboard. It was followed by a lighter step. That was when I finally sat up.

"You can come in," I called through the door. "I'm awake."

The door opened to show the silhouettes of my father and Uncle Orson. They were like a scalpel paired with a rusty hammer. They always had been, Dad joined the Army and had gone into intelligence. Uncle Orson had become, and always remained, a Marine. He was definitely the hammer.

"How are you feeling?" Dad spoke first.

"I'm not," I answered. "And I don't want to feel anything ever again."

"Yeah." He said. "I get that. But it's not the way it works."

"I know."

"I called Chuck Benson."

"I wish you hadn't. The last thing I need is more forced time off or more therapy sessions added to my jacket."

The scalpel silhouette shook its head. "I'm not sure if either of those things is true."

Dad could always be counted on to give it straight.

"But I didn't say anything about what you're going through. I filled him in on a few of the things the feds should have told him already. Then I asked him to encourage you to take some vacation to spend with us because, he and I agreed, it would be good for you and you wouldn't take it on your own."

"Work is the only thing that keeps me sane, Daddy. The only thing I understand."

"That's part of the problem," Uncle Orson chimed in. "You need to . . ." He shook his hands in front of himself like he was looking to grab the word he wanted out of the air. Finally he said, "Diversify."

That at least got a little laugh out of me. "What's that supposed to mean?"

"It means life is bigger than you. It can't all be lived in your own head no matter how hard it is to step out."

"Again," I said. "What's that mean?"

"It means you're a woman with options, Katrina." My father had found his lecture voice. "You have more choices than just about anyone on the planet. You have more resources than vets like Damon, or even Nelson had."

"I don't want to talk about Nelson," I said. "And I don't want to talk about the options he left me. He died. Even twenty years later, his war killed him."

"Do you think he wanted that for you? You were his chance at life and he was just one of yours."

"That's an awful thing to say, Daddy."

"Maybe it is in a way. But a lot of awful things are true."

"Is there a point?"

"Just a question," my father said, his voice gentle again. "With the life you have already had, and the choices you have available— heck, girl, you're rich by any standards—you can run the empire, get Nelson's paintings in big museums or on more T-shirts. Do charity work or write a book. Sit on your behind and eat ice cream until you get too fat to waddle."

"I thought you said there was a question."

"Here's a question, with so many choices at hand, you stay with the dangerous work. You wallow in the violence and the despair of other people's lives. Ask yourself if, *maybe*, you traded one Iraq for another."

That was a question I knew the answer to. I'd puzzled it out a long time ago. That didn't mean I felt like sharing or talking about it. It was something I couldn't explain, at least not well enough to satisfy myself, so I assumed it would sound like more feeling-sorry-for-myself crap if I said it out loud.

He was right though. I was afraid of being anything other than what I was, a cop in a sometimes violent world. I thought of it like fighting a forest fire with more fire. I only felt safe on scorched earth. *How terrifying is that?*

They tried to get me to talk more but I wouldn't.

Dad ended up saying, "If you feel like joining us in the shop, there's food on the grill and someone I want you to meet."

All of a sudden I felt like throwing up.

I should have done it. If I had eaten at all that day I would have lost it anyway as soon as I walked into the shop.

The woman standing next to Dad was dressed in the kind of casual clothing that cost more than the most expensive dress I'd ever worn. Worse than that was the fact that it worked for her. She was beautiful, and graceful, stylish in a way that terrified me, and she was a four-term US Representative from Missouri.

Understanding can come in a lot of ways and at the strangest times. This was a mystery in my life that was suddenly solved. After I'd been raped in Iraq, I was victimized a second time by the Army and CID. I identified the two men who had assaulted me, both captains. I was a lieutenant. It's a crime to accuse a superior officer without proper evidence. My only evidence was that I knew who they were. They had friends and were after all, officers in a combat zone.

It was an ugly back-and-forth that was about to lead to me being prosecuted and dishonorably discharged. Except for the intercession of a member of congress on my behalf.

Once my father introduced her, Congresswoman Whilomina Tindall smiled something more than warmth and barely less than sunlight. I was almost ready for a handshake, not at all for the embrace. She stepped in and wrapped her arms under mine with her palms against my shoulder blades holding tight.

"I've kept an eye on you for a long time," she whispered within the embrace.

I'm sure it was meant as a kindness, an acknowledgment that she had been the one to help me. How could she have known how vulnerable it made me feel? Two years before I would have told anyone who asked that my father was lobbyist and a veteran booster. One of those harmless old guys who looks back on his war service with fondness for the comradeship and a blind eye to any horrors. Since then I've learned so much.

The last time Army CID showed up in my life they were using me to get to my father. Could it be coincidence that both the CID and the FBI were here just as Dad was introducing me to a congresswoman with whom he's having a relationship?

"How long as this been going on?" I asked as soon as Whilomina stepped back. I tried to make it sound light and cheerful but I failed. It came out as half suspicion and half accusation. Not very light at all.

Uncle Orson was seated beside Damon at the table. It was piled with steaks and vegetables, still steaming and ready for a feast. My uncle looked at the food and for a moment I thought he was going to tell me how long dinner had been going on. But he kept his attention focused on watching butter melt over roasted ears of corn.

"It's been a while, sweetheart." My father stepped forward to stand beside Whilomina as he spoke. "It just never seemed like the time to tell you."

"A while?" I asked sounding much shriller in my ears than I did in my thoughts. "How long is that?"

"There hasn't really been a good time to tell you," he said as his shoulder nestled into hers.

"A good time?" I looked over at Uncle Orson still studying the flow of butter. "Obviously you found a good time to tell him."

"That's not really fair." Daddy was using his explaining voice. Never a good tactic when I was already mad. "Your life has been in kind of a delicate place for so long."

I laughed but it didn't sound happy to anyone I'm sure. "But it was still my life wasn't it?"

Dad looked at his feet. Whilomina looked at me. I couldn't tell if she was angry or hurt or had any feeling at all. Hers was a perfect political face, open but unreadable.

"You can't choose for me what I should know or what I'm too delicate to feel." I looked straight into Whilomina's eyes. They were as gray and firm as granite. She didn't blink. Then I said, "You knew all about me didn't you? What happened in Iraq? You helped me then." No reaction. "When I married Nelson? You knew. And when he died . . ."

"I was at his funeral," she said, and her eyes had become as gentle as her voice. "I stayed in the back and out of your way, but I wanted to be there for you and your father."

"I'm sorry," Daddy said, and he was. I wasn't sure if he was sorry enough though.

"You don't need to be sorry," she said to him. To me she said, "And you don't need to blame him. It was my fault."

"No it wasn't—" Dad began.

"Yes," she cut him off. "It was. Even if it was your choice. It was my fault. Katrina, you asked how long."

She paused and that little hesitation told me something was coming that I didn't want to hear. "We've been seeing each other—we've been together—for thirteen years."

I looked at my father and red flushed up his face.

"Don't look at him," Whilomina said. This time the granite was in her voice. "Look at me."

I did.

"Until a month ago I was married."

"Married?"

"Your father was embarrassed and I wanted discretion so that was how we dealt with it."

"I wasn't embarrassed," Dad said quietly.

"You were completely embarrassed," she chided. "You didn't want your little girl to judge you and look where it's gotten us."

It had to be all true. She spoke to him as though they'd been together for a lifetime. I had to wonder if I even had a lead role to play in my own life.

"You're telling me now because of the investigation? The CID and FBI—is that about you?"

"No and yes," Daddy said. "The investigation intersects with some work I'm doing."

"And," Whilomina interjected, "We're telling you now because we want to be married."

"But you just got divorced."

They all looked at me like I had missed some obvious point. Even Damon sitting at the table behind piles of cooling food seemed to know more than I did. Then they laughed. I think it was more out of relief than humor, but it was sudden and noisy.

Whilomina stepped forward and hugged me again. "I'm sorry. I guess we didn't tell our story very well." She retreated from the hug but kept her hands on my shoulders. "My husband, David, passed away a month ago. He'd been brain damaged and bedridden for twenty years. You father didn't break up my marriage and I didn't take a secret lover to spice up a dull life."

It was foolish to feel as relieved as I did to hear that. Then, when I realized just how foolish I felt, I doubled down, feeling foolish about being foolish. For a moment I was the girl just out of college on her way to induction, looking at her dad. There were a whole life-time's worth of expectations then, mine and his, wrapped up in everything a family shares.

I couldn't help but think of my real mother. She was a ghost in my life, a vague, misty haunting of which I rarely think or speak. She was a woman, younger than my father, a country beauty with fine, auburn hair like sunburned corn silk. Young Carmen Williams had liked the *idea* of being married to a military officer more than the re-ality. Even as a child I could feel her unhappiness. It was a sickness in our home that nothing seemed to heal.

One day, not long before I turned six, she packed up the car and told me it was for a vacation. Daddy was out of town, so it was just us girls, she said. Everything in the car belonged to her.

Carmen took me to Uncle Orson's dock and came around to open my door. I thought she was going to walk me in. She didn't. My mother's hug was hard but quick. Her breath was hard with gin.

She said, "We have to do these things like pulling a bandage off a scab, baby." Then she kissed my forehead. It was the last thing she ever said to me.

I watched her drive away. I didn't cry. I never cried for her again.

Daddy had come straight home to me and struggled to explain things in ways to show me it wasn't my fault. From then on, family had been him and me and Uncle Orson.

Suddenly, I was seeing that there was another female specter hid-den from me for thirteen years.

The girl I had been wanted to begrudge my father this new woman. The woman I was . . . well she wanted to drink. She wanted to wallow in suspicions and ask some really tough questions. She wanted to be happy for her father and, more than anything, was ashamed she wasn't.

I opened my mouth to speak with no clear notion of what words would come. There was not a chance in the world they would have been appropriate. I seemed to lack that gene.

The phone in my pocket began to ring. It was dispatch. It had lit-erally given me one of those, saved-by-the-bell moments and I stood there looking a gift call in the mouth. Everyone was staring at me as I stood, stock still, with my mouth open and the phone ringing in my pocket.

"Are you gonna get that?" Uncle Orson asked me.

"I'm suspended." I sounded to myself like a child claiming nothing could get me when I was under the covers.

"Do they know that?" he pressed.

"Who do you think suspended me?" I snapped and even before the words were gone I regretted them.

My phone stopped ringing.

"I'm sorry," I said not exactly sure to whom I was apologizing or why. "Today has been—"

The phone started ringing again.

That time I accepted the gift and answered. "Detective Williams." After that I listened without talking for a few seconds before hanging up. "I guess I'm off suspension."

Only three minutes later, even after splashing water on my face, smoothing and tucking my rumpled clothes, and resisting the urge to grab a beer off the table, I was walking to my truck. I rinsed the taste of a long day and despair out of my mouth with the orange soda my uncle handed me as I went out the door. Then came one of *those* moments. I can't describe them except to say that drunks seem to have them more than other people. They are moments of synchronicity where the things you crave and need and fear and hate and every confusing, conflicting, and ultimately dangerous, urge coalesces around temptation. Orange soda was still cold and bubbling in my mouth, when I opened the truck door to find a bottle of whiskey on the seat.

Synchronicity.

Need, temptation, and an open path to self-destruction.

It didn't matter that someone had placed it in my way. There was no way it could matter. The only thing that mattered was the choice I made. We all say we hate lies. What we mean is that we hate being lied to. What I hated more than anything were the lies I, too often, tell myself. Because of that I won't say I rejected the temptation easily.

No. It had come at the wrong time for that. Or the right time. Someone knew my weakness. Not my only one by any means, but my worst one.

In my mind, I gripped the neck of the bottle and cast it down onto the asphalt. Things in our minds are always so dramatic. There was little drama in the way I held the bottle. It was like my hands had come home to a long, lost lover. They shared the secret with my

mouth. Suddenly if felt so dry and empty it was like the dust that in-
fests my life had made a desert of my tongue.

Other people can tell you they want a drink. Drunks, like me, if
we're honest, will tell you, we want to be drunk. That was what I
wanted more than anything.

I didn't throw the bottle aside. I held it. I caressed the glass imagining feeling the liquid heat, smooth as the container, sliding down
my throat. A waking dream, of blooming drunkenness, the loss and
surrender of memory and responsibility seduced me.

But the bottle slipped.

I doubt that I had the strength to give it up at that moment so it
may have been a simple, lifesaving accident. It fell and broke at my
feet.

With a weird feeling of grateful disappointment, I climbed in my
truck and hit the emergency lights. I drove even faster than usual.

The day had died and the night seemed to be taking raucous joy in
its passing. Clouds, gray over black, had crowded into the sky from
the southwest. In the darkness they would have been invisible but for
the silent sparks of electricity they carried deep inside. The creeping
warm front looked like lighting bugs captured in milk glass. With the
windows up on the truck I could still smell the impending rain.

When the highway became a bridge I was able to look over the
blurred railing to see the scene below to which I was rushing. We always hurry, as though death is not the most patient thing in the world.
It waits and we run to it.

Shadow Rock Park was a little spit of land, a high point shaped by
the rising and falling of the lake level. It curled around under the
bridge so one side was a popular shallow water playground for
swimmers. The other side was a campground and picnic area popular with tourists and locals alike.

Another kind of lighting, man-made in emergency colors, flashed
and streaked over black water. It slashed the sheer orange sandstone
bluff that held up the west end of the bridge and the modern town of
Forsyth. Most people don't know that the area that was now the park,
was once a main part of town. That was before the dam was built and
the town moved higher. So in a sense the park was already a grave-
yard. I couldn't help thinking of the emergency lights as the leg-
endary spook lights—lost souls haunting the Ozarks.

A pair of campers had found a girl. Her body was boldly dumped in weeds along the lakeshore, in clear sight of the highway and close to the most popular swimming area. Either her killer was foolish or she was supposed to be found.

It was a messy scene with way too many onlookers. The tattooed, tank top, and flip-flop crowd was bunched around the girl's body pressing in closer than they should have. One of our deputies, was trying to keep them back and string tape at the same time. His job wasn't being made any easier by another deputy, Calvin Walker, standing in the way and arguing with both Captain Keene and SA Givens.

I was watching the frenzy when I should have been paying attention to the road. As I pulled into the park entrance I barely missed getting crushed under the wheels of the same gleaming land yacht I'd seen Reverend Bolin emerge from two days before. There was no way for me to see who was driving but I knew where to find it. Another, smaller, RV, made less impressive by years and miles was coming up behind the first, running even faster. That was a whole other story.

Two vehicles speeding away from a crime scene, even one as ripe as this one had gotten, was never a good sign. There wasn't any time for a quiet conversation about it so I stopped my truck, blocking the park's road out. Then I ignored the skidding crunch of gravel and blaring horn as I called into dispatch and requested more units.

I climbed out of my big GMC feeling pretty secure about its utility as a barricade. "Stay off that horn." I yelled at the RV driver. Had his window open and arm out so he could slap the aluminum siding. I guessed he thought I hadn't noticed him somehow. "And stay right where you are. I'll be back to talk to you in a few minutes."

I was so startled when he shouted back in what sounded like Russian, I didn't have a comeback. He kept yelling, I think cursing at me, as I walked down the hill to find an argument in English. It didn't take long.

"Help with the crowd," I yelled at Deputy Walker as I pointed at a group pushing against the tape. "Over there! Keep them away from the tape and segregate any witnesses for me to talk with. And you two—" I shoved an angry finger first at SA Givens, then Captain Keene. Truth be told, I was glad they were there. I needed to be angry with someone and they were good targets. "Get out of my scene."

I turned away then ducked under the tape to approach the body.

She was tiny, death having rendered what probably had been a vibrant body into a kind of vacant frailty. It's easy to think of bodies as houses. The one she left behind was already showing the weakness of its construction. Her brown skin was mottled and mostly the color of wheat left to rot in the field. She had long black hair that probably swept around her when she walked. Lying in the shore rushes it clung wetly to her face and draped like soggy spider's web over the weeds.

She had to be Sartaña, the girl who had disappeared with Dewey Boone. If it wasn't her, it was one of the other girls from the Starry Night Traveling Salvation Show. There just were not that many young girls, who looked like they belonged in the mountains of Peru running around Taney County.

Chapter 9

Silent lightning tracked through creeping, dark clouds, turning them into city-sized Chinese lanterns. Depending on the density of the cloud and the placement of the lightning within it, the color was rendered in pale whites or bright blues. Distant charges, the ones that streaked into the tops of invisible thunderheads, pulsed in purples and yellows. Those were not silent, but the gentle bowling alley rumbles came as much as a minute later.

I stood on the lip of the shore, looking down at the body of Sartaña. I wanted to draw out the scene but I'd left my notepads in the truck.

Footsteps, loud and angry came tromping up behind me and I knew who was there without looking.

"Who do you think you are?" Keene asked me sounding like he had rehearsed the question since I had walked away from him.

I turned around in time to see Givens put an arm on Keene's shoulder in a restraining gesture. It was gesture only. Keene shrugged it off, "This is part of an ongoing, multi-agency, federal investigation. And we will have cooperation."

"Or what?" I asked and it was almost sweetly. "What are you going to do? Share information? Tell me what you're here for?"

The two men looked at each other and it was one of those smug, we're-in-the-club-and-she's-not, looks I hate so much.

"That can't happen," Givens, the designated reasonable guy, said.

"Then you're going to take over my investigation?" I asked, again so sweet I could have attracted bees.

"If we have to," Givens answered.

"In a heartbeat," Keene added.

"Exactly what investigation would that be? I'm investigating the murder of a young girl."

"A foreign national," Givens said. "An easy, federal jurisdiction takeover."

"How did you know she was foreign?"

Both of their faces turned to stone masks.

"I thought so," I said. "And if you take over? What then? Will you do as well finding her killer as you did protecting her?"

"That wasn't our responsibility."

"You're cops aren't you?"

Neither of the men looked at me. But Captain Keene perked up at something. I turned to follow his gaze up the hill to where the sagging RV was still idling. The driver was standing outside now pacing and smoking. He slapped the flat of his hand on the side of the vehicle and shouted at someone inside. Again, it sounded like Russian.

"Is that one with you?" I asked the pair.

They both turned seeming to find the lights racing over the dark water suddenly very interesting. I looked back at the frantic Russian just in time to see another man come from behind the RV and talk with him. Given the light and the distance I couldn't swear—but I knew—it was Mike Resnick.

It's a funny thing. Many people assume, when you're a criminal investigator, you must be the kind of person that loves a mystery. They think of old Sherlock Holmes movies or books about murders on speeding trains. I've met a few cops who like those books. Never have I met one that likes those kinds of unanswered questions in real life. We get enough of that from the criminals we deal with every day. All of them think they're smarter than us. All of them think they tell a good lie.

The worst thing though, and not funny in any sense, is when the cops start pulling the mystery crap on each other.

When I turned around to face Givens and Keene, I had a finger on the crescent of scar around my eye. They were looking at me like I was something ugly and dangerous in a zoo. I had a bit of the same sense, that I was behind bars and they were reaching in with pointed sticks to see what they could provoke.

"What's the connection?" I asked. I took the finger from my scar and missed the contact immediately. "A girl from Peru and two federal investigations. I'm guessing there's nothing direct, am I right? What is her life to you? A distraction? A complication?" I could hear the rising anger in my voice but I didn't seem to be able to curb it. If I'd thought through what I was hoping for, it would have been to make them a little angry and maybe draw a few careless words out. Instead, I had shown up angry and simply kept wrapping myself up in my own ire. Had I any sense at all I would have shut up and let all of us stew a bit. I didn't have that kind of sense. "Exactly what does a murdered girl mean to your federal investigation? Or what about to you?" I looked right at Givens. Then I turned to the other one. "Or to you, Captain Keene? Does a dead girl mean anything to either of you at all?"

"That's not fair," SA Givens complained.

"You've got a rep," Keene said, his voice as flat and flavorful as Kansas.

"Tell me something I don't know."

He ignored that and went on. "You don't like the way things get done. Big picture things. They say it has to be about you."

"If they're saying that, then it must be about me," I hit back.

"They say you try to make everything personal."

"No. Just the stuff that already is personal. Murdered girls—that's personal to normal people."

"What about rape?" he asked me. His eyes had gone to match his voice, flat and without features other than the disconnect you see in some people. It was a sniper's stare.

"Rape?" I got a little bit in his face. "Is that the personal thing they talk about?"

"You were in a hot zone and bad things happened. It's pretty fucked up but it is what it is. You're a woman. You had no business there in the first place."

"I wasn't dragged off by insurgents or captured by militia to be made an American punching bag. I was taken by superior officers who simply hated women."

That was the last conversation I wanted to be having. It had already been a bad day—days—and I'd be the first to say I didn't handle murdered kids very well. Add to that, yet another Army officer questioning my experiences in Iraq. My vision was tunneling. It was focusing down until the world was a sharp but distant image framed in a cone of blowing dust.

At the exact center of that backward telescope vision was Keene's grin. He had big, yellow-white teeth in a dark-skinned face.

"That's exactly what they say," he continued. "You never let it go. Major Reach told me about you. How he investigated. How there was no evidence. Your word against theirs. But they had alibis, didn't they?"

"They had friends."

"And you didn't." His voice even though without new inflection, still managed to get hard.

"No one likes a new lieutenant," I said. "No one wanted a woman around."

"And you proved the reasons for that didn't you?" Every word was a wrecking ball battering the back of my skull.

"Screw you." Dust closed in my sight even more. It crawled out of my vision and my memory moving in serpentine curves under my clothing—under my skin. I was feeling buried.

"That's it," he said. A gleeful punch of sound. "Your answer to everything. Screw your problems. You're what's wrong with women in the military or any real hard-assed work, you want to fuck your way through the job but you still want to be the lady."

He was pushing me. I barely heard my own thoughts in the swirling wind that buffeted inside my head. Everything was a bled out brown and there was danger in the dusty fog.

He knows what he's doing.

The thought didn't help me. I reached back and put a hand on the telescoping baton clipped to my belt.

"Admit it," Keene said. His voice had become part of the wind. "You liked it. A lonely girl, far from home."

Baiting me. He wants me violent.

They say knowledge can be a dangerous thing, but self-knowledge wasn't about to keep me from being a dangerous person. When I was a child, my father told me that I had a goat in me. He said almost everyone does and it was an animal of balance. The *almost* about it was the problem. There weren't enough goats in the world to go around and someone was always wanting to take mine. If they did, it meant I lost balance and they gained it. I don't know how many times in my life growing up he told me not to let anyone get my goat.

Keene wanted me out of balance. He wanted me to act violently and knew exactly what buttons to push. I was in danger of handing over my goat and my badge would probably go with it.

I may as well have been blind. My eyes saw Keene but my mind only saw a mist of blowing dust. I could hear as well but the only sound that mattered was the roar of Humvee tires on cracked asphalt.

"Everything will be all right."

"The hell're you talking about?" Keene asked from beyond the roar and dirt.

I didn't realize I'd spoken out loud. Despite the reassurance I'd given myself, it was hard to breathe. The dust storm in my mind was tearing the air right out of my lungs and I was getting close to panic.

"Everything will be all right," I said again searching for the moment the words echoed.

After I'd been assaulted by two American officers and left for dead in the dirt of Iraq, and after I had been discovered by a truckload of militia who wanted to shoot me like a feral dog in a ditch, I was rescued by a patrol and taken into the back of a Humvee. It had been my only care or safety through the ordeal or for a long time after. That was the moment I tried to hold onto. The moment Billy Blevins looked at me with kind eyes and said, "Everything will be all right."

"Everything okay here, Hurricane?" The voice was right but the words were wrong. It was like a dream moment when you know suddenly you are asleep and all you have to do is wake up to make the world right again.

"Just breathe," Billy's voice told me.

I didn't know if it was real or not but I didn't care. I grabbed onto the sound and followed it.

"You're safe," he said. "Everything is going to be okay, just relax and breathe through it."

When I'd calmed enough to be aware of the real world around me I was sitting in the muddy shore weeds way too close to the body of Sartaña. Billy was sitting beside me with a hand on my back. Givens and Keene were nowhere to be seen.

"You hyperventilated," Billy told me.

"No," I shook my head and kind of moaned the word. "I didn't."

"Yes you did," he said emphatically. "You got angry with those feds and just got a little dizzy."

"You were there," I said on the edge of tears. "Thank you."

"No, I'm here now and helping you breathe."

"In the back of the Humvee. You told me—"

"Hurricane," he said it hard, a call to attention. Then softer, he said, "Katrina."

I looked at him, the then-Billy not the long ago, might-have-been Billy.

"You weren't in a Humvee," he explained carefully. "Not this time. You hyperventilated. Just a hard day. You probably haven't had dinner have you? If anyone asks about it, remember that."

"Asks about it?"

He looked over past the tape perimeter at Riley Yates standing beside a departmental cruiser taking notes.

"Hyperventilated," he said again. "No dinner."

I nodded and said, "Help me up."

As soon as I was on my feet Billy held out his hand. "Give me your keys."

"Why?"

"I'll put Calvin in a cruiser at the park entrance and bring your truck down closer. You'll want your note pad and a dry place to sit I imagine."

Billy knew my routine. We always have photos, but sketching a crime scene is more about seeing than recording. Even though it was dark there were enough lights to get my images down on paper. There was something else about sketching. It was a way to look busy and unapproachable but required little concentration. At least at my skill level.

I handed over my keys.

As soon as Billy started walking to get Calvin, Riley Yates was at the tape.

"You okay?" he asked in that casual way even small town news people have. Casual until it wasn't.

I nodded.

"You looked a bit put down there," he said. "Those other fellas went off in a huff too. Anything I might be interested in?"

"Which part?" I asked. "Them or me?"

"Pretty much anything I can get that won't show up on someone's blog first."

"Does anyone blog about the goings on in Taney County?"

"You'd be surprised what people find to put on the internets."

"'Net," I corrected. "There's only one."

"Youth does not always know more than experience," he answered.

I was still trying to figure the meaning of that when he pointed sideways with his index finger and bobbled it in the general direction of Billy's back. "What do you think about our friend, Billy Blevins?"

"Think?" I imagined my eyebrows had pretty much shot off the top of my face. Then I tried to pull them back in my own attempt at a casual act. "What are you asking?"

"What do you think I'm asking, Hurricane?" He jumped on that question like a stray dog on a dropped hamburger. "Is there more to the story than I know?"

"I don't even know what the story is," I said with my recovered straight face on. "I can't know anything more."

"Uh-huh," Riley nodded. He looked at me like he was reading his own headlines right through my skin. "Sheriff Benson said he talked to you."

I understood. "You're asking about the idea of Billy running for sheriff." If idiot was a liquid, I would have been the same super-sized cup that Billy kept full of soda.

"What were you talking about?" The nod of Riley's head, which at first seemed knowing, now seemed a little more educated.

"Nothing," I answered lame as a clubfoot duck. "It's been a bad day. Busy. I missed dinner . . ."

Riley laughed. It was big and loud and entirely out of place at a murder scene. I felt a lot better hearing it.

"Should I print that?" he asked, still chuckling.

"No. But why aren't you asking about what's going on here?"

"Detective Williams, what can you tell me about this investigation?"

Again, I felt like an idiot. "We don't have any comment at this time," I answered. "Got it. But what are you going to say about Billy?"

"Depends."

"On what?"

"On what people say to me about him. The sheriff thinks he's the right choice above others with more experience."

It was my turn to nod knowingly. "Like me."

"Well . . ."

"Don't bother dancing," I told him with a smile. "Can you imagine me running? Can you imagine anyone who knows my record on the job voting for me?"

"People tend to find their places in life," he said. "Like water always finding downhill."

"What's that mean?"

"I think you are the kind of person who views herself through other people's lenses."

"You're going to have to be a little straighter than that, Riley. I'm just a cop."

"That's what I'm saying. You're a good cop. It doesn't mean you should want to be the boss or would make a good one. And you're right, you have a bit of a history around here. But it serves the people of the county."

"How do you figure that?"

"Everyone tends to keep their head down around a loose cannon."

"I'm a loose cannon?"

Riley grinned. "What do you think about Billy? The right choice?"

I considered what the sheriff had said and what I knew. Then I thought hard on what I didn't *know* so much as feel. My feelings were much more aware than my mind sometimes. I couldn't say what kind of recommendation that was, but we are who we are I guess.

As I mulled the question, working through the messy mental diagram of my history with Billy Blevins, I saw a silent pulsing of light in the sky. High, and distant, the lightning illuminated the anvil shape of a stacked thunderhead.

From the sky I looked down, right into Riley's eyes. "He's the only choice I can imagine."

"You don't think older hands will have issues with a deputy stepping right on up into the sheriff's job?"

"Who cares?" I asked him with a smile. "That's the beauty of an elected position. Citizens make the call. I would be proud to work for Billy Blevins." I nodded over in the direction of my approaching truck and added, "He's on his way back if you want to talk to him."

"Not just yet,"

"Good," I said pointing into the dark sky. "A storm's coming."

On cue, a falling-barrel, rumble rolled out of the distance and new flowers of light bloomed in the black sky. Billy parked my truck and walked my notepad to me.

"Limbaugh showed up," Billy shot a thumb over his shoulder. "I left him covering the access road. That Russian guy was pitching a fit." We must have looked guilty or Billy's ears were burning because he stopped and gave us a look. "Everything all right here?" he asked as Riley wandered back to his car.

"Right as rain," I said and opened my book to a blank page.

Officially the girl was a Jane Doe, or simply, unknown victim. Unofficially there was no way she was anyone but Sartaña. For a very long time I played a game of pretend, filling the first page of my pad with nonsense scratches, staring at what I drew without seeing. I didn't want to look at the girl. I didn't want to watch the world blowing brown around me again.

I'm tempted to say the feeling passed. But it is not like that. It never seems far from me. Instead it faded once more into the background and I was able to get on with my job.

Sartaña's body was in the shoreline scrub and cattails. She was lying on her right side with her face toward the water. I sketched her out showing the orientation of her arms. The right was forward, almost pointing at something unseen by anyone living. The left was lying behind her back with her fingers and palm up. Her legs were splayed widely, giving her the appearance of leaping, as though she'd tried to escape her fate by bounding over the lake. One bare foot was in the water.

As I drew out what I was seeing, Billy mounted a battery-operated work light on a stand and pointed the beam right at Sartaña.

The LED gave everything a blue cast that gave her skin, already wan, a pallor. For some reason it reminded me of something old fashioned, like one of those Victorian photos of the dear departed. It was a trick of light only. Sartaña was wearing a short dress and it had been pushed up above her hips showing worn and threadbare underpants. It wasn't just the situation of the dress either. Her hair, dark to almost the color of the night overhead, reflected a shimmer of blue from the work light. The very darkness and the sheen communicated an ethnicity the Victorians would not have been so interested in.

Thunder rumbled so close I could feel it in my chest when I crossed below her feet to get a look at Sartaña's face. Blood ran in two tiny rivers from her scalp and her nose. It wasn't until I was wading into the water that I could see clearly enough to make any kind of judgment about her injuries.

Because of the slope of the bank and the lie of her body, her head appeared to be resting on her arm when I looked from behind. From in front it was lying over the arm twisted a little too far.

Her neck was broken.

I was certain. Not that it would be my call. The coroner's assistants were waiting patiently on the road outside the perimeter. With them was our tech and two more newly arrived deputies. Everyone was waiting on me.

I had all I needed for the moment but I kept sketching. More avoiding.

"You doing okay there?"

It was Billy asking. Was he being protective or helpful? Either way it bothered me. I didn't want to be helped or to need help. And I was certainly no damsel who needed rescuing.

"Who made you the babysitter tonight?" I asked, tinging the question with a little extra venom. I regretted it immediately and waited for a reply just as pleasant.

"You think you need a babysitter?" he asked and without the bile.

"Sometimes," I looked at him. "I honestly don't know."

"Well, when you do know, call me." He laughed like it was just a casual comment with no weight to it.

There I was, up to my knees in cold lake water, my boots stuck in mud, eight feet from a dead girl, with a man, probably laughing at me. The sheriff was right. I needed a friend. And standing there, looking across water, and death, and probably other metaphors I wasn't picking up on, it was clear that Billy Blevins was my friend. It was just as clear to me that I had never been his friend.

"Billy," I said.

When I didn't go on, he asked, "Are you stuck in the mud?"

"No." But I wasn't sure if that was true. I didn't want to try moving my feet just in case it was. Old business first. "A while back, before so much happened and I ended up with Moonshines."

"Yeah?"

"I was just wondering. Why did you stop playing music?"

"I didn't."

"No," I explained like he didn't understand my question. "You haven't even been in there since . . ."

"I still play music. Just not there."

"Oh," I said, feeling as foolish as I sounded. "Why not there?"

"Busy," he answered. I think it was the first time I ever heard him lie. Then he added, "I just never fit it in. I still play sometimes. Weekends, if I'm not on duty, down at the Dogwood."

He was talking about the Dogwood Mountain Resort. It was a lakeside development with cabins that look rustic but have room service. The whole thing is centered on a restaurant and a lounge that I just learned had live entertainment.

"Quite the place," I said.

"The people who go can afford it."

I wondered if that was a dig at me or the people who go. I'd never been. Dogwood was built as a vanity project by a rich romance writer and her third husband. It didn't take long before it was making more money than the book business.

"You like it there?"

"Why are you asking?"

Taking a genuine interest in people was harder than I remembered. I shrugged. It really wasn't possible to look very casual standing in a lake. I nodded over at the shore where I'd gone in, well away from Sartaña's body.

"Give me a hand getting out of here," I told him.

We both started making our way to the same point. Billy shoving aside the weeds to make a path. He had his feet planted and a hand out by the time I got there.

"I was just interested," I said as soon as my hand was in his.

"In what?"

He wasn't pulling. We were standing, in mud, weeds, and water, clasping hands. I was staring at him like a deer caught in headlights. The lights were behind him so Billy's face was in shadow. I had to be illuminated as brightly as a movie marquee. Like a marquee, I was pretty sure everything was written on my face.

"Can't a friend ask?"

He laughed. Honest to God, Billy laughed at me. Then he pulled and I staggered out of the water. There was a thick coating of mud on my boots making my feet heavy and slick. I almost fell but extra embarrassment was the last thing I needed.

"Is that what we are now?" He was still chuckling. His face and voice were full of good humor. Billy was enjoying my discomfort.

"Well I thought we were." I don't think there was much good humor in my voice.

"Seems to me we had this conversation before."

He was right we had. I should have left it at that.

"You don't really have friends do you?" he pressed still smiling.

"Do me a favor," I said, looking past him into the glare of lights. Up the hill, beyond the lights, shapes moved on the road—spectators or deputies. They were revealed as real people only in the white flash of light bar strobes. Outside the immediate circle of light the world seemed not to exist. Darkness reigned beyond the perimeter tape because so much energy was thrown within. It was a disorienting feeling.

In the distant overhead, cold, silent lightning stuttered in the stacked clouds. The world had a roof that seemed to be made of pain. Electricity from deep in the thunderhead flashed before breaking out into the clear. In free air it forked in jagged branches that left their impression on the eyes. In the afterimage I could swear I saw brown dust blowing toward me and the thunder was hard rubber rolling too fast on uneven asphalt.

"What?" Billy asked me.

I shook my head.

"You said, 'Do me a favor.' What favor?"

I remembered. "Go check out the Russian in the RV." I pointed but you couldn't see anything at the far end of the road through our circle of light. "Check out that story. And ask about why Mike was there."

"Mike Resnick?" he asked still a little too pleased with himself. "Another one of your friends?"

Billy started to laugh but I'd had enough. "Just do it. See what he was doing up there."

"With the Russian?" He wasn't laughing.

"Yes. I saw him."

"When?"

"Now."

"No. When did you see him?"

"When I was talking with the feds." I didn't mean to sound angry. It wasn't Billy's fault. I touched the scar at my eye then caught myself. Instead I rubbed the lids of my eyes and felt grit, like fine dust under them.

"It's not the place," Billy said.

"It's never the place," I hit back. "It's never the time."

"Breathe," he told me. But he said it gently, soothingly like you would talk to a skittish horse. "Breeeeathe." He said again dragging the word out. "It's not what I meant."

"What?"

"When I said it wasn't the place. I was talking about Dogwood. It's not the place that I like."

I took away my hands and opened my eyes.

"It's just playing. I like the music and singing. I like playing my guitar. I enjoy the people listening."

I nodded, understanding.

"It's about the music, not the place. Okay?"

"Yeah." I agreed. "I can understand that."

"You going to be okay?"

"Why wouldn't I be?" The best denial was always a good offense. "I don't need a babysitter."

"You said that."

"Then what are you doing still here?"

"Just keeping an eye on a friend."

When I was in the Army, there was a phrase that the women picked up. It was something that said more about us as women in a man's world, but still managed to convey a level of deep surprise, and stunning impact. I couldn't help but think of it: *It was like I'd been kicked in the nuts.*

What can I say? Being a lady was never my strong suit.

"I'll check on that Russian guy," Billy said. He was already walking away.

I slogged up the bank. As I went up, the tech, coroner, and deputies came down.

Chapter 10

When Billy came back to tell me that the Russian and his RV were gone, the rain broke. There was a quick scramble to clear the scene and get Sartaña into the coroner's van for transport to autopsy. I helped pull in the emergency lighting and get it stowed. All the spectators had bolted back to tents or trailers.

It didn't take ten minutes until I was alone with Billy sitting in my truck.

"Are you going after the Russian tonight?" he asked.

I started the engine and set the defroster to high. Billy was wet from the rain. I was soaked.

"How did he get past the deputy at the park entrance?"

"Limbaugh had it covered. He said, an FBI agent told him to let the RV through. So he did."

"Givens."

Billy nodded. "This is a nice truck."

"I like it," I answered not really wanting to talk about it. "It'll be a lot nicer once the defroster heats up." The moisture on our clothing and breath, and the dropping temperature outside, worked to fog the windows. I turned the fan on high and wiped a hand on the windshield. Something about being in a parked vehicle with a guy and having the windows fogged made me feel seventeen in the most awkward way possible.

"I was thinking."

Exactly like I was seventeen.

"About the defroster?" I intended it as a joke. I needed a deflection.

"About the Russian."

That time it was my turn to laugh. Not because anything was

funny but I was so relieved that there wasn't more *friend* talk. Or worse.

"What's funny?"

"The heat is finally coming through the defroster. It feels good." I didn't really think he was buying it so I pressed on. "What about the Russian?"

"You said Mike was talking to him."

"I saw Mike. At the RV the Russian was in," I detailed. "They spoke for a moment then I had to deal with the *federales*."

"So, that made me think about the fish."

"What about them?"

"Caviar. Russian. Conservation agent. It fits. And, I've heard about a Russian man who comes to Dogwood. I've never seen him, but people talk about him."

"What do they say?"

"Mostly that he's crazy and you don't want to get on his bad side. Some of the servers say he's like a favorite uncle. I don't know. I might even be confusing two people. But from what I hear, he has a wholesale bait business in that strip of warehouses north of Forsyth."

"It does fit."

The glass was clear so I turned the control to heat and hot air started rushing out at us. We both put our hands up to the dash vents.

"Something else I just thought about." He sounded smug.

"What?"

"They serve a lot of caviar at Dogwood Mountain Resort."

Even though it was only about a hundred yards away, I dropped Billy off at his cruiser. Since I was apparently no longer suspended, I could have kept working. There were reports to do and my logs to fill out. I could go out the Starry Night Salvation show to talk again with Roscoe about why he—or his big land yacht—had been at the crime scene. Or I could do a little research on the Russian. There was always work to be done when murder was involved.

I did none of that. I went home to sleep off the weight of a long day and an interesting life.

At four a.m. ghosts woke me. I entertained them for a half hour or so before I fell back into an exhausted, black sleep. At seven, the alarm ran me out of my dreams and my bed. In the shower I had an idea. With soap still in my hair, I went out into the cold bedroom to retrieve my phone.

"Duck?" I said as soon as it connected. Donald Duques, everyone called him Donald Duck or just Duck, was our lead jailer. Many years ago he'd been a lousy deputy. He made a good jailer because he liked order and sitting indoors. It just goes to show, there's a place for everyone.

"Katrina?" he answered, sounding out each syllable. That usually meant he was about to share the kind of joke that caused Human Resources nightmares.

"Don't even start," I cut him off. "I don't have time."

"Oh, you got time to call the old Duck, you just ain't got time to talk wit' him."

"I need to know about a prisoner, Duck. It's important. Has Silas Boone, that guy I put in day-before-yesterday been kicked loose yet?"

"I got papers. No arraignment. Nothin'. I was gonna put him outside as soon as I got to that end of the row."

"Do me a favor—"

"Oh, now we got time for favors?"

I threw him a bone. "I can't talk, I got out of the shower to call and I'm wet and dripping all over the floor." In my defense of using that imagery to get what I wanted from a man—it was at least true.

"Good God, Hurricane. What you need, girl?"

Yeah I was ashamed. Not so ashamed I wouldn't ask him to wait another half hour before opening the cage on Silas Boone.

I got back under the water and rinsed off.

My mood was actually a pretty fine one. Usually the mornings after I converse with my dead husband in the small hours I feel like I've been put through the gears of a machine and come out mangled but walking. That morning had been different though. What had come in my sleep were not quite nightmares, more of a feeling. I had sensed the ghost, Nelson's or someone else's, standing over me and listening as I talked. In any other life it would have been terrifying, I guess. For me it was mild. That was the reason I didn't think too much about it until I trotted downstairs to find a bottle of my favorite whiskey on the kitchen counter. Beside it was a highball glass still holding two cubes of un-melted ice.

Suddenly, the blood in my heart was as frigid and solid as the ice. I wouldn't have thought it possible to feel anything colder until I turned my back on the tempting still life. I wanted to take refuge in Nelson's painting, the one of him and me in two rowboats. It was there in the same place as always, still perched on the easel in his workspace beside the big, river-stone fireplace. It was different. There was a stripe of black paint down the center of the canvas separating us in our dark and light spaces. That stripe was like death itself lingering between us.

Whoever had attacked me that morning didn't know me as well as they thought they did. Had they left only the whiskey, temptation might have worked. The moment I'd seen the bottle my mouth watered and my center felt empty. The phrase, *one won't hurt,* was dangling from my tongue. And that's one of the most dangerous lies ever told.

It all vanished when I saw that smear of black. Vandalizing the painting made me angry enough to resist. And I know from experience, that the one thing stronger than my need for drink, is the furnace of anger that remains stoked in my heart at all times. I turned the whiskey bottle upside down in the sink then left it gurgling as I went to my truck.

As I drove I worked the phone. First, I called the SO and asked for someone to cruise by the house a few times today. After that, I called a contact from Nelson's list, a paint conservator. She promised she could fix it.

When I pulled up outside the jail, just in time to spot Givens and Keene, I wasn't scared or tempted. I was furious. They were in the same rental car. It looked slightly worse for its encounter with Kyle and Keith Dickerson.

My idea in the shower had been that since these two wanted Silas out, they might want to see where he went. I wanted to see that too, but even more, I wanted to see if they just followed or if they spent any face time with Mr. Boone.

Face time it was.

They picked him up at the bottom of the hill and took Silas to breakfast.

I made a mental note to call the sheriff and ask if he'd had that talk with the feds supervising Givens and Keene. My thought was he had and it had been a bad one. Why else would they meet openly with a man they claimed to be investigating, unless they were sure the locals had been put on a leash?

I walked into the Taneycomo Café without my leash.

Givens was the first to notice. He tried to wave me off, counting on a level of discretion it was foolish to credit me with. His face had melted to an exasperated frown by the time I got to the table. Then Keene saw me. Boone was still shoveling biscuits and gravy in his mouth.

"Cozy kind of investigation you run," I said.

"Goddamn it," Givens said.

It was the wrong thing to blurt out in the middle of the poster crowd for white, evangelical voters. Especially pointing it at a woman.

I looked around the quiet room. Boone was the only one still eating.

"Careful," I said. "You don't have any friends in here."

Keene stood to face me. "You're the one who's going to need friends—Hurricane." He sneered my nickname.

I never liked being called Hurricane. I liked it less coming from him. "Friends?" I asked. "I've got them."

"Fuckin' A." Someone behind me said. I heard flatware clattering on dishes and chairs scraping back.

Keene looked like he wanted something to happen. Givens looked like he wanted to disappear.

"What are you hoping to get out of this, Detective?" Givens asked. His tone was very calm.

"What does any investigator want?" I asked back. "Answers."

"You won't get any here," Keene said. "You're out of your pond little fish."

"Maybe," I looked down at Boone who had stopped eating to grin back and forth between me and his keepers. "But it looks to me like you're swimming in the toilet."

"You talkin' 'bout me?" Boone stood with Keene and he looked ready to pick up where we left off last time.

"In this scenario, Keene's the fish." I looked squarely at Silas Boone daring him to react. "You're the crap he's swimming with."

In the space of a sparrow's heartbeat, Givens was on his feet and he'd done something that I never saw. Whatever it was, dropped Boone back to his seat. Next thing, his hand, one finger pointed, was up in front of Keene. It was a hovering warning less than an inch from the end of his nose.

I was reevaluating the nature of their relationship.

Givens turned to me and dropped his hand from Keene's face. "Are you finished here? Because my breakfast is getting cold."

"What kind of investigation do you really have going on?"

"There are no answers for you here, Detective Williams." Givens held his gaze firm on my eyes.

"Why are you protecting a murder suspect?"

"You need to leave."

"Was the death of the girl a result of direct action by you or collateral damage?"

"You are out of line." Keene found his voice again. "I serve my country."

"Sometimes we serve best by refusing to do what's asked."

"What the hell is that supposed to mean?"

"Captain Keene," Givens said, and he had command in his voice. "You need to de-escalate this and step away."

"Fuck this bitch," Keene said. He was past being reined in by his partner. He pointed at me. "You want to call me—*my service*—into question, I'll take it out of your lying ass." The finger he had pointed at me became fingers as he spread his hand and grabbed at me.

He was angry and I was ready. When his hand touched my collar he never got the chance to take hold. I caught him with my right thumb in his palm and fingers at his wrist. At the same time, I brought my left arm up under his elbow. I turned in as I twisted and Keene went down with his face in his eggs.

After a moment like that, things can get over or they can get uglier. I was betting on ugly when I saw Boone grab up his fork. Givens reached for something behind his back and I assumed it was going to be much deadlier than a fork.

Givens could get me. But I had the satisfaction of knowing that he would not live through it. The thing is, Missouri has one of the most liberal open-carry laws in the country. The state had recently even eliminated the requirement of basic permits. Combine that with a standing mistrust of the federal government and you were looking at Ruby Ridge in the diner.

Givens cleared and aimed his 9mm at me faster than reason. There were two things about his action that were tremendously scary. First, he pulled knowing we were in a crowded, public space with civilians in line of fire. And second, he didn't blink when three other weapons, all much bigger than 9mm, I couldn't help but notice, were pulled on him.

"Let him up," Givens said, his voice slow and steady as a steamroller.

Givens was a steel spine pro. He didn't falter or show anything but resolve. Not until I glanced back at the guns supporting me and back to him. That was when I twisted and Keene gasped in pain.

"I'm willing if you are," I said to Givens. At the time, I may have meant it. He seemed to think so. I saw the front sight of his Glock, tick down slightly. In any other, less-steady hand, it would have been nothing. In that man's hand, it was everything.

I smiled.

We were all saved from my next bad decision by the tinkle of a bell and a booming voice like Moses on the mount.

"Put those guns away," the Reverend Roscoe Bolin bellowed from the café door.

Everyone, even Givens, did.

I bent over Keene and quietly asked, "Who's the bitch now?" Then I let him go and shoved a napkin at him. It wasn't so quiet when I told him, "Clean yourself up."

"Hurricane Williams," Roscoe bellowed. He released the open door and it closed behind him once again ringing the bell over it. "Is this the way you conduct the business of the people?"

"Yes, Reverend," I said, unapologetic. "One of the ways."

"And have you accomplished anything?"

I looked at Givens. "I don't know," I answered. "But I think I learned a few things."

"I hope it was worth the danger you put these people in."

"My weapon never left my holster." I was speaking more for Keene and Givens at that point. "I'll let the, assaulting-a-police-officer charge go, though. In the spirit of cooperation."

I don't think he bought it or really cared. Reverend Bolin waved an impatient hand at Boone. "Come along, Silas. Let's get back to the tabernacle."

"I never finished my breakfast," Boone complained.

"No time for that," Roscoe told him. "We have to run."

Boone tossed the dirty fork he'd been holding onto his plate and started walking.

"I'm going to need to talk with you again, Reverend." I said as the pair were headed out the door. "About last night. About the girl."

It wasn't until then that I noticed the same dark man, I'd seen earlier at the big RV. I worked my memory for the name that Roscoe had used. *Massoud.* It was a given name, nothing to run.

"I think it might be in everyone's best interest if further discussions went through my lawyer," He responded without looking back. "He'll be in touch." Roscoe went through the door and the bell tinkled again.

I followed and quickly cut in front of the stranger. "Just a moment, sir. What's your involvement with the Reverend?"

He stared at me without the slightest indication of concern.

I glanced at Roscoe who was standing at the curb waiting. There was a storm of colors in his eyes. The rest of him looked relaxed.

When I looked back at Massoud, he lifted his right hand and wiped at his prodigious mustache. Two of the fingers on the hand had large, gold rings. The one on his middle finger had a blue stone with a Coptic cross in the center.

"What's the matter," I asked. "Don't you speak English?"

He burst with a belly laugh then used that ringed middle finger to point at my face. It sounds like a simple gesture. There was nothing simple about any of it. His laugh was warm and bright. It was an easy sound. However, the look on his face remained hard. The eyes were like fixed black stones without life or movement. His teeth, tobacco stained and jagged, danced up and down in a mirthless chewing of air that had no connection to the sound escaping from behind them. Then he nodded, tucking away the laughter, but not the pointing finger. I didn't know exactly what he was trying to say, but I felt a skin crawling malevolence in the way he chose to say it.

Massoud dropped his finger and turned to step around me.

"Excuse me," I spoke louder than I intended to.

He kept walking.

"Hey!"

Massoud turned. It was a swift and sure motion. Not at all what I'd expected from a man of his stiff bearing and age.

"You are typical," he said in an East Coast American accent. "Small town, small mind assumptions." With a sniff, as if something all of a sudden smelled bad, he stroked his mustache again, then said, "If you have just cause to stop me, Detective. Do so. Otherwise, understand, I choose not to engage in conversation other than that officially required. And then, only with my lawyer present."

He turned again, and strolled with a strong, straight back alongside Reverend Bolin.

It wasn't until I had gotten out of the café, leaving Givens and Keene behind, that the reality hit me. There had almost been an honest-to-God shoot-out in the Taneycomo Café. I could rationalize it any way I wanted, but the whole thing came down to me pushing buttons just to see what would happen. That was irresponsible. More and more, that seemed to be an aspect of my nature.

I hadn't thought of myself as the loose cannon on the deck, but I was beginning to understand why others would.

The question was, what would I do with it?

I could hear my therapist asking. I could hear myself not answering.

I had a lot of time not to answer because I decided to try for a talk with Mike Resnick. I say try, because Conservation Agents get to work early and they don't hang around an office. I expected him to be out on the lake and unreachable. I got lucky when he picked up the call on the first ring. He didn't sound very happy to hear from me though.

"What do you want, Hurricane?"

"No hello?" I asked. I probably didn't sound very happy either.

"I'm working and I'm busy."

"Fair enough. I'd like to talk though. Are you on dry land?"

"I'm at Cooper Creek boat landing, checking fishing licenses and stringer counts. Can't it wait?"

"How about if it waits the fifteen minutes it'll take me to get there? I want to talk to you about Daniel Boone and Damon."

"What about them?"

"When I get there." I broke the connection, then called my destination into dispatch.

Cooper is a public landing where those who don't rent slips at a private dock can trailer their boats in and out of the water. Just like traffic cops stake out those parts of the road known for speeding, agents like Mike make random checks at boat landings and docks.

When I arrived, Mike was standing with a foot up on the fender of a trailer looking into the wells of the boat it carried. The bass boat, all metal flake fiberglass and flashy graphics was still dripping wet after being pulled from the lake. At the bow of the boat, between it and the big truck by which it was pulled, stood an unhappy-looking man.

I saw Mike counting and writing in his ticket book. It looked like it was going to be a big over-limit fine.

Instead of going over there and making things worse for the fisherman, and maybe Mike, I took my truck over to park beside the Conservation Department Ram. In stark contrast to the flashy bass boat Mike was ticketing, the department boat on his trailer was a basic V-bottom aluminum model with a tiller-steered outboard motor. No one ever said government work was glamorous.

The landing was busy. There was a boat being launched and a couple of trailers lined up waiting their turn. I saw five boats bobbing out in the lake waiting to come in. There were two that were conspicuously holding back, waiting, I thought, for Mike to go away.

Standing beside Mike's boat I couldn't help but notice the clutter in it. It wasn't that surprising I guess. I've heard stories from CAs about confiscating everything from beer to dynamite on the lake. It all has to be tagged and logged and sometimes we all fall behind in the paper work. Besides that, when you're on the water all day, you can't just run back to pick up something you need. Everything has to come with you.

From out on the main road a horn honked and tires skidded on pavement. After a second I heard someone yelling. It had probably been a close call but I didn't hear any crash so I ignored it. Something else caught my attention.

Sticking out the front of Mike's boat were two poles coming to dangerous-looking terminations. The shorter one had a gaff head. The long one had a gig. It was the same one I had noticed Monday night when we were dealing with Daniel Boone and the pile of fish. The pair were protruding beyond the prow and I almost walked right into the points.

I heard more yelling and the sound of tires squealing again. This time they were louder and getting closer.

Someone burst through the trees and ran across the broad lot, pumping his arms and legs for all he was worth. Dewey Boone. The moment I recognized him, there was a new squeal of tires and a car careened from the access road into the parking area. It spun, making the sharp turn to point itself right at the sprinting boy.

Dewey was running so fast he was basically out of control. When his foot hit a patch of gravel, he flailed and almost fell, then caught himself. Only for a moment, though. He couldn't keep his balance and overcorrected as his arms went windmilling over and over. He tumbled forward leading with his hands and his face.

Dewey hit hard and bounced into a roll then came up bloody and running again. Behind him, the car was barreling forward tracking his path. There was no doubt, Dewey was running for his life.

The car was an SUV a bit beat-up and muddy, but the engine seemed more than up to the job of catching a running kid.

I shouted his name and Dewey must have heard me. He turned and looked. At that moment I was able to see the side of his face he'd fallen on. It was scraped and bloody. Then I noticed his hands. His arms weren't swinging as strongly as they were, so I could see that a couple of fingers were bent in the wrong direction. One looked to have a bone showing through. Instead of being fisted, Dewey's hands were open as he ran. They were slinging trails of red.

Dewey won his race, in a manner. About the same time I started running at the car, he hit the water. The SUV skidded to a stop on the ramp and three of its doors opened.

Still running and with my badge held high, I shouted, "Sheriff's Department. Stop."

We pretty much have to say that and it pretty much never works. The kind of people who you have to shout that to are not great respecters of the police.

Before I ever got a look at anyone in the SUV, its doors closed and it bolted into a skidding U-turn, but took the time to try to bring me down.

I lunged to my left and rolled onto my shoulder and came up with my weapon drawn. I had no clear shot so I raised then secured the gun. The SUV had no rear plate.

A shout and a splash reminded me of Dewey. When I looked, he was standing in a boat that had been idling up to its trailer. The owner was in the water, still shouting. Dewey was backing away and ignoring the string of obscenities condemning him.

Heading for the shore with my phone out I called dispatch and waved my hands trying to get Dewey's attention. He saw me. I told Doreen, our dispatcher where I was and what had happened as quickly as I could, sending a BOLO for the SUV. At the same time I walked to the edge of the water.

"Dewey! Come back in." I shouted.

He shook his head.

"We can protect you."

Shake.

"You don't want to do this."

"It wasn't me," he finally shouted back. "I was going to help her. I was going to marry her."

"You've got to come back to make it right, Dewey."

He hit the throttle and spun the wheel kicking up a shower of foam and a deep wake behind him. I shouted again but he headed across the lake toward Arkansas.

When I gave up tracking Dewey and turned around, Mike was gone. He had offered no assistance and instead used the distraction to drive from the scene.

I wasn't feeling very kindly disposed toward Mike Resnick at that point but I knew I could track him down easily. I stayed and worked the crowd. One man reported that he'd clearly seen the front of the vehicle chasing Dewey. There were no front plates either.

As I worked I kept tabs on the BOLO and planned my next step. No one caught sight of the SUV. I was pretty sure if we did a little poking around the Starry Night Traveling Salvation Show we'd find it. I was just as sure that we would run into a federal roadblock if we tried. Reverend Bolin's evangelical movement was somehow tied up with the government and it wasn't exactly clear how. Givens and Keene never mentioned the show or Roscoe, but both were surrounded with rough-looking military types. They looked to me to be the kind of private contractors the government has been using to stretch the reach of the real military into places we sometimes didn't want official fingerprints. Somehow the entire Boone family, except maybe Dewey, was part of the team.

So the big question was, were the feds investigating or protecting these men? The next, and only slightly smaller question was, how did I move ahead?

My answer was Daniel Boone and his murder. There was something, literally, fishy there. And I was feeling that Billy had been onto something about the connections between Daniel, the fish, Mike, and the Russian.

Was Damon in that chain somewhere? One thing that was becoming certain was that Daniel Boone's death was a middle link and not an end. From him there are connections to fish poaching, Damon, and Mike. Had they become involved only since that night or was there a relationship before that was being hidden?

Following connections the other direction led from Daniel to Silas and Dewey then right under the tents of Reverend Bolin's evangelic church by way of the federal government.

It was all a confusing mess and seemed designed to make me angry. I didn't have a good history with anger. Aside from that, there was one thing I was afraid of. If I pulled both ends of the chain around would I find a termination? Or would I find my father and the congresswoman hooking things together? Did I even want to know?

Since when did anyone care about what I wanted?

I took the easy way. Once I had cleared the scene to my satisfaction—that's to say I found nothing and left it at that—I went in search of the Russian.

His name was Aton Gagarin and he claimed relation to the first man in space. He told me that over a happy smile and a countertop stacked with tubs of night crawlers.

"You are the Hurricane," he said, like it was news to me. "I know your uncle." Of course he did. It seemed like everyone knew everyone in this case, and everyone always knows my uncle.

I have to admit, and I'm ashamed to say, but I expected something closer to Boris Badenov or Yakhov Smirnoff. Aton's English was slightly accented but not the thick Russian bad-guy talk you get from a Rambo movie. I decided I needed to improve my movie choices.

"Mr. Gagarin—"

"Please, call me Aton," he interrupted jovially.

"Can you tell me anything about caviar?"

"Caviar?" He held up his hands in a cartoonish double shrug and gestured around the warehouse. "Bait, I know. Caviar—that is something else. And it is one of those foolish, cultural stereotypes to think all Russians eat caviar." Aton smiled with the dig. He was a hard man not to like.

"What about vodka?" I asked.

His face took a serious cast before he leaned in then pointed a thick finger right at my heart. "Vodka." He pronounced the V not the W like an American raised with TV would expect. But he did elongate the middle and add an upswing so it came out *Vooad-ka.* "All stereotypes start someplace." Aton laughed easily and broadly.

I found myself enjoying the joke.

"What do you know about fish poaching?" I asked still smiling.

"Ah. Now I understand it. You want to know about something more than caviar."

"Is there anything you can tell me?"

"This is a tough thing. This is a very tough thing." He stared for a moment at me then turned to look at something in his own head.

I didn't press or ask another question. People think that cops ask a lot of questions. Mostly we ask a few and wait for answers. It's the waiting, the allowing someone to get to the point, that's the toughest trick to learn.

"I know," he hesitated, and seemed to be talking himself into something. "I know that it happens. I know that the people involved in such things . . . are not good people."

"Are these people who you are afraid of?"

"They are people you should be afraid of." There was no trace of smile left on his face.

"I have a job to do, Aton. And no one is going to keep me from it."

"Please," he implored. "I like you, Hurricane. Leave this one alone."

"Have you been threatened? I can get you protection."

"There is no protection from these people. You should let it go. There is crime. There is always crime and always people looking to make a living. Things can be tolerated."

"Not murder, Mr. Gagarin."

"Murder?" Aton looked suddenly more interested than frightened. "Who is murdered?"

I pulled the intake photo of Daniel Boone from my jacket and laid it on the counter. "Do you know this man?"

He looked closely. Carefully. I couldn't read what he was thinking when he pushed the picture back. "No." He shook his head. "I don't. He killed someone?"

"He's been murdered."

That had an effect. Aton's loss of composure was microscopic. His face tightened drawing together two, thick eyebrows that were barely separated to begin with. Then he relaxed and gave me a relieved semi-smile. "Then I won't keep an eye out for him."

All of a sudden I didn't quite like him so well.

"This is a big warehouse." I pointed over his shoulder at the racks and boxes filling them. I noticed in the back was a wall and door. The space was subdivided. "Is all of it yours?"

"No. Some of it I sublease."

"To who?"

"I thought you wanted to know about caviar."

I noted his non-answer and decided to see where other things might go. "Maybe you know the dead man's brother," I pulled a booking photo of Silas Boone and set it on the counter.

This time the examination was not so careful, but Aton was just as certain that he'd never seen Silas.

"You should go," he said. "There is much work to do."

I noticed the change in his syntax. If he wasn't as careful he sounded more Russian. It made me wonder why he needed to be so careful and what was causing him to slip.

"Something else," I said, as I put the photo of Silas away. "Another man. Do you know Mike Resnick?"

"No."

His response was quick. Automatic?

"Are you sure?" I pressed.

"I am sure."

"I saw you speaking to him."

"I don't know anyone by this name."

"Mike Resnick. He's a Missouri Conservation Agent." I waited but Gagarin would neither look at me nor speak. "I saw you talking to him last night," I finally said.

"No."

"At Shadow Rock Park, I saw him come to the window of your RV and talk to you."

"No," he shook his head, seeming more sad than worried. "You are mistaken. I don't know anyone named Resnick." Once again, Aton's demeanor shifted. He turned his head up to meet my gaze, then resolutely said, "You have to go. Any other questions, I will meet you at the sheriff's office with my lawyer." There was no trace of any accent other than good old American stonewalling.

I left.

Chapter 11

My encounter with Aton Gagarin left me feeling as much confused as suspicious. His peculiar bipolar personality was a huge red flag begging for attention. Unfortunately I didn't have evidence to give him the hard look he deserved. Judges don't issue warrants for bad feelings. At least not for mine.

So I headed to the one place I knew that held some answers—Uncle Orson's dock.

When I arrived there was a good fire going in the split barrels that served as grills. Dad was helping out, turning burgers and chicken halves. Whilomina was right beside him slathering sauce on the birds. Damon was out pumping gas for a couple of fishermen and Uncle Orson was wearing a groove in the boards shuttling between the register and everything else.

"Busy day," I said as the screen door slapped behind me.

"Take a look around you," Orson said without slowing down. "What do you see?"

"Nothing different."

"The sky," he prodded. "The air, the heat, the weather. You're telling me you don't see the difference in that. It's gorgeous."

I hadn't noticed. He was right, though. It was a beautiful day and the first really nice one of the spring. That had brought the retirees and the leisure class out to the water.

"You have a congresswoman cooking your chicken dinners."

"Yeah, can you believe it?" He asked.

I couldn't.

"I need to talk with Damon," I told him.

"Now? What ever happened with your—"

I'd walked out before he could finish the sentence.

"Hey, kid." Dad greeted.

"Do you want a plate?" Whilomina offered.

Their vision of domestic bliss had my head spinning. I wasn't sure yet if I liked the congresswoman, but I was pretty sure she was here to stay. Dad looked happy and I hated that I still didn't know how I felt about that either. I should have said something nice or at least smiled. Instead I said, "We need to talk. I'll be right back." Then I went right on to Damon.

The boat was fueled and Damon pushed it away from the dock with his foot. The fisherman started the motor and idled away.

"Is Mike involved?" I'd decided to lead with the cop before the friend. Not that I'm much of a friend they keep telling me.

"I don't know what you mean—"

"Yes you do. Maybe not everything. But you know my meaning clearly enough." I let that stand there between us for a moment then asked again. "Is Mike involved?"

"I don't—"

"The federal investigation into you and your friends—what's that about?"

"What investigation?"

"What's your connection to Silas Boone? Who killed Daniel Boone?"

"Daniel's dead?"

"What?" His question put me back on my heels. The shock in his face and voice looked like it might sink into the pit of his gut and drag him to the floor. Still I pushed. "How can you act like you didn't know?"

"I didn't." It wasn't a protest. It wasn't a plea. His words were fact with baggage, a statement of loss. "I didn't . . . How?"

"What are you talking about?" My question was still an accusation. I believed his body language but not his words. "You saw him."

"I haven't seen Daniel since the Army. I was his spotter. We were a . . . team."

Again his body and his words conspired to make so much more, and so much more confusion, out of something simple. The way he said the word, *team* made me think of that kiss I caught him sharing with Mike.

We stood there, the two of us, working through meanings and words looking for understanding. My father and Whilomina had stepped from the grill and were watching us closely. Past them, Orson had his face pressed to the screen, watching and listening.

Maybe it was time to be the friend.

"Damon," I said, and I spoke his name as gently as I could. A preparation for both of us. "The man you found in the lake . . ."

"No."

"The man in the net, was Daniel Boone."

"They killed him." His words were tears. "They murdered him because he was a faggot."

The word, the hate and the bile in it filled the air around me. It was a broken word, something cracked and spilling the stench of dreams that had died in hiding. Just speaking it seemed to take a little more of the life out of Damon Tarique.

Suddenly, Whilomina was brushing past me. She put a supporting arm around Damon's shoulders and led him to one of the built-in benches that kids fished from. I felt a little better about her.

"I'm sorry, Damon." I meant it. "But I have to ask you about it. About everything."

He nodded and I understood then there would have been no keeping him from talking at that point.

"Don't ask, don't tell," Damon said quietly as if it explained everything. "I enlisted. I wanted to serve. I wanted to be better and get an education. I always knew I was gay. I had parents who let me grow and understand and never judged. The first thing they ever fought me on was going into the military. They knew."

Whilomina, sitting beside him, looked up to meet my gaze. I knew then she'd heard these kinds of stories before. I knew also that was why she'd helped after my rape, had protected me from the full weight of the Army, not simply because of my father.

"Daniel—how can you not be drawn to a man named, Daniel Boone?" Damon rambled. "He didn't know. He had been taught, all his life, queers were freaks to be hated. Imagine how he felt every day, hating every desire that rose in his heart."

"I can't," I admitted.

"Sniper teams spend a lot of time together, isolated from everything and everyone who judges. There is a lot of time to talk. To grow."

"You were involved?" I asked, feeling like an intruder in my own investigation.

"Not like you mean it. It would have been unprofessional. We never crossed that line. When we got back into contact I had hopes, though."

"How did he get into contact? You were living on your boat."

"I wasn't living on the boat then. Not until after."

"After what?" I prodded. "You're not really making sense, Damon."

"Nothing makes sense, does it? Daniel said we needed to be off the grid when things happened."

"What happened?" I had to work hard to keep the frustration out of my voice. Not that it was entirely effective.

"That's obvious now, isn't it?"

Damon wasn't really thinking about what I was asking. You could see the faraway and yesterdays in his eyes. Pushing him wasn't going to make him more responsive either. I tried an easier question. "Okay, once you got off the grid, how did you keep in touch?"

"Prepaid cell. Mostly you don't get reception on the lake, but I could come in and check messages. When I had bars, we would text."

I recalled the phone that had been in his tackle box and reminded myself to pull the records for the number. I should have done that the same night. I didn't because I never really believed Damon had killed Daniel Boone.

"What did you text about?" I asked.

"Usual things, and . . . you know . . . stuff."

I noted the evasion. The look that went with it got my attention as well. It was embarrassment more than guilt. I wasn't sure I wanted to read those texts.

"When he first told me about working with that evangelical show, I asked if he had found the Lord and lost himself again. He said it wasn't like that. It was just a job."

"What kind of job?"

"That was the strange thing," he said, mulling the thought over behind his eyes. "He was working with his brother and some other guys doing contract work. Private military stuff for oil companies and the government."

"That fits with how those guys look at the tent show." I said. "And I'm sure saving souls isn't in their job description. What's their connection to Bolin?"

Damon shook his head and watched sunfish swimming in the shadow of the dock.

"Reverend Roscoe Bolin," I repeated. "He's the one running the show."

"You don't think Roscoe is part of it do you?" It was my father asking.

I turned to see him back beside the grill moving food away from the fire. Uncle Orson was behind him watching me. I read the same question in his eyes.

"He's the man in charge," I said.

"That doesn't sound like the man I know," Orson answered.

"Maybe not, but something is going on with that operation and Jesus is not a part."

Whilomina stood from the bench leaving Damon to watch the fish alone. "You were asking about a federal investigation. What was that about?"

I told her about the FBI and Army involvement with Silas Boone. I couldn't call it an investigation but I stopped short of calling it collusion. Just barely. When I mentioned the names, Keen and Givens my father went over and whispered something in the congresswoman's ear. She nodded knowingly.

"We can't tell you everything," she said. "We can't even tell you enough, I dare say. But we can tell you that Givens is not FBI."

"What?" I asked. "An imposter?"

My father took over saying, "He had all the proper credentials I'm sure. And he does belong to a three-letter branch of the government."

"He's a spook?" I blurted incredulous.

My father's answer was giving no answer.

"That's not possible. They can't operate domestically."

Whilomina nodded, "That's a pretty fiction. And like the best fiction, it is somewhat true. The Central Intelligence Agency, and I'm not saying Givens is CIA—but as an *example*—the CIA can operate within US borders as part of a joint operation with any federal agency who takes reporting responsibility."

"Army CID," I added.

"For example," the congresswoman clarified.

I turned to my father. "You said on the phone it was about guns."

"I'd been assisting Whilomina's committee work, along with the

FBI, ATF, and Homeland in a joint investigation into the disappearance of military weapons when we discovered the possibility that they were being diverted to a Peruvian revolutionary force called *El Camino Ardiente*, The Blazing Road."

"What committee?" I asked. I think they were both disappointed I didn't get it.

"The House Armed Services," Dad explained.

"You know all this and it hasn't been shut down?"

"It's complicated." My father looked guiltier in that moment than I'd ever seen before.

"*Un*-complicate it."

"We're trying," he said.

"What's the problem?"

"Money." He looked at Whilomina for confirmation and I began to realize just how deeply their partnership went. "The secrets are in the cash. Direct government funds can be traced and shut down. But the profits from secret trades are on no one's books. If anything about this involved a finance operation, we need to know about it, what laws are being broken, and who is authorizing it."

"Finance operation?"

"Think of the 1980s," Dad explained. "Iran-Contra. The agency sold arms to Iran and used the profits to fund the Contra rebels."

"Silas Boone is not nearly smart enough to put something like that together," I objected.

"Timothy Givens is. And I imagine, so are the people he's working for." Dad turned back to the grill.

I called Billy. After the discussion with my father and the congresswoman I wanted to talk to someone smart and not directly involved. Ordinarily, that call would have gone to the sheriff. For some reason, I really wanted to talk things over with Billy Blevins.

Not only did he sound glad to hear from me, he told me to change into old clothes and he was on his way. I dug into the small closet I kept stocked on Orson's houseboat and dressed in patched jeans and a flannel shirt. By the time I got a pair of work boots laced up and tied Billy was waiting at the end of the dock ramp in his truck.

"Where are we going?" I asked as soon as I opened the door.

"Who says we're going anywhere?" He shot back. "Maybe I wanted to see you all dressed up."

"Just what a girl likes to hear. So is flannel your thing?"

"No, but it looks good on you."

I laughed and it felt good to do so. I couldn't tell if Billy was flirting. That was just as well. I couldn't exactly tell if I was either. We were making friends. That seemed more important and more interesting.

"Day off," I asked, looking into the bed of his truck. It was filled with fishing equipment. There were a couple of backpacks and camping gear as well.

He shook his head. "Wellness day. You should try it once in a while. Get out in the world. Breathe in the sunshine."

I opened my window and stared out at the sky for a long moment. It was blue with high drifting clouds. That's a bit like saying the Sistine Chapel has a nice paint job, I guess. The sky was beautiful in the way that only an amazing, spring day can make it. You can see tomorrow in a sky like that and believe it has your best interests at heart.

"How do you breathe in sunshine?" I asked.

"Well . . . We're going to learn a bit about that," he answered and no matter how I asked, he would say no more. We turned to other things. I filled him in on what I'd learned about the feds and the connections between guns, mercenaries, and the Starry Night Traveling Salvation Show.

"I want to go back to something," he said, when I paused at one point to corral my thoughts. "Someone you mentioned being in the tent."

"There was just me and Roscoe and the girl."

He shook his head. "The tech people setting up the show. You mentioned a guy called Banjo."

"Yes."

"Connor Banjo Watson?"

"I don't know is that supposed to mean anything?"

"There's a musician, a gospel and bluegrass legend. He works with a lot of big shows running the stage and musical direction. I just wondered if it might be the same guy."

"The only music I heard was on tape."

"Have you shared all of this with the sheriff?" Billy asked, as he twisted the wheel into a careful turn off the road and onto a rutted, dirt track.

"I'm telling you."

"I'm honored."

"You should be," I told him. "But don't let it go to your head. I needed a sounding board. Hey—"

The truck bounced over one of the large stones that seem to grow in Ozarks fields better than any crop. If it weren't for the seatbelt I would have hit my head on the roof.

"What you need is a keeper," Billy grinned, completely unbothered by the terrain. "What about the Russian?"

I shared my encounter with Aton Gagarin until Billy stopped the truck at a tension gate in a barbed wire fence.

"You want to get that?" He nodded out the window to the fence.

"What happened to being a gentleman?"

"I'm not sure a gentleman is what you need in your life." His voice was smiling but his face was not.

"What's that supposed to mean?"

"It means the gate won't open itself."

I stepped from the truck trying to figure if there was a deeper meaning I was missing or if there was a joke being played on me. It was tempting to let myself feel put out and maybe a little mad. He had something to say, I was sure, but he wasn't saying it. Or if he was, he wasn't doing a very good job of it. And I might have let that bother me more if I hadn't just told him about a complex investigation and left out a lot of details.

Gate was a saying a lot for the kind of opening we had to go through. Three strands of barbed wire were fixed to a post and that post set into loops of wire at the top and bottom of another post. I pulled up the top loop and drew the slack fencing aside as Billy drove through. Once he was past, I reset the post and got back into the truck.

"I'll hold the door for you any day of the week, Katrina Williams. But I never want you to believe I think you need me to."

He drove on across the field and I probably had my mouth hanging open the whole way. I didn't know what to say. When we reached a line of trees that screened a limestone bluff he stopped.

"A friend of mine owns the property. He lets me come out here but doesn't want a lot of other people knowing about it." Billy said as he shut off the engine and opened his door. "I can trust you right?"

I followed out to the back of the truck. "Trust me with what?"

He handed over one of the backpacks and tossed me a yellow hard hat. "The cave."

Behind the trees and under curtains of honey suckle was an opening in the stone large enough to have parked the truck in. Beyond the mouth, the cave tapered quickly to a ragged, maze like crevasse.

Billy led.

We had lights on our helmets and a flashlight each, but our progress was really because of Billy's familiarity with the path. Three turns and one crawl-through and we came out into a chamber. At one end water dripped and trickled, seeming to bleed right out of the stone and filled a small basin. At the other end, the basin emptied into a silent steam that disappeared into a fissure the size of my fist. In between was a flat space on which we sat. Billy pointed out shapes and features in the walls and ceiling.

"Are there bats?" I asked.

"Not all caves have bats," he answered without laughing or making me feel bad for asking. "But this one has something better. Something special."

He slipped down to his knees and put his face low. For a second I thought he was going to put his head under the pool of water. Instead, he shined his flashlight around until he found what he wanted.

"Come look at this." His voice had become a whisper.

I joined him staring into the light beam within the water. What, at first, I thought were reflections, moved away from the light. Fish. They were tiny, like minnows, but the color of bleached bone. Their eyes were small and dead looking. It was as if I was looking into a ghost world.

"Down here." Billy pointed with the flashlight then poked a finger into the beam.

There, along the line of his finger was a white rock.

"A pebble?" I asked.

"Wait."

The rock moved and the strange shape resolved into what appeared to be a tiny lobster.

"Crayfish," I said excited. It was so colorless it was practically transparent at the edges. "So pale."

"They don't need color in the darkness. They don't need eyes either."

I sat up, stunned and elated by the place I was in. "Thank you," I said looking around. "For sharing this with me."

"This isn't what I wanted to share," Billy said.

He reached to the lamp on my hard hat and killed the light. After a moment, he turned off my flashlight. Again he waited a few seconds to turn off his flashlight. Finally, after a longer pause, he turned off his own headlamp.

We were in the kind of complete darkness I don't think I'd ever experienced. It was thrilling and jarring at the same time. I reached and took his hand without even thinking. The black we were in was like distance and I wanted to be close.

"Why?" I asked.

"Look around," he answered, softly.

"It's dark," I said. "Nothing but black."

"There's no light. But absence isn't exactly black."

"I don't understand." I shook my head then wondered why.

"Some of the guys I know . . ." Billy said then stopped.

I knew he was talking about something different then, but still the same. A change in subject not in meaning. I waited, like waiting for a suspect. He had to be the one to fill the silence.

"Veterans," he continued. "Guys who were over there. We talk sometimes. They talk a lot about the things they see when they close their eyes. It's always personal. No one ever has the same experience or the same . . . vision on events. Look around. Do you still see nothing?"

I did as he asked and noticed for the first time that blackness wasn't exactly, only blackness. There were patterns of light, vague shimmers, not entirely seen, but not simply imagined, I was sure.

"Something . . ." I admitted.

"Our eyes don't like complete darkness. When there's no light to be seen, the optic nerves still fire, populating the void with specters. The thing is, your eyes won't see what mine do and I won't see what you experience. Darkness is singular. What you see, is your particular darkness, no one else's. No matter how well you describe it, no one will see it the way you do."

"You're not talking about darkness." I actually thought I heard fear in my voice.

"You're holding my hand."

"Yes," I answered, squeezing.

"Is it real?"

"What do you mean?"

"My hand. Me. Am I real"

"Of course," I said. "Why would you not be?"

"That's what I tell the other guys. We all have our own darkness within us and sometimes it gets out, it shadows our lives, the entire world we see. Those times we get so wrapped up in seeing our own thing, our own darkness, we forget the real out there beyond it."

He let go of my hand and I was suddenly untethered. I was adrift in my own darkness. It was a familiar feeling. In a way, comforting. The same way what is familiar and expected is always somehow a comfort. But I didn't want the darkness anymore. I realized I wanted his hand.

"Billy . . ."

He touched my face. Then the touch became a hold as he placed his hands to each side with his fingers in my hair. His thumb rested on the scar that framed my eye and I didn't mind.

"I don't want to live in the dark anymore," I confessed.

Then Billy Blevins kissed me.

When we walked out of the crevasse and entered the cave's mouth, the world was a circle of light to be walked into. It spread and opened as we approached. When I stepped through, I understood what Billy had said about breathing sunshine.

Billy dropped me off at my uncle's dock, but I didn't go in. Since I had been playing hooky from work for the last few hours I went straight to the SO. The sheriff was in, so I had a sit down to tell him about all the developments.

His first observation was to say that I seemed to be in a good mood.

I didn't have a response that wouldn't give away my afternoon. And I wasn't ready to answer questions about that yet. Not that it mattered. Sheriff Beeson seemed to have a sense that something had transpired to, as he put it, *pull the broom handle out of my ass.* But I made no admissions.

"I got a call a while ago," he said.

I waited. He didn't seem inclined to offer more. At the same time I had the feeling he wanted to be asked. So I did. "What kind of call?"

"From a friend of yours." His eyes fixed me. There was a little sparkle. Despite the bunched brows that shaded them I knew what had put the twinkle in his eyes.

"Marion," I said. "She's been your friend a lot longer than she's been mine."

"Yep." His agreement was quick and pointy. "Friend. Don't think I don't know why you had her call me."

"I didn't tell her to call you."

"I'd imagine that's one of those skirting-the-edge-of-truth things."

I ignored the accusation, mostly because I couldn't defend it and didn't want to try. "I asked her to look into charities, nonprofits, NGOs, anything that might be involved in relocating underage refugees in the state."

"Yeah," he nodded. "She did that too. She said she couldn't find anything registered with the state."

"It's not surprising, I guess."

"Maybe it isn't. Marion went further though." He pushed a small stack of paper across the desk. They were fax pages, stapled together.

"What's this?" I picked the bundle up and scanned. They were copies of entries from a directory with notes, handwritten in a delicate cursive, filling the margins.

"Those are federal agencies dealing with refugees that she called. After that, are the ones dealing with children. Then there are ones involved in immigration and migrants. Then there are the nongovernment, aid organizations. She even called the Peruvian embassy."

I read over the notes. Marion had detailed names and times of contact, even personality traits like A NICE GUY, or RUDE!!! beside each entry. It represented hours of work.

"I didn't expect this," I said flipping to the last page.

"Marion is not a halfway kind of girl."

My eyes were caught by Marion's last, neatly scripted comment, *Nothing. No one knows anything about these girls or anyone by the name Massoud.*

"You have no idea what you've done," the sheriff said.

I looked up from the paper, wary at his change in tone. "That's kind of the story of my life."

"*My* life."

I understood that he wasn't talking about the notes or investigation anymore. But he was still talking about Marion.

"And I don't need any help, or steering, or"—he waved his hand around in front of his face as if shooing off unpleasant thoughts—"whatever it is you think you're doing."

The hand, the quiet tone, and most of all, the lack of profanity, told me he wasn't as mad as he wanted to seem.

"Just trying to do the job," I said. "I asked Marion for a little help, that's all."

"Then why am I meeting her for coffee later?"

"She's your friend." I reassured. "She's interested in what's happening with you."

"There's only one reason an old hen is interested in an old rooster."

I smiled at him—grinned actually and asked, "You think she's looking for a little cock-a-doodle-doo?"

"What?" He almost choked on the question. "No." Then caught the joke and burst out with a hard, loud laugh. "That's about the—" Sheriff Benson stopped like he was thinking through something he'd never imagined before. Then he laughed again. "And here I was, never sure you even had a sense of humor."

He leaned back in his chair, still laughing up at the ceiling.

"I've got one," I told him. "It doesn't get much exercise though."

"Don't know it," he agreed. I thought he couldn't get any more distracted or comfortable, but I was wrong. He kicked dirty boots up onto his desk. "I think after I retire this is how I'll live out the rest of my days. Maybe get a hammock."

"Maybe you don't have to retire quite yet."

"That's the time to go, young lady. When you don't have to." He put one foot over the other and smeared a bit of mud on his desk blotter. "I'm old. I'm tired. And I'm goddamned sad. That's the worst of it. You tossing Marion at me won't change anything."

The sheriff seemed to have lapsed into a reverie to which I was not invited. Before I could get up though, he said, "They're smuggling girls, that's what you said."

I had to shift my seat to keep from talking into the sole of his boot. "Yes."

"And we're calling them refugees?"

"That's what Reverend Bolin said."

"Then maybe we've been looking at it the wrong way. Between you and Marion—"

"Mostly Marion," I rattled the pages at him.

"What if, things are not as extra-legal as they seem?"

"How do you mean?"

"We have Army and someone who won't share his affiliation. You say possibly, CIA, right?"

I nodded.

"Everything you've looked at has been about relocating refugees."

"You think the girls might be something else?" I was still nodding as I asked. "If not refugees . . . ?"

"Consider the people involved. Any way you look at it, that's a lot of government. The girls could be pawns or bait—"

"Or collateral damage," I finished.

It was his turn to nod.

"You need to check with State, or better yet, have your new step-mother, the congresswoman, check."

"She's not my stepmother."

"Not yet," he winked and grinned. "If they are refugees, they will have to register and seek asylum. That's State. Maybe Immigration and Customs Enforcement too."

I nodded and made some notes on the back of the fax pages. "State and ICE, those are good ideas. We can go a step further too. Starry Night has to be listed as a 501(c)(3) nonprofit as a church. We can check if they have a determination letter from the IRS and if they operate any other nonprofits listed as charitable organizations dedicated to resettlement of refugees."

"What will that tell us?"

"Maybe where the money is coming from or going. But if Treasury gets involved it could become too hot for Givens and Keene to put up a fight. I'm convinced it was Silas and some or all of those private military guys who killed Daniel Boone. I think they killed Sartaña too and are chasing Dewey."

"What about the fish thing? A red herring?" The sheriff laughed at his own joke and tapped his boot on the desktop.

"You know that wasn't funny, don't you?"

"See? That's what I mean about your sense of humor. It woulda killed them at the Rotary Club."

"Yeah, well, I don't know what to make of that so far, except that Daniel Boone had a history of poaching. Maybe he was just trying to get a little extra cash before he ditched the mercenaries. It's possible that he was killed for trying to get out or because he was gay. The fish and caviar thing seems like a weird coincidence at this point."

"And the CA?" He dropped his feet to the floor and sat up. "Resnick?"

"As far as I can see, there is a lot about what's going on that can be explained as *guys who don't want anyone to know they're gay.*"

"Fair enough," he said. "Let's get out of here and start a new day fresh tomorrow. I think I'm going to go see if I can buy a hammock."

"Don't forget, you have a date later."

"It's not a date," he protested too much.

Chapter 12

I wasn't ready to let my mood die and I wasn't ready to talk about it either. So I made excuses. Then I invited my father and Whilomina to dinner at Dogwood Mountain. When they asked why not Moonshines, I claimed I wanted to ask around about caviar and Aton Gagarin.

I went home to change and they came later to pick me up. It was the first time since Nelson's funeral I'd worn a dress. I was so nervous about it I asked Whilomina for her opinion. I was glad I did and wished I hadn't. Not that I looked awful it was just that I looked, as she put it, like I was hiding.

The dress I chose was long and cotton, white with eyelet lace trim. Over it was a denim shirt belted at the waist. She was right. Only my head and my hands were uncovered.

"What's in your closet?" she asked.

"Jeans and more of the same," I answered.

"You don't mind occupying yourself do you?" Whilomina asked my dad, then went off to find my wardrobe without asking me or waiting for him to answer.

My clothes took a small part of a huge closet. Another small part was still occupied by Nelson's. The two groupings hung well away from each other as if any mingling was forbidden.

"You still have some of his clothes?"

"That's all of them," I answered.

"And the rest of yours?" She asked the question like she was asking about religion.

"That's everything." I was embarrassed. My closet made me feel like I was a failure at womanhood. Then the way Whilomina looked reminded me of the scrutiny of my therapist.

It could have been my imagination too. She didn't say anything more about them, but she did dig into my hanging clothes and start shoving them aside.

"The secret treasures are always at the back," she told me and produced a mid-length floral print dress still in the store dust bag. "See?"

"I've never even worn that," I said.

"I can tell," she answered. "And that's a sad thing."

The dress itself was sleeveless with thin shoulder straps. The only reason I had ever told myself I could wear it was the short matching jacket. Still it showed too much.

"I can't wear that."

"Your scars?"

No one had ever so directly addressed the issue of my tattered skin with me. It was as stunning to me as if she had cursed in church. It must have shown on my face.

"You look shocked," she said in a way that told me that was exactly what she expected. "People think sometimes that hiding things, not talking about them, keeps the secret under their control. The opposite is true. Take it from a politician. It's the things that we bury deepest that run our lives."

"I'm not sure that's true."

"Maybe not," Whilomina handed me the dress then bent to pick up a pair of heels I hadn't even known were behind my boots and old sneakers. She used the shoes to gesture at me. "But you can choose to be pretty. Or you can choose to be beautiful. I call that taking charge. What do you say?"

I say maybe not beautiful, but I looked pretty damned good. Scars did show. From under my left arm and over the top of my left breast curled thick, pinked seams of tissue where the knife had carved into me. The cuts were savage and ragged so the edges had to be trimmed before I could be sutured. It was done in a field hospital. If I had kept my mouth shut and not accused superior officers of raping me, those wounds might have gotten more attention from a plastic surgeon once I was evacuated to Germany. Not that I'm bitter. I do still hold a grudge that there was not a single rape kit in-country when I was attacked.

I shook my head. I shook it again harder and finally saw myself once more whole and pretty in the mirror. The blowing brown of Iraqi dust receded from the edges of my vision and I let myself breathe normally.

The phrase that Billy had used earlier popped back into my head—*breathe in the sunshine*. It made me smile and, for the first time in a long season of chill and darkness, the expression worked in my mirror.

I went down the stairs of my husband's house, surrounded by his art and life. Nelson was happy. It's a foolish, sentimental thing to say, but I was sure he was pulling for me. He was a man who not only wanted me happy during his life, but expected me to be happy through the remainder of mine. It was wonderful to think I was finally ready.

Dad drove with Whilomina sitting up front with him. I told them about the girls and Massoud and the dead end that we'd hit. When I got to the part where I suggested that the girls were more tool than refugee, the congresswoman shook her head in disagreement. She didn't look back at me, although she did share a look with my father before promising to make some calls.

Regardless of the concerns I refused to be brought down. The remainder of the drive I kept my own company in the backseat and watched the passing scenery. Redbud and dogwood trees were flowering. On other trees, new leaves were beginning to color bare branches. Tomorrow would be even greener in a slow march through spring.

We walked into a new-age, log cabin. The building was split down the middle by a long and rustic-elegant lobby. The floor was made of reclaimed hardwood which made it impossible for me to ignore the irregular tap of my feet. Even in three-inch heels I was unsteady. The fact that the shoes boosted me well over six feet tall, made me more self-conscious.

As we strolled, I could feel my mind, clutching at the memories of the day like an armful of feathers in a zephyr. It would have been the easiest thing in the world to have given up. Wisps of brown wind that snaked over a low mud wall in Iraq were still burying me after so many years. Every single time I thought I had a chance at life, the dirt of the grave I'd escaped, called me back. I could have happily turned, kicked off my pretty shoes, and marched barefoot out of there and never returned. In all honesty, I could have run screaming and been relieved that the pressure to live like a normal person was gone. Being happy was a burden I was unused to.

On separate walls were two very different pieces of art. To the right, beside an arch of burnished walnut, the doorway to the Dogwood Flower Restaurant, was one of my husband's landscapes. It was full of trees and colors that never existed in the woods but should have. Across the room to my left, framed in barn wood, hung one of his paintings of a pair of worn down boots. It was a famous image both from the bootmaker's advertising campaign and from the thousands of prints it sold.

If someone had told me about that moment ahead of time, I would have said it was a little bit crystal ball, on-the-money for a sign from a dead husband. I would have been right, I guess, but knowing could never have prepared me for the feeling of presence that hit me then. My heart was breaking all over again, that time without the devastation. I was caught on the hooks of a bittersweet peace when fate, or ghost husband, or whatever was happening to me that night, decided I needed something more.

Music.

It started with a guitar. It was slow and low, but building until the strings sounded like a hundred quiet voices. Then he started singing.

Billy Blevins.

It should not have been a surprise. I knew he was playing there. It was the real reason I had come. But I had let myself become distracted to the point that the man and the song stunned me. He was singing the old Grateful Dead tune, "Brokedown Palace." Again it was just coincidence; folk and country-rock were what Billy always performed.

But.

How many people listen to the Dead anymore? Nelson Solomon—that's who.

I don't know how long I stood in my haunted rigor, my eyes staring at the painting and my ears straining for each note. When I finally broke the spell, I turned to find Dad and Whilomina staring at me. It wasn't until then I realized there were tears in my eyes.

"Are you all right?" Dad asked me.

"Yes," I answered immediately and with a strength that astonished me. It was true. "Yes," I repeated and smiled. I took the handkerchief he held out and dabbed at my eyes. "It's just . . ." I shrugged and laughed a little. Then I thought I sounded like a crazy person so I inhaled a long, deep breath. "How about if we have dinner in the bar?"

We did. During a break, Billy came over and I introduced him around. He was wearing a red satin shirt with embroidered cow skulls and pearl snaps. I teased him unmercifully about it. My father was polite but oblivious. Whilomina seemed to understand something without being told. She turned a knowing smile between me and Billy and back.

After Billy returned to his set, beginning with "Shelter From the Storm," we were served big steaks with huge potatoes and grilled vegetables. I must have gone through a gallon of iced tea. In a lame attempt to keep up the appearance of my investigation excuse, I asked about caviar. I didn't find out anything about it that I needed to know but the server seemed to be proud of their product and the sustainable practices that brought the eggs to our table. It made me think he knew less about it than I did. Still, he brought a small sample and we all tried it on a toasted cracker. At least Whilomina enjoyed it.

It was a perfect evening, the capstone of a near-perfect day and one to remember forever. We need to latch on to those moments and brand them into memory because life is never one single thing for long. Simple, plain, good—cannot last.

The server came back to ask how we liked the caviar. Before we could answer, she said she wanted to introduce the supplier since I was so interested. She suggested he could answer all my questions. The man who came through the door was, of course, Aton Gagarin.

From there, the complicated house of joy that my mind had built up collapsed in upon itself. It was pushed from outside, the forces of real life came in a panicked look and a crash of stacked dishes. Gagarin, had bolted. He turned, kicking over what the busboy had piled up thinking, I imagine, to delay me. I had not even begun to move at that point.

I shouted though. "Aton! Stop." The words were almost like an announcement that I would come after him. Why would he stop?

But he did.

He skidded, leather soles slipping on the smooth wood floor as he struggled to change direction yet again. I had risen and was still trying to free my weapon and badge from my purse when Gagarin pulled a short-barreled .38 revolver from behind his back and raised it in my direction.

Bright flowers of light bloomed with blasting thunder. The bullets sprayed, invisible lines of buzzing death. One ran a tight course along my face, so close I could feel it like I had felt Nelson minutes before—a whisper of reality. It heated the hard pucker of crescent-shaped scar around the orbit of my left eye. I heard it growl like a spinning wolf. For some reason, the thought penetrated my mind, *that's not the sound of a .38*. Then I noticed that Gagarin was flailing, his weapon arcing wildly overhead, aimed at nothing and still unfired.

Another shot. Another bloom of noise and light followed by a new flower. A bullet plowed through the fatty part of Gagarin's chest, under his left arm. It spit a mist of blood and meat forward. Behind the red haze was Dewey, still firing.

He was screaming too, but I couldn't hear him. I heard only the gunshots and the searing whip of bullets passing.

By the time Gagarin hit the floor I had my weapon pulled and aimed. I couldn't fire. Behind Dewey was the open entrance to the restaurant. I told myself later that I wouldn't shoot because it would have put people in danger. I never saw anyone. I did see Nelson's painting of a colorful forest.

"Dewey!" I screamed his name between the muzzle flashes.

He froze. "I had to," he said. In the absence of gunfire his soft voice sounded like he was speaking through a pillow. "I had to," he repeated, pleading and explaining. "He killed her. He murdered her."

"Put down your gun," I ordered. At the same time I kicked off the heels.

"I can't," he said before he started running.

I expected that and started right after him. Without missing a step, I knocked Gagarin's weapon from his hand and kept running. Once I rounded the wide door and stepped into the lobby I shouted again. "Dewey! I'll shoot."

That time I really meant it. He was no longer in front of a crowded dining room. Dewey Boone stopped and turned with his gun still low. He was standing in front of the building's front wall. It didn't matter how many people were beyond that, my bullets could not get through eight-inch logs of southern pine. "Drop the gun," I shouted one more time as Dewey raised his weapon.

I hit him twice, high up in the chest, and his gun dropped from limp fingers.

Violence like that often happens in a vacuum. There is a space in your head where your senses go to try to protect you from distraction. It keeps out the noise and motion that your automatic brain has already filtered out as nonthreatening. That means, though, when things are over, your mind throws open a door and lets the world flood back in. Rarely is what comes on that tide the good news you hope for.

I heard screaming. There was a lot of it, but one note was clearer and louder to me. Whilomina. Resisting the urge to run back into the bar, I reassured myself that Billy was in there with her. He was much better equipped to handle hysterics.

"Call 911," I shouted into the general noise. There had probably already been a hundred calls.

Dewey was trying to speak. I approached with my pistol still aimed then brushed his weapon back a safe distance with my foot.

Kneeling beside him, I said, "Help is on the way."

"I saw you," he told me through wet gasps. "I watched you drawing her."

"Sartaña? At the lake?"

"I was hiding. I went to get food. I didn't want to leave her alone in the camp, but we didn't want anyone to see her. She was so afraid."

Whilomina was the only voice still calling out in terror. An unease crept across my scalp then the question—*Why wasn't Billy here with me?*

"Why would the Russian hurt her?"

"They told me," Dewey's speech sputtered with the blood flooding his lungs.

"They told you what, Dewey? Who?"

"Katrina!" The shout came from the bar.

I heard my name. Not the meaning behind it.

Dewey reached up with his left hand. It was the one I had seen broken and bleeding as he ran into the lake. It was bandaged and splinted. First aid rather than hospital care. I took it and held on gently.

"They said," he coughed. Blood spattered his lips and clothing. "I could fix everything, they told me. Get even for Daniel and Sartaña. They said it would all work. I could stop all of it—" He choked and a thick, phlegmy line of crimson dribbled down his chin. "We have rights. The government was messing it all up. They did it all together . . ."

"Dewey." I squeezed his hand, probably too hard, but he was beyond feeling it. "Dewey, who did it all?"

"I just wanted to be with Sartaña. They killed her. They were going to destroy everything."

"Who, Dewey?"

"Katrina!" The call came again.

"Who told you to do this?" I asked a dead boy.

"Katrina!" It was Billy shouting over the wailing of Whilomina. Suddenly I understood the creeping dread that had stalked over me. I dropped Dewey's hand and ran.

The happy little bar where I'd been having dinner moments before was a scene of carnage. Gagarin was gone. My father was on the floor in a spreading smear of blood. Billy was holding wads of linen against the hole in Dad's chest. There was another lump of them under him. The bullet had gone through.

Whilomina stopped her loud crying when she saw me. With one hand on Dad's face, she reached the other out to me and when I took it, she pulled me down.

"Let him see you," she said.

"Daddy?" My voice was the same as the little girl who had gotten sick in the middle of the night or been teased for being so tall.

Clement Williams, opened his eyes and smiled at me. He tried to speak, but the lifetime's worth of love and counsel, wish and regret, would not come. It didn't matter. I heard it all anyway. Then he reached out, one hand to me and one to Whilomina. The touch was enough for him but would never be for us. He was gone.

Chapter 13

Dawn rose in a cold and bloody sky. Over a steady wind, dark clouds dragged as if a black blanket was being pulled northward. Since my father died, I had been at Dogwood, the hospital, and the SO—everyplace but at peace.

There were a lot of questions to be asked and answered. There were some that no one knew. And there were a couple that no one knew but me. When I could see and think clearly again I saw that Billy was gone. I couldn't recall seeing him once I'd knelt beside my father. The obvious thought was that he'd gone after Gagarin. That's what I told Sheriff Benson.

I didn't let go of Daddy's hand until the EMTs had him on a gurney. I followed as he was wheeled out but stopped because standing in the lobby and looking down on Dewey's body was Timothy Givens. He looked at me without a trace of even mock compassion on his face. His only reaction was a nod as slight as the tick of his gun barrel had been in the café. It was a communication, maybe warning, maybe threat. There was no *maybe* about the look I returned.

Givens stalked out the door my father had just been taken through. By the time I got outside the EMTs were loading Daddy into the ambulance. Givens was nowhere to be seen. That, I didn't share with the sheriff. I was already planning on keeping some things personal.

I drove my father's car, back to Uncle Orson's place as the sun struggled into a sky that seemed to be rejecting it. Whilomina had gone with my uncle after Sheriff Benson had called him.

When I got to the dock, still wearing my bloody clothes, I had every good intention of taking a hot shower and letting myself cry until sleep took me away. But good intentions and the road to hell

and all that . . . The first thing I did was dig behind the counter searching for the last of Clare Bolin's homebrew whiskey. It wasn't there.
That was when I noticed the liquor shelves were empty too.

"You won't find a drop here." Clare himself was sitting at the
table in the corner. He looked like a man waiting patiently for his
dinner. "Not liquor, not beer, and not that awful wine your uncle
keeps. Orson called me. I came and cleared it out."

I wanted to tell him he was wrong about me. I wanted to shout
that the last thing I wanted was to drink when my father was dead. It
would have been a shameful lie and we both knew it. I wanted a
drink more then than I ever had.

"Daddy's dead," I told him as if it explained everything. Maybe
it did.

"I know." Clare nodded in the semidarkness of the morning
gloom. "And he was proud of you as a man could be. Proudest when
you set the whiskey aside. You don't want to pick it up today."

"I need it, Clare."

"I know you think that. But let's get past today and decide. What
do you think?"

"I think—" I was empty. There were no words. No feelings. I had
thought for an instant, there weren't even any tears. I was wrong.

I cried, I blubbered in loss and grief and God bless 'em, Clare
Bolin got me to bed without being drunk. If it wasn't such a horrify-
ingly pathetic moment for me, I would have been amazed at what he
did next. Without looking or even making me much aware of the
process, he reached under the blanket with a pocketknife and cut my
bloody dress off me.

As he carried the rag away, I think I said, "Goodnight, Daddy."
I'm not sure.

When I woke after a couple of hours the sky had cleared into a
cold blue that had an ominous weight. A confusion of winds crossed
the lake constantly shifting direction and falling still before coming
back in heavy, wave-whipping gusts. The dock and houseboat undu-
lated on the churn.

I don't recall getting dressed, but when I stepped back into the
shop I was ready for work. At least my clothes were. I'm pretty sure
my face reflected the way I felt. That much was easy to read in
Clare's face when I walked in.

"You want some breakfast?" he asked, without moving from the table. He knew the answer.

I shook my head anyway. "Have you been here all night?"

He held up a book. Not one of my uncle's, it was one of the trashy, sexy things by Drury Jamison I like to read, but don't want anyone to know about.

"Where'd you get that?"

Clare pointed to the minnow tank. "It was by the bait well. I think that black fella was reading it."

"His name is Damon."

I must have had an edge to my correction because Clare said, "I was describing him, not judging him."

"I know." And I hoped he heard the apology in my voice. It was the best I was going to give. "Where is he?"

"Haven't seen him."

"Since this morning or . . ."

"Not since I got here last night," He filled in. "Is it a problem?"

"I doubt it." I shook my head as much to clear it as anything. My thoughts seemed as if they were being telegraphed on bad wires.

There was an electronic chirping from his pocket and Clare put down his book to pull out his phone. When the connection was made, he looked right at me and said, "No need. She's already awake." Then he disconnected.

"My uncle?"

"Your boss." Clare put his phone away but didn't pick the book back up. He looked like he was waiting for something.

I figured I knew what it was. "Is your brother part of this?"

The bob of his head and the look down at his fingers told me I was right on target with his expectations.

"No," he answered quietly. "But that's me believin', not me knowing."

I nodded, understanding. There was not a more honest man alive than Clare Bolin, despite his politics and bootlegger past. I had wanted to believe the same about his brother but that had gotten harder every day.

"I'll be honest, Clare. I don't know what to believe. But there are a hell of a lot of questions."

"You'll have to ask him. And I know you will."

Again, I nodded. I didn't want to put him in the middle of something he really had nothing to do with. But that's pretty much the nature of family, isn't it?

"Thanks for last night." It was an awkward change of subject, but the best I had.

"Glad to do it." He hit me with a sad, little smile that said more than his words. Regret, obligation, friendship, and concern, were all wrapped up in his face. It was a good look. "Are you still wanting a drink?"

"With every beat of my heart."

We talked a little more and we sat without talking even longer until Sheriff Benson's boots *clomped* up the walkway to the shop door. We followed his footsteps and could even see him through the door panes but he didn't come in right away. Never a good sign. Chuck paused with a hand on the knob and looked out over the lake like he was wishing he was someplace else. I imagine he was.

When he opened the door, his hat was in his hand. It was his we-need-to-talk look.

"You can't be bringing any worse news than I've already had, Sheriff. Just put it out there," I told him.

He did. "We can't find Billy."

"What do you mean?" I asked. It struck me at that moment, how denial almost always starts with a question.

"You said, Aton Gagarin was shot by Dewey Boone."

"Yes."

"And that, after your father passed, you didn't see Billy."

"I lost track of things. It was . . . I don't know what happened. Honestly, I can't say how much I remember after Daddy died and I woke here."

"But Billy was gone?"

"Billy was gone, I know that. So was Gagarin. The Russian had to have gotten up and tried to run."

"But you don't know?"

"I don't know. My father died and I can't even say how long it was till I looked up again. The EMTs were there. Whilomina was crying. I looked—Billy was just gone."

"Did you look for him?"

I realized as soon as he asked the question, I hadn't. And I should have. A fresh knot of guilt wadded up and stuck in my throat.

"It's not your fault." Chuck made it a statement of fact. A hard truth that didn't leave room in his estimation for equivocation. "No one would have done any different or better than you did in the situation. And Billy was not your responsibility."

It was good of him. It was the right thing to say and the right way to say it. That doesn't mean that I believed it.

"There was something . . ."

"About Billy?" he prodded when I faded.

"I don't know."

He waited as I tried to work through memories, timelines, and my personal subterfuge. I didn't want to admit it, but decided that I had to.

"After . . ." I began, then didn't want to say again after what. "After. The EMTs were there, other officers had arrived. I went back out to the lobby because I didn't want to let him go. I remember telling myself, I should stay with Whilomina. But I was only thinking about Daddy."

"You don't have to make any excuses," the sheriff reassured.

"I saw Givens out there. He was standing over Dewey's body."

"Did he see you?"

I shrugged. "He must have."

"Did you see anyone else?"

I shook my head. "There were a lot of people around. I didn't see anyone who I recognized as a part of the investigation."

"Well . . . I'm not sure what we can do with it, but I believe it answers one thing."

"What's that?"

"There was no weapon with Dewey's body."

"Givens took it." I accused with certainty.

"I can't say why, but it'd be my bet."

"I know why."

Sheriff Benson didn't look surprised. He did reach into the ancient cooler Uncle Orson used to keep sodas on ice. He pulled out one of Clare's homebrew root beers, then sat like he was ready for a story.

"Dewey was using an M9. Your basic military sidearm. I got a good look at it when I kicked it out of his reach. Givens and Keene are either investigating or facilitating the smuggling of military weapons. I'd bet Dewey was using a pistol that would raise a lot of questions if we had it."

"Yeah, well, there're going to be questions." The sheriff took a long pull from the bottle then sat it down with a loud *thunk.* "And neither of us is going to like them or the people asking."

"What are you talking about?"

"Isn't it obvious?"

I shook my head and looked from Chuck to Clare and back. "Not to me."

"Congresswoman Whilomina Tindall."

I waited.

"*Congresswoman,*" he repeated. "She was involved in a shooting and the man she claims to be engaged to was killed. That's news and it complicates everything."

"She and my father were getting married. There was no *claim* about it."

"Maybe," he nodded. "But I get the picture that it was, if not secret, at least not well known."

"So?" I raised my hands, palms up.

"Just more grist for the mill, honey."

"And . . . you want me to stay out of the mill."

"Want's got nothing to do with what I have to do."

"Suspended?"

"Vacation." He took another drink of the root beer. "If you come in and make an issue out of it, the desk. But you are no longer involved in investigating anything to do with, the Boones, the girl—"

"Her name is Sartaña."

"Yes. Sartaña. Or any other part of this cluster-fuck we got going on here."

"What about Billy?"

"We'll find him."

"You're damn right we will." I pronounced it like a judge's sentence, final and righteous.

"You're on leave right now, Hurricane." The sheriff told me. "Don't make me come back here and take your badge and weapon."

I read that as *don't get caught.*

Five minutes later Chuck Benson was gone. He went hesitantly back into a world of trouble that, I felt sure, existed because of me.

When the hard *thump* of the sheriff's boots disappeared from the bones of the dock, Clare finally broke his silence. "What are you going to do?"

"I'm going to set fires until everyone is in the light."

* * *

Gagarin's warehouse was crawling with cops when I got there. Not just because it was of potential investigatory interest. Mostly the extra officers were there to handle the pressure of media. There were live trucks from Springfield, reporters and cameramen from the big news channels and networks. Pushed off to the side, I noticed Riley Yates watching the scene and scribbling in his little reporter's notebook with a stubby, chewed pencil. When he saw me his eyes got wide and he shook his head like he was trying to tell me something. Too late I understood he was trying to tell me not to be there.

Almost like a switch had been flipped, I was recognized. Every camera turned in my direction and a dozen people shouted my name. There were a mixture of deputies and even city cops on loan from Branson holding them behind a line of yellow tape.

I rushed past without looking and headed for the warehouse door. Sheriff Benson wasn't there. I was glad of that. Our officer-in-charge was Ambrose Houseman. He was an old-school cop, almost as close as the sheriff to retirement, but good at his job. He wasn't happy to see me.

"What're you doing here, Hurricane?"

"You know what I'm doing here." I answered just as gruffly. "Did the sheriff tell you to keep me out?"

"He told me to have you dragged out in cuffs when you showed up. Not if, but when. You're not exactly unpredictable."

"So? Are you going to do it?"

"You saw the reporters. What kind of idiot would I be to throw blood into that water?"

I pointed to the open door at the back of the room. The same space I'd asked Gagarin about. "Then let me in there without making it hard for all of us."

"Why would I do that?"

"Billy is my friend."

Houseman laughed but didn't sound amused. "You know why he's Billy? Not William. Not Deputy Blevins. Not any of the dozen other ways people could refer to him."

I shook my head.

"Because Billy Blevins is everyone's friend. You're not nearly as special as you think you are, Hurricane. If I, or even the sheriff was gone, people might be sad, but they'd go on. If you were to suddenly disappear, a lot of folks might just give a breath of relief. But Billy—

hell, losing him would be goddamned tragic. So don't be thinking your personal shit is gonna carry any weight here."

That was a revelation to me. A shameful one. I'd seen Billy only as he related to me. Almost at the moment I began to see him as more than some backstory to my own life, he becomes a casualty. But that wasn't the time for another of my staring into the brown wind moments. It wasn't time to make anything about me.

I did it anyway.

"Look, Houseman." I touched the scar at the edge of my eye then jerked my hand away. I'd been about to tell him how nasty it was going to get if I didn't get into that room. And how only I could find Billy. But that was ego and bullshit. Anger was not the way to make anyone see it my way.

"Houseman," I said again. "You're right. Right about Billy and you're right about me. But you don't know it all. I'm not here because of some righteous anger and revenge thing."

He looked justifiably skeptical.

"Not entirely." I looked at the floor. The truth is a hard thing. When I brought my face up to look right at Houseman, I decided—truth at all costs. "I'm here because Billy kissed me."

Houseman looked like I had just opened my shirt and asked if he liked girls. Then he looked like he was going to curse.

"That may be hard to believe. It was hard for me to believe too. But I want him to do it again. I want a chance. And you're right, it's still about me. Just not the way you thought."

"That's the thing about you, Hurricane. I never know if you're a *master* manipulative bitch, or a normal, everyday one."

"If you figure it out let me know. I really need to see what's back there."

"No you don't," he said. "And for the record, it's not about the investigation. It's about you."

I didn't understand until I walked into the room. Houseman had stopped at the door and called the techs and deputies out. When it was clear he'd gestured for me to go ahead and said, "You know the drill. Don't touch. And don't say I wasn't trying to do you a favor."

I'd already visualized the room as a kind of dormitory. Beds and chains for the girls taken from Peru. Without really thinking it through, I had already chalked up a much-needed win fantasizing happy families brought back together. Perhaps I'd even allowed myself to think Billy, or at least the information to find him, would be inside.

It was a shock. And nothing even remotely expected.

The room smelled of death, blood, and old fish. It was set up with four tables. All of them had hoses leading to a drain in the floor. Drain was more of a hope than a fact. The holes of the iron grate were rusted and clogged with the offal of innumerable slaughters. Everywhere flies were buzzing and maggots were wriggling on the stained concrete under each table.

In the back of the room was a bank of glass-fronted refrigerators like you would see in any grocery store. The difference was the contents. These were stacked with dead animals. On one shelf I saw the heads of two bald eagles hanging from brown paper wrappings. On another was an alligator snapping turtle the size of a manhole cover. There were the severed heads of deer, bighorn sheep, and an elk along with un-butchered wolves. Among it all were fish and canisters of what I instantly assumed was caviar.

As gruesome as the refrigerator inventory was, it was behind glass and separated from us. The wall to the right was populated with the finished products. Stuffed birds, eagles, falcons, even a whooping crane. All endangered species. I peeked into bins standing under the birds. In one was a collection of bear paws in another was a pile of individual claws. There were also drawers that I imagined were full of other body parts. I didn't open them but one was labeled DEER PENIS.

"Poaching for traditional Chinese medicine?" I asked Houseman.

He didn't answer.

"And the rest of it—" I peered into a misted refrigerator door. "It's like Hannibal Lecter's taxidermy shop," I said, brushing flies away from my face. "This is what he was hiding?"

"Hurricane," Houseman said too gently. "This isn't what you're here to see. Turn around."

I turned.

At the front of the room, in the far corner I hadn't even glanced at, the walls were red with broad spatters of blood. Someone had been beaten there and badly. The spray was splashed in places from impact and rooster tailed in others, slung from fast-moving fists. Centered in the corner was a metal chair, hanging with bloody shreds of duct tape. Draped over the back, wet and pasted to the metal, was the red satin shirt with the cow skulls.

I don't know how long I'd stood there staring at the shirt and the blood. And I have no idea how much longer I would have remained there, transfixed by the image and the feeling that I had brought another person into my own particular darkness. Houseman broke the spell when he appeared beside me. He didn't touch me but he stood close—support if I needed it. He was a gentleman even if I refused to be a lady.

"In my experience," he started carefully, "something like this happens for one of three reasons. Somebody wants something that the victim won't give up easy. To send a message. Or for sport."

He waited a long, quiet moment waiting for me to say something. I wanted to. Everything felt frozen. If I took the breath to speak, my chest would have cracked.

"Now . . . I wouldn't put it past some people to take things out on a cop, just because. But I don't get that here. I hate to ask it, and forgive me, Hurricane—are you getting a message from this?"

Chapter 14

It was a message all right. And it was to me. Problem was, I couldn't read it. I didn't know what Gagarin wanted or even if it was from him exactly. There were too many spoons in the stew. I did know where to go to stir the pot though.

The circus outside the tents of the Starry Night Traveling Salvation Show made the melee outside the warehouse look like a warm-up act. There were satellite trucks crowding every bit of grass and cars lining the roadway in. The sheriff was here and he didn't look very happy to see me pulling up with my emergency strobes flashing.

"You're on leave," he shouted in my direction as soon as my door opened.

"I want to talk to Roscoe," I shouted back.

A hundred lenses, like one big, compound eye, turned my way. I heard my name and shutters clicking feverishly. Some of the reporters beckoned, me some bellowed questions. I did my best to ignore them all as I marched forward to the big tent.

"I don't think you're going to get that chance today, Hurricane," the sheriff said with his hand held up at my chest.

When I got close enough, I could see Reverend Bolin within the tent standing in the spotlight on stage. It looked like a rehearsal. He struck a pose with his arms stretched out in mimicry of the cross hanging behind him.

"Reverend," I shouted. "We need to talk."

He didn't answer, not precisely. I doubt he even heard me. However his amplified voice rolled out of the tent. It sounded like joy, suddenly released from a black dungeon expressed in one word. "Hallelujah!"

It was followed by a murmur of other voices and the flashes of cameras. For the first time I noticed how full the tent was. There were as many reporters inside as there were outside. It wasn't a rehearsal. It was a press conference.

From out of the shadows at the back of the tent, four men appeared. They took positions blocking me from getting in or reaching Roscoe. One of them was Silas Boone. He was grinning in a way that would get most people committed.

"Woo wee—" he sang out. "Look a'—well, look a' look a' here. What we got?"

I started forward with hate and murder on my mind. The sheriff stopped me but Silas put up both hands and gestured me on. The three men behind him put hands on weapons concealed under oversized sports coats.

"You're not going in there," the sheriff told me. The strain in his voice was obvious. I got the impression there was something more going on than me making another mess for the department.

"No. No." Silas mocked. "Come on in. Jesus is waitin'. And he's armed."

"Hallelujah." Reverend Bolin intoned the word again and it sounded to me, again, like joy and being grateful for it. "I asked you here, to share in our celebration of life—"

"I know all about your little weapon, Boone," I taunted right back. "You won't be shooting anyone with that."

"Fuck you bitch." He dropped all pretense and opened his coat putting a shoulder slung MP7 on display. He didn't buy that at the local Bass Pro.

"Are you attempting to intimidate a police officer in the performance of her duty?"

"Katrina..." the sheriff tried to calm me but Boone and I were two angry dogs barking through the fence.

"Children," Roscoe said and the word struck me. It sounded like a sermon as much as a press event. "Children of war. Children of poverty. Children of innocence sold away, for the price of power. It is a crisis—"

"But you ain't a cop now are you?" Silas laughed like the joke was on me. "And you ain't in performance of any duty."

"How're you gonna be laughing when I make you chew that weapon?"

He laughed again, harder. Then he jerked a thumb back at the interior of the tent then pointed to the outside gallery of reporters. "They gonna get that on camera? Psycho bitch, going all Waco on the church tent—how's that gonna look?"

The sheriff was right in front of me now, pushing hard. At the same time he was restraining his voice, trying to make it seem like a discussion because of the spectators. "Katrina," he whispered my name. Then he put his hands on my shoulders and shook me saying, "Katrina. He's working you up. Don't play it."

In the quiet moment of thinking about consequences Roscoe caught my attention again.

"Christ," he pronounced, then let the name hang. "Lives in action. Quiet words—are for personal contemplation. Differences in the world—those come from following him, with a hammer in your hand. With a shovel. With clean water and schoolbooks. I want to talk to you of Christ, as a verb. Uplift. Enlighten. Feed. Teach. Free!"

"What do I care how it looks?" If I could have snarled at that point I would have. I was ready to jump in and damn the consequences.

"Oh you care, little lady." Silas was not grinning as he said that. "You care a bushel and a peck. Because life is a hard, hard road without a little music in it. Ain't it?"

"The hell did you say?" I was sledgehammered. Boone was telling me he had Billy. "What the hell did you say to me?" That must have come out louder than I thought because quite a few heads turned my way.

". . . because we are put into this life to become the people who deserve heaven." The reverend's preaching filled the void I left with my cursing. "We earn it every day. Not by prayer. Not by faith alone. We earn—we truly live—by action. Our task is to make the world as close to paradise as we can. And we build from the bottom. Uplifting those who are in need."

"We have a letter, Hurricane," the sheriff told me. "The department has an order from the US Attorney and DOJ to stop our investigation citing homeland security."

"He has Billy," I said.

"We don't know that."

"He just told me."

Boone was grinning again. "You're gonna to take your orders, missy," he said to me. His voice was just loud enough to carry. "And you're gonna keep your mouth shut about it. About all of it. Or the music ain't never comin' back. You got it?"

I reached for my weapon but the sheriff caught my hand. His fingers, bony and callused, gripped as hard as regret. While he held me, he whispered, "Take another road."

"We lost one girl to a tragic accident," Reverend Bolin said on stage. His voice had come down to match the thought. "We mourn her. But we celebrate the thirteen other girls we have delivered into the refugee program. Thirteen girls, safe and protected in secret U.S. locations."

Girls?

I walked back, almost staggering in the trampled pasture, putting some distance from myself and the tent. Then I took a long, hard look around me. None of the girls were there. All the small, frightened girls—children—were gone.

Finally it hit my reeling brain, Roscoe was talking about the girls from Peru, like Sartaña. He said they were in a secret location. My thoughts were jumbled. Trying to order them was like counting socks while the dryer was running. There was something about the girls, though—a connection not yet made.

The frustration—the anger—inside me got to be too much for silence and thought. I lashed out at Boone one more time. "I'm going to burn your secrets down around your head."

"Katrina!" Sheriff Benson shouted a warning at me.

Faces turned, along with them came lenses and microphones.

"Another word—one more word—and I'll have to take your badge for good," he finished.

"You can't." I answered weakly.

"Yeees sir-ee," Silas yipped. "You made your bed now."

Without giving the sheriff that additional word and the excuse to take my badge, I turned, and trod past the reporters without looking anyplace but straight ahead. That was a fortuitous circumstance because crossing ahead of me, creeping in a battered little pickup, was a man, not old, but too old for his longish blond hair and John Denver glasses. It was the guy called Banjo.

Banjo was an easy tail. He didn't know, and didn't seem to care, if he was being followed. Most people don't when they go to the hardware store. I watched to make sure I didn't have a shadow. Once

I was reasonably certain, I went in and found Banjo with a basketful of lag bolts and measuring out lengths of chain.

"Building something?" I asked, sounding something between nosey and dangerous.

He looked at me and I could almost feel him checking me with mental radar. "You're that cop that has it out for the show."

"Who says I have it out for anyone?"

Banjo started to answer, then seemed to think better of it. I couldn't tell if it was because he didn't trust me or his source. He looked a bit like he couldn't tell either.

"What do you want with me?" he asked without sounding quite innocent.

"Questions."

"Yeah," he said, making sure I could hear his disbelief. "It always starts that way."

"You've been in the system?"

"I ain't no big stripe, if that's what you're askin'."

"What did you go down for?"

"That the question you wanted to ask me? Or is this just the warm-up?"

"Just getting to know who I'm talking to," I told him. "Are you Connor Watson—Banjo Watson?"

He stared, giving nothing up.

"I was told about you . . . a friend . . . He said you were a legend in gospel and bluegrass music."

He almost smiled. "You a fan?"

"I . . . have an appreciation."

He broke and chuckled a little. "Don't we all?" Then he solemnly nodded at me and said, "Give it a chance."

"My friend is a deputy. He plays guitar, sings old Dylan tunes and Ozark Mountain Daredevils. But he's in trouble now."

"Well . . ." Banjo looked me over with an appraising eye and I think, for the first time, saw something other than a cop. "He's got good taste in music. But that ain't what kind of trouble you're talking about, is it?"

"No."

"Grass."

I shook my head, not understanding.

"I was in a van—on our way to a gig in the wrong part of

Arkansas. Lots of wrong things that day. Wrong kid drivin'. Wrong cop with the wrong ain't-gonna-take-shit attitude. A pound of grass I didn't even know about, ended up takin' away almost five years of my life. But I took Jesus in with me and took him out. So I'm suspicious of cops, but I understand trouble."

It was a bold and honest confession so I honored it by laying my cards out for him. "Some of the people you work with are not so close to Jesus."

His look turned to my eyes, hard and piercing. He was afraid.

"It's a strange sort of situation, isn't it? For the Salvation Show to be carrying guns."

"It wasn't always like this." After he spoke he glanced around.

"How is it?"

"Your friend?" he asked. "Is that the kind of trouble you're talking about?"

"I'm not exactly sure about the what. But I'm pretty sure about who. The Boone boys. And a couple of feds, Givens and Keene."

Banjo shook his head slightly then paused like he had a thought. "No," he said. Then he shook his head hard enough to whip his hair. "I can't. I don't know what it is; I just know what it isn't. And it ain't right. But you got the right folks, mostly. Ol' Dewey just did what his brother told him and his brother followed his cousin. You know that's why Silas brought Daniel in, don't you?"

It was my turn to shake my head vigorously. "No I—What?"

"The gay thing. They wanted to pray it away."

I think I blushed. Not at the words but the thought. I was ashamed for all of us that such things still went on.

"Reverend Bolin did that?"

"There's the front-of-house religion and there's the back-of-house kind. That was back-of-house. It was double worse for Daniel being one of the gunmen. He had the Reverend praying over him half the time and the rest he was stuck with the big macho boys. They didn't pray. They cursed him as less than a man and showed him so much hate he could hardly stand it."

"What did he do?"

"He went fishing. He used to catch these big ol' catfish-looking things that had long noses instead of whiskers. They tasted pretty good in corn meal and fried in lard but he didn't care about that. He was selling the eggs to the Russian guy."

"Gagarin," I told him.

"I never knew his name," Banjo shrugged then caught himself, remembering to be afraid. "I don't know anything for sure except that the Russian had some kind of deal with Daniel about the fish. I always thought that was strange."

"Everything about this is strange."

"Maybe so," he said, hefting up a bundle of chain. "But having that guy in charge of kids is the strangest."

"What? What do you mean?"

"The Russian guy is the one who takes the Peruvian girls once we bring them into the country."

"Takes them? Where?"

"The Reverend told me it was to an orphanage."

I shook my head confused and angered by the feeling. Confusion and rage seemed to be the only true emotions I could maintain and they kept feeding off each other. "Roscoe told me it was the other guy, Massoud who took care of the girls."

"I don't think so," Banjo hefted more chain as he considered the question. "He works with the government. He's the one in charge of the military contractors." He looked down and pulled links through his fingers before shaking his head again. "No. The Russian guy worked out the deal with Reverend Bolin. We were pretty small time then. He was the one that said we needed to do mission trips down to Peru and smuggle back the girls. Everyplace we would hold a tent show in the States, he would meet us and take the girls we brought in to his charity camp."

"Charity camp?"

"He said he had it all set up. Relocation, school, a good life for the girls."

"And you believed him?"

"I never talked to him. I believed the Reverend." Banjo's shoulders slumped. He rattled the chain in his hands. "The cross needs more support. My own money."

"Believed?" I asked. "You said you believed the Revered. Don't you now?"

"When you say some things out loud it's hard to say you don't understand or don't believe."

"What is it you don't believe, Banjo?"

"That this is God's work."

"I think you might be right about that."

"What do I do now? I'm caught in the wrong van again, ain't I?"

"Not if I can help it," I told him and I meant it. "But I still need your help. Do you think Reverend Bolin is involved?"

"He's running the church and it's running him. As far as I can tell he believes the best and thinks the gun boys are there to protect us from the socialists in Peru and the government here."

"The government here?"

"He said there's a congresswoman who was going to ruin the whole deal."

"How?"

"I don't know."

"Okay. One more thing," I reassured. "The two other names I mentioned. Givens and Keene—they mean anything to you?"

"Nope."

"All right. Listen, Banjo, I have things to take care of. Can you get to a safe place?"

"I'll go back to the show," he said, although he looked leery of the thought. "Once your eyes are open, you can't go back to blindness. The Reverend needs me. Maybe just to talk things through with."

"Talk through what you need. Don't share what we've talked about, though."

"Don't worry about Reverend Bolin. He'll come down on the right side when he knows the truth."

"It's not his placement I'm worried about," I said.

Back at my truck I called Uncle Orson. He picked up before the first ring completed and asked, "How are you doing?"

"I'm fine," I said. "How is she?"

"Are you really?"

I thought a long time and he waited without pressuring. Finally I answered carefully. "I'm fine enough for what I have to do."

"You don't have to do anything." His words were just as careful. They perched on a tightrope trying neither to push nor pull me.

"Do you believe that?"

"Yes. I believe it. I know it's a foolish belief. Some things just won't be let go of."

"I miss him already," I said and the admission sounded like a whisper from far away, even to me. "It's like there's a huge crack in the world and everything is falling in except me. I keep standing on the edge, staring into the nothing."

"We all miss him."

"I wasn't a very good daughter."

Orson laughed and a hot flash of anger burned my face. I wanted to shout. I wanted to scream at him—at everyone because what I felt had to be shared and spread around. Instead I asked quietly, "Why?"

"Your dad was talking to Whilomina before you met. He was happy and excited to introduce you. He told her you were the best daughter he could imagine a man having in his life."

The heat in my face faded. It drained as liquid sorrow from my eyes and started to drip from my nose before I grabbed a tissue.

"I have to fix this—" I said, then stopped. "I have to make them pay for what can't be fixed."

"I know you do."

Then I cried a little bit and my uncle listened without saying a word. When I could speak, I asked, "Where is Whilomina?"

"She's on her phone in the kitchen. She's making arrangements and calling people that she shouts at and cusses their asses raw. I'd hate to be on the other end of those lines. She's a hot-barreled pistol."

I was careful again asking, "Do you have a gun?"

That time, Orson put all of his care into silence before he finally said, "Not on me. But I can get one pretty quickly. Do I need one?"

"I think you should have it on you."

"What's happened?"

"I need you to get armed and sit down with Whilomina to have a talk. Tell her that I think Daddy was not exactly the messy accident it looked like. But I think she was the target. Tell her that they were upset about her investigations and the Russian who was shot at Dogwood is the man who has the smuggled girls." I gave him the few details I had about Gagarin then told him to ask Whilomina to make the kinds of inquiries only a member of congress can. "I've already asked her to check on charities and refugees, but everything was slanted toward Reverend Bolin and that guy Massoud. This thing, all of it, is tangled up. It's going to take someone smarter and more connected than me to pull it apart."

"Charities? Refugees?"

"Or not. I don't exactly know what those girls are. I think they're in danger though. But any investigating I do may raise more alarms than answers."

"In that case," he said with a new edge in his voice. "Do you think the phones are secure?"

I was reminded of the first call my father had made to tell me about the connection between military weapons and the Salvation Show. He said he didn't want to say much on the phone. "I never even thought about it. Assume they aren't."

"You know the black ops stuff was your father's bag. I'm just an old marine."

I told him, "You're the most dangerous man I know." Then I hung up.

Chapter 15

I started driving with no clear idea where I was headed. Sometimes the drive itself is the answer. At least it seems to help me think my way to one. After having warned Uncle Orson and gotten Whilomina on the track of the charity, I felt—not better—more prepared. The question was, how to turn feeling into reality?

Billy was the start. He was my first and greatest concern. But he was a string with no pull. I had to find him by tracking the other people involved. As I twisted through Ozarks roads it was like splitting into two people. One part of my mind did the mechanical work of driving the truck. Another part did the heavy tasks of thinking through the connections. There were moments—there were fractions of thought and feeling that took me into the crevasse that I'd told Orson about on the phone. I'd lied to him. I think he knew that, although he was sensitive enough not to mention it. When I had told him I was standing on the edge of the crack and looking in, it was into nothing. It's never nothing. When I stare into the abyss, it is always looking back in a swirl of brown dust.

Memory is a dangerous thing when you can't leave it behind. For the first time in a very long time, maybe for the first time ever, I saw my world occluded by the dead, dust of Iraq—experienced again my rape and mutilation by two superior officers—then came back with a clear mind and heart.

I came back for Billy. But I needed Mike Resnick. Since he was already avoiding me, I knew Damon had to be my first step. I made a call to the SO to check with our impound lot. One of the few pieces of paperwork I'd accomplished was a release for Damon's boat. Sure enough, when I talked to the gatekeeper he confirmed that Damon had signed for it that morning. He also told me he'd seen the boat hitched up to a Ram truck with a Conservation Department logo on the door.

They could have put the boat in on Taneycomo or Table Rock, either one has hundreds of miles of fingers and coves to in which to hide. Below the Powersite Dam, Lake Taneycomo connects to Bull Shoals in Arkansas. Ozarks lakes were giant unmarked highways with a million secluded hiding places. But it was on Table Rock that Damon had found Daniel Boone. I was betting that he'd go back to that lake if not to that exact spot.

That spot was the first place to look. The news that the body he'd found in the lake was his old partner, had hit Damon hard. People are drawn to places of meaning when they are on unsteady feet and turmoil seemed to define Damon's life almost as much as mine.

I flipped on the emergency strobes mounted behind the grill of my truck as I turned around. Driving with lights but no siren, I blasted through miles of blooming spring.

In a few minutes I was parking again at the end of the failed development. Everything was back at the place where this whole thing began. Maybe it was time for a fresh start.

I left my jacket in the truck. Before I closed the door I checked my weapon and reseated it in the holster making sure there were no obstructions. I trod carefully, picking my way through the rough trail headed for the little cove where Daniel Boone had been found wrapped in a net.

Tape, tattered and torn, was still stretched from undergrowth that was sprouting new growth. I breached the perimeter with my hand resting on the butt of my service weapon. Once I pushed through the brush and got close to the lake, I found the boat. The bow was pulled up onto the mud shore and tethered to a tree. Other than Damon's meager possessions, the boat was empty. From the water I worked in a broad half circle around the scene looking for anyone hiding behind the budding trees and greening ground cover. I was disappointed to find myself alone.

As soon as I relaxed, and took my hand from the gun a voice said, "You're about as stealthy as a skittish mare in a mirror shop." It was Damon. Until he stood up, covered in limbs and leaves he was invisible. Once he did stand, I noticed something couched in both of his hands and it was disguised as well.

"What's that?" I asked.

"I thought you were a country girl. You don't know horses?"

"I'm not talking about horses. What have you got there in your hands?" I pointed.

".30-06," he said, holding up the scoped rifle.

"Are you expecting to need it?"

He cradled the weapon in his arms. "Why are you here, Hurricane?"

"I'm looking for you. I obviously misunderstood why you would be here."

"I'm going to do what you can't." He said it like you might say *I'm going to the grocery store.* If you expected the grocery store to shoot back.

"What is it I can't do?"

"Not just you," he explained with venom in his tone. "Regular cops. People with rules."

"You don't have rules anymore?"

"Daniel was my friend. He was a lot more than that. We owed each other our lives."

"And now you feel like you owe him revenge?"

The termination of his stare was someplace behind my eyes. I could feel it looking at my hypocrisy and the roiling desire to hurt those who hurt my father and Billy. Sometimes though you have to protect people from the same mistakes you march happily into.

"I need your help," I said. "Billy needs help."

Damon kept staring, but didn't say anything.

"Who are you going after?" I asked, trying another tack that did nothing to break his gaze. Then I nodded at the rifle. "You get that from Mike?" That got a reaction. So I charged ahead. "You have a relationship with him. It's not a stretch to figure he gave you the rifle."

"You don't know as much as you think you do," he said, but not as sure as before.

"Maybe. But I know more than *you* think. I don't know who you're going after though. Silas Boone and the contractors? Or the Russian?"

"You know about the Russian?"

"I told you. I know more than you think." I told him trying to keep the confidence in my voice. "Now, how about setting that rifle aside?"

"I don't want to have to fight you for it."

"How about if I promise you won't have to. You stay there and I'll stay here. We can work things through better if we're not worried about things getting too hot."

Damon thought about it a moment, then sat on a pulpy log, leaning the rifle next to him.

"Whose idea was it, yours or Mike's?"

He shrugged, an exaggerated gesture, and looked away.

"Mike wanted you to do this?" I pushed. "Why?"

"Nobody's telling me to do anything. I'm not taking orders anymore."

"Then what are you doing? Because I'm hard-pressed to understand anything you could be planning."

"They killed Daniel because of what he was."

"Who?"

"All of 'em. Silas. Reverend Bolin. They were always talking about perversions and cleaning the queers out of the world. But it was the Russian who did it."

"This seems like something bigger than homophobia, Damon."

"The only reason Daniel was fishing was to get away from them. He needed some money to break free."

"How do you know it was the Russian?"

"Mike told me. He told me the Russian is after him too." Damon looked at me with an expression all mixed up with worry and anger.

For the first time I could really see the warrior within the man. Damon had plans for the Russian.

"Mike said we wouldn't be safe until the Russian is gone because he knows who I am."

"Who you are? What does that mean?"

"It doesn't matter." Damon pulled his rifle close and stood it between his knees. "None of it matters anymore."

"You're not making any sense. This isn't about praying the gay away or about killing homosexuals to make a point."

"You don't know," he said with angry certainty. The fingers of Damon's hands curled hard around the stock of his weapon. "He's already trying to force Mike out. The Russian is going to get him fired. He's going to ruin everything for us if he doesn't kill us. He's got to be stopped."

Damon was getting worked up and angrier by the moment. I gave him a little space and time as I tried to understand. None of it made sense to me.

"Damon," I said as gently and still keeping my distance.

Then I thought again about what I wanted to say to him. He was enraged and confused, but we had the same target, Gagarin. I didn't know to what degree adding more information to his suspicions would rile Damon, but I was certain it would be fuel on the fire. The shame of it was I never thought if I should. I only considered how it would affect my plans.

I'm not proud of it, but I said, "I think the Russian is holding Billy." I had the entirety of Damon's attention then. He was locked like a stalking cat on my face and my words. "He might have some girls, too. A lot of people are in trouble."

"That's why you're here." It wasn't a question.

I shook my head anyway. "I wanted you to tell me where Mike is. The Russian is hiding. Mike might know where."

"He knows. He told me."

I realized that I was staring into that pit again. Inside it were choices, consequences, the difference between the right thing and the one with the result you need. I made my choice and asked an unstable man with a rifle, "What are we waiting for?"

Sometimes you can fool yourself. You can make plans and pretend you don't know where events will take you. We can talk about chance or pray for outcomes. Sometimes, some rare times, your feet are held over the fire by someone who won't let you lie to yourself.

Damon said, "This isn't cop's work." He looked at me as he rose and lifted his rifle, staring, daring me to flinch from the truth. "No badges. No rule books. No forgiveness and no mercy."

When fate holds that mirror up to your face, you can either surrender to your better nature or do what I did.

"That was my plan," I admitted to my darkness.

Gagarin had a place on the lake, far off-road and secluded. It was also across the lake. That put it in Stone County. There was nothing legal about what I was thinking. I can't imagine why the thought of a jurisdictional infraction bothered me, but it did.

Even the way I drove it would have taken a couple of hours to make the loop around the north end of the lake and back around to the other side where Gagarin's place was tucked in among the junipers and hedge apple trees. It has already been longer than that since I left the Starry Night Traveling Salvation Show and the day was wearing thin. We took Damon's boat.

Thirty-five minutes later he cut the engine and we coasted into an over grown finger of the lake about a half-mile from where Damon said Gagarin had a cabin. We hadn't spoken the entire trip.

When the outboard was quiet and we were tied up to a root, I pulled my phone and turned it off. The last thing you need when sneaking up on someone was your phone ringing. I didn't even want it vibrating. No distractions. When I put it away I finally addressed another distraction by asking something that had been on my mind. "Why was your file redacted?"

He didn't answer, but he looked away so intentionally he had to have heard and understood the question.

"I saw your file. Both the Boone cousins' too. They were all redacted. Why?"

"We have to be quiet getting through the undergrowth," he told me. "Think you can manage that?"

"Don't worry about me," I said, making sure he knew I was annoyed at the question. "What about you?"

"What about me?"

"Are you going to answer me about the redactions?"

Damon stepped out of the boat a different man than the one I had known. The confusion and all sense of timidity was gone. In a thirty-minute lake crossing, the battered civilian had somehow been subsumed ng by the soldier. He stood on the shore, straighter in the back and harder of aspect.

"What do you want to know?" he asked. "You know what kind of men they are, what kind of operations they would have been involved in, by knowing what they became after the service. Regular grunts might get corporate security work. But you said yourself, there's something more going on."

"Yes. I did say that."

"So you know what kind of men they are—black ops contract workers. You know what kind I was. Files like ours end up with a lot of black ink on them."

"Yes, but—"

"What do you want me to say, Hurricane? That there is one simple secret that will make everything make sense? Has your life ever worked that way? Mine sure hasn't. The secrets are just markers of places and times like points on a map with no boundaries and no legend. You can follow from point to point all your life and never know where you are."

"There have to be reasons," I said, not even convincing myself.

"Let's go."

Damon started treading through the undergrowth. Even though the sun was sinking by that point he made almost no sound as he went.

We came out of the woods into a clearing but remained screened from the house by an outbuilding and a stack of firewood. From where we were we could see the front yard and half the front porch of the cabin. It was a kit house, the kind you buy from the lumber store and have set up on your foundation. It was a step above a mobile home but not a huge step. At the back was a covered stoop that served as a back porch and past that was an empty carport. Any later in the day, any less light, and I would have bought it. But screened by a huge, widespread magnolia I saw the protruding bumper of a late-model pickup. I would have pointed it out to Damon but when I turned from it, my attention was stolen by the horizon.

The sky, that had been nothing but shadows under the canopy of white oak and walnut, was a wall of ruby in the west. The contrails of jets made roads that disappeared when the travelers passed. It was an amazing sight but somehow full of portent that I was compelled to deny.

When I was a girl, my uncle told me the day was a pig running through the sky. When we saw a beautiful sunset, he always said it was the curly tail of the pig jumping a fence. It was a thought, something normal and wonderful to take hold of and cling to. That was what I chose to do.

I looked at Damon and he was staring at the house the way I think Ulysses must have looked at Ithaca after so many years. It wasn't a good sign.

"Damon?"

"I'm ready," he said without looking at me.

"What exactly are you ready for?"

"Anything," he answered flatly. "Everything." The addition was just as featureless.

Nothing was right. I suddenly knew it as surely as I knew that western purple would soon be black. I had thought the need to get Billy was everything. I'd compromised my responsibilities and used Damon to get me where I was. When it came to it, I didn't want to use him any further. Or maybe I didn't want him using me for whatever was in his head. Either way it was all wrong.

Damon stood and looked around the woodpile. The first shot came from a window and sent oak splinters flying. Some of them protruded from Damon's cheek.

A fire flared in his eyes, and I heard it crackle in his voice when he said, "Fuck, yeah."

"Damon—" I tried one last time and failed to stop the avalanche I'd set to falling on us.

"Go that way," he said, pointing around the other end of the shed. "Run fast and low. I'll make sure he keeps his head down."

He put his rifle between two quarters of wood and fired. Before the sound had stopped its echo, Damon had pulled the bolt and reseated the next cartridge. Feeling like I was caught in a strong current, I ducked and ran.

He fired again and this time I heard the breaking of glass. His third bullet hit the unlighted window when I was half way to the cabin. By the time that sound had died I had my back to the wall and was creeping up under the window.

When Damon didn't fire a fourth shot, the barrel of what appeared to be an AR-15 poked from the broken pane and fired a triple shot. Damon wasn't there. He was at the same corner of the shed I'd come around.

I held up a hand for him to hold. Then I pointed my weapon up at the window before showing Damon three fingers. Once he nodded, I counted down dropping fingers as I went. On three, I fired into the window. My bullets went harmlessly into the cabin's ceiling, but if the man inside had any sense he was not watching as Damon crouch-ran to the cabin.

Once engaged there was certainly no turning back. But there was no chance I was going to let Damon be the first into that house either. Part of that was worry for his safety. Part of it was fear that he would kill whoever was inside before we had a chance to talk.

So, as soon as Damon hit the wall next to me, I said, "Cover the window." Then I went for the back door without waiting. I got to the small porch and nodded my readiness before taking position at the door.

Damon, fired again into the window and as he did, I breached the back with my boot. Times like that I was glad I wasn't a dainty girl. The door was flimsy and cheap. It buckled rather than the frame bursting. I had to kick two more times to sweep it aside. As I did so, dishes clattered and a key rack fell from the wall.

I had come into a small kitchen that was exposed to a great room by open counter space and a wide arch. First I cleared the corners then ducked behind the lower cabinets. As I went low, the air above my head sizzled. Three metal-jacketed rounds punched through the sagging door and the wall behind it, probably without slowing.

Damon's rifle fired again from outside. I didn't know if he had a target or was shooting blind. It didn't matter, I was up and moving before he had the bolt back and a new round chambered. With a firm two-handed grip I left the kitchen keeping my back to the wall and my weapon out front.

One more time Damon used his rifle for suppressing fire and I saw it was aimed. He was standing at the window edge targeting a huge leather couch. I darted to the opposite wall and made sure that he saw me before I took a knee and sighted the top edge of the center cushion.

I saw the AR-15 muzzle rise before I saw the man behind it. It popped up just where I was aiming then hesitated. I shifted my sights right, to the far cushion, where the butt of the weapon would be tucked under a shoulder. Before I could call him out, Gagarin jumped up. I don't think I was who he expected. I saw surprise on his face as he tried to shift his momentum my direction. He might even have been trying to stop bringing his weapon to bear. He never got the chance. That's to say, I never gave him the chance. I placed two, center mass.

Things like that happen quickly. It wasn't until his carbine went flying over the furniture and Gagarin dropped behind it that I understood he was wearing body armor. My 9mm would not have pierced most vests, but he was going to be hurting. That wasn't enough for the moment. I dashed forward and around the far side of the couch, approaching from behind his head. Even hurting it was possible that he could pull a handgun.

Gagarin didn't have any fight left in him. He was gasping for air and scratching at the hook and loop straps that held his vest in place. Not for the first time, I wished Billy was here. He would have known exactly what to do. I didn't know if it would be best to take him out of the armor to let his chest expand better or if the vest was keeping pressure where it was needed. I opted for removing it.

Pulling the straps made a loud tearing sound. That was when I noticed that the rest of the world had gone almost silent. That happens after a gunfight. It's like the force and violence is a surprise to everything. No birds were chirping outside. Inside, the house was silent. Even Gagarin, once I had the vest off of him, was breathing more quietly. Although each breath he took came with a small rasping, bubble sound. I opened his shirt and found the skin of his chest a vicious looking red that was already streaking black. I believed his sternum was broken.

"Where's Billy?" I asked. My voice sounded louder and more frantic than I would have hoped. Self-consciously I looked to see if Damon had heard.

He wasn't with me. I sat up to look over the back of the couch for him. Nothing. I was alone in the house with Gagarin.

I opened my mouth to call out, then heard the engines. They were approaching fast from the land side of the cabin. Under the motor sound was the crunch of dry limbs and foliage. Two vehicles, maybe more, were approaching fast and not worried about staying on the path.

"Damon!" I shouted, both a question and alarm. That got no response so I turned back to the man stirring uncomfortably on the floor. "Where is he?" That time my question to Gagarin was followed by a shake applied by gripping his loose collar.

The pain contorted his face into bright surprise. "Who?" He managed to gasp.

"The man you beat up in your back room," I dragged the explanation from the center of my chest and it came out sounding like a snarl. Then I tried shaking understanding back into him. If the pain in his chest would have let him scream, he would have. "The deputy you took from Dogwood."

"I did not take. He saved me." His accent was thick again and tinged with panic. Gagarin appeared to be close to tears, although from fear or pain, I couldn't tell. I never even considered the possibility it was from remorse. "He saf-ed me."

"From what?"

He started crying.

"From what?" I asked again, jamming a thumb into his chest. I didn't have time for his tears.

"Them!" His shout was all force and no volume. And as he fell into quiet wailing I heard the vehicles stop.

I ran to the shattered window and looked outside. That I could see, there were two SUVs stopped and idling on the grass. One of them was the same one I had watched chase Dewey into the water. Silas Boone stepped out of that one.

"Hey you, Russian son of a bitch," Boone called toward the house. "The time for retribution is at hand." He laughed like he had made a great joke. "Come out and take it like a man."

"Do not let them have me." Gagarin pleaded in a rough whisper. "Please."

"Why do they want you?"

He didn't say anything.

I went from the window to stand over him and asked again "Why. Answer me or go to them." I told him.

It was good he believed me because I meant it.

"They say—I killed—one—of theirs." He punched the sentence out in gasping breaths.

"One of theirs?"

"You asked me," he was still pleading. "You showed picture."

"Daniel Boone?"

Gagarin nodded. "Yes."

"You killed Daniel Boone?"

"No," he said. "No. But they believe."

"Why?"

Chapter 16

Gagarin never got to answer me about why the mercenaries thought he killed Daniel Boone. The moment I asked him, a burst of automatic weapons fire ripped through the walls of the cabin. I dropped to the floor then rolled to where he'd dropped the AR-15. I ejected the magazine and cleared the chamber to check the count—nine. I reloaded the free round, seated the mag, and pulled the charging bolt, all in a few seconds. Some things you never forget.

Then I went to the front door. Before I went through, I had to pause and breathe. Anyone who tells you, confrontations like this don't bother them, is psychotic. I'm not that far gone. I was terrified. The thing is, being afraid is okay. Looking it, is not. Men like that crew will eat you alive if they think you're not fully ready to fight every inch. So I went out the door.

There was one man standing at the passenger door of Boone's car and three men at the other SUV. They all looked like shadow-specters beyond the yellow wash of high beams. Judging from their reaction, they must have thought the same about me when I stepped out into the glare spilling onto the front porch. In the moment of surprise I raised my weapon and killed the headlights of the second SUV. All five of the men dropped almost in unison.

"What do you want with him?" I shouted into the echoing quiet after the gunshots.

"The fuck?" Boone practically screamed at me as he got back onto his feet. He must not have taken my restraint as guaranteed because he kept the vehicle between us.

Keeping behind cover was the right thing to do. Or it would have been. I think he was conflicted by the idea of hiding from a woman. His body was behind the SUV but from the shoulders up he was wide open. I sighted his throat and had to convince myself not to pull the trigger—yet.

"Don't you know when to quit?" he shouted across the yard at me.

"No," I answered without shouting. He heard me okay.

"Just give us the Russian."

"Why do you want him?"

"Just leave us to it and we'll do your job for you." Boone sounded like a man trying hard to be reasonable.

"I've already done that job. You're the next one on my list." I doubt that I sounded very reasonable to anyone at that point.

"You don't understand the situation here—Hurricane." The name seemed to taste bad in his mouth. "We have the guns and the men. What have you got?"

I didn't really have an answer for that. I was a suspended cop out of my jurisdiction with a, possibly unstable, civilian backing me up. I wasn't even sure about that. Damon had disappeared.

"I've got this—" I displayed the Ar-15. "And I've got more balls than you ever had." Goading him may not have the best idea. Fear brings out the worst in me. At least in the bad light they couldn't see my hands shaking.

A couple of his buddies laughed and Boone shot a look that shut them up. Next he turned back to me and said, "What about the deputy?"

Despite my determination not to give him any reaction, something must have showed in my face or body.

Silas Boone, grinned a fun-house expression at me then cackled murderous glee. "That got you all shut up, didn't it? There something going on there? Deputy boy, your man?"

"I've called for backup, Boone." I lied hoping my shout would help sell it. It didn't.

"Bullshit," he yelled right back. "If that was true you wouldn't tell me about it. Besides that, who do you think you're messin' with? We monitor your frequencies. There's no one coming."

At that moment I heard the sound of another truck approaching. There was not a chance in hell it was someone coming to help me.

"We—on the other hand," he cackled again. "Oh, *we* got a deep bench with hitters on deck."

"Didn't anyone ever tell you, sports metaphors turn girls off?" At that point I was simply talking to buy time. I was out of ideas and about out of hope. Damon was gone I was sure, wisely fled back to his boat.

"Bitch," Boone shouted as the third vehicle pulled to a stop. "I'm going to turn you off for good."

Before he could get his weapon trained on me, someone came staggering from around the side of the house. Gagarin had his vest back on but hanging loose from the shoulders. His hands were behind his back. He was crying as he stumbled into the light.

"Do not shoot me," he begged through the tears and the snot. "Do not shoot. I did none of the things you think. I am not your man."

Boone cackled like a crazy chicken. "Oh—you ain't a man all right. But you're mine."

"Gagarin—don't," I called.

He ignored me. "Please. Please do not shoot me."

When he was beside the porch I could see a bit of wire dangling from his clasped hands. His wrists were bound behind his back. I hadn't tied him.

Damon.

"Come back, Gagarin," I shouted. "Don't go to those men."

"I am have to," he cried. The man was terrified but more afraid of what was behind him than in front. He kept moving forward.

When Gagarin reached the front of the SUV, Boone grabbed him by the arm and dragged him around to the passenger door. "I guess you are just not very good at your job, are you, Hurricane?" He taunted me as he shoved Gagarin in the vehicle. Once he slammed the door shut, he thumped his chest and shouted louder. "What're you gonna do now—bitch?"

I lowered my sights and put a high velocity round right through his damaged leg. The frail bone must have disintegrated because the leg bent the wrong way and Boone pitched forward onto his shocked face.

Before he hit the ground I was dropping behind a porch column and the other men were firing wildly. Those who had just arrived, were firing from behind open truck doors. Wood shattered and splinters rained down on me as I tried to make myself as small as possible. In the staccato rumble of automatic fire, I caught the single bark of a .30-06.

One of the gunmen dropped.

From someplace hidden, Damon fired another round. It removed another shooter from behind a truck door.

The killers shifted focus from me to shoot into the woodpile by the shed where Damon and I had first come to the clearing. A head high stack of oak piled in three rows was better cover than an SUV. Other than the engine block a car is mostly empty space covered with glass and sheet metal.

With no one shooting at me I was able to move to a safer position off the porch and cover behind the stone corner of the cabin foundation. As I moved I was able to see one of the men helping Boone up and into the back of the truck. That man then ran around to the front of the SUV with Gagarin in the front seat.

I aimed from a prone position planning on shooting the man if he started driving. I never got the chance. The man in the driver's seat turned to scream at Gagarin. It was an explosion of rage but silent outside the cab.

Damon's .30-06 blasted again. Even through all the gunfire I could pick out the one hunting rifle. That time though, I saw no one hit or fall. From where I was I could see the barrel sticking out beyond the wall of firewood but when I tried to follow the line of sight it seemed wrong. Like he was aiming into the woods beyond the fight.

When I looked back to the cluster of cars and shooting men, I saw something I hope to never witness again. Gagarin's head exploded within the SUV showering blood on the passenger side windows. For an instant, the man in the driver's seat was paralyzed by shock. But only for an instant. He was a professional.

But so was Damon.

The man jerked the shifter down and into drive. The wheels spun in the grass for a moment. On that melee there was no missing the sound of the .30-06. I heard the shot and saw the man drop onto the steering wheel. That time there was no burst of gore simply a gunshot followed by death.

The other SUV and the truck surged forward spinning into tight turns. Dirt and weeds flew from behind them in broad sprays as they fishtailed. In a moment they had traction. The two vehicles left the one stuttering to an idling stop.

The quiet in that moment was almost intolerably deep. As it lay over me, an insulation against the world, it was also an echo chamber for my thoughts.

How had it come to this? Why?

Nothing, no thought I could muster, made any sense to me.

I'd let my anger and fear tempt me into a gunfight with the men who, I believed, were holding Billy. I qualified that because I was no longer sure of anything. Gagarin was involved but not involved. He said he didn't kill Daniel Boone and that he was rescued from the mercenaries by Billy.

I was waiting for Damon to show. He'd restrained and then released Gagarin but had he killed him too? I tried mentally replaying the fight and couldn't piece things together. The .30-06 had a report distinct from the automatic weapons but there were so many bullets fired.

Where is he?

I had expected Damon to come to the cabin after the vehicles had carried away the danger. Then I wondered if he'd been hit. Or maybe he thought I should come to him.

I didn't stand right away. I couldn't. It's hard to give up cover when you have it so I scooted along the cabin's foundation until the whole scene was blocked. Keeping to a crouch, I made my way back to the shed and woodpile ready to drop at any moment.

No one was there. I scanned the fight scene, staying behind cover. After that I watched the gaping windows and crushed back door of the cabin, scanning for any movement. Nothing.

The first sound I was aware of for fully five minutes came as a rustling of dry sticks in the woods behind me. I followed, thinking Damon might be after someone. Or the opposite might be true. Either way . . .

The trip back to the boat seemed much quicker than the slow stalk we had made away from it. Mostly that was because I had given up the idea of stealth as a personal impossibility so I ran. That is, I jogged as well as I could through dark underbrush. It was all for nothing. When I got to the covered lake finger where we had secreted the boat—it was gone.

With no choice, I made my way back to the cabin as quickly and loudly as possible. By that time, the darkness under the trees was so thick my jog had become a careful picking of steps. I'd started to think I was still back in the cave with Billy. Or was I hoping? That time though, the cavern mouth was illuminated by firelight not sunlight.

The cabin was on fire.

It wasn't a huge blaze—yet. The front was boiling with bright flame and the back, the crashed open door and broken windows were flowing with smoke. Above the roof, the columns of soot looked like black snakes silhouetted by stars.

At the edge of the clearing around the cabin, I waited, watching. I wanted to cry. The snakes weaving over everything in starlight, were laughing. They wanted me to cry too. Or they wanted me to drink. Glittering on the front porch rail, barely beyond the licking reach of flaming tongues, was a bottle of whiskey. Worse than that, the SUV in which Gagarin and the driver had both been shot, was gone.

Life, karma, or something was continuing to taunt me.

I broke cover and ran. This time I didn't crouch. Around the back of the cabin I bolted and up the three steps. There on the little porch I got to hands and knees and crawled under billowing smoke to search the floor. It took a lung-charring moment, but I found what I was looking for. There were a couple of sets of keys that I had knocked from a holder when I kicked the door in. Only one had a car key with a remote fob.

Behind the magnolia, I started the Ford truck and sat, once again, in quiet fear. Eventually, after I really had started crying, I dropped the shifter into drive and left the burning cabin as quickly as the truck would take me.

After a firefight is the dangerous time for your sanity. Your body, pumped on adrenaline, becomes a limp rag as the chemical energy fades. Some people want to sleep. Some become giddy and laugh uncontrollably or make inappropriate jokes. I've heard some people describe it as arousing, a sexual feeling. There is no telling how your body will react. One thing that you can be sure of though, is the brain. In the time after the conflict, every violent moment gets written into your memory like something carved in hard wood with a dull knife. That's why the most common phrase you hear in support of a troubled friend is *Try not to think about it*. But everyone thinks about it.

That's the hard thing, knowing how close your story was to the end. Of course that begs the questions. They all begin with the word *why*. Why me? Why them? Why didn't I—

As I found the dirt road, my adrenaline charge was trickling away. I was asking all the questions. It was gone completely as the truck bumped up onto asphalt. I was picking apart and second-guessing each moment since Damon and I had first taken cover behind the woodshed.

Miles burned away under my tires as I dissolved into depression. Headlights swept over the faded yellow lines on the county blacktop illuminating nothing but my past. The truck, and the sound of tires, carried me from one violence to another. Before I knew it I was surrounded by the blowing brown dust of Iraq. I was splayed out on my belly and when I opened my eyes, I saw the stain of my blood. It was already mixed with the dirt, surrendering its color into the dun shades of the desert.

My worst wound was below the shoulder blade. The knife had been thrust straight down while I was pinned by the weight of the man on top of me. At the time, there was no telling how bad the wound was—but it was bad. It was probably the reason I'd been left discarded so blithely. Either I was believed already dead, or ready to die.

My uniform had been cut and stripped away. Leaving me naked was another way to demean me. It also left me separate from the *real* soldiers. The men who had raped me were Americans too. Hating women crosses all borders and faiths. I knew who they were, that was the worst thing. The devil you know—

If Americans had found me dead, they would assume I was a casualty of the insurgents. If I was found alive by any insurgent, I would be raped some more and condemned to die for the sins of being female and American.

Wind pushed rippling waves of dust over the mud wall I was behind, slowly making my grave. I don't know how, but I refused the tomb. It took a long time of hope and tears. Eventually I rolled from under the accumulating soil rising to my hands and knees. Every part of me shook with the effort. My head throbbed and gold flashed in my eyes with each beat of the pain. I vomited.

When my gut seemed ready, I opened my eyes again. The puddle of puke under my face, like my blood, was being devoured by the dead land, becoming simply, more of the brown.

Careful not to put my hands in the mess, I backed away. That was when I felt the cuts in my backside. The captain had slapped and cut my behind with the knife as he sodomized me. When he bucked up against me, moaning with his release, he thrust the blade deep into my right buttock.

I let my head sag so I could look down the length of my body. More blood. More wounds. The entirety of my ribcage was bruised—black finger marks on pale skin. A lot of attention had been paid to my breasts. A long gash, starting high on my chest, ran under the soft flesh causing one to hang lower and at an impossible angle. On the other, my nipple was sliced and twisted. There was another laceration in the pubic hair, a violent, jagged gash, and a bare strip where the darker red curls had been stripped away. The lieutenant had taken a souvenir.

Blood flowed from me. A river, undammed by my movements, rushed over the crust between my legs. Fresh fluid trickled down dead-white thighs and spread into dark galaxies of bruising. The new blood was coming from my vagina. The lieutenant, before cutting his souvenir, had punching between my legs several times before shoving his fist inside.

I cried. For a short time or a long one, I wasn't sure. Maybe it was a short time that only seemed equal to all the time I had lived so far. I stayed there on my hands and knees because it hurt too much to move, and I cried. It poured from my frothy lungs, a quiet, keening wail that sounded almost like a meadowlark, but there was no answering call.

Even the silence became too great a weight to bear. I started gathering clothes and doing what I could to cover myself. The only thing worse than being raped and left naked behind some mud wall and shack in Iraq, was being found naked in any condition by the local faithful. A naked woman in that part of the world was a whore. The men there neither resisted nor respected whores.

I found tattered pants and a bloody T-shirt, no boots and no underwear. Still it took almost ten screaming minutes to get the clothing on.

When I stood, my head lurched again and the guts followed. There was no fighting it. I draped my body over the low wall and puked in hard spasms. Gold starbursts patterned my vision. I smelled bile and copper.

I never remember rising again. Nor do I recall walking away from the wall. The next thing I really remember was finding a road and hoping I'd turned the right direction to find a checkpoint. Before I made it a hundred yards down the road, a white dot appeared on the horizon. A vehicle.

If it wasn't green it wasn't safe. I dropped into the shallow ditch. When I hit, something popped in my chest. It was physical and audible and started a cascade of wrenching pain. Later, a doctor told me that a nick in my lung must have torn through. Air was escaping into the chest cavity at the same time blood was running into the lung. Each breath was a loud, gasping rattle that brought in little air and almost as much dust.

The white pickup truck slowed on shrieking brakes. It carried three men up front and six in the back. All were armed. They looked at me like a wolf looks at a wounded calf.

I said good-bye, in quiet thoughts, to my mother and father. All thoughts had become prayers. Everyone who had ever done me harm, I forgave, except the men who had put me where I was. Then I waited for the real death.

One man jumped down from the truck bed and the others stayed behind, shouting. The bolt on an AK-47 was pulled. Everything went silent for a few moments then the shouting started up again. The man with the AK ran back to the truck. He sprayed a wash of rounds at me without aiming as the truck left the road and took off across open ground.

A moment later, I watched a column of Humvees stop on the broken road. A squad of men piled out and formed a perimeter. One man shouted, "We need a medic and a litter up here."

In the back of a Humvee, the medic's eyes were wide with fear and embarrassment. He had never worked on a woman before and certainly never one so intimately harmed. He looked all of nineteen. Working as quickly as he could, he put in a line to drain the air and blood from my chest. Once I could breathe, he followed the lines of cuts on my body, filling them with hemostatic powder. When he cut my pants off and spread my naked legs to pack those wounds, his eyes rimmed with tears. While he touched me and bound the lacerations that could be bound, he talked. Mostly he said everything would be all right. He said it like a mantra more for himself than me.

"It'll be all right."

"Everything will be all right."

Outside, the thick, hard rubber of the Humvee's tires roared loudly on cratered asphalt.

"It'll be all right," Corporal Billy Blevins said again.

Chapter 17

Sunrise was a blue-orange gap between a newly greening nadir and a marching gray zenith. Thunder rumbled faintly. I had lost the night to violence, both fresh and aged. That wasn't so terrifying, I'd lost more than my share of nights hiding from the brown haze in whiskey and tears. Drunks like me know about lost time. No, the terror came from two realizations that came one foot in front of the other. First shoe—People needed me, the girls, *Billy*, needed me, and I had fallen into the darkness again. Second shoe—there was a new bottle of whiskey, still in the brown bag clutched in my hands.

I had not so much as taken a drop. I knew that, not because the bottle was still sealed, but because of the fact, I was not intoxicated. At that point I was not going to trust my eyes. I did trust my sense of myself as a drunk though. There was no chance I had started drinking without getting completely wasted away.

I opened the truck door and unlimbered myself from the cab. It's a scary thing to realize, you're hoping the whiskey in your lap was placed there by a stalker hoping to intimidate you. It is even scarier to suddenly know that it was something you did in the turmoil of a flashback and dry drunk. The truck was parked in the gravel lot of an all-night liquor store. Worse yet, it was one I recognized as being in my own county.

I wanted to cry again, I may have done it if the man leaning over my tailgate hadn't spoken to me.

"We need to get you out of here," Captain Alastair Keene said.

"You need to go fuck yourself," I hit him right back. When I'm that tired and heartsick I'm not up to my usual level of banter.

"I'm not kidding," he informed me flatly, then continued in the same bland tone, "Shit's happening."

"Then you should feel right at home." I felt better about my repartee with that one. "Why are you here? And how?"

The how part struck me like God's whisper in a prophet's ear—*he was at the cabin*. I dropped the bottle and reached to pull my weapon from the holster. It wasn't there.

"I have your pistol," Keene said. "For my own safety."

"Why?"

"Because I didn't want you to shoot me."

"The other why," I blurted out. "The big why."

Keene opened his mouth slowly like he was building the answer with his teeth before letting it out. I didn't give him that much time.

"And if you think I need a gun to put you on your ass, you're fooling yourself."

His mouth stopped working the words over. A shadow of anger rolled over his face and his eyes narrowed to dark fissures. For an instant I thought he was going to take me up on the challenge and I regretted my inability to hold my tongue. Then he relaxed and grinned, showing me bright white teeth. It was an expression I honestly couldn't read. Some of that may have been the scent of whiskey coming up from the broken bottle at my feet.

I lifted my feet high, stepping over the liquid like it would drown me if I touched it. It might have. I didn't know and I didn't want to risk it.

"So—Hurricane—" Keene stepped over the nickname as carefully as I had the spilled whiskey.

"Why." I punched with the word.

"Why. The big why. I don't have that. Just a lot of little ones and you're going to have to help me out on the ones you want."

"Start with this." I kicked gravel and dirt at the broken glass and blotted liquid. "Why have you been leaving it in front of me? It's a real dick move."

"You did that."

I knew he wasn't lying. I knew the truth before I asked the question. I needed it to be him without believing it was.

"You bought it last night and came to this truck and sat in the parking lot. The clerk knew who you were and finally called the sheriff. That was how I found you."

"Sheriff Benson told you?" I made sure he could read the disbelief in my face and voice.

"Things have changed."

"Things always change, but they never really do."

"This thing changed. Your uncle killed a man trying to break into his dock."

"What? When?"

"Last night. While you were off the radar. Your phone's been off."

I pulled the phone from my pocket and remembered turning it off before starting the walk through the woods to the cabin. There were over thirty waiting messages. I put it back in my pocket.

"Tell me everything," I said.

"A shooting involving a sitting member of congress gets a lot of attention. A second shooting...well, let's say that shakes the branches hard enough for all sorts of things to fall out."

"Is Whilomina okay? What about Uncle Orson?"

"She's fine and he's about the toughest bastard I've ever met. I don't think he can be hurt."

"He's hurt," I said, thinking of my father.

"I guess your uncle took the congresswoman to the dock for defense. It wasn't a bad idea. There's only the one narrow ramp for someone to walk in on and, with all the lights on, no boat was sneaking up."

"But?"

"No but. Two men tried to run up the gangway. Your uncle, dropped one and the other swam for it. Orson said he hit that one too."

"If he says he hit him, he did," I said with admiration. "That doesn't explain how you got into the mix and why you're not here to make my life a little more miserable."

"Can we talk about it in the car?" He nodded at the dented rental parked way behind Gagarin's truck. "If I found you, the mercs can too."

"They already found me," I said. "Last night."

"What happened?"

"I'm the one here, aren't I?" I held out my hand and waggled my fingers at Keene demanding my weapon.

"They said you were a hell on wheels and ten miles of dirt-road bitch." He took the gun from his belt and handed it over.

"Who said that?"

He shrugged, "Everyone."

"How long have you been in the service?"

"Full twenty, next year."

"So you've saluted women? Superior officers."

"Of course."

"Did you ever salute one you didn't think was a bitch?"

He stared at me without answering.

"That's what I thought." I checked my weapon then returned it to the holster. After that I pulled my phone again and called the sheriff. I gave a quick rundown of what had happened and asked him to call the Stone County Sheriff. He repeated basically what Keene had told me about Uncle Orson and Whilomina. He added that the congresswoman was not doing as well as she pretended to be. I quietly admitted that I wasn't either.

"Come back in," he said. "This is getting a lot bigger than us."

"I would . . ."

"But Billy?" he asked and answered.

"Yes. I'm going after him."

"How?"

"I'm walking straight into that tent and kicking ass until I find him."

"If you do, I'll have to arrest you myself," the sheriff said quietly. "And I mean it."

"Yeah," I answered. "We all pay prices."

"No one says we have to buy the pig in the poke."

"What's that mean?"

"It means," he said, "that you don't know if he's there or even if anyone there is involved. It means you're holding a bag. It's big. It's alive inside. But you don't know if you're holding your pig or not."

"You're right," I deflated as I said it.

"Be careful."

"It's too late for that, Sheriff." I disconnected before he could say anything else. Keene had been listening in as I talked. His face was stony. There was no way to tell what he was thinking.

We left the truck in the liquor store parking lot.

"Do you know where Billy is?" I asked as soon as Keene had the car moving. He looked at me. Every line of his face could have been set by a level. It pissed him off that I asked even though he understood. "So explain it to me," I said.

"I told you"—he heavy footed the accelerator and we hit the road—"things get a lot of attention when a member of congress gets involved. Especially one on the House Armed Services Committee."

"So Whilomina put pressure on your boss?"

"She didn't have to. Once it hit the news everyone wanted to get on the right side of things."

"You're still not saying what things. What knots were you tying the Constitution in?"

"This time, I can honestly say I was as much in the dark as anyone. The CID—I was just a screen for the domestic part of a CIA black-bag operation to provide Army weapons and munitions to El Camino Ardiente."

"Why?"

"I wish I knew. For deniability? The weapons were listed as stolen from the Army. My job was *investigation*."

"By not investigating," I said.

He nodded. "That and making sure no one else did any investigating."

"You mean me."

"Yeah."

"And you took a look at my file and thought . . ."

"I thought you were a troublemaker with a grudge against the Army. To be fair though, you didn't do much to change my mind."

"To be fair—kiss my ass." After that we sat in silence for a few twists of the Ozarks roadway. After one sweeping turn that Keene took wide and almost into an oncoming truck, I asked. "What's it all about? The big picture?"

"The guns—"

"Not enough," I cut him off. "This whole thing is about as clear as the sky above us."

Keene craned his neck to look up at the darkened clouds. "Another storm," he said. "The weather is weird here. It's warm one day, cold the next."

"It's spring," I told him. "Storm season. The cold air is spilling from the north or rolling off the Rockies. Warm air is rising up from the Gulf. Everything between the mountains out west, and the Ozarks plateau is tornado alley."

"How do you know when a tornado's coming?"

"Watch for the sky to turn green."

He looked out the windows again, trying, I imagined, to find green in the lowering gray.

"It's not even a storm yet," I reassured him. "You'll know when to look."

Keene kept driving and, mostly resisted the urge to scan the skies. "What did you mean, 'it's not enough?'"

"Think about it," I said then took my own advice for a minute. "You can't just steal weapons from the Army and cover it up without a lot of people being in on it. Congresswoman Tindall and my father knew some of it. Not enough to understand or stop it. The Army is involved, so is the CIA and a team of outside contractors."

He looked like he was doing what I'd asked—thinking about it. Or he was thinking about the impending storm. Either way, his face was fixed and his head nodded gravely.

"You'd know better than me," I went on. "But it seems that our government supplies weapons to regimes and revolutions all the time. What is it that makes this operation something worth shooting at a member of congress or killing other American citizens?"

Keene stopped nodding. "It would have to be very big or very illegal."

"Does what you know, fit that description?"

He was driving even faster at that point like he was running from the conversation or the impending storm. His hands were at ten and two on the wheel but his mind was working other roads. After we leaned into a squealing turn, Keene shook his head. If it was to say no or to clear it, I wasn't sure until he said, "No. What I've seen has been basic stuff—that's to say, basically illegal, but explainable. I'm pretty sure that the guns would not be sent to Peru and the rebels there without congressional approval."

"That means Whilomina knew about it, I'm betting. She and my father tried to warn me without giving too much away."

"Too much of what?"

"I'd ask if I thought she could tell me."

"Could or would?"

"She would if she could. Now." I turned into myself thinking about my father and his relationship that had been a secret from me. Finally I said, "She doesn't know."

"Know what?"

"That's the thing. She doesn't know the end game anymore than we do. But my father said something about a finance operation. What do you know about Iran-Contra?"

Keene shrugged. "Before my time."

"Mine too. But my father said the CIA sold arms to Iran and used the profits to fund the Contra rebels."

"I don't think there are Contra rebels anymore."

"Maybe not," I said. "But I'm sure there are plenty of other groups we might want to fund quietly."

"But why use an old Army chaplain and mercenaries to do it?"

"Army chaplain?" I had the sickening feeling that I'd missed something important.

"Roscoe Bolin was a divisional chaplain with the Army. He was deployed into Iraq to help the local command with religious issues as the new Iraqi government was forming."

"Wait. Religious issues?" My mind was swimming around something that wouldn't hold still long enough for me to get ahold of. "But he's not Muslim."

"He wrote a doctoral thesis that got him the job. Something about the common source of fundamental beliefs and how they can unify the big three religions."

"Religious fundamentalism as a moderating force?" I asked incredulously.

"Hard to believe I know."

"Impossible," I pronounced. "Wait—" It was a fortuitous pause. The car rounded a curve out of the valley between two steep rock cuts and into a cleared hilltop. As soon as it did, we were hit by a hard blast of rushing wind and the gritty tick of carried dirt against the metal.

"Whoa." Keene sounded like he was calming a startled horse. "Are you sure that storm isn't here yet?"

At that moment his voice was lost in a different wind. So was I.

"Hurricane? Hey—are you in there?"

I don't know how long Keene had been trying to call me back, but the car was moving a lot slower by the time I left the blowing dirt of Iraq behind.

"Keep going," I said.

"You okay?"

"I'm fine," I snapped a bit, but didn't feel the least bit bad. "Just keep going."

"What happened?" He ignored my tone, but did speed up. "Flashbacks?"

"Forget about it."

"You're sure a hard girl to be friends with."

"I've got all the friends I need," I said ignoring the fact that my life seemed to have acquired a theme. Being annoyed with Keene was actually a blessing. If I was alone, or with anyone else, I think I would have melted down into a mass of pain and tears. Everything about me, but that spark of anger, wanted to dwell on my father and Billy. It was good to fan the flames. But there was an even better target.

"Reverend Bolin," I said, dragging him to the front of my mind. "How many of the contractors did he have contact with in Iraq?"

"I don't know. Most of those files are black ink. All of those guys were involved in some pretty bad stuff. Givens knew things, but he didn't share."

"We have to find Damon."

"Damon Tarique? Givens was worked up when you mentioned him but would never tell me why."

"Because he knows things," I said, guessing. "He hasn't shared it yet. But all these guys are connected somehow."

"Okay. We have a target. Where do we find him? Hopefully before the storm breaks."

"That's not the storm you have to worry about." I pulled my phone and called the sheriff. I asked him to contact the Department of Conservation and find out where Mike Resnick could be found.

I expected a long wait, but Sheriff Benson called back in a few minutes with the news that Mike had not reported to work that morning.

"I know where we're going," I said as I put the phone away.

All the light of morning had faded to a heavy murk under oppressive clouds by the time we pulled up to Mike's place. Mike's truck was in the drive, hitched to his boat with the driver's door standing open. That wasn't a good sign.

I pulled my weapon and looked over at Keene to be sure he was ready. I needn't have bothered. His pistol was out and in a two-handed ready position. His dark eyes were scanning the house, moving quickly from door to window to the corners and back. I couldn't help thinking that if Damon wanted us hurt we'd already be on the ground. I didn't share the thought.

Keene moved carefully to the truck and checked the cab before moving on to the bed. Both were empty. From where I was I could see the inside of the boat. It was still cluttered with all the gear that Mike always seemed to fill it with.

"Ow—goddammit." Keene's exclamation was a breathy stage whisper of pain.

Keeping his eye on the house, he'd walked right into the tines of the long handled gig protruding over the bow of the boat.

It was one of those moments of understanding that take you entirely by surprise. Little things that had no meaning fell like tumblers in a lock to open a door. Behind it was a sickening shock.

I bolted past Keene and up the few steps to the house's front porch. Without stopping I pushed through the gaping entrance and inside. Mike Resnick was dead on the floor. Damon was sitting nearby with a gun in one hand and a sheaf of photos in the other. The warrior I had seen the night before was once again the gentle, damaged soul I had taken to my uncle for help.

Keene rushed in behind me, moving fast but carefully—professionally. I heard him shuffling and his breathing as he cleared corners and checked the other rooms. There was no point, I knew.

"He killed Daniel Boone," I said quietly. I kept my weapon ready, but pointed at the floor.

"Yes," Damon said. "How did you know?"

"I didn't until Keene walked into the gig sticking out of Mike's boat. Daniel had three holes in his abdomen about two inches apart. Exactly like the three tines of a fish gig. It was in front of me from that first night."

"It was in front of me too," Damon said, sounding both horribly sad and disgusted. "I thought he—" The rest of that thought was unexpressed but obvious.

"Why?" I asked as gently as was possible.

Keene sidled up behind me with his weapon ready and trained on Damon. He had questions in his eyes but didn't speak.

"Fish." Damon expelled the word like a curse. "It was all about fish." He started crying. "The Russian told me when you were outside the cabin. I worked it out of him. How Mike was poaching the fish he was supposed to protect and selling caviar to the Russian."

"And Daniel started doing the same thing."

"That's right. Mike didn't want to share so he killed him. I thought he cared about me, but he only wanted to be sure I didn't know anything."

Damon's tears seemed to come from a deeper place then. His back shook with the effort of wrenching the sound and pain out into the world. He gasped like he was taking a last breath, then howled the word again, "Fish."

"Damon try to—" I never finished. Soothing words are no salve for the kind of hurt he was suffering. He had his own comfort in mind.

"Fish," he said sounding almost surprised as he raised the pistol.

I put up my hands, one of them empty with spread fingers the other gripping my weapon without aiming. Once again I was coming too late to understanding, but still following the motions.

"No," I said speaking to Keene more than to Damon.

Neither man listened. Keene shot and killed Damon with two closely spaced rounds in his chest.

It was more for confirmation than investigation when I checked Mike Resnick's service weapon still in Damon's hand. The safety was on.

Chapter 18

It would be a lie and a disservice to Damon to say I didn't understand why he would want to die. When I saw the guilty second-guessing of himself in Keene's eyes, I wished that Damon had found another way. Still, I was glad it wasn't me who had pulled the trigger.

This was another of those, if-I'd-been-alone, situations. What would have happened? I never targeted Damon. Would I have shot him? Would I have passively allowed him to kill me? It was a scary thought that I couldn't find a true answer in my head or my heart. I've thought the same thoughts that must have been haunting Damon.

Tears were filling my eyes. *So much death*. I wanted to cry, to break down and give in. I wanted to sit in the darkness with Billy and tell him about the ghosts and the fear I lived with. But at times like that, we're each alone in our own skins.

At the same time, Keene and I secured our weapons neither looking at the other or at the dead men on the floor or couch.

"He wanted me to . . ." Keene couldn't finish the sentence.

"Yes."

"Why?" The question was feeble, grasping at straws. "There has to be a pretty big reason someone would do that."

"No big reason. Tiny ones that stack up and weigh you down. A million of them. A million-million. Reasons are like sand—or stars. Uncountable."

"You sound like maybe you—"

"He had pictures in his hand." I pointed at the scattering of photos that had fallen when Damon died. "Memories. Old ones or new?" Using my fingertips on the edges, I lifted and examined the images one by one. They were the same ones I'd seen in the bottom of his tackle box that first night.

"You're one shoe-leather tough woman, ain't you?"

"You have no idea."

I refused to let Keene see me wipe my eyes.

"Look at this." Without looking at him I handed over a photo.

It was a real photograph, not a print of something digital. I knew a few guys who would get disposable cameras in the mail and send them to family when they were full. No one cared if one of those got lost and for someone on deployment, there is still something about snapshots.

"Do they look familiar?"

In the photo, a group of men in desert camo were lined up and grinning in two rows, one crouched and one standing. Despite many of them wearing sunglasses you could still recognize Silas Boone and several other faces I'd seen recently. On the end and noticeably apart from the others, Damon and Daniel Boone stood together. In the back, wearing a *shemagh* around his neck and under a bushy beard was the Reverend Roscoe Bolin. Next to him, in an Iraqi military uniform bearing stars, was Massoud.

Keene flipped the photo over. On the back was an inscription in pencil, ALL OF US WITH THE REVEREND AND GENERAL MASSOUD—STARTING SOMETHING BIG.

"Starting something big?" he read and questioned. "What?"

"Massoud's a general." I said. "I didn't expect that."

"Why not? He's the one footing the bill for the mercenaries."

"That's what Banjo said."

"Banjo?" Keene sounded surprised. "The guy from the revival show?"

"Yeah, the hippie." I answered thinking of Banjo's John Denver look. "He said the Gagarin was in charge of the girls and Massoud had the reins of the mercenaries.

"Givens spent a lot of time with Massoud. Cash changed hands. I don't know anything about your Russian."

"What do you know about Massoud?"

"I just told you everything."

"Now that you know he was an Iraqi general, can you find out more?"

Keene hesitated long enough to let me know that he wasn't following my orders then said, "Give me a minute." He went to another room with his phone.

As he talked I stared at the picture. Something about it bothered me. It was nothing obvious. There were no big clues or secret weapons. The background was blue sky and dirt.

I turned it over and reread the inscription.

ALL OF US WITH THE REVEREND AND GENERAL MASSOUD—STARTING SOMETHING BIG.

What was so big, I wondered. There was no answer to that. Not yet anyway. I ran through the rest of the notation. General Massoud and the Reverend were clear. Nothing there. Then I got stuck on the phrase, *All of us*.

Once more I flipped it over and examined the picture. That time I really looked, moving carefully from face to face looking for ones I recognized. Many I did. They were the contractors I'd become familiar with the last few days.

That was what I expected. Maybe that was also what was bothering me. Sometimes when you expect things to look a certain way, they fit perfectly or they perfectly don't fit. Context can be like a straightjacket. You see what you expect to see the way you expect to see it. You see a man in uniform and you see a soldier. Take him out of uniform—

There he was, front row center, crouched with a cradled weapon and sunglasses up on his head, Connor Banjo Watson.

I couldn't help it, the opening few notes of "Dueling Banjos" from *Deliverance tinked* in my reeling brain. "This time you did get into the wrong van," I muttered.

At that time, I felt pretty smug. I'd caught the lie and another tiny piece fell into place. That feeling disappeared when I reran the conversation I'd had with him in the hardware store. He kept pointing me toward the Russian. Distraction. Disinformation. When I took the words out of the memory though, I caught what he'd really been hiding in plain sight. Chains. Banjo Watson had been measuring out lengths of chain as we talked. Looking back at that moment, I knew without any doubt that the chains were to hold a dozen girls in bondage and in secret.

"Have you ever heard of Rojava?" Keene asked from the doorway.

I must have looked as blank as I felt.

"Syrian Kurdistan," he clarified. It was still mud.

"I'm not sure I care anymore." I spoke the words. The feeling behind them was more like a sigh. Resignation and acceptance. The world is a terrible place.

I held up the photo with my middle finger perched above Connor Watson's face. "Do you know this guy?"

"He's the one you were talking about, Banjo."

"Right. What do you know about him?"

"I never liked him. Two-faced. He worked for Givens I think."

"What? How?"

"Givens never told me. But we met him several times away from the tent show."

"What did they talk about?"

"I never knew. I waited outside when Givens went into the trailer."

"What trailer," I asked, and I felt the fire blooming in my eyes.

"You really do need to hear about Massoud," Keene explained as he drove.

I was dialing my phone and nodding, not exactly ignoring but not giving him much attention either.

Using the phone to point, I indicated the intersection ahead. "Take the left. Go three miles and we'll turn right. And get on it. We're in a hurry."

Once I pressed the phone back to my face it connected to Sheriff Benson. Without wasting any small talk, I told him where we were heading and that I believed we would find the girls and Billy held there. The sheriff had questions. I didn't have a lot of answers so I disconnected.

By my silence and angry staring out the window, I'd hoped to hold off any more conversation. Keene wouldn't shut up though. He kept trying to engage me. Finally he said, "It really is a big thing."

That caught my attention. I lifted up the photo I'd set on the dashboard and read the back again. ALL OF US WITH THE REVEREND AND GENERAL MASSOUD - STARTING SOMETHING BIG.

"Yeah, that's the big we're talking about," he said.

"Okay," I relented. "Tell me."

"Rojava, is the name of a part of Kurdistan. The western region that encompasses northern Syria."

"Okay."

"So, Massoud is General Massoud Masum, an Iraqi Kurd and Kurdish nationalist."

"You said, Syria."

"That's part of the big thing. Kurds are the largest ethnic group in the world without a home state. Historic Kurdistan is a region that includes huge sections of Syria, Turkey, Iraq, and Iran."

I don't need a history lesson." I pointed again. "Turn there and get on the highway."

"Everyone needs a history lesson on this. It's one of the reasons the Middle East is constantly at war. And it turns out, some people think it might be a path to peace. Or at least, some peace, for the region."

"I don't follow."

"The Kurds are one of our strongest allies in fighting Daesh." He pronounced it Da-ish not Dash.

"He's an Iraqi Kurd. Two reasons to fight the Islamic State insurgency, not necessarily to have any loyalty to the United States," I said.

"He's not loyal to anyone but Kurdistan. And since Kurdistan is little more than an idea on a map, he's willing to make himself valuable to anyone who might help make the idea a real state."

"I can't claim to know a lot about US foreign policy as it relates to Kurdistan. I won't even claim to care. How does it fit into what we have going on here?"

"I don't know." Captain Keene steered into a long curve.

I caught him stealing a glance into the sky. The clouds had lowered and darkened. It was the middle of the day, but the only light that reached the ground was a filtered twilight. Branches on trees, both the evergreen junipers and the budding sticks of oak and cottonwood bent in a hard wind. Old leaves, the cast off of the previous fall, skittered across the road.

As if we'd driven past an invisible boundary, the tone of the gloom changed.

"Is the sky getting green?" Keene asked.

His unease and the blue-gray mist crawling toward us caused a prickle to rise over my back and shoulders.

"That's just rain," I reassured.

On cue, the water rolled like an unfurling wave across the windshield. With it went even more of the day's light.

"I don't like this." He stated the obvious.

"Where're you from?"

"Portland."

"Oregon gets a lot of rain."

"A lot of rain, not a lot of storms. I've never seen a tornado."

"You're not seeing one now either. This is a spring storm. We have bigger things to worry about."

Keene's hands were locked on the wheel in a grip so tight the dark skin of his knuckles were noticeably paler, like each little joint was giving its all, even its color, to keeping him connected to the car. His back was hunched up, a mockery of his usual posture.

I can't say why I said it, but I told him, "There's no shame in what you're feeling."

Keene didn't say anything. He did straighten his back and loosen his grip. Both hands stayed on the wheel though.

"Sorry," I said. "I was reading something that probably wasn't there."

"I could say the same to you, you know."

He looked like he was going to say more. I headed it off. "What do weapons, girls, and Peruvian revolutionaries have to do with an imaginary Kurdish state, missionaries, and mercenaries?" By the time he was ready to say anything I was pointing again. "Turn there," I said. "We're here."

The long, unpaved drive needed grading and a new covering of gravel. Rain, by that time, blowing in a sideways slurry, was already making muddy basins in the ruts. We followed the loop through the trailer park to the most distant arc, where the weeds grew and the road turned back as if in shame. There was one double-wide, white trimmed in faded black and rust stains. Leading up to the door was a staircase of stacked cinder blocks. They matched the dry stack supports showing under the unskirted trailer.

"You know how a tornado is like a divorce in Taney County?" I asked Keene.

"No."

"Either way, somebody's losing a trailer."

He laughed, a nervous sounding grunt, probably pity.

"Stop," I told him. "We're going in."

"We're not waiting for backup?"

"I'm not."

"What if we're wrong about this place?"

"Either way, somebody's losing a trailer."

As soon as Keene had the car stopped in a track of crushed grass and weeds that served as a driveway, I was out in the rain with my weapon at ready.

If my life was a book or a movie, what happened next would have been perfectly scripted. Squalling rain died, swept aside by the same wind it was carried on. Overhead, the black blanket was pulled gently aside and sunlight made bright pockets in the gaps. In one place, a beam, feeble illumination that looked, none the less, like a strong promise, stroked trash and weeds in the yard before moving on to paint the tops of trees.

Keene was beside me, even though I'd never heard him get out of the car. "Does that happen a lot here?"

I was angry with myself when I realized that the awe in his voice reflected my own feelings. Signs. I'd been seeing them lately. Both good and bad. Life had taught me only one thing about signs and omens. You only see them when you're looking and you're only looking when the real world is too ugly to offer the hope you crave.

"Let's get inside," I said, suddenly absolutely sure that nothing short of nightmare waited inside.

"Just wait."

"For what?"

"Them." Keene jerked a thumb over his shoulder at a snake of cop cars hurtling up the mud track. They were running lights, no sirens. Behind the front three Taney County Sheriff's vehicles there were two other civilian vehicles.

The feeling I had about impending nightmare got stronger.

"Captain Keene," I spoke louder than I needed to. "Can they stop us?"

"Stop us?"

"There is an order from DOJ keeping the department away from the tent show and the people there."

Keene's glance felt like a long stare. When he nodded the movement was almost imperceptible. Its meaning was impossible to miss. He looked away and toward the double-wide. I suspected, like me, he was looking for signs.

The snake of cars came sloshing to a stop in the road with everyone piling out like a single unit. Aside from the sheriff in the lead car and deputies, men I knew and mostly trusted, Massoud and armed contractors stood before me. The last civilian car was my father's. Uncle Orson and Congresswoman Whilomina Tindal stood beside it. That's how it was for a moment. All action poised but not yet triggered.

Then the moment was over.

Massoud shouted first. I followed, stepping on his words with accusations. The sheriff and Whilomina joined in next. We were all yelling with all the breath we could muster and none of us hearing.

I'd forgotten that I still had my pistol in my hand. When I raised it to point at Massoud the three men in tac gear lifted their weapons and joined in the shouting. I might actually have dropped my weapon if Orson had not been behind the men. He pulled the .45 that he'd brought back from Vietnam and oiled like a baby every Sunday night since.

Orson didn't yell or threaten. He didn't do anything to turn the mercenaries to him. If things didn't ease up, he would just pull the trigger. Two of the men would drop before they could even turn and I was pretty secure in my feeling that he would trust me to get the third.

Sheriff Benson raised both hands and strode into the center of the shouting match. It actually worked. I lowered my weapon and stopped shouting. The mercenaries raised theirs to the sky and quieted.

The only one who kept making noise was Massoud. He shouted, "No!"

But he was directing it beyond me. I turned just in time to see Captain Alastair Keene kick aside the trailer door and step inside.

Chapter 19

Even with the clearing of the clouds, there was enough of a pallor to the day that the two gunshots from within the trailer flared like flashbulbs.

No one was yelling anymore. In fact it had gotten so quiet I realized that the rain had not stopped completely. Thick drops were falling with sporadic spits of sound as they impacted leaves or mud.

Keene stepped back into the open doorway and waved. "You need to see this, Sheriff." He shouted.

I holstered my pistol and waited for the sheriff to come along side before I started walking. He held up a hand to tell me to stop. As he kept walking he continued holding the gesture until he got to the steps. By that time Massoud had tromped past me without looking. His mercenaries looked. In fact they gave me serious stink-eye as they followed the money.

Probably, I would have said to hell with it and gone on in if Whilomina had not put a hand on my shoulder. Uncle Orson gave me a quick nod then tilted his chin toward the car. Neither said anything, but Orson still had his .45 in a two-handed ready grip. He followed Whilomina and me to the car, backing all the way.

"I suspect that Army officer took a big hit for you back there," Whilomina said as soon as Uncle Orson had the car rolling. She was seated with me in the rear.

"How do you mean?" I asked, looking back through the rear window. I could see nothing but weeds and battered trailers.

"You're not a cop anymore," Orson made it an angry pronouncement.

"How?" I wasn't really surprised and not as disappointed as I might have expected.

"DOJ has been putting pressure on the sheriff. Pressure they've been getting from other departments," Whilomina explained.

"What departments?"

"Defense. Homeland. State. Departments doesn't really sum it up very well. We'll simply say, the executive branch."

"The president?" That time I was surprised. Impressed actually. I was about to say so when Uncle Orson took a hard turn from the county blacktop onto a private farm road. "Where are you going," I asked gripping the back of his seat for stability. He had not slowed at all. In fact I think he sped up.

Without answering he twisted the wheel and shot through an open gate into wet pasture. The sedan was not built for off-road, but it dampened the irregularities of the rough field admirably.

"Who are we hiding from?" I asked.

"We're not entirely sure," Whilomina answered. "I only hope it is not from our own forces. I couldn't stand that."

"Is that possible?"

"A few days ago I would have said never. Now . . ."

Orson pushed the car from one field to another. We crossed over and along farm roads and bits of asphalt, twisting over crooked country. More than once he stopped to open gates. At one in particular, a soft gate of post and wire, I suddenly realized where I was.

"I'll get it," I told him as he stopped in front of the same gate Billy had brought me to just days before.

I unhooked the post and dragged the wire fencing aside. When the car was clear, I brought the gate back around and latched it carefully. Back in the car, I didn't say anything about why that gate or why I lingered. They didn't ask.

We didn't talk anymore until we were back at the dock.

Clare was there waiting for us in an idling truck. As we passed through the short downhill drive into the parking lot, he pulled across, blocking the road, and parked. I noticed when he got out of the truck that the old moonshiner carried an ancient M1. He walked slowly, keeping a careful eye out as we went up the long dock ramp.

The first thing I noticed inside the shop was that all the liquor was still absent. They didn't trust me not to get drunk. I wasn't sure if I was resentful or grateful. Too much of one and not enough of the other probably.

Once Clare joined us inside, Whilomina told me, "You need to know what this is all about."

"Rojava?" My question was also an answer.

She looked stunned for a second then nodded. "How did you know?"

"I don't. Not really." I sat at the table. Uncle Orson was there already with an opened bottle of Clare's homemade root beer. He and the bottle got the kind of look I usually reserve for ketchup on a hotdog. He ignored the rebuke in my face and pushed the bottle closer to me. "I want something stronger."

"I know," he answered. "Me too."

"You're going to keep me dry?"

"You can thank me for the root beer later."

"Katrina," Whilomina spoke my name gently. "What do you know?"

"Not as much as you, I'm sure." I took a mouthful from the bottle. You know that feeling of surprised disappointment you feel when you pick up the wrong drink? Somehow, despite my knowledge of the contents, there was another part of me, the drunk, expecting the amber satisfaction of an American lager.

My tongue and throat wanted to reject the liquid. The drunk screamed inside my head and the noise set spiders to dancing under my skin. I choked, but I got the root beer down. Where has your world gone when even a drink of soda pop feels like both a small penance and a bullet to the head?

To my credit, I only cried for a minute or two. To everyone else's—my uncle, Whilomina, Clare—they all came close and embraced me or touched my hands with no pressure for me to stop. Clare handed me a napkin to wipe my eyes and running nose.

Finally I said, "Tell me about Rojava. What was so important that my father had to die?"

Saying that was not an accusation in any way. But un-careful words are like bullets. Once loosed, there is no control. Whilomina looked for an instant like she'd been slapped. She recovered before I even recognized the look. I had to remind myself, she was hurting as badly as I was about him. And she carried the burden of one thought I didn't, *Why did the bullet miss me and take him?*

I opened my mouth to apologize.

Before any sound could come out Whilomina said, "Rojava is a piece of a puzzle. The other piece is the Kurdistan Autonomous Region of northern Iraq. Put the pieces together and you have an idea whose time, many powerful people and forces think, has come."

"A Kurdish state," I said.

"A nation," she corrected.

"How?"

"*How*—is startlingly easy. Between the Syrian civil war, our invasion of Iraq, and the rise of the Islamic State, there is an entire swath of ground with no working civil authority. All the Kurds need to do is declare it theirs and a nation is born."

"It can't be that easy."

She shook her head sadly. "You're right. Nothing is easy. Least of all this. They declare and face instant opposition from Turkey, Syria, Iraq, Iran, and Daesh."

"How could it possibly work?"

"The Kurds, particularly those of northern Syria, are politically committed to acceptance of ethnicity, religion, and gender equality." It was a statement that seemed, at first, to have nothing to do with the question I'd asked.

Then—"That's . . ." I couldn't finish the sentence or the thought. None of that represented any kind of world I was exposed to in the Middle East.

"Indeed." Whilomina seemed to be agreeing with thoughts that I could not even complete.

"What had been unthinkable a year ago, a separate, Kurdish nation, could be birthed and supported by a coalition of forces including us, Israel, most of the NATO nations, the Vatican, and even Russia. It's a shot at stability and a political reasonableness that the region hasn't seen since the map got jiggering after the First World War."

"As amazing as that is, how did it end up here in Missouri with mercenaries and murder?"

"I can answer part of that." Clare Bolin was sitting across from me. The hands that he'd held mine with earlier were under the edge of the table, hidden but nervous. Their fidgeting was given away by the motion of his arms. His eyes were turned down. Also hiding from me.

"Roscoe told me some of it." His confession was quiet. "I never put it together with what was happening here. It all seemed so removed." Clare looked up and at me then huffed out a snort that communicated disgust. "Who am I kidding? It sounded like bullshit, apple-pie-in-the-big-blue-sky dreaming."

"You and your brother are not the only ones guilty of dreaming," Whilomina said.

Just as she had a few moments before, I experienced a slap from words that turned out not to be aimed at me. It was her own dreaming that she spoke of not mine. The emotion covering the words was grief not the rancor I imagined.

I wondered if she was as angry as I was. *Is anyone?*

"Go on," I said to Clare.

"It started when Roscoe was an Army chaplain. He told me about cooperation between Sunni and Shia Muslims, Christian missionaries, and local Assyrian priests. Did you know there were so many religious sects living in the same area? Even Yezidi and Zoroaster communities. The thing was, all these religious people were talking. The only thing they really had in common was the desire to live and worship how they wanted. Maybe that's enough?"

"No," Whilomina answered him with absolute certainty. "Not in a war zone. They need weapons."

"The United States is giving them weapons?" I asked.

"Oh no." She shook her head in a tight, disappointed looking negative. "Turkey would never allow that. They're a NATO ally with military bases and airspace we need. The Assad government in Syria would fight it too. And they're allied with Russia. What government there is in Iraq, won't willingly give up territory or control either. They expect us to push out the Islamic State and leave the country just as it was under Saddam Hussein."

"Iran-Contra," I interjected.

"In this case, it's Peru-KDR."

"KDR?"

"Kurdish Democratic Republic. That's the dream."

"And we can't be seen supporting that dream because it might offend other friends," I filled in.

"That's the crux of it. The real pity is that it's as worthwhile a dream as that part of the world has had in a long time. A homeland for a people who have been stateless for a century. An island of tolerance in a sea of religious and ethnic differences. And a possible stabilizing buffer against Bashar al-Assad and ISIL."

"That's over there," I said. "Here, once again, the United States has gotten itself involved in morally dubious transactions, absolutely against our own laws, to sell weapons to one group and shunt the profits to another."

"That's right. It's the profits that got your father and I involved. They're sitting in a Pentagon slush fund. And I've got the money tied up with a congressional subpoena of records. We're going to get answers."

"But it's different this time, right?" Clare asked. "I mean the Kurds aren't Contras. And the end goal is something that could serve the whole world."

"What profit to a man, that he should gain the whole world and lose his soul?"

It was the first time Uncle Orson had spoken since he'd pushed root beer on me. It was a stunning contribution not only because it seemed so on target, but because I could never recall him making a religious reference in my life. He rose from the table and went to peer carefully out the front door. Orson startled us again by saying, "They're here."

At the mouth of the parking lot, three black SUV's were stacked up the ramp blocked by Clare's old truck. The improvised barrier didn't stop them more than a moment. A man jumped out of the passenger side of the lead vehicle and checked for keys in the truck. Finding nothing he waved the driver forward then stood aside. He kept a weapon ready and his gaze moving.

Easing the wheel over and the SUV forward, the driver brought the nose of his vehicle to touch the bed of Clare's truck at the back bumper. Once contact was made, he dropped the transmission into low and gunned it, nosing the old truck aside almost gently.

As soon as the road was clear the caravan darted into the lot then spread out. They stopped well apart from each other forming a rough semi-circle around the dock's gangway. All the doors on the front and rear vehicles opened to disgorge dangerous-looking men. They all wore black tactical gear and carried automatic weapons. The middle SUV sat idling, motionless for a long moment before the front doors opened. First out was the passenger, General Massoud Masum. He stared up at the dock but didn't move from behind his open door. The driver got out and without hesitation or any looking around, strode toward the gangway. Timothy Givens.

Both Orson and Clare were ready to shoot him down before he had a chance to set a foot on the ramp. Whilomina warned against it although without much force. I asked them to wait on the shooting. I had the feeling he wanted to talk to me. I knew I wanted to talk to him.

"But," I warned them, "don't take your aim off of him."

I pushed through the shop door as Givens marched up the gangway.

"That's far enough," I told him at the halfway point. "What do you want here?"

"You're a surprising one," he said, trying hard to keep it light. His hands remained open and spread out from his body. "I would have never believed you could get Keene on your side."

"I was wrong about you two from the start."

"How's that?"

"I had you pegged as the smart one."

His laugh was almost genuine. He sounded like a man who was trying to keep a good face on a small problem. It made me dislike him even more.

Givens raised his hands again, showing me the empty palms as if he could feel my renewed animosity. "That's yet to be seen, isn't it? Keene is already on his way back to CID, HQ. He has a lot of explaining to do."

"Don't we all?"

He laughed that same, almost real, almost good-natured laugh again. "That's it, isn't it? Do things right and who cares. One little thing goes bad—there's a world of explaining to do."

"What's wrong, Givens?" I nodded in the direction of Massoud who was staring bullets in my direction. "Get a spanking from your sugar daddy down there?"

He didn't like that. I could hear it in the laugh again. That time it was a cold, sneering sound. The same sound echoed when he said, "The girls are safe. You accomplished that much." The way he said it, the contempt in the tone and the flat look in his face said, I'd accomplished nothing in his estimation.

"How do I know that?"

"It was stupid really. Nothing that should have ever happened in the middle of"—Givens shrugged and rolled his head like he was trying to encompass the whole world in a gesture—"bigger things."

"I guess we all decide what's big in our own eyes."

"That's such a bitch thing to say." He waited for a reaction that I didn't give. "Anyway, Keene killed Banjo. And you want to talk about stupid—Banjo? What the fuck? Who goes around letting the world call them, Banjo? And anyway, the case stops there. Connor—Banjo—Watson was acting alone to traffic the girls whom Reverend Roscoe Bolin, in good faith, and with the most"—he sneered again—"*Christian* intentions, saved from the poverty and violence of their homeland."

"Is that a press release?"

"Close. It'll be the official report."

"Who's going to buy that?"

"Everyone who needs to."

"So what's the truth?" I opened my hands and held them both as if I was weighing out two invisible quantities. "Were you selling girls to fund the nation building? Or was the Reverend doing it to fund the church building?"

"Say now, Hurricane." He grinned like a great thought had just come to him and he was dying to share. "You remember that movie a few years back? Everyone saw it. Seemed to be the only thing people talked about for the whole year. You know the one—with the slow guy and the box of chocolates? Well he got it wrong. It's not *life* that's like a box of chocolates. It's truth. You know—you reach in and take the one that tastes best. Life? Well that keeps going on and doing its own thing."

I looked out at the vehicles and armed men. Then out at the lake that I loved so much. "Situational morality from a spook," I said before turning back to look at Givens. "What a surprise."

"Smug, self-righteousness from a cop. The world is full of surprises. But no one cares. Things happen. Things are complicated. What's important to most of us is what cash is coming our way and how can we feed little junior, son of a bitch. And that's fine. It makes my job easier."

"And what exactly is your job here?"

"I serve my country."

He must have seen the look on my face as soon as he said it. He must have read the words forming on my lips or the fire that bloomed in my chest, because he laughed again. That time it was a machine sound. It had no heat. It carried no chill. The sound was mirthless and lifeless and I thought for the first time that I was seeing the true man.

"Don't give me that look, Hurricane," he said once he swallowed away the laughing sound. "I serve. I sacrifice. *I. Do.* When people like you fail or cry or run to daddy, I do the dirty work that keeps the taps flowing for my country."

From behind me, I had the sense that Orson's finger had tightened slightly on a trigger. Any more and Givens would be dead. If my uncle could beat me to it. I suddenly realized that my hand was all but strangling the grip of my pistol.

"We're working beyond the law here, aren't we?" I asked him quietly. "Your boys aren't going to the police no matter what happens."

"You're getting it now."

"But you understand—if my badge doesn't protect me, it doesn't protect you."

"You don't have a badge anymore. No badge. No uniform. No daddy."

It's possible he believed that I wouldn't do anything with guns pointed at me. Possible but foolish. He didn't have time to react when I pulled the pistol already in my hand. I imagine that he had some sense of satisfaction at having provoked me. I imagine also that he pictured me standing with my gun aimed at him while he talked and taunted some more.

Whatever Givens expected it wasn't the hard contact of my pistol barrel with the side of his face. It hit his right temple above the orbit bone gashing as it passed and turning his head to the left. I know he didn't expect what happened next. I followed through, letting the arc of my swing die low on my left side then pulled back, leading with the gun butt and striking it right on the bridge of his nose.

He was tough. His knees trembled and got a bit rubbery but Givens didn't go down. He should have. Instead he shouted, a sound of pain and anger without words. He still thought he had some control.

I took that belief away when I stopped his cry with the point of my weapon. It clacked against his teeth as I jammed it into his gaping mouth. That was the moment he understood.

I pushed harder, choking him on the barrel.

He had the sense not to fight or pull away. His legs, wanted to crumble under him but his brain fought back. I could see the struggle in his eyes and I enjoyed it.

"You want to run to your daddy?" I asked.

Givens didn't answer.

"Let me tell you a little something." My voice was too small to carry the rage with which it had been burdened and so had faded to a ragged whisper. "No one ever served a nation by facilitating its crimes. And you be careful whose experience you belittle." I rattled the gun in his mouth like ringing a bell. "Because there is still room for you to learn exactly what I went through in service to my country."

I took a deep, slow breath. The focus of my eyes widened out, so I was able to see more than Givens' fearful eyes. Massoud was walking up the gangway with his hands raised.

Chapter 20

The front sight of my 9mm took two teeth with it when I pulled the barrel from Timothy Givens' mouth. With his hand cupped over his gushing mouth, he crumpled and finally fell to his knees as I turned the weapon on Massoud Masum.

"General," I said.

The wind chose that moment to return. It brushed past me on its way to the shore whipping my hair. Rain was once again carried on air that was warmer than expected.

"Let Mr. Givens go," he said in that surprising American accent. "I believe your true concerns are with me."

"I believe that too." I looked down, tempted to spit. I didn't. I'm at least that much a lady. "I never said he couldn't go. Givens got caught up in the conversation, that's all."

Massoud nudged Givens with the toe of an expensive-looking shoe. "Go back to the cars."

Givens spit blood on the gangway. Even from the floor and dripping from the mouth, he managed to look surly, holding up a finger to put the world on hold as he sputtered out another stream of red.

Massoud toed him again. That time instead of waving the finger around Givens turned to spit into the lake. Bad timing or it wasn't his day. The wind surged again blowing the stringy mess back into his face.

I wanted to laugh. If he hadn't beat me to it, I might have. It was that same, lifeless sawing of sound he'd produced before. That was the real Timothy Givens. I knew it then.

He stopped and shook his head as if he was the only one in on a joke. Then he dropped and reached into the lake and washed his face with the cold, green water. Without another word or look at either of us, he rose back to his feet and walked away.

It wasn't until Givens had reached the SUV that I returned my gaze to Massoud. I got the impression that he'd never taken his eyes from me.

"This is a dangerous point in history," he said, still sounding more like Harvard than Red Guard.

"History is nothing but dangerous times," I gave back.

He shook his head. "No. Not times. Places. Events. *Sides*. The times simply are history."

"Why do I get the feeling that you're trying to say something more?"

He stroked his mustache like a silent movie villain while looking me over as if considering a used car.

"You are an interesting—" Massoud shook his head behind the fingers on his mustache then used the same fingers to point at me. "No. Remarkable. You are a remarkable woman. The sobriquet applies. *Hurricane*. You remind me of the Kurdish women. They fight. There are many women in the Kurdish Defense Forces, did you know that?"

I didn't. Not that I was going to respond. I wanted him talking, not a conversation.

"They are treated with respect, fighting alongside men for the same cause." He touched his mustache again, then he said. "Not like your story."

"Careful," I warned. That was when I noticed that the pistol was still in my hand. I'd been so unaware of it I had to tap my finger to reassure myself it was outside the trigger guard. As I reseated the weapon in its holster, I reminded Massoud, "Remember what happened to Givens when he tried to provoke me."

"He was clumsy, a butcher knife, something that cuts through bone and sinew. The delicate work is done by scalpel."

"You sound like Lex Luthor. Did your commission come with a super villain handbook?"

"And you sound like a petulant child." He slapped the words at me. "A girl who can't get her way kicking out and screaming at things you don't understand. You are selfish with no real understanding that the world does not revolve around you."

"Are you going to tell me it revolves around you?"

"It revolves no matter who is in the center. We are irrelevant. Only the things we build are important and last."

"A nation?"

"A people."

"And what do I have to do with it?"

Massoud laughed. Everything about it was the polar opposite of Givens' dead amusement. The general barked a loud guffaw, all round edges and surprise. Then, as quickly as it had burst forth, he sucked it back in with an audible gasp. Delight remained in his eyes as he said, "Nothing."

That caught me off guard and I was forced to think about what he'd admonished—*the world does not revolve around me.*

"Then what . . . ?"

"Disorienting isn't it? When one finds themselves a spear carrier in their own play." He laughed again enjoying my confusion. "You stumbled into something." Again he lifted the finger and pointed at me before putting a hand within his jacket.

As he moved I reached to put a ready hand on my pistol.

Massoud nodded and slowed his movements. When his hand came out from his jacket pocket it held a pint of whiskey. "You could have staggered," he continued. "But you showed amazing restraint. Believe me, it is not a quality you are known for."

"You." I understood then that he'd been the one leaving the temptations in my path. If not his actual hand, he was choreographing.

"Not me," he said. "Always you." With a quick twist he cracked the seal on the bottle and held it open under his nose. He smiled from behind the glass and his eyes danced, black lights in a dark face, taunting.

"Put it away," I told him.

He set the bottle on the handrail and the cap beside it. Even in the rising wind I could smell the rich liquid. It settled into my chest like an old friend—my father's cologne—the lake at night. I was tempted.

I touched the scar at my eye. It was my past and a talisman. Somewhere between memory and need, I found a bit of strength. When I lifted the bottle, the warm wind rushed, whipping little, lapping tongues up in the lake. I poured the whiskey into the water. "You never understood me."

Massoud nodded, the humor still in his eyes. "Apparently," he agreed. "As I said though, it is not about you. Your involvement was all an accident, all errors without comedy. Who knew that faggot, Sergeant Boone, was going to get himself killed and drag us all into his impure hell? Fish eggs and faggots. Useless girls and a man who calls himself Banjo. You. And a mere captain. These are the small things. Small people. But even small matches too close to the fuel tank can make a big fire."

"You're forgetting my father, and the congresswoman."

"No. I'm not. If you were a match they were the gasoline. They matter. She is an adversary. You are a pothole."

"I'm the one you're here talking to."

He burst again with that laughter that bristled with secret knowledge. "Clearly, failure to understand is a defect we both share." He turned and looked at the still-running center SUV.

Givens was standing beside the closed rear doors. It was impossible to miss him. Even through the gloom and bluster the smear of blood still showed on his face. He raised a hand and slapped the roof of the vehicle. The far door opened and Reverend Bolin stepped out.

Behind me the shop door opened. Clare was trying to get out.

"Don't, Clare." I blocked his way.

"They have my brother."

Massoud's laugh turned vicious. Then he said, "No." He turned to look down at the car again. "But we have him."

I followed the gaze in time to see Givens with the second rear door open. He reached inside and jerked out a bound man, with duct tape over his eyes and mouth.

It was Billy.

It was the Reverend Roscoe Bolin who moved next. He marched around the vehicle and up the gangway with the rising wind blowing his silver hair into a shimmer of tarnished light.

"You should go inside," I told Clare without taking my sight from his brother.

"I want to talk to him."

"I know you do. But I don't think you want to hear what he has to say right now."

Massoud stood with his back to Roscoe and looking over my shoulder. At first I assumed he was looking at Clare. But he smiled and tilted his head in a small bow. I heard Whilomina speaking softly to Clare and I heard the door open, then close again as she drew him back inside.

Once more, Massoud shifted his eyes to mine. "So you see?" he asked. "You are not the one to whom I am speaking, at all. I was talking through you, not to you."

Roscoe stopped his march behind the other man's shoulder. Regardless of what the general had said a few moments ago about being irrelevant, history, and nation building, it was obvious, even before he said a word, that Reverend Bolin was the true believer. His disturbing eyes, couldn't contain the fire that blazed behind them. The air that had brought chop to the lake, swirled around him seeming to touch only his hair.

"Hurricane," he said.

I wasn't sure if it was my nickname or a pronouncement of impending storm.

Before I could say anything, Massoud squared his shoulders and stroked his mustache as he projected his voice, through me, to Whilomina waiting within the shop. "If action is not taken, there will be hearings. The money promised to my nation will languish and the hope of a people will be lost to committees. That is a tragedy I cannot suffer for the *conscience* of *Americans*."

It was impossible to gauge if he put more disgust into the word conscience or Americans. I expected more, but, abruptly, Massoud turned and slipped past Roscoe heading back down the ramp.

"Is that how you feel, Reverend?" I asked Roscoe.

"Judgment hangs easily off your shoulders, Katrina. But some things are worth fighting for."

That time I struck with an empty hand. When I did, the shards of color in Roscoe's eyes flashed with internal lighting. He said nothing.

"People who don't fight find it easy to talk about what's worth the sacrifice of others." I looked past his shoulder and watched Billy. He was bloody and teetering on his feet. "But there *is* going to be a fight."

"No, there won't. At least not for you. That's why the deputy is still with them. He'll remain safe but in their care until the funds marked for the cause are released."

"And why are you here telling me?"

"I want you to understand."

"Oh I do."

"You don't. You're angry. You see the battle but don't see the ending or the result."

"I see murder, slavery of girls, and kidnapping of a cop."

"I had no part in what was happening to those young women."

"Children," I corrected.

"Refugees from war—whom I brought to peace."

"You abandoned them to predators."

"I acted in faith that the girls would be cared for."

"You're lying." I said it to his glaring face. "On behalf of liars. Turn around and look."

Roscoe turned his head. Givens was forcing Billy back into the SUV.

"Those men are criminals. Do you really believe they will release Billy when they don't need him anymore?"

"Criminals?" The question came as a bellowed refutation, as though the suggestion itself was suspect. "Crimes." He all but shouted, spreading his arms as if at the pulpit. Around him, the air charged. Above, the clouds lowered. Dark tendrils, like living mist, reached for the tops of hills. Roscoe whipped out his arms again. "You speak about infractions of man's law. I endeavor to uphold the desire of God. Ending a war for millions. Think of it. Imagine the suffering that will end. Then complain to me about petty crimes."

It was a Cecil B. DeMille moment. I wasn't drawn in. "So," I asked in soft counter to his bluster. "You wonder, would I sacrifice one girl to end a war that hurts a million?"

"That's the question, Hurricane."

"I thought some things were worth fighting for."

"Smart words will not wrench you from the jaws of the devil. And make no mistake, the devil is in the questions."

"How's *no* for a smart word?" I asked him staring right into those flashing eyes. "I wouldn't take the life of someone innocent to stop your war. I would pick up a weapon and fight."

"Your morality is too poor a coat for the Lord to wear. His plans are not those of men."

"Maybe so. But I don't claim to speak for him and my morality is one I can live with. I doubt you can say the same when the accounts come due."

"We'll see, Hurricane. Perhaps you will come see me in the new Kurdistan one day, and we can talk about it again."

"How about if we make it a little sooner, like when I walk into your tent show and drag you out in cuffs?"

"You'll never get in. Outside, your own department will stand against you. Inside, there are men who already hold a pretty firm grudge against you. You would be a fool to try. And tomorrow, we'll be gone."

"Then there's only one thing left to do."

The Reverend's smile was part surprise and part victory. "Are you suggesting prayer?"

"I'm saying, have a talk with your brother."

I turned then opened the door. Clare was waiting. I've never seen a man look so broken or disappointed in my life.

He stood aside to let me through and I heard him say, "I don't have words to tell you how ashamed I am." Then the door closed.

The moody gloom of the day was draining quickly into a twilight full of threat and darkness. I'll never be able to say if what I was feeling was about the weather or the situation. They seemed tied together as if one was a distant echo of the other, both amplifying the darkness carried within the other. I watched from behind a display of fishing lures in the window as the SUVs careened up the short road and away.

"I'm sorry, Clare," Uncle Orson tried to console his friend.

"I never expected something like this from him. Roscoe was always the believer." Clare Bolin spoke into the floor, hiding his face and his mourning. I suspected that the brother in his memory was as dead as my father was to me. Change can be a kind of death. Maybe that's why we fear it so much.

"So what are we going to do?" Orson asked with a hand still resting on Clare's shoulder.

"Nothing." The answer came from Whilomina. "We wouldn't do anything even if they weren't holding the deputy."

"Billy," I reminded her. "His name is William Loraine Blevins. Everyone calls him Billy and no one has ever made fun of his middle name. He's one of the good ones."

"I understand, dear. And we will fix this. But I'll do it in Washington."

"That'll be too late for Billy." It wasn't an argument. I said it simply as a statement of fact, more to be understood than to be considered in her plans.

My plans were different.

"Katrina . . ." Whilomina said my name carefully, like it might be a spark in a gas station. "What are you going to do?"

I went over to the old television on the wall behind the counter and turned it on.

"I'm going to check the weather." The set was an old tube type, very old. It still had dials to turn and said ZENITH on the front. As it hissed and the picture jittered into shape I asked my uncle, "Can you take Whilomina back to Nixa?"

"I can," he answered making his suspicions clear. "Why?"

"Yes, why?" Whilomina added.

On the television a picture popped into view. I twisted the dial around the few local channels until I found what I needed. One thing you can always count on in the Midwest, local TV tripping over itself to be the first with a bad weather report. "That." I pointed at the screen. The radar map showed a cycle of morphing blobs that looked to be creeping toward Taney County. "And Daddy."

"Your father?" Whilomina looked like she had been caught at something. All the activity had distracted her from the grief she'd been feeling and she was suddenly feeling guilty about it.

"The arrangements you were making for him. I wouldn't know where to begin." It was a lie. One I hoped she wouldn't catch. I'd made arrangements for Nelson not so very long ago. I was uncomfortably familiar with the routine of death. Before she could think it through I went on. "And your work. You have to get something in motion to slow down the delivery of the cash to Massoud. We need time to stop them."

"Stop them and save your friend." Whilomina said as if I needed reminding.

"Yes. I want them stopped and I want Billy safe. He'd do it for me."

Chapter 21

Uncle Orson gave me looks that were both knowing and accusatory as he helped Whilomina gather her things for the drive north. He understood that I needed her gone and out of the way so I could do what I needed. He even understood that it was for her as much as me. A member of congress had no business in the mess I was about to kick up. He didn't understand why I was sending him away as well. Orson needed to bring some hurt for the sake of his brother every bit as much as I needed to do it for my father. The difference was, he wasn't thinking about failure. I was. It would be impossible for me to survive losing him so close to Daddy.

They were selfish thoughts, I know. Had I bothered to think about it, I would have known that losing me would have devastated him. My anger and my ego were such that losing my own life was not even a consideration. At least not one I allowed to myself to acknowledge. That doesn't mean I was unaware of the possibility. The refusal was to care. Had I let myself think about the risk to myself, I would have had to accept that there was more than a little wishing to go rest between my husband and my father.

"Clare," I called him over as Uncle Orson and Whilomina packed up. "I need you to do something for me."

When they were ready to leave and I walked out with Whilomina and Orson, she asked where Clare was. She seemed to buy it when I said he had things at home to attend to if there was a storm coming.

"I've never been in a tornado storm before." Whilomina wrapped her arms around herself against the still rising wind.

The air was a strange mix, at one point chilled then a moment later, warm. At least it was warm in comparison. Rain trotted out in streaks following the line of gusts. When the wind died, so did the spray of water.

"I'll make sure you're not in one this time," Uncle Orson told her. To me, he leaned in and whispered, "Be careful."

"Nothing to be careful about," I told him. "I'll go home and watch the weather. If it gets bad I'll go for the cellar."

"That's not what I mean," he said and he looked hurt to have to say it. "You'll need me."

"Not this time," I told him trying to sell it with a weak smile. "God grant me the serenity to change the things I can . . ."

"And the serenity to accept bullshit when I hear it."

"Stop it." It was Whilomina. She had tears in her eyes but a straight and strong back. "I don't care what either one of you thinks you need to do." It was clear she hadn't been fooled by any of the pretense. "I can drive myself." She stepped forward opening her arms to pull us both into her embrace. "You're all the family I have now. I don't want to lose anymore."

We stood together for a moment before the clutch had its effect on me and I melted into the hug. Orson's big arms encircled us both. The warmth and closeness was the best kind of prayer.

It was too short when Whilomina let go and said, "Take care of each other. Whatever you think you're doing. I'll do my part and we'll make the bastards pay."

That was the moment I truly knew what my father had loved about her and I loved it too.

She drove away leaving me and Uncle Orson standing in the parking lot at the bottom of the gangway. Her car became nothing more than moving headlights quickly in the stirring mire of the weather. The front was approaching quickly. It was pushing air ahead of it like the pressure wave off the bow of an immense ship. The high clouds were invisible but the low ones, the line of snarling vapor was lit from below by the lights from Branson and from within by clashes of lightning.

"Give me a second to get armed," Uncle Orson said before heading up the gangway and leaving me alone.

Solitude in a rising storm seemed to be a metaphor for my life. It was the first time that I'd been alone to my own thoughts since waking up that morning with the bottle in my hands. That had been a million years before. I realized that being alone was overrated. I touched the scar at my eye and for a moment felt grit in the wind that was only in my memory.

The first thunder rumbled. It was distant but still vibrated my chest. Surprisingly it was soothing. It made me think of the recent sensations of a presence in my life. I suppose thinking about the presence in your life is a form of feeling that presence. I didn't know and I wasn't trying to sort it out. I was thinking about two men—Nelson and Billy. For a fraction of a second I felt guilty knowing I was thinking of them rather than my father. Just a fraction—because he was the one who always pushed me to life and living.

No. I was thinking about Nelson and Billy and I was not allowing any guilt about any of it. There was something there. Something greater than my fear and anger. Greater maybe than that moment in the dirt of Iraq.

A shimmer of yellow caught my eye and I looked skyward. The clouds looked to me like a giant jar of lightning bugs like those from my childhood.

Change.

The thought came to me not in a flash of light, but in a creeping finger of wind that stroked over my scar just as I had done a moment before.

That was what I was really thinking about. The storm. Not the weather but the storm, the turmoil of my life. If I was honest with myself, I would admit that in a normal life I would not have been married to Nelson. He was rich and vibrant with life. I was a cop defined by the dun color of desert dust. I think I would have loved him given the chance, but we had met when he was already dying and I was wrapped in my own pain and alcoholism. If I was going to love him it had to be quickly and passionately. Could years have sustained that?

And Billy? I've been drawn to him and fighting the feeling for a long time. Why have I fought? Could it be that I loved Nelson because, no matter the pain involved, it required no change in me? In my life perhaps, but not in my living. If I give in to my desire for Billy—that would change everything.

Lighting flashed. That time it was a crackling bolt that crashed instantly.

And in between the two men was the storm.

Uncle Orson started tromping down the gangway carrying an M14 and a metal ammo box.

One storm at a time.

First we had gone to pick up my truck, then together we'd crossed some back roads and through a field to get to a bald patch of wild meadow surrounded by tangled woods. Behind the screen of trees and vines we found two other vehicles. One was Clare's old truck, the recent damage from serving as our gate still showed as the only bits of bright metal on it. The other was the little car driven by Riley Yates.

"It's not a fit night for man nor beast," Riley said as we walked over after parking.

"Nor for any of the rest of us," Uncle Orson said. "Why is the fifth estate joining us?"

"I had the same question. Clare said it was important. And that no matter what, I wouldn't regret being here."

"He's right," I said. "I asked him to bring you so the story gets told."

"What story's that?" He asked.

I pointed over to my truck and said, "The one I'm about to tell you."

Even though he had a tape recorder Riley took notes on a little pad in a tight, fast script I doubted anyone else could read. He asked surprisingly few questions and those he did ask were mostly to clarify something. Riley listened as I told the story of the past week leaving nothing out. I made sure to emphasize the DOJ injunction against the sheriff's office keeping them from acting and that I was no longer a part of the department. Everything I did from that point on I did as a private citizen. The last thing I wanted was to cause problems for the Sheriff Benson or the SO.

"Why tell me all this?" Riley asked after almost half an hour of my narration.

"I won't let them win," I said. "If a nation—our nation—is going to stand for anything, it has to live by its own laws."

"Fair enough," he answered. "But why out here—in a storm? And what makes you think any story I write can make a difference?"

"Difference or not," I said looking out the window at the rush of leaves in a gust of wind that shook the truck. "Tell the whole story."

"The whole story? Is there something you haven't told me?"

"It hasn't ended yet."

Out of the woods and into my burning headlights came Clare. He was carrying the old M1. I rolled down the window as he approached. Once the glass was down, a small typhoon of wind and mist filled the cab.

"It's happening," Clare shouted against the currents. "Just like you said, the sheriff's deputies and the city cops are all being called off for storm patrols. The clouds are lowering more, too. When the lighting flashes to the south, it shows a deep green sky."

I nodded thanks then put up the window. Riley was still writing in his pad. I started the engine before leaning over past Riley to open his door.

"You should get out of here or become part of the story. Some of the other reporters are still at the tent show. I think there will be plenty of witnesses."

As he climbed out I shifted the big truck into four-wheel drive and considered for a second dropping the transmission into low. There was no road where I was going. The extra power could help me ease through the overgrowth.

Screw it, I decided. *Nothing about this is going to be easy.*

I killed the headlights, leaving only the running lights, and hit the gas. The GMC slung four muddy rooster tails from the tires as it shot from the meadow into the brush. I bumped into a shallow ravine then back out as I gained speed. Small trees bent under the frame of the truck. Larger ones broke. Ropes of grape vine caught the grill and bumper. They snapped then coiled like snakes in a fire before dragging under the tires.

As soon as I could see some lights through the foliage I switched off my own. The last hundred feet was a maze of dark trunks in a dark night, but I wasn't trying to find my way through. I was knocking down the walls.

Growling like a demon snarling at the storm, the working truck's powerful engine shot me through the last of the dense brush. Between the final trees and the pasture that held the Starry Night Traveling Salvation Show was a four-strand barbed wire fence.

I went through one old post. Several more broke away from the drag of the steel wires that sunk rusted teeth into the body of my truck. Finally everything gave way and my path through the pasture was smooth compared to the trek through the woods.

From the fence to the tents of the show was about two hundred yards—two football fields. Halfway through, the storm broke. There was a flashing blast of lighting and a sound thousands of times louder than the cracking of trees under my truck. Immediately after the sound faded, the rain fell. It was a colorless sheet of water thicker than Irish melancholy. The drops banged the metal hood in an impossibly fast cadence that more than doubled when the hail added in.

I turned my lights back on. It didn't matter at that point. No one would be looking for me. When I did, I saw two sets of lights behind me come to life. Orson and Clare were following.

I got close enough to see people within the lights of the main tent. They were scrambling to ropes and poles. Some were running away. Out in the darkness I noticed the headlights of cars headed across the hail-speckled grass aiming for the roadway. There must have been some faithful stragglers who didn't believe until the last moment God would rain on their revival.

When I got closer, I could see a knot of people on the stage at the far end of the tent. They looked to be having a party.

That was something I'd seen before. People, with no idea what a storm like this could bring, hoping to see a tornado in person. Sure enough I could see bottles in hands raised in salute. A couple of people ran to the flapping edges of the tent to look out at the sky, then back in to the party dripping wet.

I wasn't expected. Why would I be? I'd been warned and there was a storm raging. They must have seen my lights headed toward the entrance. I was close enough then I could see the trucks and RVs parked around the tent. There was still one satellite truck that had not been called away for storm coverage. Around it were nervous-looking engineers and celebrating reporters.

In a moment they'll have something to celebrate.

Then I hit the brakes. They grabbed the discs but the locked wheels kept sliding on the wet grass carrying me right into the tent.

The stunned paralysis of the contract men lasted only until the truck came to a stop and I stepped out.

Like roaches scattering when the lights come on, they ran for their guns or to put distance between themselves and the men at the center of the stage. Reverend Roscoe Bolin and General Massoud Masum.

I raised my weapon and pointed it at Massoud. In the time it took to clear the holster and aim, the hail then the rain stopped its patter on the canvas. In the sudden quiet I screamed, "Where is he?" My rage was darker than the storm.

The Reverend moved first, blocking my line of fire. As he advanced he lifted his arms with the great cross behind him.

"You can't do this here."

I didn't fire the first shot. It came from outside and it was a single round not automatic fire. Either Clare or Uncle Orson were covering me. I wasn't the only one who read the sound. Most of the contractors I could see turned to the threat in their rear and began firing. The ones who didn't regretted it. One lifted his weapon in my direction. Before I could take cover or sight my weapon, his head popped open in a red splash.

Massoud darted out from behind the Reverend, leaping from the stage then bolting for an open flap. I shot as he ran and missed.

My gunfire attracted another of the mercenaries. Three rounds passed so close, one through my hair, that the hornet *whiz* of their passing tracked heat on my skin. His next three rounds went through the peak of the tent roof and out into the night as he fell with a hole in his throat.

"The storm," Reverend Bolin shouted out into the house of violence. "When the disciples went out on the Sea of Galilee, the storm raged and they despaired, calling for their master to save them. Jesus appeared calming the waters."

"I know this one," I called back to him as I went carefully to the open flap through which Massoud had gone. "This is where Jesus admonishes them for having too little faith."

"Knowing is not the same as understanding, Katrina."

"Preaching to the choir," I told him as I stepped out into the steady rain and settled wind. All the hairs on my body stood straight up. It's the calm that tells you to worry. As long as the wind howls and the rain blasts, it is a storm. When the sky calms and you feel your skin crawl, you know hell is coming.

I ran to the big RV. Its door was standing open with bright yellow light pouring from it. Automatic fire started chewing the ground in front of me leading, and walking back as I ducked and rolled. I fired two rounds of suppressing fire at where the muzzle flashes had been then ran for the open door.

I made it in as gunfire collapsed the front tire.

The RV was one of those big rolling houses that cost more than most people's regular home. Inside it was fitted with plush chairs, and HD television and a better kitchen than I've ever cooked in. Way in the back, Billy was bound by silver tape and seated in a chair. His mouth and eyes were still covered by the duct tape as well. I was unable to keep myself from imagining what he might be seeing in his darkness.

"Come on in," a voice from inside invited. It was Silas Boone.

"I'd kind of hoped you were dead," I said.

He cackled as if that was the funniest thing he'd heard in a long time. "Ya know," he said. "I hoped the same thing about you, Hurricane. You can come in. My gun ain't even pointed at you. I'm sure you know where I'm aiming."

"I do." Silas and I were separated by a partition that held mechanical and hydraulic equipment to push out the entire side of the vehicle. He was in that cove of space. From where I was crouched in the doorway, I could see him clearly reflected in one of the big tinted windows. Silas was reclining on a couch propped on one arm and aiming at Billy.

"What's the matter?" he asked me still focusing on Billy. "Cat got your tongue?" Then he cackled again sounding like a demented hen laying a square egg. "I bet a bull dyke bitch like you likes a little kitty on her tongue." He laughed harder.

"That's why your cousin is dead." I taunted. "You know he was fishing to get away from you and all your hateful crap."

"He was a fag."

I could see Silas moving higher up on the couch. The effort was obviously painful. Stretched on after him was his lifeless leg wrapped in thick bandages.

"He wouldn't give up smokin' the bone so why should I care what happened? And it don't matter. We got the Russian that killed him."

"Russian didn't kill him. You got the wrong guy. Givens and Massoud let you think it was the Russian. Tried to make me believe it. They didn't care about him any more than you. They wanted the investigation to go away. They sent Dewey to kill the congresswoman but everything went bad when Gagarin showed up. Dewey believed the Russian killed Daniel and Sartaña and lost what little control he had."

"It was you shot the boy."

"I shot him. But they sent him to get shot. Givens never would have left him alive."

"Girl," he shouted to the ceiling. Then in a normal voice, still staring at Billy, Silas asked, "You tryin' to appeal to my family side?"

"Obviously it isn't working. So how about I appeal to your self-interest? Toss your weapon out and I'll let you get out of here alive. I can't promise you'll walk out after the last time we met."

"Oh yeah, you're a funny woman all right. Shoot me in the knee. My bad knee. I'll never walk again."

"They're doing amazing things with prosthetics these days. Or put up a fight. I'll take the other one and you can get some of those space age running things. Maybe get into the Olympics."

"You get off on talking tough like a man?"

"One of us has to." I actually made myself chuckle with that. "Listen, I can keep outsmarting you all night, but I don't want to be in here when the wind starts howling. Why don't you come out and live through this?"

His answer was a gunshot that ripped a hole through the window I'd been watching him through. In the enclosed space the sound was a brutal kick in the eardrums that sent my senses into a void. I shook my head with my hands cupped over my ears, opening then closing my mouth hoping to pop some life back into them. The first thing to come back was a squealing tone then a rush of sound like waves against rocks that kept getting louder.

It wasn't waves and it wasn't the after effects of the gunfire either. The sound built like an onrushing freight train and the RV began to teeter then really shake.

Tornado.

Chapter 22

As the RV trembled in the wind I heard Billy screaming through the tape over his mouth. At first I thought it was panic. When I looked I saw that he was jerking his head to his left and the screaming was one muffled word. It sounded like *ow-un*.

Down.

He was telling me he was going for the floor.

"Go," I shouted and he did.

"What the hell?" Silas hollered.

It wasn't clear if he was reacting to Billy falling or me standing up and rushing into the unsteady cabin. He fired at Billy and missed, the bullet tracking high as he fell to the carpet.

I didn't miss Silas. I didn't wound him either.

By the time I got my hands on Billy the trembling of the RV felt like an earthquake. Instead of lifting him up. I was kicked to the floor right on top of him. Then everything moved at a strange angle and crashed back to level with a howling scream of wind and rending metal.

We had to get out. If the RV went over we would be like a couple of shoes in a dryer. The lights flickered and the huge vehicle teetered again. I jumped to my unsteady feet and pulled Billy up after me. When I jerked his arm to make him follow, he fell. His ankles were bound. I helped him up again then knelt at his feet. My teeth were the only tools I had to tear through the duct tape.

With a hand on his T-shirt collar I pulled and he ran after me. We jumped from the RV as it rolled away behind us. We ran. There is no telling where we were going or even how long we remained upright. Anything I could see was distorted by movement. Everything was shaking, trembling, swirling. Streaks, mostly colorless runs of gray sliced through black. All the while, the freight train of sound, huffed and squealed. It was an avalanche of sensation.

We fell. There was no place to run so I pressed Billy into the mud and grass covering him with my body.

I don't know if he heard me, but as we huddled in the rage of wind, I kept telling him, "Everything will be all right."

Once before in my life I had hunkered under a wall as wind whipped the dust of eternity over me. That time I was alone in my growing grave.

With Billy under me I wasn't as fearful. It was dirt and wind, it was all the swirling loss of my life. But it wasn't alone.

Everything stopped.

It was as if we were dropped into a thick sack of wet darkness and silence. When I finally looked up, the feeble light from three still burning bulbs illuminated what was left of the stage. The great cross was fallen. It reclined on its side with one arm still raised. Draped over the long end, was the black-clad body of Roscoe Bolin.

The sight, and the silence, made me think, *this is what the prophets felt when God's voice went quiet.*

I didn't think such big thoughts for long.

Billy said something from under the tape and I was pretty sure it was *Get this tape off.* So I worked it as gently as possible from his mouth.

He gasped, gulping long breaths of air before he finally said, "What the hell was that?"

"Tornado," I answered.

Then Billy Blevins kissed me. It was a good kiss too, happy and grateful, and full of life. I let it go on as long as he wanted. Honestly, I was a bit disappointed when he broke it to say, "Get this tape off my eyes and free my arms."

The tape was in his hair and eyebrows so I didn't pull it all away. I tore it off his nose and eyes. There was no point in tackling his arms without a knife so he stayed bound up as I helped him up one more time.

The first movement we saw was actually a news crew, two men with a camera stalking through the remains of canvas and stage lights and the bodies of dead men with bullet holes.

"What happened?" Billy asked and the question was too big to answer.

"It's a long story," was all I could say.

Someone moaned loudly and black moved in the light. It was Roscoe. He was unfolding himself from the cross and standing on shaky legs.

The video crew caught the movement as well and rushed into the space the main tent had occupied and focused on the Reverend. He ignored them pointing his finger at me.

"You." he accused with the John Brown light in his eyes. "I blame you."

The camera followed his accusation. Is it vanity that I tried smoothing my hair?

"No more blame." The voice from beyond the circle of light was equally weighty. Clarence Bolin stepped out of the night. "Unless you point that finger at yourself."

The camera turned to Clare then back to Roscoe and to Billy and I then back to the Reverend. I bet all the while they were seeing Pulitzers as they taped the end of our story.

Clare came closer followed by my uncle. Both still carried their rifles.

No one was saying anything. We may have been too exhausted or stunned by the storm that came back as a gentle, straight-falling rain at that moment. It's tempting to say it was a glad-to-be-alive moment, the same feeling I had sharing that kiss with Billy. But the truth, I believe, is that everyone knows that things aren't over until they're over.

And our story was not yet over.

A charging bolt was pulled back, chambering a round in an automatic weapon. Then Massoud staggered up behind us and jammed the barrel into Billy's spine forcing him forward.

"Someone bring me a car," he said. To Orson and Clare he said, "Drop your guns." Next he turned Billy to keep him in front of me. "You too. Drop the pistol." Into the air he shouted, "A car. Get me a car."

"It won't do you any good," I said, displaying my empty hands. "It's over. You can't get away and there's no chance the government will support your cause now."

"Governments. Governments don't rule the world like you suppose. They certainly don't rule America. At least not America beyond her own doorstep. There are other people. Other ways of doing things."

As if he had said some secret word, the video camera, which had been tracking Massoud since he showed up, shattered in sparks and glass.

I caught the muzzle flash in the distance, but didn't see the shooter. I didn't need to. Givens.

"Do you see now?" Massoud's thick mustache twitched as he asked the question. "That's how it is. The people in the dark and shadows who run this world. Inside the light—under the tent you have the show. That's your government and your God."

"I don't accept that," Roscoe pronounced from the stage. "I don't believe. It's not what you believe, Massoud. It can't be. If we serve nothing higher we can never rise above the dirt."

"We build with the dirt then we serve what we create and build higher. Only the people matter." Massoud turned to me. "*My* people."

I understood that was the cue for a bullet to pass through my head. There was time for the understanding and the regret that I hadn't lived more. If I'd had another micro second I might have accepted. I didn't.

Massoud's head split at the temple coughing out a spray of red and gray. His body crumpled into a small pile on the trampled grass.

Givens wasn't following Massoud's orders. He was cleaning house.

"Roscoe," I raised my hand with the shout, but too late.

The last bullet of the night pierced his heart and the Reverend dropped backward, collapsing again onto his fallen cross.

Epilogue

I kept my Monday appointment with Dr. Kurtz. I had a lot to share and tell. And a lot I kept to myself too. Maybe I didn't despise therapy as much as I once had. That didn't mean that I trusted it entirely either. Sometimes we need things we don't like or want. That's a whole other conversation.

I wore a dress when I went to see her that time. I don't know why and I felt silly when she complimented me. She sets an impossible standard, I informed her. She smiled a bright lipstick-beaming smile and said, "So do you."

Daddy's funeral was the kind of event you dream of for the people in your life. It was filled with military men and their stories. Flowers bloomed from every space. One arrangement was from the White House. So much of his life was secret from me. What was clear though was that I had gotten the best of it.

The service was officiated by my friend Clarence Bolin. Clare was ordained just like his brother and they had both found their own ways to challenge the faith. A few days later I joined him at the private ceremony for his big brother.

"Brotherhood is a tough relationship," he told me. "Family of any kind is hard." After that, he went off with my Uncle Orson who had also lost a brother. I think they got drunk on homemade whiskey.

Whilomina Tindall wore her grief, beautiful black, and never took it off. She really loved my father. After the funeral she remained a part of my life. She had to, I roped her into helping me create a non-profit to support and protect refugee women. I finally felt like I had something to add to and a reason for Nelson's fame and wealth. I'm still probably the richest working cop in the country.

I didn't expect to be a cop, but the depths of governmental denial ran deep. Riley Yates became famous for a while as the reporter who exposed the plot to fund a new Kurdistan. Since it was a covert campaign that worked against the interests of NATO partners and regional allies it was all publically investigated and publically smoke screened. Reverend Bolin, Massoud, and their mercenaries took the blame for what was called, an independent and *freelance* operation.

That was probably why Givens had left us alive.

After an unpaid vacation I got to return to work. Ultimately nothing changed in the department. Sheriff Benson stood for election after all. Billy's injuries and the new spark of life the sheriff got from Marion Combs convinced him to change his mind. At least for the time being. Houseman retired and Sheriff Benson gave his job to Billy. He became Detective Billy Blevins.

After a lot of thought, and a lot of therapy, I decided that my life was like the tornado that scared a mile of the county that night. But all the wind was my own. I lived in it. In the conflict and the swirl. After my assault in Iraq I had hated the world and blustered against it. When I met Nelson, I ran into love and marriage as if I could own the storm and keep the pain at bay.

I refused to rush or run with Billy Blevins in my life. We went slow, healing and laughing. He didn't even kiss me a third time until weeks after that night.

But what a kiss.

The first in a gritty new series by author Robert Dunn,
featuring sheriff's detective Katrina Williams, as she
investigates moonshine, murder, and the ghosts of her
own past . . .

A Living Grave

Katrina Williams left the Army ten years ago disillusioned and
damaged. Now a sheriff's detective at home in the Missouri Ozarks,
Katrina is living her life one case at a time—between mandated
therapy sessions—until she learns that she's a suspect in a military
investigation with ties to her painful past.

The disappearance of a local girl is far from the routine
distraction, however. Brutally murdered, the girl's corpse is found
by a bootlegger whose information leads Katrina into a tangled web
of teenagers, moonshiners, motorcycle clubs, and a fellow veteran
battling illness and his own personal demons. Unraveling each
thread will take time Katrina might not have as the Army
investigator turns his searchlight on the devastating incident
that ended her military career. Now Katrina will need to dig
deep for the truth—before she's found buried . . .

Read on for a special excerpt!

A Lyrical Underground e-book on sale now.

Chapter 1

Therapy is not for the weak. It is spine-ripping, devastatingly hard work that shines a light on all the secret parts of your soul. We are all vampires at the center of ourselves, I think. Those bits of ourselves, the secrets that are protected by ego and self-delusion, burn like phosphorus flames when the light finally pins them down.

I didn't choose therapy. The sessions were a requirement of keeping my job with the Taney County Sheriff's Department. I'm the only female detective in the department and the only one required to attend counseling.

There had been an incident—

There had been incidents—

I guess the final straw that I had tossed onto the sheriff's back was what I called a "justified adjustment of attitude." It wasn't that I minded so much the trouble setting the wife-beater straight got me into. What really got to me was that the wife, with her two raccoon eyes and broken nose, picked him up at the hospital and took him right back to the familial double-wide. Some things no amount of adjustment can fix.

My therapist said that I was violent toward the man but exhibited more anger at the woman. Those were the kinds of things she said and I had to listen to. That was easy to blow off, but sometimes she said something that stuck like a bit of glass in my eye. That morning she had mentioned my clothes in the way only a woman in pencil skirts and strappy shoes can bring up another woman's choice of jeans and boots. I work for a living and being pretty isn't part of the job. Sometimes her questions and observations made me want to grab a fistful of perfect hair and adjust her attitude a little.

I didn't, though, because sometimes—just sometimes—she shines a light that I guess I really need to see. Maybe I need the burning away.

Sessions were over at ten, but I took the mornings off until noon. The doctor was in Springfield and the Taney County seat was Forsyth. It was close to an hour drive each way the best of times. Post-session was never the best of times, so I usually went through home. Nixa, Missouri has little to distinguish itself to the rest of the world, but it was my hometown. It was where I went after the Army, and it's where I return every few days just to touch something that was gone. There really aren't words for what was gone. I didn't know the thing, just the absence of it. That's the kind of crap you learn in therapy. Home didn't fill the hole, it just let me walk the edges without falling in. I learned that on my own. Something else it did for me—it let me eat without feeling like a complete carb whore. Sometimes I would pick up Dad and take him to the Drop Inn Café for a late breakfast of biscuits and gravy. If it was a bad day, I had the big plate of eggs, runny over medium, with sides of grits and bacon and toast. Therapy to get over therapy. That morning Dad was gone, off again to D.C., where he still did consulting work for the government twenty years after retiring from the Army. He never told me anything but happy stories about his time in the service and I never told him anything but happy stories about mine. My therapist says we're both lying to ourselves and each other, but honestly I think I'm the only one with lies to tell. I missed him as I sat alone in the café and had the eggs and bacon with extra grits.

Missouri roads are some of the worst in the country but have some of the best curves. There is so much up-thrust sandstone and limestone karst topography that straight lines had been impossible for anything but federal road projects. I would have made better time on Highway 65. It was a bland seam of government concrete, no joy at all. But I wasn't looking for progress. I was looking to grind time under my wheels and kill it with horsepower and dangerous turns. Going through Nixa kept me on 160 the whole way. The long way back to Forsyth, but even in a truck, the curved path is more fun.

Already the sun was high and burning languid heat into the day. I like to drive with the windows down on the pickup. Nixa is my hometown, but the entire Ozarks region is home. And I like the feel of home on my skin as I drive. The moving air smelled of cut grass and horse manure. Despite the heat, it was heavy with humidity.

When the cell phone vibrated on the console I stared at it hard, hoping it might back down. It didn't. I put the windows up and turned on the air before answering. I needed to hear clearly. The only calls I ever got were from the office and never casual.

"Yeah," I answered. I wanted her to know how I felt about the intrusion. Not that it would do any good.

"Hurricane. It's Darlene."

I gritted my teeth at the sound of the nickname and took my calming breath. I always imagined every woman named Katrina picked up the same extra baggage after 2005. It sounded kind of action-movie lame to me, but I knew a lot of male cops who would love to be tagged with it. Just another of the things that make me different.

"Yes, Darlene. It's always you," I said back into the phone. Darlene was the most professional dispatcher on the planet. Nothing much seemed to ruffle her panties, which means people like me feel almost all right dumping our moods on her. "What have you got for me?"

She gave the location of a call out to a farm road south of Walnut Shade and on the south side of Bear Creek.

"What's the call?" I asked.

"Just see-the-man. No name. No complaint. He said it was an emergency but didn't need EMTs."

"Did his information show up on the computer?"

"He didn't call 9-1-1. Used the office number."

That told me he was one of the longtime residents. A lot of people around here remembered party lines and there were more than a few left who could tell you what it was like to walk miles to the only phone that you had to crank. They were the ones who remembered the sheriff's department office number but never seemed to get comfortable with 9-1-1.

"I'm on one-sixty coming up on the Reeds Spring cutoff," I told Darlene. I had passed the cutoff at least a mile back. "Don't you have anyone closer?"

"Closer but not available. Almost everyone else is up at Walnut Shade looking for that Briscoe girl."

"Briscoe girl?"

"Thirteen years old, reported missing when she didn't come home for dinner last night. Sheriff has everyone not already tied up and about forty volunteers checking the dirt roads and late night dirty-tango spots."

"I've got it then. It gives me an excuse to drive fast."

"You need an excuse?" Darlene asked before hanging up.

Walnut Shade was one of those towns that had been something less than a town for a hundred years until the lake region exploded along with Branson in the 1990s. Now it was what we called an *unincorporated community*, subdivided and paved, but remaining something less than a town. The old-timers don't want change and the new-timers want the illusion of rural life. What that means for us is the sheriff's office getting called every time a mobile home with a leaking septic system floods the yard of the McMansion next door. Still, a call is a call and I had a job to do.

There was no direct route to where I needed to be. If I stayed on 160 it would take me right into Walnut Shade. But since I needed to be below there and on the far side of Bear Creek, I had to take 65 where the two highways crossed. After that, it was mostly hunt through the unmarked farm tracks and fishing paths until I found someone who looked like they'd been waiting an hour.

It didn't take an hour; it only took about forty minutes. The old guy was sitting on the open tailgate of an early-sixties GMC pickup that looked like it had once been painted Forest Service green. When I pulled up and parked he waved a fishing pole in greeting. He was polite but unenthusiastic about dealing with the cops. We get that a lot.

When I introduced myself, he looked me up and down without trying to hide the appraisal. Since he didn't leer, it wasn't clear if he was checking me out as a woman or as a cop. He was pretty old and since he didn't make any comment, I gave him the benefit of the doubt and assumed it was cop first, female second.

"You want to let me in on why you called?" I asked him.

He looked at his feet and spit a stream of tobacco into the weeds. It wasn't me bothering him. You get to know, as a cop, when you're the problem with someone. When you're a woman cop you get to know a few extra problems.

"I'll show you," he said before dropping off the tailgate. His name was Clarence Bolin. Everyone called him Clare, he told me as we walked. He was the kind of old-timer who the Ozarks had been both commercializing and trying to live down for a generation. Hillbilly. Of course, nowadays that was an epithet to be avoided. Like being drunk and slovenly was the role an oppressive government forced on him. He wore a T-shirt that had once been white under overalls that were un-buttoned at the side to provide room for his huge belly. If it weren't for the belly anyone would have thought the man had no weight on him at all. He had thin arms and legs that flapped like wings in the big legs of the overalls when he walked.

Clare led the way as we tromped over the fallow field. When we got to the border of overgrowth that bounded the cultivated land and separated it from the creek, he held back and waited for me to take the lead.

He walked behind me on the narrow path of crushed foliage for a few yards before he said, "You're the one they call Hurricane, ain't you?"

"Why do you say that?" I asked without looking at him. I was curious to see where this would go.

"People talk about the big-ass female deputy."

I turned around then and gave him a look with crosshairs in it.

"I don't mean to say you got a big ass . . . I mean—it's just a way of talking . . . Oh hell, you know what I mean—there just aren't that many six-foot-tall women that pile on boots with a cowboy heel."

Just to keep him squirming, I kept the look locked on the old man for a long time, then I said, "Detective."

"Huh?"

"Detective. Not Deputy." Clare relaxed a bit, his shoulders coming down to their usual slump. "Are you sure you don't want to make a comment about my boobs now?" I asked.

His shoulders tensed again and his eyes remained aimed exactly at mine. He didn't answer. It was obviously all he could do to keep his eyes off my chest.

"Good man, Clare. There might be hope for you yet," I told him and then turned away, not caring where his look wandered.

From behind me I heard him say, quietly, "No need to bite a man's head off." Then Clare started walking. He kept muttering to himself and it was like Popeye in the old cartoons; you knew he was saying something—you just couldn't understand it. I stopped and in the quiet I heard him say, ". . . not like I had a very good day myself."

I understood why. There was a girl on the ground in front of me. She was dead. I looked at Clare and he wasn't looking. Not at the girl, not at me. He had turned to look into the high branches of the covering trees, but I got the feeling he wasn't seeing leaves.

There wasn't any doubt in my mind who she was. It had to be the Briscoe girl. Death—this kind of death—just wasn't common here. The chances we would have one missing girl and one, unrelated dead girl within a few miles were nonexistent.

I took another look at her but didn't linger. Something that felt like fear, a hot wave of nausea, and a pounding drumbeat signal to run boiled from my stomach into my throat. It lingered as a flush on my face, but made my feet feel as though they were growing roots into cold ground. This was the abyss the philosopher Nietzsche talked about. The one that stares back if you stare too long into it. A girl left dead and alone. For an instant, the forest floor was desert dust and the girl was me. Just for an instant. Then I regained control.

This is my job. I can do this.

She was flat on her back with her hands up and to the side. Down below her legs were together and her feet splayed. Death was always pigeon-toed. Her shoes were well-worn flats and her skirt a medium-length denim that covered her knees. The knees were scratched and scraped with old injuries and new wounds. Those that looked old also looked normal, benign. One expects kids to have scrapes on knees and elbows. Scabs are the hard-earned badges of youth. Those other marks, though—the ones on the lower part of the knees—were ripped skin with the ground-in detritus of the woods. Black soil and flecks of bark were embedded in the wounds. Bits of leaves glued with the girl's blood were clinging to her limbs. I checked her hands. They were scratched and caked with black soil as well. She had crawled before she was put on her back.

I tried. I worked very hard to focus on her knees. It was important to see those wounds and keep them in my mind. I needed to remember those knees because if I didn't, the image I would always recall was that of her face. It was all but gone.

"Stay here with her," I told Clare. "But stay back where you are. And don't touch anything. I have to make a call."

Making a call required walking back to the high ground at the edge of the woods and fishing the air for a signal. I was glad for the distance. I needed it to pull myself back into myself and focus on the job. As soon as I got a couple of bars, I called Darlene for a description of the girl. She read what she had and told me the name was Angela Briscoe. Then I told her Angela was here, and dead. I asked her to call the sheriff to get help out to me. After hanging up, I stood there for a few moments and waited for the tears that, as always, hit a roadblock and piled up just behind my eyes.

At that point I was mostly waiting for the system to get in motion. It's like a living thing: Something lumbering and brutish that has to unlimber itself, have coffee, and work its way up to a task. You needed to overcome its inertia, get it moving with enough energy to carry it to the end. The sheriff would make calls, talk with the family, the press. Deputies would secure the scene. Investigators would help collect evidence and the ME team would collect the body. I was part of the system too. Because I was first on scene and had awakened the death system, I would be responsible for finding who did this. The trick with this system was to move it without getting it stuck on the wrong paths. There were always more wrong paths than right ones.

How many paths were there that lead to murdered little girls?

I sucked it up. There had been more than a few dead bodies in my life. Some even children. I had been on the investigative team in Iraq when those soldiers—Americans—had killed a family, then raped, killed, and burned the body of a fourteen-year-old girl. People talk about the stress of war driving good soldiers to do bad things. It's crap. It drives bad soldiers to do terrible things. That's what happened to this girl, Angela Briscoe. Someone bad did something horrible to her. I could make it stop.

A few minutes later I was standing over her body again. This time I looked at her, really looked. I had no camera with me so I pulled out my pad and pen and started writing and making a diagram. Photos fix things in the mind; the notes and drawings I make for myself keep things more fluid. They let me recall what I felt at the time, the truth of the moment more than the truth of the scene.

I had noted before that her legs were together, but this time I took note there were no clothes separate from the body. Specifically underclothes.

"Look away," I told Clare. He did, and I noticed he turned completely away without making any attempt to see what I was doing.

What I did was to grab a fallen branch and break off the smaller twigs and leaves until I had a long, crooked stick. I used the stick so I could stay back from the body and lift the girl's skirt. Her panties were where they should be. She probably hadn't been raped. She was wearing a white T-shirt printed with the phrase *All Girl All Awesome*.

The blood covering the top half of the shirt showed clearly the out-line of a bra that was in place.

I wrote in my book some more, telling myself all the whys about my belief that there was no sexual assault. Scribbling quickly, I drew out her hand and noted where something had been chewing at her fingers. There were tracks of bird's feet on the arm too. Probably a crow had walked through her blood and then perched on the arm to peck at the fingers.

"You can turn around if you want," I told Clare.

"I'd just as soon not," he answered. When he spoke you could hear a thickness to his voice that had not been there before. My esti-mation of him went up a few points.

"I have a granddaughter about her age," he added.

I wrote it down that he said *her* and not *that*. Then I noted he had no visible blood and he had called it in and waited maybe an hour for someone to show up. At the bottom of that little column I wrote, *Clarence Bolin, not very likely.*

"When I get home, I'm gonna call her. I get annoyed sometimes, thinkin' that she oughta call me. I'm her grandpa, after all. I don't think I'll worry much about that anymore."

He still had his back to me and I heard him blow his nose. I'm pretty sure he didn't have a handkerchief. In my little notebook I cir-cled the word *not* in the last sentence I had written.

"I know your Uncle Orson," he said. "Been fishing with him more times than I can remember."

I crouched to be close to the ground and kept poking around the body with my stick, then sketching things in the pad. Clare's talk was actually soothing to hear. Normal, even though he was doing it to keep his mind off of something not normal in his life at all.

"Your daddy too. Way back when."

I think I nodded, reacting more to the sound than his words. Toss-ing my stick aside, I stood, then circled the body. Each time I stopped I added to my sketches. I had to force myself to look into the face. Into where the face had been. I sketched. Then I looked away. I sketched her hair. Then I looked away.

"There are monsters in the woods," Clare said, his back still to me. I was listening then. "It used to be a joke. When I was a kid, peo-ple talked about Momo, the Missouri monster. It was like a local Big-foot. But the real monsters are people, aren't they?"

I didn't answer him.

"Perverts." He spit the word out. "Monsters that do that to children. There isn't hate big enough for them nor a hell deep enough. This will rile some people up. He lives in one of those piece-of-crap mobile homes in that big development off of F Highway. You know, over by the McKenna farm."

"Who does?" I had stopped writing and was paying very close attention to Mr. Bolin at that point.

"The guy. The rapist."

"Turn around and look at me, Clare." He did. "Tell me what, and who, you are talking about."

"He's on the sex-offender site."

I let my breath out slowly.

Clare went on talking. "One of those Web sites with the names and addresses of all the kiddie guys. He's listed on it. Lives just a few miles from here."

I hated those listings. Someone thought it would be a good idea to let everyone know where the sex offenders lived. Problem was in some places you were prosecuted as a sex offender if you stepped into the woods to urinate because toilets in the park were broken. Most of the bad ones, the ones you really had to worry about, didn't hang around with a big neon sign pointing at them. I'd check the guy out but it already felt like a waste of time.

"Clare," I said, "I don't think this girl has been sexually assaulted."

"No?" he asked. I could see the certainty drain out of his face. It wasn't pretty. That's the thing about certainty: It makes everything easier. When it goes, you're left with a wide-open landscape of horrible possibilities and it's hard to find any comfort in doubt. It seemed to hit Clare pretty hard. "Who . . ." he started, then faded out. Then he drew up his breath again. "Who would do something like this unless it was for . . . ?"

"I don't know," I told him. "I'm going to find out." I tried to sound certain.

"I hope so," he said. "But I don't see how."

"There's always something. Evidence or witnesses. Usually criminals do something stupid or they'll be like your sex offender. Part of the system. I'll check him out and anyone else in the area who stands apart from the crowd. Anyone new who might have been hanging around the girl or even around here."

Clare was starting to look a little deflated and sick. He swallowed hard and looked back off into the green again. The grip on his fishing pole had turned to a hard white. As much as I wanted to ask him what was wrong, I didn't. He wanted to say something; that was clear. I wasn't going to push.

Just let it come.

I looked away to give him some thinking room. When I did, I noticed something that had escaped me before.

Leech.

The word was freshly carved in ragged letters on the trunk of a white oak.

"This mean anything to you?" I asked.

Clare came closer but kept a wary distance. He had changed in the last few moments. Change was something good in witnesses; it means a connection; it means they know something or they think they know something. Whatever it was that Clare knew bothered him. I didn't have any doubt it bothered him enough to spill it. The question was how much line he would take before letting himself be reeled in.

He was looking hard at the carving. Harder than it probably deserved. I almost asked him if it was my badge or my big ass that was making him uneasy. He wasn't ready to have the mood lightened up.

"No. Kids carve all kinds of shit on the trees around here," he said.

"Sure," I agreed and I ran my fingers over the lettering. "But why *Leech*?"

"Who knows?"

"It's an odd word. Capitalized like a name."

"What about bikers?" he asked.

"What about them?" I kept my gaze and my fingers on the carved letters.

"You think bikers could do something like this? If there were any around?"

"Oh, there're always some around. Some good ones and some bad ones—mostly they all try to look bad. Makes them hard to weed out, but if I have a reason, I'll sure look into anyone who needs looking into."

Clare looked away, casting his gaze to the creek bank and up the little trail that ran alongside it. Then he looked at me and quickly looked back to his feet. "Okay if I get on out of here?"

"Thought you were going fishing." I nodded to the rod he still carried in his hand.

"Not with all the cops that'll be around here. Who needs that?"

I almost said "the little girl there," but stopped myself. It would have been needlessly cruel in more than one way. Shaking my head, I went back to stand close to the body, maybe a little possessively. "No. I'll need you to stick around for a while."

The girl was close enough to me now that I could feel her presence without looking. Death has a gravity and Angela Briscoe was pulling at me. Even so, I didn't move any closer. I didn't want to cause any contamination to the scene. Each step I took in proximity to the girl was where I had carefully stepped before.

I looked at Clare and caught him looking at the girl. He was trying to see a face where there was just red and splinters of white. Even her corn-silk hair was fanned out away from the face as though in surprise at the violence that had erased it.

Clare walked toward the creek bank and the sound of running water.

I had to pull myself away from the girl too, or orbit her tragedy forever.

It was full summer and everything along the riverbank was green and dappled yellow with sunlight. Within the banks were flat stones and smooth-tumbled gravel from black to white with colorful scatterings of pink and molted greens. The water that ran over it was so clear, if it were not for the ripples, it would be invisible. There was an empty space in the mud where a stone had lain, half in and half out of the water. At the edge of the space were the marks of fingers where the stone had been lifted. Small fingers.

A woman's? Or could Angela have been forced to choose her own murder weapon?

Water tinkled where the shallow flow ran over stones.

"Why were you up here?" I asked Clare.

"Like I said," he raised up his pole to reinforce his point. "I was sucker grabbin'."

I nodded and then reached up to push aside a strand of hair that had fallen with the movement. For the sake of my pale skin, I usually keep my hair under a hat when outdoors. No matter how hard I try though, every summer my nose burns and my hair goes from a deep reddish brown to summer red. Unconsciously, my finger found the scar that started in my left eyebrow and followed the crescent of the orbital bone. It was a small scar. Small wasn't the same as meaningless. As soon as I realized, I pulled my hand away. It was a bad habit. The slight discoloration barely showed to anyone but me. When I touched it, though, when I was aware of touching it, the ridge of skin seemed like a jagged, red wall I had yet to climb over. No one else has climbed over it, either. A couple have tried. Only a couple. Both had made the mistake of saying it gave me "character." It was as much of my character as they ever got to see.

When I lost myself in thought, or when there was a puzzle, I had the habit of touching the scar like a little talisman. Just then I was puzzling about sucker grabbing. Sucker were big, carp-like fish. Bottom feeders, they were hard to catch on a bait hook. They're mostly caught by weighting a line with a big treble hook and dropping it into a congregation of fish. Then you jerk the line and grab them with the naked hook.

I carefully stepped back from the water, checking the ground for any other evidence of the girl's last moments, and then started hiking downstream.

"Follow me," I told the old man. He did, but he set his own path and pace. Slow.

The woods were thick with wild grapevine and poison ivy running under the mantle of oak, walnut, and hawthorn. The ground was lumpy with softball-sized hedge apples. Along the bank, just skirting its edge, was a path. Bare dirt littered with cigarette butts, beer, and soda cans.

Kids come to party and drink.

Down in the streambed, the water deepened. Here it had eroded more than gravel. Large, flat slabs of sandstone were all along and under the water. They were the remains of an ancient shallow sea that now defined the shape of a spring-fed stream. Here the water was silent. Another two hundred yards down, the cold flow dumped into the deeper, swifter water of Bear Creek.

"I mean, why were you up there?" I almost had to shout to be heard, Clare had fallen so far behind.

"What?" he hollered back.

As I stood waiting on the old guy, I caught myself fingering the scar again. There's another reason it's a bad habit. Every time I touch it, even when I don't realize it at the time—*especially* if I don't realize it—I get pissed off. That little scar is kind of a trigger. When things don't add up or they start to churn in my head just a little too much, I reach up and pull it.

"Get your old ass down here, Clare." This time I did shout. I was getting tired of the waiting game with him. And I'm usually such a patient person.

As he picked his way through the path, I was rubbing the rubbery pucker of skin around my eye and thinking, not for the first time, how everyone seemed to have lies that had to be worked out of them. Watching Clare work his way forward, like if he moved slowly enough I would forget about him, made my dark mood churn.

"Now, I want to know why you were up there," I said emphatically, "where the water's way too shallow for sucker grabbing. And not down here at this pool, where I can see at least thirty fish just waiting on you to pull them out."

Clare opened his mouth to speak, then seemed to think better of it. There was something there. It was impossible to miss. I decided he just needed a little more pressure at his back.

"That's good, Clare. Saying nothing is better than lying. But saying nothing won't let me know you had nothing to do with this."

"I called ya, didn't I? I brought you out here. Why would I do that if it was me that hurt the girl?"

"Happens all the time. Lots of people get the bright idea to throw off our scent by being the first to report. It pays to consider the motives of the person that calls. Especially when that person is not completely forthcoming."

"I don't know what you're talking about." His words said one thing but everything else about him said another. It was an interesting change. I wondered what he was protecting.

Who?

For a long moment I stared at him and then turned away to point downstream. "I bet the kids have a name for their little party spot, don't they? That clearing by the fork."

"Whiskey Bend."

That says something.

"When I was seventeen we called it Budweiser Corner." Clare looked like he was trying hard to remember seventeen. "Kids been coming here for years. For a while I heard they were calling it Coors Corner. Course, back when I was a kid, you couldn't get Coors this far east. You ever see *Smokey and the Bandit?*"

"Why whiskey, Clare?"

He stopped smiling and his eyes got that same caught-in-the-crosshairs look. "Huh?" was all he managed to get out.

"Whiskey. Kids like beer. It's what they usually start with. What they can get away with. My old man kept a refrigerator in the garage filled with the stuff. He never noticed when a couple disappeared."

"So?"

"So, now they call it Whiskey Bend. I have to wonder where the whiskey comes from."

Clare was thinking. He had the look of a man weighing options. Heavy ones. I kept watch on him from the corner of my vision as his face squirreled around itself. He had nothing to do with killing the girl; I was sure of that. But the girl was dead and that left no room for anyone's secrets in my tally.

Leech.

There it was again, carved into another tree. This time the word was more than written, it was stylized like a logo or brand. The capital L was formed with arrow points at each termination and the rest of the word inset within the angle.

"I don't want no trouble," Clare said. "And I don't want to start nothin' where there ain't nothin'."

I just looked at the man and nodded. He needed to know I was listening, but interruptions had a way of derailing even the smallest of confessions. To give him a little thinking room, I turned away again to examine the carved graffiti. This time I pulled a pen and notebook. Both the word and the style went onto the paper.

"I don't give it to 'em or sell it, either. But they're kids. Kids get into things."

When I finished my rendering of the carved mark, I wrote the word *whiskey* beside it. I added the phrase *kids get into things* as well. Then I lowered the pad and looked right at him again. I didn't speak; silence did the talking.

"It ain't me you gotta worry about anyway. I just make a little for fun. For me and friends and I only sell to the old-timers."

"I think it's time you spit it out, Clare. This is one of those only-the-truth-will-set-you-free moments."

"My mama used to say, 'It's time to come to Jesus.' You kind of remind me of her."

The old man's eyes wandered down and, for a second, I wasn't sure if he was falling into memory or checking out my shape again.

"Clare!"

"There's another guy that's been coming around here. He busted up my rig and he's been telling me to shut it down. A real badass-biker type."

"By rig, you mean a still?"

He nodded. "Small-time. Just for fun and to make a few extra bucks. I never believed it could cause things like this."

"What are you talking about, Clare?"

"The biker. He said if I didn't stop, someone was going to get hurt."

LYRICAL
UNDERGROUND

A
KATRINA
WILLIAMS
NOVEL

A LIVING
GRAVE

ROBERT E. DUNN

About the Author

Robert Dunn is the author of the Katrina Williams series, including *A Living Grave* and *A Particular Darkness*, as well as the novels *The Red Highway*, *The Dead Ground,* and *Behind the Darkness.* He can be found online at robertdunnauthor.blogspot.com or on Twitter at @WritingDead.

Printed in the United States
by Baker & Taylor Publisher Services